Destiny by Design
Leah's Journey

Mirta Ines Trupp

To my children: you are my greatest inspiration.

In Jewish history there are no coincidences.

—Elie Wiesel

Prologue

Driving along the elegant tree-lined streets, Molly, who had studied the Russian Revival period of design, as well as the Byzantine with its mosaics and cupolas, couldn't help but admire the striking estates. She was certainly well prepared for the display of notable architecture, but she was anxious to reach the Abramovitz home and hoped that the neighborhood they were seeking wasn't too far off. As the car stopped in front of an impressive structure complete with gables and colorful domes, Molly found herself pleasantly surprised.

"This is where my family lived? It's so…majestic."

Galina rushed to the massive door eager to get them out of the rain. She pulled out an antique skeleton key, turned it in the lock, and pushed the door ajar. With a sweeping motion of her hand, she welcomed her client.

"Vhat? You vere expecting *shtetl*? This is not *Anetevka* and your great great-grandfather was no *Tevye*."

Molly took a moment to appreciate the grandeur of her family's estate. Galina was right. She had allowed her imagination to paint in bleak, broad strokes. If people thought all their ancestors were stereotypical characters in a Sholem Aleichem play, that was an innocent, if not an ill-informed, misconception. That *she* allowed herself to visualize her family living miserably in a wooden shack at the edge of a fictional village was shameful and immature.

"Vell, don't standt there. Come in! *Come in!*"

The two tentatively crossed the threshold and began looking for a light switch. Galina explained that the house had been updated in the late 1940's—after the war—but didn't go into further detail. Molly made note of the year and, because of the history of that time period, didn't push for more information. The years following the Russian Revolution were times of misery and famine under Soviet rule. The subsequent years brought the Nazis and near annihilation of the Jewish community. Her family had thankfully been long gone by World War II. The fact that the house survived the horrors of that era was extraordinary.

If these walls could talk...

Chapter One

November 1900 ~ Odessa, Russia

*L*eah scurried by the gold leaf, floor-to-ceiling mirror before leaping down several steps to the main landing. As she passed the stained glass window at the top of the staircase, she heard her mother call out.

"If you cannot moderate your wild disposition, my dear, in future you will not be invited to our family meetings," Malka said as she regally glided down each step. "I will not have you galloping about the house."

Summarily chastised, Leah regained her composure and waited on the landing. "Yes, Mamá," was her rueful reply.

"My dear, I realize you are pleased with your invitation, but do *try* restrain your exuberance," Malka chuckled. "Can you imagine the look on Avram's face if you bolted through the door in that high-flying manner?"

Knowing the family was even now assembling in the drawing room, Leah nodded her understanding and held her tongue. She would not give rise to further reprimands. Her eldest brother, Moishe, had called a family meeting and extended a request that she join them. That could only mean one thing. She was to be accepted into their society and join their ranks.

Her eighteenth birthday was next month and Leah had been concerned that preparations had not yet commenced for a grand celebration. Unleashing her vivid imagination, she had fancied a surprise party was to be arranged. But after receiving Moishe's missive, she thought perhaps the adults were assembling in order to discuss her coming out party. Avram, and several of her more pious brothers, would not favor a ball where men and women danced together. Perhaps Moishe would overrule their objections—he was the head of the family business, after all. *Perhaps Mamá would support a debutant ball*—complete with an orchestra for dancing! There was no need for further speculation for; finally, the time had come.

Malka opened the door and allowed her youngest to lead the way. She smiled as they stepped into her favorite room of the large estate. The library upstairs, with its dark wood paneling and sumptuous leather divans had been designed for her beloved husband, Solomon. The drawing room, however, was her retreat. Pastel coverings enveloped the space with fanciful lace and billowing tulle. Fresh flowers, along with diamond-paned windows and a luminescent chandelier gave the room an air of whimsy.

It was here that Malka enjoyed her evening tea. A lifetime ago, Solomon's brother had sent the young couple an impressive samovar and a set of *podstakannik*. The fine glasses were enfolded in delicate work of silver and gold filigree. She favored this set above all others, not for its marked artistry but for the cherished memories that the wedding gift evoked.

Now seated in her particular corner by the bay window, Malka observed her large brood as they assembled for their customary forum. In his later years, Solomon had established the practice with the hope that his children would continue to work together, equally sharing the burdens and the rewards of the business. Observing her twelve offspring—with the additional spouse here and there—filled Malka with a deep sense of accomplishment. *Shepn naches fun di kinder,* as Solomon used to say. She did, indeed, derive much pleasure from their children.

Leah observed her mamá sitting prettily in her favorite chair. Impeccably dressed in a gown of black silk and her salt and pepper *coiffure* braided into a crown, Malka Abramovitz looked every bit the queen. To be sure, Leah had always known that her mamá had held court alongside her beloved husband from that very chair—discussing business, politics, and family matters to her heart's delight. When her papá passed away, over five years ago, these duties had been relegated to her brothers. That the men still looked to their mamá for counsel pleased Leah to no end.

Moishe was the last to enter the room, and as he closed the door, he gestured for all to be seated. With his raven-black hair and sapphire blue eyes, Moishe was the replica of their late father. Leah smiled upon seeing his countenance, knowing that whatever he was about to share with the group, it would be imparted with sincerity and good will.

"Thank you for making yourselves available for this evening's gathering," Moishe began. "We do have quite a bit to discuss. I welcome Aaron, as our chief accountant, to bring forth a most pressing matter."

Moishe's younger brother—*younger by minutes*—stood and offered a dossier of invoices and statements as substantiating documentation. Although they were fraternal twins, the men did not share the exact coloring and features, nor were they quite the same in character. Aaron was meticulous and structured, probably more so than his brother. He had no qualms presenting facts and figures; however, he was uneasy tonight as his speech entailed sharing troubling news.

"As you very well know, the Abramovitz Manufacturing Company must be certified each year by the State. That certification proves that our company continues to be useful to Mother Russia," Aaron said pointedly. "Our accounts must show a balance of at least 50,000 rubles in order to qualify for certification and, needless to say, we must be prepared to pay taxes on this year's profits."

"That shouldn't be a problem," Ysroel interjected. "Every time Avram and I have asked you to join us at *yeshiva*, you and Moishe have begged off stating you were too busy to study!" He laughed at his own joke, as his brother Naftali joined in.

"I presume you will not find it amusing when I say that the *revizor* has already paid us a visit," Aaron rejoined. "Indeed, I found myself in the uncomfortable position of having to request an extension. And, as it is our custom, I now offer this pressing matter for discussion."

Avram, prickly and eager to return to his books, shook his head in confusion. "I don't understand. We have paid this fee year after year without fail. Why is there need for debate?"

"It is not the customary fee, Brother. The new mandate stipulates that *each* member of the family, who is eligible to inherit the estate, must pay for certification in their own right."

"Heavens! You make it sound as if we are destitute, Aaron!" Leah exclaimed. Are we finished speaking of taxes and officials? What of my party?"

As far as Leah was concerned, they ought to have been planning her long-awaited, coming out. Indeed, it ought to have been planned months ago. She had hoped for a debutant ball equal to the Poznanski girl or the Konig sisters. Heavens! Everyone who was anyone was *still* talking about Brodsky's gala event. At the very least, Leah believed she was entitled to the same soiree as Lazar Brodsky's daughter.

With controlled patience, Moishe raised his hand, silencing his sister before she could say another word. "We have not forgotten your birthday. Indeed, I asked you to join us this evening in order to discuss the matter."

Leah nearly squealed with delight, but caught herself with one look from Aaron. His grim face cautioned her to refrain from being overly zealous.

Moishe cleared his throat and continued. "You *will* have a celebration, and it will be an elegant affair, to be sure. It will just be relatively simple—certainly nothing comparable to Clara Brodsky's ball. There is nothing to be done for it. The family must economize."

Leah stomped her satin-slippered foot. "Of all times, why must we economize now? You do realize that a successful coming out might lead to an excellent match. Clara married one of those wealthy Saint Petersburg Gintsburgs. They are *practically* royalty. Indeed, she is now a baroness!"

"Our family is not in the same sphere as the *Sugar Kings* or the Gintsburgs—"

"You probably will marry the match manufacturer," cackled Benjamin. He was always at the ready to jab and prod. "Or better yet, Shlomo, the butcher."

So very accustomed to her brothers' taunts, Leah did not hesitate with her retaliation. "And you, Benjamin, will no doubt suit quite nicely for Olga, the tanner's daughter."

Malka paid no attention to her bickering children and, instead, turned to her eldest. "Are we in such dire straits, my son?"

"With these unforeseen expenditures, Aaron and I find we are not comfortable putting out a large sum for a birthday celebration. Indeed, there is talk of more trouble with the tax ministry; therefore, I must insist that we plan accordingly. We cannot afford to lose the title of Manufacture Councillor."

"Oh no! We wouldn't want to *lose a title!*" Yosef mocked. "This is 1900. I cannot fathom how we *still* rely on Peter the Great's feudal system."

Moishe stared at his brother in disbelief. Once again, Solomon's youngest son was challenging the family's way of life—Russia's way of life. "Need I remind you, Yosef, it is *only* because our grandfathers were allowed entry into the First Guild that we are allowed to live outside of the Pale? They had to purchase their entry—they had to *prove* their worth. And due to their combined extraordinary efforts, Papá was awarded the title of Merchant Councillor. I assume that even you appreciate what that implies."

"Yes, yes. I know—I know it by rote! As Honorary Citizens, we cannot be drafted. We cannot receive corporal punishment; we are not required to pay a personal tax..." Frustrated, Yosef thought of another line of defense. "Let me you ask this, Moishe: do you only think of money?"

"On the contrary. I think of Papá's achievements. I think of this family's sacrifice. I think of those poor souls held captive in the Pale of Settlement with no hope—with no future. Papá was named Manufacture Councillor after twenty-five years of dedicated work. He understood the game and ensured that we, his heirs, would inherit the title. A *hereditary honorary citizen*, Yosef! Would you truly give that up?"

"Remember our friends with lesser designations do not fare as well," Efraim offered. "If their business is not successful, they risk losing their ranking as Merchants. If they *are* successful but cannot pay their taxes, they lose everything."

"Yes, yes. I also know that Jewish merchants have been charged twice as much tax! Mother Russia will have her share—especially from us *foreigners*!" Yosef exclaimed. "What color must we bleed to be considered Russian?"

Efraim nodded in acknowledgement, but would not back down from making his point. "That ruling was abandoned almost a hundred years ago. If you wish to debate, make sure you are up to date on your facts."

"*Touché* Brother, but we still face the fact that Honorary Citizens and Merchants must hold an estate certificate—and there is a price to pay for said privilege."

"Papá had paid a sum of 50 rubles yearly until the time of his death," Moishe acceded. "As his heirs, we are all listed on the certificate. But now, as Aaron indicated, we must *each of us* pay for the distinction."

"And that money is supposed to be held in a trust by the government—in whom we all have complete faith," Yosef added with not a little disdain.

At the mention of unfair taxation, Avram was eager now to contribute to the conversation. "Let us not forget the *korobka* tariff. Every pound of kosher meat sold in the marketplace, not to mention, our ritual clothing—including each and every *yarmulke*—has been taxed. The income from this toll was supposed to be devoted to the maintenance of our Jewish schools..."

"Yes and what is your point?" Leah asked. She desperately wanted the conversation to return to the matter at hand—*her birthday.*

"I simply beg to pose a question, if I may," Avram mockingly bowed to his sister. "Millions of surplus rubles from the *korobka* funds have been deposited in the government's coffers. *Where are the funds?*"

Yosef doubled over in laughter smacking Avram heartily on the back—an action not taken very well by the reserved brother. "Good point! I read these surpluses totaled over 3,000,000 rubles! *Where are the funds*, he asks? We are surrounded by corruption and money grabbers! Pray tell me, my exalted brother, why should we continue to pay into this system?"

"It is quite simple, Yosef," Moishe sighed. "To do so, allows the family to live in the manner with which we are accustomed. To refuse, means we lose everything Papá built. And there is something else I've yet to mention. There is talk amongst the Guild members—of retribution."

"What do you mean?" Leah asked, vexed and impatient.

"I am speaking of *pogroms*."

Avram gasped. "Not again—not *here*?"

"Yes, I'm afraid so," Moishe said, rubbing the disillusionment from his eyes. "Two months ago, Perchik Feinstein was not able to pay for his certification. Not only was he fined an exorbitant amount, but when word got out that the Feinsteins were in peril of losing their ranking, their factory was taken over by rioters. When Perchik complained to the police, the captain said there was nothing to be done."

"Then I must suggest, once again, we speak of immigration," said Yosef. "Or do you propose we wait for another series of attacks? We simply cannot be idle. We must *do* something."

"Such as?"

"I have been contacted by several men who wish me to join their organizations. There are people who wish to affect a change in Russia. They refuse to be rounded up like cattle and corralled in the Pale. They refuse to be bullied into paying more than their fair share. *They refuse* to be made the scapegoat for every mishap and disaster—"

Malka had heard more than enough. Her husband had secured a prosperous living for the family and she was not about to give it up for the musings of her modern-thinking son or her daughter's self-indulgent rants.

"*A sof*! That will be enough. I am not convinced that we must leave our home and livelihood behind. The time may yet come, but for now, we will pay for our Merchant certification and keep our ranking— *antiquated as it may be*. With regard to these organizations, Yosef, I do hope that you are being sensible and researching with whom you wish to align yourself."

"I have not joined up with anyone, as of yet, *Matushka*," Yosef replied softly, using his mother's favorite term of endearment. "Like the pendulum in our maladjusted clock, their politics swing too far in either direction. I will not put myself in that perilous position."

"I am grateful, at least, for that bit of news." The matriarch adjusted her black shawl about her shoulders and grinned. "Aaron, do you have further information you wish to impart?"

"Unfortunately, Mamá, I do need to bring another matter to your attention. About our profits…"

"We did splendidly last year, surely," stated Rivka, the eldest daughter. "The last shipment of brocades we sent to the Spaniards must have brought in a pretty sum."

"While we were fortunate to contract with that up-and-coming house of fashion," Moishe answered, "it may be a long time before we see that kind of business again. Many competitors have taken issue with those of us who deal in foreign trade. Furthermore, there are those who wish to curtail all efforts of modernization. Even the Russian Technical Society has begun condemning many of us for working with Western European technology."

"I wouldn't be surprised if the grievances originated with the Morozov family—"

"What does all of this have to do with the budget for my birthday celebration?" Leah demanded.

"The Ministry for Commerce and Manufacturing of the empire is one of the leading advocates of Russian protectionism. It wishes to curb our trade with all of our international customers," Aaron offered, confident that his comment was sufficient explanation. But seeing a glazed look on his sister's face, he thought better of his judgment. He would have to further enlighten the silly girl. "They are imposing tariffs and restrictive quotas, Leah, which will make it impossible for us to make any significant amount of profit. Do you understand? Less profit means less money for your fripperies, flowers and fancy dinner."

"Indeed," Moishe said, as he came to his feet announcing an end to the debate. "You have heard our report. We hope you have a better understanding of the situation. We must be wary. Our future is uncertain."

Malka nodded once in Moishe's direction and came to her feet with resolve. "Never fear, my son. We will follow Aaron's budget to the letter. And Leah," Malka continued with a severe look towards her youngest, "there will be no theatrics."

The evening ended on a somber note. Each family member quietly exited the room and dispersed to their own quarters—all except for Malka. She poured herself another cup of tea and took to her chair once more. The news was unsettling, to be sure. She recalled the first day Solomon spoke of their new home. As a surprise, he had purchased the estate and had it refurbished to his precise specifications. More than the extravagance, or the unexpected gift, Malka had been overwhelmed by how far they had come.

Their families' meager beginnings from Lithuania to Novorossiya to Odessa had been quite a journey. It had taken over a century—if truth be told—for the families to create a niche for themselves *and* for the government to grant them the liberty, not only to leave the Pale of Settlement, but to be prosperous and thrive. Prussian principalities had issued patents of nobility to a tiny number of wealthy Jewish families. These patents were later ratified by the Russian state. Slowly, the emergence of a small, but persevering, Jewish *bourgeoisie* was tolerated. Russian officials still considered Jews to be foreigners, but realized if permitted to succeed in their business, the boon would be beneficial to government coffers. The Abramovitz family had grown to such financial heights that when, in 1865, Solomon offered for Malka's hand in marriage, he pledged she would be treated as queen—a designation quite fitting as it was the exact definition of her name.

As the children began arriving, the family's success was not only measured by their financial growth, but by the many blessings *Hashem* had bestowed on them with the birth of each healthy child. Once again, her husband made a solemn vow—his wife and children would forever remain together. They would live in comfort and safety all under one roof. Solomon felt that they were more secure in this manner, rather than spread across the land—separated by distance and the stringent traveling regulations placed on Jews. When he presented her with the keys to the grand estate, his heart was full of satisfaction. Malka's own heart was overflowing with love and admiration.

They had raised twelve children in that happy home. They had celebrated *Shabbos* week after week and commemorated the appointed holidays throughout the years. They had received new daughters and sons when their children married and then, they welcomed their grandchildren with open arms and bursting hearts. Such *naches*! Of course, they had their share of problems—with twelve children, there was always something with which to contend. A broken bone, a troublesome fever—a belligerent adolescent, but there was nothing that Malka and Solomon couldn't overcome. When the *oblast* was gripped with typhus, and Solomon succumbed to the disease as many others in their region, Malka's world came to halt. It took all of her reserve and faith to face a future without her beloved, but she found the strength. *Hashem* was with her— and Solomon, she knew, never really left her side. Yet, what was to become of them *now*?

The world was spinning out of control once again. Malka knew they had led a privileged life, but she wasn't afraid of losing the wealth or the position. She was afraid for her children's future. Whether they lived on a grand estate in the center of fashionable Odessa or in a shack in the middle of a *shtetl*, they were Jews. Imperial Russia was not going to forgive them for that fact. *What God decrees, man cannot prevent*. If they were meant to stay and prosper, it would be. If they were meant to flee and start anew, it would be. Having mused and pondered enough for one evening, Malka set down her now tepid cup of tea and went off to seek her bed. Tomorrow would be another day and she still had to plan *something* for her youngest—silliest—daughter.

Moishe was up bright and early the following morning and, as was his custom, he headed for the factory before the rest of the family had arisen. Admittedly, he looked forward to facing the daily challenges and coming up with innovative solutions and creative designs. With the machinery humming in the background and the feisty chatter coming from the workers, Moishe found he enjoyed the demanding pace. Most days, it was only his grumbling stomach that told him it was time to go home.

Although it was quite a distance across town, Moishe didn't bother ordering the coach with its retinue of footmen. His favorite mode of transportation, rather, was on his much-loved Orlov Trotter. A present from his wife on the occasion of his thirtieth birthday, Moishe had been overjoyed with Devora's selection of the jet-black beauty. He named the stallion *Abastor* after the legend of Pluto and his four black steeds—suffering Devora's warnings *not* to abduct young maidens or try to outride the stars.

With Abastor's easy trot, Moishe arrived at the factory just as his employees were settling down to business. As the previous night's conversation was still fresh on his mind, Moishe was nonplussed—to say the least—when he found the *revizor* napping outside of the building. Indeed, he approached the man with not a little trepidation and cleared his throat just loud enough to coax him to awake.

"Good morning, Inspector Reshetnikov," Moishe said with a smile that did not reach his eyes.

Mikhail Reshetnikov uncrossed his portly legs, and with exaggerated theatrics, made a great effort to stand.

"Moishe Solomonovich! You caught me napping while on duty. No doubt," he chuckled, "this little *faux pas* can remain between us?" The inspector's hands gestured back and forth. "What's a little secret between friends, eh?"

Moishe nodded his assurance.

"What do you say—will you not invite me in?"

Still shaken by the early morning visit, Moishe was at a loss for words. He handed Abastor over to a young groom he kept in his employ, and silently escorted the inspector throughout the maze of aisles and corridors. Upon reaching his office, Moishe opened the door and stepped aside, as the official sauntered into the room. Making himself comfortable in a worn, leather armchair, he proceeded to twist his thick neck to the left and then the right, before Moishe finally found his voice.

"May I be of service, Inspector? Are you looking for something in particular?"

"I don't suppose you could offer me something to drink?" the man said, fussing with his shaggy mustache.

"Some tea, perhaps?"

"*Nyet*! I don't care for the stuff. I was thinking of something stronger, my friend, but do not fret. I will not hold it against you."

"Something stronger? At this hour..." Moishe stumbled. "Ah—do forgive me, Inspector. Of course, you keep different hours than a simple merchant as myself."

"Come now! Do not play a part for me. We both know that you are not a *simple merchant*—not by any means."

Moishe, choosing to ignore this comment, ventured to change course and attempted to bring an end to the visit. "Inspector, what can I do for you?"

"Spoken like a true businessman. A tradesman through and through! I have to hand it to you, Moishe Solomonovich—you *evrei* are very good at what you do," the revizor said, as the armchair creaked under his weight.

Moishe clamped his mouth shut. *Evrei* was better *zhid*. If the official had used that derogatory term, he would have been hard pressed to keep a civil tongue. "Yes, well—" he stuttered, "I know you must be very busy, Inspector Reshetnikov, and I have yet to start my day..."

"Fine. No small talk. I am here to discuss your taxes. I fear the amount you were previously quoted was incorrect."

"I don't understand you, sir. I have already discussed the matter with my family. We are prepared to pay the required sum."

"An additional adjustment has been made to your tax obligation. It could not be avoided. The farmers have been hit hard this year...poor crops and all. The coffers are at an all-time low. The municipality can scarcely afford to pay its own workforce."

"While that may be true, Inspector, I am not able to meet the increased demand this quarter. If I may be allowed some time to retrench, perhaps there is something we can do."

"Unfortunately, I cannot guarantee the safety of your business in these stressful times. The police are overworked and underpaid themselves," said Reshetnikov, scratching the wide expanse of his belly. "Who knows what occurs at night, when we are safely tucked in our beds."

Stunned, Moishe pulled the chair from behind his desk and slowly lowered himself into a secure, seated position. Could he be hearing the man correctly? Was he being threatened?

"I am sorry. I know what happened to your friend— that Feinstein fellow. Several factories over in Kharkov have also seen a change of hands."

"A change of hands?"

"Just like Feinstein—the proprietors could not meet their tax liabilities, you see. Their rankings were revoked and their businesses were foreclosed. Of course, we did our best to find suitable replacements—it makes good business sense to install one of our own."

"Am I to lose my business?"

"Look here," he whispered, "I will be honest with you, for we have always fared well together. I have heard from state officials, that soon all *yid* business will be targeted. They need the locals to prosper, rather than you foreigners. You must understand."

"Inspector Reshetnikov, with all due respect, we *are not* foreigners," Moishe dared to rejoin. "My siblings and I were born in Odessa. My grandparents, and those of their generation, were practically *invited* by Catherine the Great with the partitions of the Polish-Lithuanian Commonwealth. How can we be considered foreigners when Lithuania, Belarus,

Ukraine, and Poland were assimilated by Mother Russia? We *are* Russian citizens just as the Moldavians, the Tatars, the Albanians..."

The inspector wearily came to his feet. Moishe's ardent declaration would not change the situation for any of the parties involved.

"*Mr. Russian Citizen*, I leave you with this final message," he muttered. "Things are going to start heating up again, and when they do—God help me—I will not be able to come to your aid."

Chapter Two

A whirlwind of activity had taken over the tranquility of the Abramovitz household. Moishe, overwrought with concern for the family business, had said very little when presented with the various invoices for Leah's celebration. A few more rubles here or there would not make any difference in the grand scheme of things, at least, that was what he told Aaron when his twin came to express his concern. The men discussed the conversation Moishe had had with the tax inspector; nevertheless, they decided to withhold the information from the family until after the festivities. They had no desire to dampen their sister's spirits or that of their mother's.

It was during tea, one quiet afternoon, that Leah presented her mamá with a folio containing names of potential guests, suggestions for the menu, references for florists, musicians and extra domestic personnel. Sokolov, the majordomo, would probably object, but Leah would insist on an extra footman or two. She had even taken the liberty of designing the invitation and provided her mother with a sample for her approval. Leah's only regret was that the family would not be hosting a ball but, rather, an elegant dinner party. Although the matriarch was of a mind to allow the younger set to partake in the pleasures of dancing, her pious son had made a strong case against the suggestion.

"Mamá, you know very well that there are rabbinic interpretations regarding mixed dancing," Avram proselytized. "In order to refrain from any sort of lewd conduct, or even the *temptation* of such a thing, our Talmudic sages have had much to say upon the subject."

"I respect your knowledge, Avram. Heaven only knows that I am not qualified to have a learned discussion on the matter, but tell me," Leah pleaded, "where is it *explicitly* written that men and women are forbidden to dance? Why must you be forever so old-fashioned?"

Avram chortled. "Well, at the very least, I can agree with you on one point—you are *not* qualified to have a learned discussion..."

"You needn't be offensive," Leah quipped.

"I would have you remember the incident with Lieutenant Yegorov, dear sister. You did not show any signs of maturity in that matter," Avram accused. "I dare say, neither did our house guest, Miss Marina. After all, she did assist in you stealing away—"

"It wasn't Molly's fault...oh dear! I mean to say *Miss Marina*!" Leah cried. "After meeting Lieutenant Yegorov on three separate occasions, I believed myself in love...*oh dear*! I only mean that she meant to protect me."

"Marriages have been arranged for less!"

"Avram, you must believe me. The lieutenant disturbed me greatly, but he did not injure me. Now, this business about prohibiting dancing—in this day and age—it is nonsense."

"My dear, it is a *minhag*," Malka interjected. "It is an accepted tradition, and whether or not it is in the *Torah*, I am not willing to allow an activity in our home that makes any family member uncomfortable."

Knowing that his mother would keep her word, Avram left the drawing room confident that the remaining organizational details were safe in her hands. It was not his intention to be old-fashioned. He did have Leah's best interests at heart, and Avram was certain that keeping the traditions of their faith intact would ensure her future happiness.

With Avram's departure, Malka turned her attention to her daughter's detailed manuscript. As she flipped through the many pages of clippings and hand-written notes, she was not at all surprised at Leah's organizational skills, but couldn't resist a chuckle or two when she came to the section entitled, 'Judith-Lady Moses Montefiore.' Leah had scribbled across the page the title of a book attributed to Lady Montefiore: *The Jewish Manual: Practical Information in Jewish and Modern Cookery with a Collection of Valuable Recipes & Hints Relating to the Toilette.*

"What have you here?" Malka asked.

"Oh, Mamá! I am truly pleased you noticed that entry! I've been researching Jewish gentry throughout Europe, in the hope that I might find some direction on how they lived in society—you know, among those who were... *not*." Leah giggled.

"And what were you able to discern, my dear?"

"Lady Montefiore wished to offer a cook book which represented a 'distinctive Jewish cuisine' for those genteel persons socializing in exceptionally cosmopolitan circles," said Leah, quoting her notes. "However, it is much more than a book of recipes! She offers practical advice for one's *toilette*, as well as one's table décor. Did you know, Mamá, she was of Portuguese lineage? She includes *both* Ashkenazic and Sephardic recipes."

"I was aware of Lady Montefiore's heritage, but, Daughter, I do not believe I have ever seen you so *impassioned*! Duvid will be quite impressed to hear you extolling the merits of the written word."

"Do not jest—I was simply mesmerized from the first page. It was as if Lady Montefiore was speaking directly *to me*! This book presents the 'cuisine of a woman of refinement' and that is *exactly* what I wish to be."

Malka skimmed across the page, reading various recipes and nodding her head here and there. Leah took this as a sign of encouragement and continued.

"Now I know what you are going to say, *Matushka*. The Montifiores were not necessarily strict in their adherence to the dietary laws, but apparently theses lapses in *kashrut* were only when they were away from home. Even then, Lady Judith mentions that 'all over Europe, the greatest chefs began to learn, if not a downright kosher, at least a *baconless* cuisine.' This was due to the many Jewish families in the highest social circles, such as *the Rothchilds*! Can you imagine?"

"What does your research say about their religious observance, Leah? Does it match our own?"

"Match our own?" she repeated. "We are such a large family, Mamá, all of us living under one roof—it is not possible for *all of us* to share the same belief! Not truly—not *deep* in our own hearts. Do you not agree?"

Malka smiled at her daughter's passionate nature and restated her question. "What have you learned of their beliefs, Daughter?"

"The newspaper clipping says 'English Jews of the elite and upper middle class were casual, inconsistent and pragmatic in their observance.' There—that is not *so* different from our own attitudes, is it?" Leah asked. "It says that this behavior was meant to be 'a compromise with the social and economic demands of English life.' I find that this speaks to my own way of thinking. If I am of age now—an adult, privy to my *own* thoughts and counsel—should I not formulate my own philosophy?"

Sighing, Malka recalled her own youthful rebellion. Questioning was part of becoming an adult and, most definitely, an integral part of being a Jew. "Your grandfather, a learned man and a beloved rabbi, taught me many things, as well you know. One of his most meaningful lessons was regarding our personal connections with Hashem. All the books, the interpretations, and regulations, *mean nothing* if they do not bring you closer to your Creator." Smiling, Malka gestured for her daughter to nestle along her side. "Come, let us look through this impressive catalogue of ideas and get to work."

From that afternoon until the night of the festivities, Leah's excitement couldn't be contained. The flowers were ordered and the invitations were delivered. Malka hired musicians—a string quintet—and even Avram approved. The evening's menu had been another point of discussion as Leah requested a formal French meal, served *à la russe*. Everyone in the household, from her brothers to her young nephew, Duvid, teased Leah over her fascination with the French; nonetheless, she would not be denied.

From fashion to cuisine, she adored all things *à la française*—except for manner that they served their meals. While the French custom was to serve all the food at once in an impressive display, Leah preferred the Russian practice where the various courses were brought to the table sequentially. Once the matter had been decided upon, the task of coming up with a suitable menu was attempted. Malka allowed Leah to join in the conversation, as well as several of her older, more experienced, daughters. The kitchen was taken over by the Abramovitz women and Mrs. Kraskov was not overly happy with the matter.

"I am sure I don't need your interference in preparing a meal, *Baryshnya* Leah," the feisty cook proclaimed.

"To be sure, I do not recall being asked to share *my* opinions for my coming out," Sara interjected with some disdain. "It is a bit shocking for Leah to have a say in the matter—"

"My daughter means no disrespect, Mrs. Kraskov," Malka assured her faithful servant. "We have enjoyed every meal you have prepared for us these many years, and Sara, dearest; you are a married woman and enjoy many rights and privileges that Leah will not experience for some time to come. I see no reason why she should not be allowed to put her creative mind to good use."

Leah tenderly embraced the old woman, ignoring her sister's pugnacious comments.

"In truth, it is not a slight against your skills, Mrs. Kraskov. Since I am not to have a ball like so many of the other girls or a Grand Tour across Europe, I wish to have a Parisian celebration. One day, I plan to visit the City of Lights—perhaps I will own a grand House of Fashion and everyone will know my name—but until that day, won't you help me create an enchanting evening à la française here at home?"

Sitting on a stool alongside the massive kitchen table, Leah had paper and fountain pen at the ready, as well as, Lady Judith's manual. The cookbook would come in handy if they needed a clever auxiliary ingredient or a refined suggestion to compensate for a *treif* course; and although she had promised herself to accept what her mamá and sisters suggested, Leah thought there was no harm in having a bit of fun.

"I wish to start the meal with something absolutely decadent. I believe we will begin with Clams on the Half Shell," Leah dared to say with a straight face.

"Have you lost your mind, *devushka*?" Mrs. Kraskov cackled, as she sat peeling a bushel of potatoes. "You cannot serve shellfish to a room full of Jews—and I don't care if they are accustomed to dining with the Tsar himself!"

Leah bit her lip, desperately trying not to laugh. "Well, then, what say you to caviar?"

"You cannot be serious? Even Lady Judith with all her tricks and substitutions, cannot make a sturgeon *kosher*!" Adjusting her apron, and throwing a handful of potatoes into a boiling pot of water, Mrs. Kraskov continued. "No—*Baryshnya* Leah, write this down— we will have a selection of hors d'oeuvres: *Pate maison*, *Melon Frappe*, *Saumon Fumé* and a refreshing, tomato salad."

The ladies looked around the kitchen table and bobbed their heads in agreement.

"Very well!" Leah acceded and set aside her jokes. "A soup course should follow. Shall we serve a clear *consommé* or a *veloute*?"

"We will serve *consommé julienne*, garnished with strips of root vegetables," Malka suggested. We do not want to serve a thick *veloute* with all that butter, dear."

"After which, there should be a crudités platter followed by some sort of fish," Rivka proposed.

"Yes," said Mrs. Kraskov, "followed by the entrée—I suggest a chicken dish—*poulet saute chasseur*?"

"It all sounds divine," Leah squealed with delight. "And then to cleanse the palate, I wish to have a Champagne sorbet."

Malka agreed "That would do very nicely, and now, on to the main course. For the *releve*, I suggest a hearty, but not too heavy, lamb dish. What do you say to *navarin d'agneau*?"

Mrs. Kraskov approved as Leah scribbled ferociously. "Afterwards," the cook added, "we will serve roast quail and *champignons grilles*."

"That ought to be followed by a course of *salade vert* and cold *poulet roti*," Leah's sister-in-law, Bluma opined.

The dessert course came together with a fit of laughter and indecorous squeals:

"*Ananas flambés au kirsch!*" said one sister.

"Crystallized dried fruits!" shouted another.

"Chocolate bonbons!" offered Leah.

"Cognac for the gentlemen!" gurgled Sara, allowing herself to be reeled into the excitement.

"Fine liqueurs for the ladies and...*shoyn!*" said Mrs. Kraskov most definitively. "That is more than enough!"

With much deliberation, and some giddiness as well, the ladies of the household had managed to come up with a sumptuous French menu that both Russian Ambassador Alexander Kurakin *and* Lady Moses Montefiore would have approved. Staff and household were at the ready. Leah had whipped everyone into such a state, even Gitel—one of the housemaids—was overheard saying, "You would think the Tsar and Tsarina were coming to dine!"

The *pièce de résistance* of the entire affair, of course, was to be Leah's evening gown. She had had the privilege and pleasure of wearing many beautiful dresses throughout the years, but this one was special. It was the fulfillment of a dream—a gown of her own design. Moishe had helped select the fabrics and only the top seamstress from the factory was allowed to assist in the creation.

Leah had worked diligently on the design of the skirt which was made of luxurious cream satin. She was pleased that the new fashion called for cleaner lines. The architecture of the silhouette was softer— more feminine. Leah had hand-embroidered delicate silver flowers with fine metallic thread on a net overlay. With every movement, light would catch the shimmer of the flower petals reminding one of twinkling moonbeams. An emerald green *faille* silk train was sewn over the cream silk and lace, descending down the back and wrapping the bodice in a lattice fashion.

When she dressed for the evening, Leah placed an emerald brooch at the center of the bodice. It was her father's final gift to her at the age of twelve, and upon recalling that bittersweet occasion, she was overcome with emotion.

"I am ever so grateful, Mamá," she said contemplating her reflection in the mirror. "I only wish..."

Malka knew her daughter well and understood the sudden melancholy. "You are a vision, my dear. *Such talent!* You have an eye for fashion. Papá would have been the first to acknowledge it." She reached for Leah and gently clasped both of her hands. "I am certain that he is with us in spirit. Do you not feel his presence? I know that he walks beside me each and every day."

Leah turned back to gaze at her image in the mirror. Her fingers lightly skimmed over the multifaceted cool stone. "I often wondered Mamá about...about *his spirit.* Do you truly believe he is with us? And if so, would he truly be proud of me? Would he find me deserving?"

Unshaken at these queries, Malka sought the words to console her daughter. "Did you know that emerald brooch was a favorite of your grandmother's? You always did remind your papá of Chanit. She was a strong woman, with piercing green eyes and a personality to match!" Malka smiled. "Her strong character might have been considered off-putting to some, but she was a leader *and she followed her instincts.* I believe your dear Papá saw these qualities in his enchanting—*mischievous*—daughter. He would feel that you deserve this and so much more."

"I do hope he is looking upon me with pride, but...that is to say...would he be ashamed of my reprehensible behavior with Lieutenant Yegorov?"

"Why would you think upon the matter—tonight, of all nights?"

"*It is the brooch*! The emerald reminds me of...of the fateful night when I urged Molly to accompany me to that miserable ball. Do you recall it? I'm certain that you do. You were all so very angry with us," Leah cried. "Molly wore Rivka's white satin covered in tulle and silver and I wore my cream chiffon with the emerald paisley applique—"

Realizing that she was rambling, Leah paused and tried to focus on what she wished to relate. "Oh Mamá! *I miss Molly*—I mean Marina! *Heavens*! I suppose it doesn't much matter what I call her now. I just wish she would return to us. I wish that I could have followed her back to her home. I can't stop thinking of all of the missed opportunities!"

Malka released a deep sigh and prayed for guidance on how best to approach the subject of Molly Abramovitz—or rather, *Marina Davidovich*, as the family had come to know their mysterious houseguest.

"We vowed not to speak of Molly's visit. Goodness. Even Duvid hasn't brought up the subject, and we all *did* agree that it would be for the best in order to avoid any disagreeable enquiries. Trust me, my dear," Malka said, as she smoothed out an imaginary crease in Leah's skirt. "You ought not want to follow in Molly's footsteps. You will have your own chance to be put to the test and be triumphant. In any case, Molly's visit was a lesson—an awakening to something that Hashem meant for her alone. At least, that is my interpretation of the circumstances. We should not assume to understand Hashem's divine plan."

Leah picked up a handkerchief that lay on the vanity and dabbed away at the silly tears she had allow to escape. "You are right, of course, Mamá. I am not being reasonable. Perhaps it is the excitement of the evening that has me in such a state."

"Yes, my dear. Tonight is a night of celebration. Let us not dwell upon matters which we may not control, let alone, comprehend," she implored. "Now then, are you ready to make your entrance? I am afraid your guests might believe you have changed your mind and have run off to Paris, after all!"

The women shared a giggle and left the room arm and arm. From the main landing, Leah witnessed the controlled whirlwind of activity. Outside, liveried footmen were at the ready as carriages rambled up the gravel path to the portico where elegant passengers alighted. Leah's guests, resplendent in their finery and jewels, mingled and meandered their way throughout the grand foyer accepting *coupés de champagne* and delectable canapés.

Her mamá descended the grand staircase looking every bit the queen of the realm. Dressed in black silk, as was her custom, Malka deemed it appropriate to wear the diamond and pearl brooch with matching earrings that Solomon had presented her on the occasion of Leah's birth. Handsome in their formal attire, both Moishe and Aaron waited for their mother as she reached the main floor, and with noted gallantry, presented her with a delicate wrist corsage. Malka turned to the chamber ensemble and they, witnessing her regal nod, began to serenade the guests with music both lyrical and light.

Only a moment or two passed before Leah made her appearance at the top of the stairs. On an impetuous whim, a young gentleman began to applaud, and quite spontaneously, family and friends joined in. They gathered around the majestic balustrade which had been polished to a lustrous glow and welcomed Leah as she gracefully descended—her silk train gliding lightly upon the steps.

"*Bienvenue mes amis*," Leah called out with unbridled joy. "Welcome and thank you! Thank you for coming to celebrate *mon anniversaire!*"

And with that, a throng of young ladies dressed in multicolored gowns of silk and satin came upon the birthday celebrant with shrieks of glee and felicitations. The family observed that their Leah—usually impish and not a bit *overly* reverent—had transformed before their eyes into a young lady of sophistication and refinement.

She glided in and around the crowd, greeting each guest with a kind word and exchanging kisses in the traditional manner. She paid compliments to the gentlemen and lavished praise on the ladies for everyone was looking quite their best. Upon greeting Hannah Rivkin, Leah was overheard showering her friend with congratulations. Hannah had recently become an aunt for the first time to twin boys. A moment later, she was noted consoling Rachel Lipovesky whose grandmamá had recently taken a fall. But when Leah was observed graciously listening to the rabbi's longwinded story, the family knew that they were *indeed* witnessing a true transformation.

Just then, Tamar Bezkrovny, Leah's lifelong friend and neighbor, came rushing upon her leaving her betrothed Mikhail Roitman trailing behind. Mr. Roitman did not seem too perturbed at being abandoned as he was accompanied by a gentleman who, although was simply dressed, had the look of a rake about him.

Realizing the young man was not of her acquaintance, when Leah leaned in to greet Tamar, she whispered most discretely, "Who is this handsome stranger?"

"Dear Leah," she gushed, "did you not receive my note this afternoon?"

"In truth, I do not recall. Gitel has worn herself out bringing me all manner of gifts and cards that were delivered today. With all the preparations, I simply did not have time to look at everything! What did the note say?"

"Only this—I wrote to impose on your kind hospitality," said Tamar. "Mikhail informed me only this morning that his good friend, Lazar Vaisman, had arrived from Kiev for an extended visit! We could not abandon him on his first night, and I simply refused to miss your birthday celebration. We had to bring him along."

"Tamar, you are a silly goose! Mr. Vaisman will be a charming addition to our table. He is rather dashing, isn't he? Let me advise Sokolov to add another setting —*next to me*—so that I might make him feel welcome."

"Leah, please *do* listen. I am not at all acquainted with Mr. Vaisman, and while he *is* rather dashing, he has shown himself to be, let us say, uncouth."

"Whatever do you mean?"

"I am merely trying to warn you, my friend. Do not allow yourself to become infatuated..."

"Really Tamar! What do you take me for? Tonight, as a true pupil of Lady Judith, I am the paragon of virtue and sociability," Leah said, hiding a muffled laugh behind a gloved hand.

Excusing herself, Leah sought out the majordomo and provided him with a revision to the seating arrangements. Moments later, Malka caught her daughter's eye and nodded a silent message. Understanding her meaning, Leah turned and called out to her guests, "Shall we go in?"

Malka led the way with Moishe at her side and Leah linked arms with her brother, Aaron. With family and friends trailing behind, they made a regal party indeed.

The staff had outdone themselves in preparation for the evening. A magnificent contrast of colors greeted the happy company as they followed the guest of honor into the grand dining room. It truly was a thing of beauty and Leah was overwhelmed to see her plans come to fruition. The stark white damask linens she had selected brought out the sheen of the fine, dark woods, and as she had requested, crystal vases arranged with roses of every hue were perfectly situated along the center of the table. The chandelier and table candelabras provided an almost fairy-like luminosity that flittingly played upon the glistening *niello* goblets and gilded tableware she had chosen from her mother's collection.

The Abramovitz household numbered nearly thirty adults and Leah had invited thirty more. The luxury of being able to seat sixty people at one's dining room table seemed slightly ostentatious at first, but after further reading of Lady Judith's social gatherings, Leah felt the number was quite modest after all. Mamá had approved the list and Avram, apparently feeling a bit guilty for ruling out a debutant's ball, had acquiesced.

Leah had requested that the children dine early and remain in the nursery, although she extended an invitation to her young nephew, Duvid, as he had become a Bar Mitzvah and could readily be considered an adult. Duvid declined his aunt's request to dine with the grownups, as he had *far better things to do with his evening than sit around and eat rich foods while discussing politics.* Leah had laughed at his naive remarks and promised to save him some treats from the dessert course; however, she unequivocally denied that they would be sitting around her elegant table discussing politics.

"Who would be so coarse as to speak of such horrid topics whilst dining?" she exclaimed.

After the initial *oohs* and *aahs*, Leah's guests spied their names printed very prettily on silk cards. The ladies were assisted in taking their places and the gentlemen were seated. A *serviette* in the shape of a *fleur de lis* had been placed at the center of each setting, and when Malka gently placed the napkin upon her lap, the party followed suit. After a brief benediction, the dinner service commenced while music spilled in from the foyer, intermingling with the pleasantries exchanged across the wide expanse of the Abramovitz dinner table.

Sokolov had seen to Leah's request and Mr. Lazar Vaisman had been seated to her left. Curious to learn more about her friend's houseguest, she turned slightly to face the gentleman, whose good looks had caused more than one young lady to blush. Mr. Vaisman, however, was not prepared to entertain Miss Abramovitz as he seemed to be conversing with a passing footman. Leah found it odd that a guest would strike up a conversation with a staff member. It was rather rude to the other guests and inconsiderate to the footman who, after all, was attempting to complete the task at hand.

As the footman scurried away, with his wig askew and trembling tray, Leah faced her guest once more only to find him exhibiting a shocking want of decorum. Slouched in his seat, Mr. Vaisman allowed his long legs to stretch under the table—brushing his foot alongside of Leah's satin slipper! *Heavens*! She chose to ignore this faux pas and attempted to speak with Mr. Lev Gobenko, a particular friend of the family, who had himself just recently returned from Kiev. But as Leah shifted in her seat, she witnessed Mr. Vaisman wildly scratching his head—just as she had seen the stable boy do on many occasions after napping on a bale of hay. As Leah sought to catch Tamar's attention, the footmen brought in the soup course.

Each man carried a silver tray which held a heavy urn and ladle. When the footman approached, Mr. Vaisman not only lifted the ladle and took a whiff, he asked the domestic if he had already supped and if the food had been to his liking! Fortunately, the chatter around the table was lively. Leah's guests did not overhear the remarks nor did they witness the man's outrageous behavior. As a gracious hostess, she could not reproach Mr. Vaisman; and so, Leah simply asked the footman to carry on hoping to avoid causing a scene at her exquisite table.

Just then, Mr. Vaisman sat up in his seat exposing his full height and broad shoulders. "Is that Brahms?"

"No," Mr. Gobenko replied, "I believe it is Shubert."

Mr. Vaisman wiped his moustache rather brusquely and tossed the *serviette* onto the table. "I dare say the musicians could scrounge up a proper Russian score."

"Let us not disparage the evening's entertainment, sir," Mr. Gobenko suggested. "Perhaps the next piece will be Tchaikovsky. Will that be more to your liking?"

"It is not a matter of it being to my liking, sir. I am simply pointing out that Mother Russia has a multitude of talent. Why must be entertained by foreigners?"

Yosef, sitting nearly at the other end of the table, began to notice Leah's distress. Unable and unwilling to shout across the expanse, he urged his like-minded brothers, Ephraim and Benjamin to pay close attention to the matter unfolding. He had not been introduced to this Mr. Vaisman, but Yosef was leery of the stranger's audacity. The simple fact that the man chose to act out, whilst attending a dinner party for a young lady, was ample reason to be vigilant.

"Sir," said Ephraim, "Mother Russia does indeed have a wealth of artistry. I, myself, am not proficient in the world of music, but perhaps we can request a piece by Anton Grigorevich Rubinstein or Samuel Moiseyevich Maykapar? Not only are they Russian, but they are Jews!"

The chit-chat around the table had dropped to a minimum as guests had become aware of an indelicate situation taking place. The footmen began bringing in the next course. Leah was distressed that the food she so carefully selected was not receiving its proper accolades; but Mr. Vaisman was determined to continue his topic of conversation, and no one seemed to have the slightest interest in the delicacies Mrs. Kraskov had prepared.

"Ah—*Rubinstein*," Mr. Vaisman smirked. "There's an interesting choice. Jewish, you say? I believe their family were forced to convert. If ever there was a confused man..."

"Perhaps we can enjoy Tchaikovsky *and* the *poulet saute chasseur*," suggested Leah.

Vaisman harrumphed at Leah's comment and looked Ephraim straight in the eye. "Have you not heard Rubinstein's ramblings? Allow me to quote: *'Russians call me German, Germans call me Russian, Jews call me a Christian, Christians a Jew. Pianists call me a composer, composers call me a pianist. The classicists think me a futurist, and the futurists call me a reactionary. My conclusion is that I am neither fish nor fowl—a pitiful individual.'* As I said, a most confused individual."

Benjamin, trying to move the subject off the music, turned to another topic. Unfortunately it, as well, was not to Leah's liking.

"I agree wholeheartedly. We should enjoy Russia's gifts. It is in keeping with the *Haskalah* that we take pride in our country. As educated, enlightened Jews, we should advocate that our community speak the language of our countrymen. Yiddish is a rich and delightful language, but here we are, conversing in Russian—and am I happy for it. Russia is *our home*. In order to prove our loyalty and commitment, we must assimilate."

"Not everyone in our community lives as we do," said Ysroel. "People who are not of our rank deserve our assistance, our compassion and understanding. It is possible that they do not assimilate, as you say, due to a lifetime of ridicule and ostracization."

"It is incumbent upon us to educate those beneath us in social standing," Benjamin retorted. "We need not allow ourselves to be looked upon as a separate and unique entity. We should endeavor to integrate with our surrounding societies, and this, of course, includes the study of the native tongue, values, and fashion."

"I'll tell you what we ought to be doing. We ought to be waltzing in your ballroom to a masterpiece by Tchaikovsky or some such!" Mr. Vaisman interjected. "We *ought to be* enjoying the Russian caviar that flows with such great abandon in the homes of our neighbors and colleagues—not this foreign, French fare."

Leah recoiled at this last comment. The servants had continued bringing course after course; and yet, her lovely Parisian meal had been spoiled by the ramblings of an uninvited, and clearly, unrefined guest. And now, as the staff cleared one set of plates and set out the next course, the rabbi—a guest of Avram's—prepared to join in the conversation.

"If I may, I believe that the gentlemen are forgetting a key component. Aside from the minority of Jews of your rank, and the multitude of Jews enslaved in poverty and serfdom, there is yet another group we ought not forget. We, of the rabbinate, cannot approve of those who wish to eliminate or minimize the preservation of traditional Jewish values and mores. Indeed, that behavior will surely lead to the extinction of our faith."

"All this talk about religion and societal estrangement is *secondary* to the real problem," Yosef stressed. "The people are frightened of the economic downfall, not the social or political clamor. It is the crop failure, which leads to famine and illness that is stirring the masses. If the empire cannot sustain its citizenry, then rich or poor—*Jews or non-Jews*—will seek a solution to their economic crises outside of Russia."

"Economics?" Mr. Vaisman shouted. "Have you not read *The Protocols of the Elders of Zion*? It is probably the most widely distributed piece of anti-Semitic propaganda ever created."

"Yes, yes, the *Okhrana* are doing their bit as the secret police to help strengthen the Tsar's authority," said Yosef. "They believe by stirring the pot with this rubbish, our Christian neighbors will feel threatened that we Jews are conspiring to dominate the world."

Benjamin snickered. "Funny that—dominate the world while our mouths are gagged and our hands are tied behind our backs. That's quite a magic act."

Malka placed her utensils across her plate, signaling that she had completed her meal. Raising a goblet to her lips, she asked Mr. Gobenko to update the company on the goings on in Kiev. "Had you the opportunity to visit the opera house, Mr. Gobenko?"

"Yes madam and I arrived by way of the new-fangled electric tram. What an adventure! The opera house, in all its splendor, was shadowed by the journey," he replied. It cost me 35 kopecks—which I willingly paid—for the opportunity to arrive to my destination compressed as a sardine in a tin can. To be sure, the car was overly crowded with many courageous and eager passengers."

"Oh, do tell, Mr. Gobenko!" Leah asked, relieved at the change of conversation. "How were the ladies dressed for their evening at the Opera?"

"The ladies and gentlemen of Kiev were wearing the latest fashions brought in from Paris—no doubt, created by your very own fabrics, Abramovitz," he said directing his comment to Moishe. "It would have been in an extraordinary evening in its totality, had it not been for a brief scuffle on the tram."

"Scuffle? What happened?" Leah asked. "Is it appropriate to share with mixed company?"

"I dare say with everything else that has been discussed tonight, you fair ladies will not mind hearing this last bit!"

Leah's heart sank as the footmen brought in the *Ananas flambés*. Her guests were simply engrossed by the conversation, and no one seemed to notice as the dessert was set alight by Sokolov, causing a flare of blue-tinged flames which quickly dissipated as Mr. Gobenko continued with his tale.

"As we traveled from Poshtova Square and crossed the Nicholas Bridge, we realized a troop of soldiers were following us at high speed. The tram conductor brought us to full stop and spoke briefly to the captain. It was a curious and uncomfortable turn of events, to be sure. Just as the soldiers began boarding the car, a gentleman seated in the back row bolted and ran off! The soldiers followed in hot pursuit; but as the conductor was given leave to continue, we were not privy to the conclusion of the incident," Mr. Gobenko concluded with great flair.

"Do you know who they were pursuing?" Yosef asked.

"No, nothing was explained to us. However, later in the evening, there was a bit of speculation over the gentleman. It seems there had been some political activity in the city, some unrest over domestic servants and their rights as employees. Several gentlemen indicated that the man was not caught and that he was able to leave the city without further confrontation."

Leah let out a gasp and peeked at Mr. Vaisman underneath her lashes. It was a strange coincidence that he should arrive at Mr. Roitman's doorstep unannounced and uninvited. She daren't think such things, but it *was* too provocative to say the least! She was saved from making further commentary as Malka suddenly arose and the gentlemen followed suit.

"Ladies, shall we retire to the drawing room?" Malka proposed. "Let us leave the gentlemen to their engrossing conversation, along with their port and cigars."

The ladies, obliging and relieved, accepted the gentlemen's assistance and began their withdrawal to the sounds of Liszt's String Quintet in C major. The music, *allegro ma non troppo,* reflected the ladies retreat—quick, but not too quick. Leah turned with the intention of asking her brothers not to dawdle for too long, when a loud crash of glass startled the party. The men rushed to the shattered windows where Yosef picked up an empty bottle of vodka. A note was tied about its center with a blood-red ribbon.

"Death to the Jews! Out with the foreigners!"

Chapter Three

$\mathcal{F}$ollowing a brief investigation of the surroundings, the men sent for the local officials as guests hurriedly piled away in their elegant conveyances and drove off into the cold mysterious night. Shortly after the constable arrived, his assistants, along with one or two of the rattled footmen, secured the premises. Recording the damage to the shattered windows, as well as the devastation to the grounds, the officer advised the family that a report would be submitted. He emphasized that they ought not have any expectation that the perpetrators would be found. All across the *oblast*, he noted, there had been reports of uprisings and attacks against the local gentry. Shrugging his shoulders, and with a cheeky tip of the hat, the constable bade everyone a goodnight. His men followed suit.

Very little sleep was to be had that night. Family members tossed and turned in their beds, fearful for what had transpired and anxious for what lay ahead.

The light of dawn brought with it not only further proof of the damage done to the estate, but of the damage done to the family's outlook. Leah, distraught and humiliated that her presentation into society turned out to be another incident on the constable's evening report, was inconsolable. As one by one they staggered into the family breakfast room, Mrs. Kraskov filled their cups with steaming hot tea and placed before them a simple repast of toasted bread and honey, *maslenitsa* with jam and butter and a variety of fresh fruits.

"Will there be anything else, *Barynya* Abramovitz?"

With a practiced glance, Malka interpreted her family's demeanor. Not only was there a lack of appetite, the absence of chatter was deafening. Poor Leah's face said it all. They were overwhelmed by anger *and fear*.

"That will be all, Mrs. Kraskov," Malka quietly replied. "After last night's extravagance, a simple meal will do."

With expansive multi-paned windows facing the rising sun, the intimate chamber was awash in morning's golden glow. While the breakfast room usually leant itself to animated conversation and witty repartee, the mood of the current inhabitants would not defer to the decor. Even the scattered arrangements of sunflowers and daisies could not add any measure of vivacity to the room. The despondency was complete. When Aaron cleared his throat and made a fuss of adjusting his place setting *just so*, Malka was relieved that, at last, someone would break the silent gloom.

"There is something you wish to say, *Aaronka*?"

"You are correct, as usual," he replied with a wistful smile. "Moishe and I made an unwise decision in keeping some information to ourselves. We did not wish to ruin the festivities, you see, but as we have now been victimized, and have witnessed firsthand that which Inspector Reshetnikov had forewarned, we have no choice but to discuss the matter."

"You had spoken with the inspector?"

"Not I, Mamá. Moishe had an unexpected visit to the factory."

The family turned and looked to Moishe. Seated at the head of the table, he had been stirring his tea the entire time Aaron had been speaking. The clinkety-clank of his spoon against the porcelain had gone unnoticed until just then.

"Yes—well," Moishe began. "There is no other way to say this, I suppose. We are not only facing government regulations and international pressures, as was previously discussed. I was certain that we would be able to weather that particular storm, but you see, the issue we are facing—"

"Yes, Moishe—out with it!" cried Yosef.

"Inspector Reshetnikov believes that Odessa will be witnessing an increase of violence, the likes of which our people tragically have already experienced."

"And so? Is anyone surprised at this information?" Ephraim asked. "After the *pogrom* of '71, Peretz Smolenskin wrote several articles questioning the belief of Jewish integration into this society. Then came the *pogrom* of 1881, followed by the one in '86! How many more humiliations must we suffer? How many more deaths will it take?"

"It was only a question of *when* the violence would start up again—*not if*," Benjamin interjected. "I, for one, am tired of living in such of state of anxiety."

"Precisely," said Ephraim. "We must constantly be vigilant of what we say, with whom we are seen, how we do business—or *not* do business. This is no way to live."

"What do you two suggest?" asked Sara.

Benjamin looked to his side and shrugged. "Yosef speaks for us."

Solomon's youngest son slowly folded his napkin and placed it purposefully under the edge of the plate. Standing, Yosef pushed the chair back into place and gripped the engraved wooden spindles. He knew what he wanted to say—he had practiced over and over in his mind; yet now when the time had come to put forth his proposition, Yosef found that he was at a loss for words. He looked to his mother who sat patiently with inquisitive eyes. She had always respected them enough to know whatever idea they had formulated, it was one worth considering. The curiosity sketched across her face, coupled with her calm demeanor, somehow gave him the incentive to begin speaking.

"We have been on a downward spiral for some time, both in financial and political terms. It has now become personal. Let us not forget that, in truth, this was not the first attack against our family. Our factory has been a target of vandalism and, on both occasions, the officials refused to take action." Yosef noticed the family nodding their recollection. "Our very existence is questioned by those who we would call compatriots. I think it is time we leave."

Leah, sitting quietly at the edge of the room, was stirred into action upon hearing Yosef's words.

"Are others of our position leaving?" she demanded. "Do the Brodskys speak of immigration?"

"The Brodsky family has connections to other industrialists, such as Artemy Tereschtenko," Benjamin replied. "Their resources for financial stability *and* personal safety far surpass our own. You are forever comparing us to that family. When are you going to understand? They are practically royalty—*we* are not."

Leah disregarded her brother and posed yet another question. "What of Kharkovs or the Poznański family? I do believe that their textile production plant is quite lucrative."

Yosef simply shrugged his shoulders. "You can go down your list and name all the Jewish industrialists—the Zaitsevs, the Balakhovskys, the Halperins—I still will not have a satisfactory response to your question; and furthermore, I care not of their arrangements."

"If no one else is speaking of leaving, I don't understand why we have to broach the subject. I do not wish to leave my home or my friends. Believe what you will, but I have my own dreams...my own plans."

"And who are you to have dreams and plans already?" demanded Sara. "You are a *shmarkatka*—a snotty nosed little girl just turned eighteen. I suggest you keep silent and listen to your elders."

"Look," said Yosef eyeing both of his sisters with growing annoyance, "do you not understand? We live in a nation that does not have a constitution! We do not have elected representatives or a democratic process. There is nothing *or no one* that can restrain the Tsar. Whatever he decrees, his ministers, and bureaucrats implement. If we manage to survive this episode of violence—and we know it is coming—we will only have to deal with the next one. Our children—*yours and mine*—will live in this vicious cycle."

"Son, what do you propose we do?"

"There are forward-thinking men in South America—*men with vision*," said Yosef, waiting for the gasps and scoffs to conclude before continuing. "I suggest we go to Argentina. It is a new country, but these men—Alberdi, Sarmiento, and Mitre—realize that the rich flat lands are calling out to be civilized. They need to grow their population and develop the country. They are asking—no—they are begging for European immigration."

"But do they want Eastern Europeans?" Avram challenged. *"Do they want Jews?"*

Yosef was prepared for this question. He had studied the situation from all sides, knowing that each of his brothers would challenge his plan from a different perspective. It was strange that, when he had first started learning about Argentina and Baron Maurice Hirsch, the family had received an unexpected—and shockingly well-informed—visitor.

Marina Davidovich was introduced as the daughter of a business associate from Lviv. She was a beautiful young lady, charming and educated, but she was rather odd. She spoke of things that most young ladies wouldn't dream of discussing. Yosef had become leery of her. He had gone as far as suspecting her of collusion with some of the more aggressive activist groups, but he had been mistaken. In the end, her explanations and concerns with regards to the family and factory, seemed to make sense, and in one aspect, her visit spurred his interests in Baron Hirsch.

"As a matter of fact, Avram, the answer to your question is a definitive: yes. I've been researching an organization called The Jewish Colonization Association," Yosef explained. "A nobleman by the name of Maurice von Hirsch has been assisting Jewish immigrants in Argentina since 1882."

"Why would he put his money into that strange and far-away land?" Ysroel asked. "Why not put it to good use right here?"

"He tried! He offered to donate a fortune to the Jewish community, to build schools, hospitals—to alleviate the poverty in the Pale, but the Russian government wanted to have control of the funds."

"That would have been absolute insanity!" Ysroel cried.

"Precisely. Having given up trying to negotiate with the government for the safety and well-being of Russian Jews, Hirsch decided to use his wealth by establishing an emigration and colonization society. He, along with several great philanthropists, realized the importance—*the significance*—of this plan soon after a certain gentleman by the name of Carlos Calvo contacted them. After learning of the horrific pogroms of May 1881, Calvo, who was the representative of the Immigration Department of Argentina in Paris, advised several key people that the fledging nation was open to emigration," Yosef said with increasing enthusiasm. "The Argentine government is beckoning us to join them! We could be part of something historical—not only saving our own lives, but creating something of worth for the future."

The room was silent as Yosef finished his dramatic speech. To ease the solemnity, Malka choose to direct the conversation in a more positive vein. "I believe, children, the situation calls for a Spanish tutor—post haste!" she said with a hopeful grin.

Dejected at the turn of events, Leah groaned. "We already are quite proficient in Italian and French...oh! Now *that* is a brilliant scheme! Why not immigrate to France?" She looked at her siblings and urged them to rally around her suggestion. "At least we know the language and have connections with designers and manufacturers...oh, but *what of England*? Papa had made many connections on his travels there, and with Queen Victoria's relationship with our royal family, perhaps we would be well received! Of course, I would need to improve my English accent. I admit I struggle with the syntax—"

Yosef stared in disbelief as his sister continued to ramble on.

"But, if we were to go to Paris, perhaps I would be able to study under the tutelage of Charles Worth! Imagine working with the father of Haute Couture. Oh Mamá—to be in *La Chambre Syndicale De La Confection Et De La Couture Pour Dames Et Fillettes!* I can envision myself working alongside the most elite of designers."

"Yes, of course," said Benjamin. "You would go straight from our drawing room into one of the top couture houses known to the modern fashion world. Do try to be a bit more humble, sister dear."

Leah knew, of course, she would have to prove herself, but the thought did not intimidate her. She believed her passion put her on equal footing with those who had the experience. One could be taught a skill, but without the heart's involvement, the end result would suffer for it. Her father had taught her that lesson. Leah held on to the concept as a beacon to help weather the storms of sibling taunts and skepticism.

"I am a fairly good seamstress," Leah declared in rebuttal. "Better still, I own that I am quite talented with embellishments. I might begin in an important *atelier*. The workers in those intimate shops are given exact instruction. I would be well directed, and one day, I might be able to show Mr. Worth my designs."

"And he will fall on his knees and beg for permission to include your work in his next collection." teased Benjamin once more.

"*Oh you*! Naturally you must goad me, but at least, I have aspirations. I don't understand why we have to go to Argentina, when we could do perfectly well in France. We have friends there to welcome us..."

"No, that is out of the question," Malka firmly stated. "I wouldn't dream of contacting our business acquaintances and putting them in such an awkward situation."

Yosef shook his head. "Up until now, I have said nothing about your obsession with French fashion, or your choice of menus, for that matter. But here, at least, I must draw the line," he railed. "Leah, do you have any idea of what is going on in France?"

"I know we have been in business with many well-connected people in that country for decades. You make it sound as if we are still at war with that self-proclaimed little emperor!"

"You are being nonsensical. I am not speaking of the Napoleonic wars or anything having to do with the military expansion. Have you not read, or even heard of, *Le Petit Journal*? *La Patrie*? Those popular journals are dripping with anti-Semitism. Jews are not safe in France today."

"I would have you know, Yosef, that I do read—maybe not the periodicals that you find so enlightening," Leah retaliated. "In one of my fashion journals, I read that there were over forty thousand Jews in Paris alone, and that they were highly integrated into society. Are you telling me that forty thousand people in the City of Lights are not safe?"

"I have three words for you. The. Dreyfus. Affair."

"What about it?"

"*What about it*? It only happens to be one of the worst political scandals of that nation!"

Yosef was so overcome that he began pacing about the breakfast room looking to his brothers for support. Ephraim decided to take on the matter. He asked Leah to take a seat and he approached her as if she were a witness on trial.

"This hideous scandal began just a few years ago in '94," Ephraim began. "Captain Alfred Dreyfus, a young artillery officer—a Jew—was convicted of treason. He was sentenced to life imprisonment for allegedly communicating French military secrets to the German Embassy in Paris, and was imprisoned on Devil's Island in French Guiana. When new evidence came to light, and a Major Esterhazy was named as the true culprit, several high-ranking officials suppressed the information. Not surprisingly, a military court unanimously acquitted Esterhazy and accused Dreyfus of *additional* charges!"

Leah sat silently as her brother circled around her. He was such a bully—just like the others, she thought.

"Thankfully, two years ago, a letter was published in a Parisian newspaper accusing the court of framing Dreyfus," Ephraim continued. "The letter was written by famed author, Émile Zola..."

Leah's head popped up as she gasped in recognition of the name. "Émile Zola? The author of *Au Bonheur des Dames*?"

"I suppose he is one in the same..."

"Oh, I just finished reading that novel—it was *tre magnifique*! It takes place in the most delightful department store, *The Paradise* or some such, and it is filled with every exquisite item you could imagine..."

"It is impossible to speak intelligently with the girl!" Ephraim exclaimed. "Just know this: the scandal has divided French society between those who supported Dreyfus and those who condemned him."

"Can you expect to make France your new home?" demanded Yosef. "No! Argentina is the place for us."

"Even Theodore Herzl has claimed that Russian Jews only have two choices—the Holy Land or Argentina, Aaron offered. "Knowing our community's painful history under tsarist rule, one can only imagine what lies ahead."

Avram noted the many voices in agreement and sought to have his share of the conversation. "I realize that most of you have been won over by Yosef's impassioned speech, but I do not wish to leave Odessa. We have built a community here. There are those less fortunate who rely on our leadership and good works. I would propose that Hashem has placed us here for a reason, but perhaps it is time for us to part ways—each of us following our own path."

"Your father, may he rest in peace, insisted we live together under one roof. If he didn't wish the family to spread across the city, the *oblast*, or even the empire, I can only imagine he would not want us to be separated by an ocean," Malka decreed. "No. We must all go. I fear darker days are ahead—darker than even my passionate son believes."

"How do you know this, Mamá?" asked Sara.

"How does one define trust?" Malka murmured. Sighing, she paused but a moment. "I have often said that there are things which are inexplicable. We are suddenly being presented with a barrage of dilemmas. I believe that these obstacles are messages from Hashem and it behooves us to pay attention."

"Others in our same position do not seem to be in a rush," Sara insisted. "Why the urgency?"

"Why hesitate, Daughter? I do not wish to be as the Israelites escaping their brutal masters in Egypt, and perhaps there is something better waiting for us in Argentina. *Gam zu l'tova*—this too is for the good."

"Are you willing to take a chance with our future based solely on faith and dictums?" Leah presumed to press on.

"You may believe that I am taking a leap of faith, but I have been listening to my children and paying close attention to those in our community. My sons are at risk of becoming more attached to certain radical groups. Our brethren are trapped in the Pale. There is talk of impending revolution amongst our own people and war against Japan. Our business is at risk and our future is not secure. These *must* be signs from above, and I do not choose to ignore them. My only stipulation in this scheme is that we all leave together. No one in the family should remain behind."

"What of Gitel and the rest of the household?"

"The staff is free to choose their own path, but Gitel has a place within our home much like no other."

"She is a servant, Mamá," replied Avram.

"She *is not* just any sort of servant, my dear. Gitel was but a child when she came to us, and has now become indispensable. She has trained with Mrs. Kraskov and has become of great use to her in the kitchen. She has helped me in the garden with my herbs and has become quite the alchemist. She keeps house as well as any other and is an exemplary ladies' maid. And besides, I have taken a liking to her. She reminds me a bit of...me," Malka said with a chuckle. "Gitel has no other place to go. Who knows what will befall her if we leave her behind. No—Gitel comes with us."

"As it appears that the family has agreed to this adventure," Avram conceded, "how do we proceed?"

"We will need to get our papers in order," Moishe stated. "As Jewish merchants we have permission to travel within the country; however, we will still need to research the matter as it pertains to emigration."

"After the last series of *pogroms*, officials have turned a blind eye on the flight of—let us just say—*undesirables*," said Yosef. "Naturally, we will have to apply to the Jewish Colonization Association. Our government has approved a ten-member committee headquartered, here, in Odessa. Now that I have the family's support on the matter, with Moishe's assistance, that's where we shall begin."

Chapter Four

The following morning, Moishe and Yosef made their way into town. It was a matter of good fortune that the J.C.A. had seen the benefit of establishing an outpost in Odessa, as a trip to Kiev, or worse yet, St. Petersburg, would have meant a delay in their plans. Leah had taken umbrage at the insinuation that the J.C.A. would have looked down their noses at opening a branch office in her beloved city. Odessa was the fourth largest city of Imperial Russia after Moscow, St. Petersburg and Warsaw. The *Pearl of the Black Sea* was considered Russia's southern capital, she reminded her brothers. If ever there was an appropriate location for an important government entity, it was Odessa.

The men traveled in silent reverie, each lost in their own private musings. As the eldest, Moishe felt the burden of leading the family. He envisioned calamitous developments occurring in either of the two scenarios. If he urged the family to stay, would his be the hand to seal their fate to a life of violence and degradation? If he counseled the family to make the journey to Argentina, would he be responsible for leading them into a life of penury?

Yosef—full of vigor and hope—had no idea what was plaguing his brother. He only thought of what he would say to the committee's representative. Yosef had put to memory every pamphlet or article he had come across. In fact, such was his passion and understanding of the material, he could very well represent the J.C.A. if the venerated agent ever wished to return to St. Petersburg.

With the horses keeping an easy gait they reached Deribasivska Street soon enough. The men were impressed to find the J.C.A. office on the popular thoroughfare in the heart of the city. Prestigious limestone buildings, shops, and cafes lined the street, and a charming park provided a welcomed respite to the surrounding gravel and concrete. Upon discovering the correct edifice, the brothers dismounted and secured their horses. Eagerly taking the steps up to the second floor, they soon found the appropriate door. It was slightly ajar, beckoning visitors to enter.

Knocking first to announce their arrival, the brothers entered without being prompted. A man, middle-aged and haggard, sat at an impressive writing table nestled in-between two prominent portraits. Above the man's right shoulder was a framed portrait of the Tsar and Tsarina alongside their daughters, Maria, Tatiana and Olga. To his left, hung a portrait of Baron Maurice de Hirsh and his wife, Baroness Clara. The remaining accommodations, as well as décor, were sparse and unassuming.

"Good morning," began Moishe. "We were hoping to speak with the representative from the Jewish Colonization Association. Might he be available?"

The man pushed a stack of papers to one side, effectively clearing the center of the desk. Taking a fresh sheet, and with pen in hand, he waved the men in and had them take a seat.

"I am Leonid Sverdlov, agent of the J.C.A. I will take your application."

"Thank you, sir," the brothers answered in unison.

"Name?"

"Moisei Solomonovich Abramovitz."

"Yosef Solomonovich Abramovitz."

"Occupation?"

"We manufacture textiles. We own the Abramovitz Manufacturing Company," said Moishe, not with a little pride.

"Hmm—that is one I have not heard before," the man said, as he scribbled his notes. "I am certain this will be the first time I have to ask this question... what is your ranking?"

"We are Merchants of the First Guild and hold an honorary hereditary citizenship."

"How many in your family?"

"We are twenty-five," Yosef replied, "not counting the children."

"Twenty-five—" Leonid Sverdlov said and drummed his fingers lightly on the desk. "Your manufacturing works supports this family?"

"Yes, indeed," Moishe answered. "It has done so, quite satisfactorily, up until recently."

"Mr. Abramovitz, do you understand that thirty-seven percent of this city's population is Jewish?"

"Well—yes, I am aware that we compromise a significant number."

"Do you have any idea how many of those Jews have come through that door *begging* for assistance? Destitute, or nearly so, they come here looking for a way to escape the hardships of Russian life," the agent said, as he crumpled up their application. "I am afraid that your family would be denied by the Association. I see no need..."

"Sir, if you permit me," Yosef interrupted, "your very own mission statement, as noted in Article Three, indicates that the Association's purpose is 'to assist and promote the emigration of Jews from any parts of Europe or Asia, and principally from countries in which they may, for the time being, be subjected to any special taxes or political or other disabilities—"

"Yes, yes, Mr. Abramovitz. You are certainly correct, and I am duly impressed by your recitation, but your family fails to meet the requirement of *dire* necessity."

"Mr. Sverdlov, unlike my brother, I am not a man accustomed to study or debate. I am a merchant. My concerns are for maintaining the business my predecessors built by sheer determination. To be blunt," said Moishe, "we are being *pushed* out of business. There is no future for us here, and my interest in this venture is to investigate the possibilities of starting fresh in the New World."

Yosef attempted to hide his chagrin. Always the businessman, Moishe only had the factory in mind.

"Sir, you speak of those needing to escape the hardships of life in Odessa. We are well aware of our brethren and their plight," Yosef insisted. "My family has done their utmost to alleviate this strife through acts of charity and goodwill, but we will be helpless to help *ourselves* soon enough. We are compelled to leave."

"I sympathize with you, gentlemen. I am a Jew myself—these are, indeed, dismal times," Mr. Sverdlov allowed. "Perhaps, you will allow me to suggest an alternative?"

The brothers nodded in agreement.

"You certainly have the funds to secure your own passage. *Go to Argentina.* Purchase your own land. Set up whatever sort of business you wish on your own terms—without interference or direction from the fairly omnipotent J.C.A.—and without having to compromise your lifestyle by living amongst the colonists."

"I am sorry," Moishe responded, sharing a confused look with his brother. "We fail to comprehend your meaning, sir."

"How do I put this delicately? The vast majority of the colonists are impoverished, and certainly not as educated as yourselves. You will find that Yiddish is the language most commonly spoken, and then, there is the issue of your clothing—"

"Let me reassure you sir! We are not of noble stock. Our parents, grandparents, and those before them, slaved away to build what we have today," Yosef maintained. "While my family speak Russian in our day-to-day lives, we are, *of course*, fluent in Yiddish. Several of my scholarly brothers are experts in Hebrew and Aramaic, as well. As for our clothing and accruements, I assure you that we will strive to fit in with our neighbors. We are well prepared to work in any capacity! With such a large family, you will find that we have a variety of skills."

Even after hearing such an impassioned plea, there was nothing to be done. Mr. Sverdlov declared, most emphatically, that the Jewish Colonization Association would be doing a disservice to the community by assisting a family of such noted means. He reiterated that which Yosef had already known; the Association adhered to the strictest of regulations when approving applicants for the agricultural colonies, not only in Argentina, but in Canada and Palestine, as well. He could not, in good conscience, present their application to the committee; nonetheless, if the family insisted on leaving Russia, they were free to do so by their own accord. He jotted down a name of a man who had connections in Buenos Aires. Boris Zhirinovsky, he suggested, might act as a go-between for the family.

"Mind you, I have not worked with the man," cautioned Sverdlov. "My colleagues in St. Petersburg, however, have done some business through his contacts."

The Abramovitz men shook hands with the agent and took their leave. The meeting had not gone as planned; nevertheless, they were armed with advice and a possible contact. At least *that* was something for which to be thankful. Regrettably, the family meeting would prove to be problematic. Yosef and his brother were not of one mind and the lack of unity would most certainly cast an ominous shadow on their schemes.

Tea had been ordered as the family sat waiting impatiently for the men to return. Lectured at length by her sisters, Leah had been allowed to remain in the drawing room, but only after being sternly admonished. After all, Sara was keen to point out, Moishe and Yosef were doing their utmost to secure their safety. Grateful to be included, Leah vowed to be on her best behavior.

She glanced at the opposite end of the room and caught her mother's smile. Peering over the rim of her teacup, Malka gazed about the room and took inventory of their present situation. Her youngest daughter was a vision of angelic serenity, with her hands folded prettily and her countenance at peace. Malka smiled and wondered how long the well-executed charade would last. She was, however, quite pleased to see Avram and his wife, Bluma, seated side by side. This was a happy circumstance, for it appeared that her son and her challenging daughter-in-law were working towards reconciliation. Now, if only her boys would bring good tidings from town...*may it be God's will.*

The men arrived in due time and greeted the family with strained smiles. Moishe took a seat next to his wife, Devora, and allowed his brother—who seemed to have been born to lead—to communicate the news.

Yosef repeated Mr. Sverdlov's assessment, keeping his narrative simple and without embellishment. Quickly, before his family lost their teetering nerve, he shared the alternative which the agent had proposed. The family listened intently to his short speech. Yosef was certain that the idea of immigration would completely fold, as no one muttered a word. Finally, there was movement from the corner of the room. Aaron set down his plate of honey cake and wiped the crumbs from his lap.

"Perhaps," he stated, "it simply is not meant to be. "If Mr. Sverdlov could not see the value in our departure, why do we not take some time to reevaluate the situation?"

"Do we truly need to deliberate the matter further?" Ephraim exclaimed. "Putting everything else aside— the taxes, the restrictions on our commerce, the threats of impending violence to our community— *there is talk of war*! With this building aggression between Russia and Japan, they will surely be calling for conscripts again."

"What if they come for our boys? Would they take our Duvid?" Devora cried. "He is just a boy of thirteen!"

"Another war?" repeated Bluma in despair. "Can we withstand another Crimea?"

Aaron reminded them that, *Baruch Hashem*, the evil and depraved cantonist policies had long been abolished by Alexander II, and besides, the family held an honorary title. They were protected from the draft.

"They will find a way to challenge that decree!" said Ysroel. "Somehow, if it entails sending Jews to the front, you mark my words, they will find a way."

"We must act now," Yosef said in a soft and foreboding manner. "While it is true we are in no immediate danger, we cannot deny that the noose is getting tighter by the day."

Malka served her son a cup of tea, which he promptly sipped and set down before reminding his engrossed audience of the dangers they faced. Many of Yosef's contemporaries had recently returned from top universities in France, Germany, and Great Britain. They now eagerly pushed for change and worked to see their dreams of a constitutional monarchy come to fruition. Others proposed a different route and supported socialism and labor unions. They promoted their radical views among the working class and spoke of overthrowing the Tsar altogether. Both factions met in secret, risking their lives all the while. If the Tsar's secret police, the *Okhrana,* found them out, they would be accused of treason—no threat to the Romanov dynasty would be tolerated.

"This is why I recommend we leave now," Yosef pleaded.

Leah sat quietly, taking in each comment and storing it away for deeper consideration. Once alone in the privacy of her bedchamber, she would be free to think on the matter without reproach. Her mother's censure was stern, but usually meted out with kindness—depending on the transgression, of course. Her siblings, however, were another matter. Being the youngest, Leah not only had to concern herself with parental discipline and expectations, but with a whole household of siblings who felt it necessary to comment, criticize, and command her every thought and action. This talk of leaving home was both exhilarating and terrifying at once. Leah did not feel equipped to make an educated comment as of yet. Her eldest brother, however, had no qualms to speak his mind.

"I have tried to weigh the matter with some equanimity," said Moishe, his eyes reflecting the burden he carried. "Truth be told, it would break my heart to turn my back on everything Papá has built. We have an obligation to fight for what is ours! Avram was correct—there are people less fortunate than us in our community. Who will come to their aid? Who will help fund their schools and hospitals, if the upper class turns tail and runs away? Our people have survived worse. We can, perhaps, weather this storm by staying and defending what is ours."

"Twelve years ago," Yosef began in a whisper, "the Supreme Commission for the Revision of Current Laws of the Empire Concerning the Jews concluded their five year investigation. Do you know what their findings were, Brother?"

"No," Moishe sighed. "But I am certain you will enlighten us."

"Suffice it to say, Count Pahlen and his Commission concluded that the Jews should be given a wider berth—they even suggested that the Jews *gradually* be allowed equal footing with the general population. However, *and this is important*, the Tsar did not agree!" Yosef now roared. "His cohorts continued to spread lies and filth about our people. *Jews are parasites*. Jews are aliens who only wish to inculcate the spirit of the West into Russian society!"

"I am still not convinced—" Moishe said.

"You, *yourself*, have said the time is ripe for another uprising against our community. We are neither peasants nor are we nobles—we are simply a family who has made good through the hard work and vision of our father. We owe it to his memory to *survive*! Moishe, I don't know what is coming; but if we stay, we will not fare well."

Malka stood then, motioning to her sons to stay their discussion. Now that the idea had been planted in their minds, perhaps it would be wiser to spend some time in prayer and contemplation. Leah listened with gratitude, and not a little relief, as her mother suggested that they postpone any further discussion for the time being.

Yosef stormed out of the room. Moishe and Aaron, holding their heads together, continued a private conversation as they followed their young brother's footsteps. The others trailed behind, and as it would be some time before dinner, Leah climbed the elegant staircase to her room. She welcomed the solitude in which to hold a private debate, where she could draw her own conclusions. Of course, it was an exercise for her personal benefit. No one, it seemed, was interested in her opinion.

While a disheartened Yosef battled against his frustration, his brothers continued their quiet debate on their own. In fact, by the end of that week, the men decided that Aaron would accompany Moishe on a visit to the *revizor* himself. They needed clarity. A battle could not be won if the enemy was not plainly understood or clearly defined.

Finding Inspector Reshetnikov behind a mountain of paperwork and scowl upon his face did not inspire the brothers to believe that their meeting would go well. They had been announced, however, and given leave to enter the cramped and untidy headquarters; and so, they stood quietly waiting to be addressed.

"The brothers Abramovitz," the official stated with great flair. "To what do I owe this unexpected pleasure?"

Aaron cleared his throat before answering. "We are honored that you have allowed us this audience—"

"Nonsense, you have done me a favor by coming to see me this day. I had been given instructions by my superiors to pay you a visit. Thankfully, I am now spared the trip. Please, gentlemen, sit down," the inspector offered with a wave of his hand.

The men shared a worried glance with one another before each taking a seat. Moishe opened his mouth to speak, but was interrupted by the inspector's sudden movement. Dropping a heavy ledger upon his desk, Inspector Reshetnikov grasped the leather cover between two fat fingers and began flipping through the pages.

"Gentleman, this is the history of your business. It holds the records of your stated income, the taxes you have paid thus far, and of your estimated value to the empire."

"As you can see Inspector, we are up to date..."

"I would ask that you refrain from interrupting, Moisei Solomonovich Abramovitz."

Hearing his full name shouted in such a manner, Moishe simply nodded his understanding.

"Point in fact, your payments are *not* current. You will recall our previous conversation where I addressed the matter of the necessary increase. In addition, not only have your profits declined in the past quarter, you have been showing a loss for quite some time."

Both men, now, silently nodded.

"You are also aware, no doubt, that the Tsar—in his infinite wisdom and generosity of spirit—has allowed you and others like you, to live outside of the Pale of Settlement because you were deemed useful. I believe that your community has accepted this so-called Russification as a means to improve your lot in life. Your *kupechestvo* status enables you to travel and to do business throughout the land. You speak Russian, your children are sent to Russian schools...in fact you consider yourself Russian Jews. Do you not?"

"Yes, sir, but..."

"Let me finish!" The inspector shouted unexpectedly. "You may believe as you wish, but I do not find this pleasant." Clearing his throat, he began once again. "It has been brought to our attention—by a private citizen—that your business is floundering. You are fully aware, to be sure, that the empire requires you to maintain a certain level of success. You risk losing your status as members of the First Guild by not keeping your end of the bargain. If you are not successful, you cannot pay your taxes. If you cannot pay your taxes, you lose your business."

Aaron, unable to stay silent, jumped from his seat. "If we have not shown a profit, it is because the empire has restricted our trade!"

"Aaron," Moishe hissed. "Sit down."

"Who was it?" Aaron demanded. "Tell us who was so eager to enlighten you with news of our purported demise?

"I am not at liberty to name names, Aaron Solomonovich. Suffice it to say, it was one of your competitors. Somehow, they have managed to stay afloat during these trying times..."

"Yes, but most likely, they are not Jews!"

"Aaron!" Moishe exclaimed, surprised at his brother's uncharacteristic display.

"They are Russian patriots, to be sure. And to be quite frank, they are appalled at the trade your family has been known to keep with Western Europe. They have made their case to the Commission and the matter is being reviewed as we speak."

"The matter? *What matter*?"

"The revocation of your family's status and honorary title, naturally," the inspector stated.

"And who will benefit from our loss?" Moishe said, finding courage to voice his revulsion.

"It is only too clear, Brother. Our competitors, *the Russian patriots*, will benefit. They want what they perceive to be intrinsically theirs. We are not Russian. We don't deserve to partake in the benefits of being members of the First Merchants Guild. We don't deserve—"

"Come now, gentlemen, the times are changing. In truth, I don't understand it all myself," the inspector sighed. "Nothing has been decided as of yet, but with the new policies coming from Alexander Palace...well, it doesn't bode well for your people."

"How long do we have?" Moishe asked gravely.

"I would imagine that you will be advised within a month, maybe two. Be on guard. Once word gets out, well—*you already know*. I don't have to tell you. Your people have a way of attracting this sort of trouble."

"Of course, Inspector," a weary Aaron replied. "Our people are well versed in the concept of *mea culpa*. Perhaps, we should try harder not to draw attention to ourselves, as we simply go about the business of living—"

Moishe cautiously eyed the revizor before grabbing his brother's arm. "Come. Let us go home."

The men walked away without further commentary. The inspector made no attempt to stay their course. There was nothing left to be said—not without risking further provocation—and although the brothers would not have believed it of him, the inspector had hoped that their departure would be swift and orderly. At the very least, he would spare them the shame of being shackled and dragged before the magistrate for disrespecting a government official.

In a state of shock, Moishe was unable to verbalize a clear thought. They would have to inform the family, but what could they possibly report? How could they explain that, in one fell swoop, they were on the verge of losing everything? Aaron was the first to find his voice, but it was only moments before crossing the threshold of their beloved home.

"We must go to the bank immediately," he said in a slow and even tone. "We will need to have a source of income at our disposal until we can arrange a transfer of funds."

"But, what will we *do*, Aaron? What can the future hold for us now?"

No words had to be spoken—they both knew the answer.

Chapter Five

*L*eah clutched the edge of her seat as she listened to Aaron's testimony. Although he and Moishe had visited the inspector with the hopes of coming to some sort of an understanding, they had been ensnared—a bloodless coup had taken place instead. She could hardly believe it. That someone of their acquaintance could despise them so. It was unconscionable.

"I wager it was those Morozovs!" cried Benjamin.

"It doesn't serve a purpose to indiscriminately point fingers," replied Moishe. "We must look at the facts of the matter. Clearly, our competitors questioned our loyalty because we wished to do business outside of the empire. They questioned our methodology. Our projections for improvements seemed too farfetched. Our vision for a modern textile industry rattled the old-timers and enraged the protectionists."

"If we lose the factory," Leah whispered from her quiet corner of the room, "what will become of us? And if they hate us so, why would we stay?"

"That is precisely my point," Aaron replied. "Yosef's proposal to immigrate to Argentina seemed radical at first, and with the J.C.A.'s rejection of our application, it appeared that our plans were foiled. I am suggesting we follow Mr. Sverdlov's approach. We will establish the Abramovitz Manufacturing Company in this land of Yosef's dreams. We shall close the house, sell off what we can, and start over in this so-called New Jerusalem."

"You mean to live in Buenos Aires? Not on the *pampas* with the colonists?"

"If your heart is set on working the land, Yosef, then I suggest you follow your friends to Palestine," Moishe replied. "What do we know of farming?"

"It is a once in a lifetime opportunity, Moishe! To work with our hands, to build something out of nothing..."

"But we *will* build something—a new factory. We will build a legacy that will endure for our children and our children's children!" Aaron exclaimed. "In Buenos Aires, we can rally again—*without* the restriction and interference of the Tsar."

"It is has been decided, then?" Leah ventured to interrupt. "It is not to be Paris or London?"

The seemingly innocent—if not repetitive— question led to a series of rebuffs and refutations by her learned brothers who were all too eager to provide a detailed analysis. Paris, having already been discussed and discarded in a previous meeting, was summarily set aside. The rising anti-Semitism in that nation was not to be ignored, no matter how well connected the Abramovitz Manufacturing Company appeared to be.

Yosef next tackled the subject of England's political and economic outlook suggesting that the urban centers of London and Manchester were facing deterioration on a grand scale. Tenements were popping up throughout every major industrial center, prices were stagnant, and workers were losing faith in their representatives as militant trade unions and organizations were on the rise.

"In Italy, starving workers are demonstrating against their government," Yosef continued. "Germany is economically sound, but they're creating an authoritarian political system that might be as horrific as what we already experience under the Tsar."

"Yosef," Leah cried. "I was simply asking..."

"Yes. You asked, and I'm attempting to explain. Europe is seeing her glory days come to an end. The Americas are the future. Argentina is a *trading giant*, rich in animal products, grains, and minerals too."

When at last the family came to an agreement, beaming with pride and enthusiasm, Yosef forgot himself and revealed a secret that he promised to keep. "Oh, and one more thing, he said. "Sofia and I are getting married."

"Mazal tov," grumbled Aaron, "another mouth to feed."

"Make that *two* more mouths to feed," Yosef replied with a grin. "Her father is coming with us."

A meeting with their advisors was immediately arranged to discuss the factory and the necessary legal transactions. Moishe had suggested creating a writ that transferred ownership to his best lead man, Yuri Ivankov. The idea of selling the works, or letting the officials simply take it over, was out of the question. Making his case, Moishe empathically stated that he'd rather give it away to someone who would see it prosper, than to sell to their covetous conspiratorial rivals who—out of ignorance and greed—had so eagerly stabbed them in the back. As Ivankov was a Russian citizen through and through, the Abramovitz attorneys would not run into any difficulty with the government officials, or the ignorant hooligans bent on destroying Jewish property.

With no knowledge of purchasing land or establishing residency in Argentina, they turned to the one contact available—Mr. Boris Zhirinovsky, the man the J.C.A. agent proposed as a reliable intermediary. Yosef owned that it was a great risk surrendering their faith, and their money, to a relatively unknown entity; but based on what the agent said, Zhirinovsky had done business in South America and was familiar with the lay of the land. They sent the man a note via messenger, and four days later, he appeared at their door.

Boris Zhirinovsky was a bear of a man with big, beefy hands and shoulders wide as the Dniester River. He wore a black wool suit with a checkered vest. The fabric was top quality, Leah noted, but the tailoring left something to be desired. The sleeves were nearly two inches too short, as were the cuffs of his trousers. Perhaps it was not the tailor's lack of skill, she thought. Perhaps Mr. Zhirinovsky was a difficult man to clothe. She took an immediate dislike to him, but decided it best not to make her feelings known—she would rather not be on the receiving end of one of her sisters' reprimands.

Although Leah believed that the interview with Mr. Zhirinovsky would be held in the drawing room, where the entire family would have a chance to hear the man speak, she quickly learned that her assumption had been in error. Moishe, Aaron, and Yosef escorted the gentleman into the library where the family's attorneys had already been seated. Once the party crossed the threshold, Aaron closed the door quite soundly. It was nearly three hours later, after the tea tray had been sent in and refreshed twice, that the men emerged from their cave—so fitting for Mr. Zhirinovsky, bear-like and all.

There was a great deal of hand shaking and back slapping as her brothers escorted their new emissary to the door. Sokolov stood at the ready with the man's derby hat and ivory topped cane. Upon Mr. Zhirinovsky's departure and the attorneys' retreat, the brothers returned to the library, and shortly after, the others began meandering in. Everyone was anxious to hear the news. Leah assumed she would now be welcomed and followed in their trail. Aaron had a bill of sale in his hand and was waving it about in a most comical manner. As Aaron was *rarely* comical, the action was twice as amusing.

"*Mazal tov* to us all! We are the proud owners of *Villa Esperanza*, our very own Argentine estate!"

When the exclamations and the hullabaloo quieted down, Aaron continued on with the details of the property. According to Mr. Zhirinovsky, the home had been built in 1830 during Argentina's colonial period. It was located just about an hour outside of the capital, which would prove to be beneficial for establishing their new enterprise. Buenos Aires was a bustling port city. This was a tremendous opportunity for a manufacturing family interested in the export business.

"Do stop being so practical, Aaron, and tell us of the house itself!" Leah cried.

"Mr. Zhirinovsky had nothing but praise for the ranch house and its location," Aaron allowed. "The original owners, *Spanish aristocrats* I might add, built the house at the end of long drive, beautifully lined with acacia trees. The estate boasts enough rooms to house us all. There is a well-stocked library, a gallery which opens onto the park, a summer dining room *and* a formal dining room, stables, of course, and—for Duvid—it even has a guard tower," he said with chuckle. "Imagine that!"

"It sounds too good to be true!" Leah exclaimed.

The family nodded their heads in agreement; but recognizing the disquieted looks upon their faces, Aaron acknowledged that it did indeed sound too good to be true.

"Our lawyer, Mr. Bobrinsky, was invited here today specifically to review the documents. His assessment of the property deed and other legalities concerning the purchase were favorable. After careful deliberation, we agreed to provide Mr. Zhirinovsky with a down payment—forty-five percent of the total asking price."

His announcement was met with silence. Aaron glanced at his brothers for support, but their hesitancy to add to the conversation caused an awkward pause.

"We will inform Mr. Zhirinovsky when our passage has been booked, at which time he will contact our man in Buenos Aires. They will meet us at the port, and the estate will have been made ready for our arrival."

Malka nodded. "It appears that the plan is sound, but—we shall see how it all unfolds."

"Why such restraint, if you claim the plan is sound?" Leah asked.

"Because, my dear, as much as we would like to organize and prepare, and make all manner of extraordinary arrangements, we do not have the final word on how it will all turn out. What God decrees, man cannot prevent."

Avram nodded his head in agreement, and stealing a glance at his wife, he said a silent prayer. Bluma and he had suffered greatly of late—a miscarriage and a babe that survived a Cesarean section delivery only to be taken shortly after his *brit milah*. There had been months of grieving and of prayer, but nothing seemed to make sense. Bluma had all but cursed at the One who created their lives in the first place. Heartbroken and desperate, Avram had tried to console his wife with words of faith and hope. She would have none of it, until one day, everything seemed to turn around. Bluma had had a chance meeting with their unexpected houseguest, Miss Marina Davidovich; and although Avram was not privy to the conversation, he noticed an immediate change. And now, his mother just repeated the words he had been saying all along...*what is meant to be, will be.*

Aaron's voice jolted Avram out of his silent reverie. He shook his head and blinked several times to focus on his brother's words.

"We need a concise projection of our available funds," Aaron was saying. "I suggest we keep several good pieces of jewelry in our possession—pieces that we would be apt to sell if need be, and of course, a decent amount of silver and gold coins. We are preparing letters of credit to transfer our funds; however, I believe we will lose quite a significant amount in the exchange to Argentine pesos. We must be prepared to adjust accordingly."

"If our requests to travel are denied, what then?" asked Ysroel.

"There is no reason to believe that they will deny us—not yet anyway. We are still citizens in good standing," Yosef replied. "That being said, there have been cases of people sneaking across the border—many on foot, others by train."

"I do not wish to sneak *out* or *in* of any country," Bluma stated, wrapping her shawl tightly about her shoulders to emphasize her opposition.

Aaron reminded the family that Jews—no matter their rank or social position—who had gone abroad without a legal exit permit were stripped of their citizenship and not allowed to return.

"We will do whatever is possible to leave properly, but *leave*, we must," said Yosef. "Our countrymen head west and make their way towards the coast. I think that is our best option."

"Why go to all that trouble?" Leah asked. "Why don't we leave from our own port?"

"It is not as simple as it seems," declared Yosef. "As a matter of fact, I suggest the first leg of the journey should be to Lviv. Perhaps we might pay a call to our houseguest, Miss Marina Davidovich. She had shown quite a bit of interest in Baron Hirsch and the Jewish colonies. Miss Marina resides in Lviv, does she not? She may have some insight to share with us."

A brusque *No* came unexpectedly from the corner of the room.

"I don't believe that will be possible," Malka stuttered uncharacteristically. "She is...traveling."

"She and her papá are on the Grand Tour," Leah added for good measure.

"That is a shame. She was a strange young lady, to be sure, but very knowledgeable. No matter. I still suggest that we travel to Lviv, and from there, head to Trieste."

Trieste had become the most prosperous Mediterranean seaport in the Austro-Hungarian Empire, he noted, and it was no small part in thanks to Isacco and Giuseppe Morpurgo. The brothers owned three steamships, and for the past twelve years, had been providing transportation to South America without fail.

"Trieste offers far more contemporary and luxurious ships to Argentina than the port in Odessa," Yosef explained. "The ships are not only modern, but *faster—*"

"The journey will take no more than fifteen days on a steamship," said a child's voice from the opposite of the room. Duvid poked his head from around the wing backed chair. "It will depend on how many screws the ship contains."

"What are you doing there?" Moishe demanded, a smile softening his tone. "You should have made yourself known."

"I was reading, Papá," the boy said.

"This is an adult assembly," Avram reprimanded. "We are discussing family matters of great importance..."

"I am part of the family," Duvid answered boldly, "*and* I am a bar mitzvah. If I am old enough to chant Torah, am I not old enough to attend a family meeting?"

Yosef laughed and slapped the youngster on the back.

"Well said young man! I say we allow Duvid to remain. He will help me explain our mode of transportation, seeing that he is an expert in the field."

"Well—not *an expert* to be exact, but I know that sailing ships were made obsolete over thirty years ago with the invention of the steamers. Which company are you researching, Uncle? Do you know the ship's name?"

"We are looking at the Lloyd Austriaco Company. The pamphlet I picked up listed several ships that make the journey to South America, but I like the *Umberto I,* in particular. Is she listed in your book?"

Duvid jumped out of the chair and eagerly searched for a specific book of maritime facts and historical chronology. He had recently been leafing through the tome and distinctly remembered reading about the shipping giant. Finding the book, he pulled it off the shelf and skimmed through until finding the Lloyd Austriaco and the particular ship his uncle mentioned.

"It says here the *Umberto I* was built in 1878 for *Societa Rocco Piaggio & Figli* of Genoa. She has one funnel, two masts, and a single screw."

"What does that signify?" Leah asked impatiently.

"It says she has a speed of 13 knots," he continued without responding to Leah's query, "which should allow her to reach Argentina within 12 to 15 days."

"Fifteen days on a ship?" Bluma cried out. "But we have heard such horrors of the lack of privacy and decent food...*and clean bedding*. I will not travel in the belly of some tub with hundreds of strangers. I am sure that thing will be crawling with mice and other vermin."

Leah observed Bluma's face was flushed, and although the room was quite comfortable with a cheerful fire to keep them warm, her sister-in-law was cocooned beneath a large woolen shawl. In any event, Leah was apt to agree with Bluma on this one point—if nothing else—she did not want to spend 15 days in the belly of a ship.

"Calm yourselves," Yosef replied. "The *Umberto I* is a luxury liner. She can accommodate ninety-eight First Class passengers!"

"The pamphlet indicates that there are salons and libraries, and even a theater. With our considerable party, we will surely take up the majority of the First Class accommodations—that is to say, if our family's accountant agrees to pay for that luxury," Moishe said eyeing his brother.

"*Trieste*? Are you certain?" Malka asked.

"There is a large Jewish community in the city, and I have reason to believe, we could find assistance within that quarter if a problem should arise," said

Yosef. "What do you say, Mamá? Do we you have your approval?"

"I say..." Malka hesitated for only a moment, before raising her chin with determination. "Papá would be very proud of you, my son—of all of you. I am grateful that you give me the final word, but in truth, it is not mine to give. *You* are the future. Your lives and those of your children are at stake. If you are all in agreement, then as you mother, I only can say this: Lead on."

In a whirlwind of activity, the factory had been left in the deserving hands of Yuri Ivankov, just as Moishe had advocated. The employees had been given a bonus for staying on and working under a new master. She accompanied her brothers to bid farewell to the workers—most of whom had known Leah since she was a babe. It felt as if she was saying goodbye to her papá once again. Leah had to remind herself that her own dear father would be happy to see them go, if it meant their safety would be secured.

As Moishe had handed her up into the carriage, she turned back once more to look upon the treasured workplace and noticed a man, silent and stalwart, sitting upon a restless horse. He was just a few yards away and, although she couldn't make out his countenance, it was obvious that he was observing their departure. Leah had asked her brother who the man might be. Moishe turned and grimly replied, "It is Inspector Reshetnikov."

The bittersweet finality of it all had been in celebrating Shabbos, one last time, in their beloved home. Every action, every thought, was filled with her papá. The sense of abandonment was tangible. Leah was overcome with emotion thinking *this was where Papá would have me stand for his blessing and this is where Papá would sit to recite the Birkat Hamazon.*

He had been gone for these five years, and yet, living amongst his things, passing by his favorite chair, or picking up his cherished momento, her papá seemed to be with them. How could she leave, Leah thought, when the house was full of his spirit? Even with her mamá's reassurance that he would follow wherever they would go, Leah's heart was heavy—and of course, she was not alone in her grief.

The Shabbos blessings and rituals had been completed, the meal was served and consumed, but the usual joy and sense of fulfillment was missing. Avrum took it upon himself to remind the family that the beauty of Shabbos was to be in the moment with Hashem. There was no need to ask for anything more, there was no need to worry for what was to come. The day of rest was meant for celebrating the completeness of it all. Everything was as it was meant to be. Nonetheless, for the pious and for the less so, the holiness of the day was shadowed by heartache and regret.

The house had been packed up. Linens had been placed over the furnishings; non-essentials were stored away or given for charity. For quite some time now, Leah had accompanied her mother on her quarterly visits to the various charitable organizations in town. Those that helped the sick, the poor, and the orphaned would gratefully accept their household items, clothing, and knickknacks. With no need to sell the estate—they had not received any further demands from the officials—the family decided it best to simply close it down. There was no telling what the future would hold, and following Malka's pronouncement, it was best to prepare for every eventuality. Who could say if they would return one day?

Leah mostly stood aside as she watched her mamá and sisters carefully decide what to bring with them and what would stay behind. The last few days had sped by with such intensity, she could only now reflect and admire her mother's capacity for completing a task with the utmost care and respect for all those involved. No detail had been overlooked; no element was too small or insignificant not to warrant consideration.

Malka set aside a few family heirlooms—her very own great grandmother's candlesticks, a set of silverware that belonged to Solomon's family, a tablecloth she had embroidered as a bride. So many memories lovingly stowed away. Each adult had their own dome-top trunk filled with traveling necessities, as well as their personal belongings. Duvid, to no one's surprise, managed to fill his allotted chest with an assortment of favorite books, but in truth, few accessories or luxuries would be taken. The family had been advised that there would be limited space available on the voyage. Aaron assured the women that they would purchase whatever they would require to set up a proper home, once they reached the shores of Buenos Aires.

The family said their final farewells to friends and neighbors who, in turn, bade them an easy voyage and the best of luck—all the while, skeptical and afraid. Leah, in a moment of frustration, came to believe that one or two of their anxious acquaintances might have given them the evil eye, for there had been confusion and delays even before their departure had taken place!

Such a large traveling party was bound to call attention, and so it came to pass that an official detained the group as they were preparing to board the train. With pointless circumlocution, the inspector stated that it was his duty to review their travel documents and proceeded to enquire after each member of the family. Once satisfied, with great self-importance, he placed his seal over the exit stamps previously administered by the city's bureaucrat and made a notation in his own ledger: The Family Abramovitz—Odessa. Departure approved: 4 of April, 1901.

Releasing a communal sigh of relief, the family proceeded with their embarkation while the station master glared at them with increased derision. Emotionally spent, the family sat in stunned and reflective silence as the train sped across the terrain to Lviv; however, turmoil would continue to cast its shadow upon their journey. Upon reaching their destination, they found themselves at the center of a chaotic construction site, for a new and modern railway station was in the process of being built.

Under normal circumstances, Leah would have begged for an opportunity to have a look around and admire the Art Nouveau style, but with the family in the midst of such an emotional undertaking, she made do by accepting an illustrative brochure which a paperboy was distributing along with the evening news.

The old neo-Gothic structure would soon be replaced by a first-class train station befitting the capital of Galicia—one that would represent the importance of the region. Leah appreciated the architect's vision that combined steel, stained glass, and twin cupolas on either wing. She wondered if, one day, she would return to see the completed work. In the meantime the laborers, equipment, and rubble made for a most uncomfortable sojourn, as the anxious family waited for their next train. They had yet another day and a half before reaching Trieste, and the chaotic environment only added fuel to the fire. The Abramovitz family members were each lost within their own frenzied thoughts, equally filled with torment and expectation.

When, at last, they boarded and situated themselves into cars equipped for overnight travel, the family settled down for the night. As the train headed speedily towards their seaport destination, Leah was certain that the excitement and strain of the day would not allow her to rest, but the train's cyclical reverberation calmed her nerves and she was lulled to sleep before Mamá had finished her evening's ablutions.

Earlier that day, Leah had thumbed through one of her nephew's history books, reading of colonial ladies and their attire. She learned that an Argentine lady never stepped foot out her door without covering her head. The quality of lace used for the veils, in addition to the detailing of the high combs, were sure giveaways of the lady's social standing. The greater the height of the *peinetones,* the greater was the lady's consequence. Leah's imagination has been stirred by these images, and so she dreamt of strolling down the cobble stone streets of Buenos Aires—her flaxen locks covered with an exquisite black lace *mantilla* held in place by a *peinetone,* wider and taller than any other of her acquaintance.

In her dream she walked purposefully, for a clandestine assignation awaited her. A dashing young soldier met her under a street lamp. The gas light combined with the evening fog, setting an ethereal stage for the two young lovers. Leah coquettishly waved her jeweled fan hither and thither, enticing her young man to come closer. Preparing to receive her first kiss, she tilted her head ever so slightly and lifted her eyes—full of longing and excitement—only to cry out in horror. The handsome soldier holding her in his arms was none other than *Lieutenant Yegorov*! She felt his hold tighten as she cried out—the words rang true to that eventful night so long ago.

"Dmitry, you are frightening me! How can you treat me so?"

"Very easily my dear." His fingers dug deeper into her soft, delicate skin as he spewed out his venomous speech. "It is I who am the injured party. I have been humiliated. I have been manipulated into consorting with a zhid! You are nothing but a lowly Jewess trying to pass herself off as a lady."

Leah woke up with a start just as the train conductor sounded a warning horn. Her trembling hand reached up and pushed aside the crushed velvet drapes. Although her heart was still racing and her eyes were wet with tears, she resolved to put aside the Lieutenant and the doubts he had implanted. There was no time for that now. They had arrived in the Adriatic seaport of Trieste.

Chapter Six

April 1901 ~ The Imperial Free City of Trieste

*A*rrangements had been made for an overnight stay in a nearby inn. There had been much talk of late of inadequate housing for the many emigrants coursing through the city. Sanitary inspectors divulged that public accommodations were overcrowded and outbreaks of infectious diseases, including small pox and typhoid, were on the rise. The family had taken rooms with the well-known Austro-Americana Company; however, after reading a scathing editorial against the proprietors, they changed their plans and consulted with one of the local Jewish organizations who were happy to direct them to a more *heymish* destination—a cozy home-away-from-home.

The Abramovitz clan took up the entire space in the intimate lodge run by an elderly couple, but neither proprietors nor guests complained. The following day, the family returned to the port and joined the queue with hundreds of other passengers. It was then, they were informed that the *Umberto I* had been caught in tumultuous storms at open sea and would fail to meet her new passengers in time for the voyage south.

The port master allayed their anxiety in short order. Happily, he informed the discouraged passengers that the Sofia Hohenberg was readily available and equally up to the challenge of transporting such refined travelers. Taking the port master on his word, Leah's brothers confirmed their passage and prayed that the Sofia Hohenberg would live up to her reputation—it would be a long and uncomfortable crossing if she proved otherwise. Leah wondered again at their misfortune, but knew not to complain, for her mother would have only answered: *What will be, will be.*

With the travel arrangements completed, the family prepared to board. Standing in one queue or another had become rather monotonous and Leah was anxious for the voyage to begin. The sooner they departed, the sooner the ache in her heart would begin to heal—at least, that was what she was led to believe. Once they set foot in Argentina, she could begin working on reinventing herself; and then, she wouldn't have time to dwell on the pain of leaving her home. Maybe it was all for good, like her mother continually said. Perhaps it *would* all make sense in the end. She had been destined for a bright future, growing up in the upper echelons of Odessa. Surely she could still make a success of it.

It was then, hearing familiar words in Yiddish, mixed in with Polish, Russian and German, Leah became aware of a rag tag assembly in a separate queue. She noted their clothing and their modest bundles. Their children were hungry and restless, their elderly huddled together clinging to the few precious bits of home. They sat on boxes tied with multicolored strings while reciting their traveler's prayers, shooing away evil spirits from troubling their journey. It was clear to Leah at once, that while the ship offered accommodations to its high society clientele, there were hundreds of passengers who would be traveling in far different circumstances.

Moishe had extolled the Sofia's luxurious amenities. The family would have their choice of two social rooms on the upper deck, a library, two dining rooms and various leisure salons. Leah felt grateful and awkward at the same time. The poor souls in steerage would experience cramped living quarters with little light or fresh air. Leah realized that she was blessed in more ways than one, and offered up a *bracha* of thanks on her family's behalf and a prayer for those less fortunate.

Malka kept a close eye on her youngest daughter. The other children were guarded and guided by their own dutiful parents, who had their hands full keeping their youngsters from falling overboard or some such calamity. As a young woman of quality and unsettling beauty, Leah had been inciting interest from the moment she set her pretty little booted foot on board. Malka was ever present to ward off the uninvited, yet ever persistent, attentions of the young male passengers.

Her mama-bear's intuition was alerted to another peculiar circumstance as they approached the end of the first week on the Sofia Hohenberg. Her daughter-in-law's continued absence grew more and more evident. Bluma had been overly quiet prior to their leave-taking, never once offering an unsolicited opinion nor a stinging rebuttal. Malka noted that Bluma had become slovenly with regard to her coiffure and manner of dress—she seemed particularly attached to a rather large drab woolen shawl. These changes were quite a departure from her habitually fastidious character.

Bluma's absence from the ship's activities had been dismissed at first as being due to seasickness. The constant rocking and bouncing of the ship was playing havoc on more than one passenger. When Avram asked his wife—for the third time in one afternoon—if she would care to take some air, he was summarily rejected and dismissed. Afraid that she may do herself a harm, having not eaten for three days straight, Avram beseeched his mother to look in on his wife.

"She refuses to leave her bed and rejects any assistance on my part," Avram admitted. " I have tried to make her comfortable, but she won't even allow me to remove that *shmata*—that horrid shawl she has taken to so fanatically."

With Leah tagging along, Malka arrived at her son's cabin door, knocked once, and entered. What she saw upon crossing the threshold was doubly startling. Firstly, she witnessed her daughter-in-law, lying upon her side *sans* the wretched piece of fabric. It was quite clear that Bluma was in the family way. Secondly, Malka was astounded that her son hadn't seemed to notice!

"My dear!" Malka cried as she went directly to Bluma's side. "Why on earth did you not tell us?"

Bluma burst into tears, and for the next quarter of an hour, was quite incoherent. Malka allowed the woman to have a good cry. She stroked her back comfortingly and took the time to assess the situation. Apparently with all the angst of moving away, and the added fact that Bluma had always been troubled, Malka had missed the telltale signs. There was no doubt about it now, and certainly no need to cover the increase of Bluma's girth under the hideous wrap.

"How far along are you, *Blumale*?"

Bluma mumbled into her pillow. Leah leaned in closer to try to make out the words. Malka shook her head *No* and shooed her away. Leah felt childish. Embarrassed with the intimate nature of their visit, she knew her mamá would, at any moment, request that she leave the *women* to the business at hand.

With a soft caress, gently moving Bluma's hair away from her face, Malka whispered once again.

"Blumale *sheine,* how far along you?"

"I'm not sure. I suppose six or seven months," she cried. "The pains started a few days ago—but, it is too soon! I fear I will lose the child."

"Seven months!" Leah exclaimed. "How could we have not noticed? How is it possible that Avram did not know?"

"It's not his fault. I was not certain for quite some time." She paused as a sharp pain took her breath away.

"Do not be frightened!" cried Leah.

Malka shushed her young daughter and turned again to Bluma, placing a cool compress on her forehead.

"Can you go on, my dear? Help me to understand..."

"After the loss of our son, I simply did not pay any heed to my—my monthlies. I was never regular, and in any event, I was ever so disconsolate to care—that is to say, until Miss Marina Davidovich come to visit. There was something special about that young lady, however strange we thought her. A conversation I had with Miss Marina truly affected me, and I was persuaded to look at my life in a different manner."

"I'm glad that Moll—I mean *Miss Marina*—was of help to you," Leah stammered."

Bluma nodded weakly. "It was at that same time, Avram began plying me with Mrs. Kraskov's good food—so concerned was he for my wellbeing. I believed that my sudden weight gain was due to the copious amounts of noodle *kugel* and potato *knishes* I was consuming."

"To think, we will never have the pleasure of eating Mrs. Kraskov's knishes again..."

"Leah, please." Malka admonished at her daughter's interjection. "Go on, Blumale."

"Avram would have put a stop to the plan of our immigration, if he knew of my condition. I didn't want to worry him—I knew how important it was for the family to remain together. Even when I felt the child move, I refrained from telling anyone. I was so afraid to tempt fate—to invoke the evil eye. And now...now the baby is coming and it is *too soon*!"

Bluma let loose with a nightmarish scream and Leah, paralyzed with fear, screamed along with her sister-in-law. Malka busied herself about the room looking through Bluma's belongings for a nightdress, extra sheets, and towels.

"Leah, go at once and find Gitel," Malka commanded in a calm and clear voice. "Tell her to bring my portmanteau. She'll know which one I want, we packed it together with items from the apothecary. Ask her to attend me immediately, and then go fetch Avram and advise him of the situation but, under no circumstances, do I want him in this room. The two of you go in search of the ship's doctor, and if he is not too busy with the wretched souls in steerage, let him know that we are in need of his services."

Despondent and rejected, Leah exited the cabin. She made a fool of herself just then and would be banned from all further excitement. Once again, she was delegated to the role of the innocent. Leah made quick work of finding Gitel, and together, they located her mother's bag. Malka had come prepared for the journey, bringing all manner of herbs and remedies. Gitel found her way to Avram and Bluma's cabin, as Leah went off in search of her brother. Gitel knocked on the door and waited to be asked to enter. Quickly ascertaining the situation, she knew instinctively what Malka would ask of her and began preparing ingredients for a poultice.

"Which tea do you require, mistress?" Gitel asked. "Is it to be the raspberry or the Motherwort? I shall have to fetch some water..."

Bluma murmured, "What? I don't want tea..."

"Hush now. It will help you relax and that will improve the efficiency of your labor." Malka thought for a moment and decided to have the Motherwort prepared. It had a refreshing minty taste, which her daughter-in-law would appreciate—nauseous as she was—and the soothing liquid would alleviate the anxiety of labor.

"The doctor cannot come!" Avram shouted as he burst into the room. "He is performing an emergency appendectomy on a poor child not yet ten years old. Mamá? Whatever are you doing?"

Malka smiled at her beloved son and continued applying the poultice that Gitel prepared. "I am massaging this mixture of oil, chamomile, and lavender onto your wife's back...unless you care to do it?"

"What? Me? Ah—no. I...I will wait outside and allow you the space in which to work," Avram answered, his pallid face suggesting he would do better elsewhere. "You *do* know what you are doing, Mamá?"

"The massage will relax the muscles and ease her labor, and son," she said with a proud smile, "do not forget—I have had twelve children." And with that, Malka waved him away and turned her focus back on Bluma and future grandchild.

The family gathered together in the main leisure room. While Avram vacillated between pacing and reading psalms, the others attempted to pass the hours reading, playing chess, or trying their luck at a game of whist. Leah sat alongside of Duvid who was nose deep into a book of the Argentine pampas, and although she attempted several times to strike up a conversation with her nephew, he could not be persuaded to abandon his reading.

Much to Leah's chagrin, she was quite bored with her situation. Shunned from the birthing room, snubbed by an adolescent, and turned away from cards, Leah began looking about the room for some form of entertainment. How propitious that at that exact moment, a gentleman entered the salon. Dark and slender, the man had a foreign look about him— Leah was reminded of picture she has recently seen of a Spanish *matador*. Not wanting to appear brazen, Leah turned her head and quickly picked up a periodical she had just thrown aside.

Flipping the pages without deliberation, Leah found she could not resist taking a peek at the distinguished stranger. Unfortunately, just as she raised her eyes to look upon his fine physiognomy, he chose to look upon her as well! The stranger smiled revealing two dimples on either side of a very mannish square chin. His eyes glanced about the room, noted the stillness and inactivity, and quickly turned to exit. Leah released the breath she hadn't realized she was holding and tossed the fashion journal aside once more.

Nothing exciting ever happens to me!

"What do you mean nothing exciting ever happens to you?" asked Duvid. "Aren't we at this very moment on a steamer ship heading to a new country? Aren't we moving into a colonial *estancia* complete with a guard tower? Aren't we waiting to hear about Bluma's baby?"

Leah hadn't realized that she had spoken out loud, and now hearing Duvid's reprimand, she was quite put out.

"The difference," she sighed, "is that these things— exhilarating as they may be—are happening whether or not *I* had any say in the matter. We are forever being told what to do, how to do it, and when to do it! Don't you ever wish that you could choose for yourself?"

Leah huffed and stretched as she grew restless in her chair. She suddenly realized, if she wanted something of interest to happen, she would have to create it herself. The fortunate circumstance of the moment could not be ignored. She was presently not under Mamá's hawkish eye and her family was quite occupied with their tiresome activities. Now was the time to act! Leah pretended to stifle a yawn and said rather loudly, "I'm going to take a nap."

Sara glared at her for her unladylike mannerisms, but nodded once and returned her attention to the cards in her hand. Duvid continued reading without a second thought to his aunt, and in a blink of an eye— most advantageously—Leah found herself alone and unattended. She took the path back to the cabin, but at the end of the long hall, she turned right instead of left and found herself on the promenade.

Leah walked along allowing her fingers to glide lightly above the railing. The cool breeze was refreshing after sitting so long indoors and the easy movement of the ship no longer caused her to feel light-headed or dyspeptic. Feeling wonderfully free, she allowed her senses to revel in the cool mist of the waves and in the delightful chatter coming from the water below. Curious to discover the origin of the high-pitched clicking sounds, Leah leaned over the railing to investigate and was rewarded with a most pleasing sight of frolicking sea creatures.

"Careful Miss. You wouldn't want to fall overboard."

Quickly releasing the rail, Leah stepped back and turned to find the handsome gentleman standing in very close proximity. *Too* close.

"I couldn't resist getting a better look," she replied in the same lyrical Italian he had articulated. "I've never seen such creatures..."

"Aren't they magnificent?" he replied. "According to the ancient Greeks, spotting a school of dolphins riding in a ship's wake is considered a good omen."

"Dolphins, you say? How fortunate that I happened to be walking this way—such an opportunity might not present itself again!"

"You have the right of it, Miss..."

Giddy at her own audacity, she replied. "It is rather improper to introduce ourselves—without a third party to do the honors—but perhaps, as we are at sea, we can dispense with such formalities. I am Leah Solomonovna Abramovitz. How do you do?"

Nonplussed, he bowed over her delicate hand. "Very well, thank you. Miss Leah Solomonovna Abramovitz? You are Russian?"

"Yes," she said, as she dipped into a small curtsey and wondered what her mamá would think of her behavior. "You have cleverly deduced my nationality by the sound of my name, but you have neglected to introduce yourself."

"Quite right. Miguel Luis Maldonado del Castillo—*a su servicio, señorita.*"

"A Spaniard, then?" she laughed.

"Precisely so."

"Nonetheless, you have addressed me in Italian."

It was his turn to laugh now as he explained that he thought her to be an Adriatic princess—she looked so regal strolling down the promenade. Leah turned to hide her blush and struggled to think of something to say in response. Since he was a Spaniard, she thought she would put her skills to the test.

"I am not Italian, nor Austrian, *nor a princess* for that matter. However, I am to be adopted by the Argentine people."

Smiling, he revealed the dimples Leah had noticed earlier. He complimented her language skills, and since he had been adopted by the Argentines as well, señor Maldonado del Castillo stated he was most assuredly qualified to dub her quite the *porteña*, as the citizens of the port city were known.

"You flatter me, but I doubt that I emulate the accent well enough to pass as a Buenos Aires local. I do have an affinity for languages—at least that is what my papá had always said. We've had lessons in French, of course, and Italian. We speak Russian at home—Yiddish, as well..."

"Yiddish?" he interrupted. "I am not familiar with that word.

Leah froze at his response and immediately chided herself. She knew better than to converse with a complete stranger, alone and unchaperoned; but to speak to a stranger who obviously was not Jewish, she became paralyzed with fear. She thought of Lieutenant Yegorov and all those evil men in Odessa. What if he concurred with their horrid beliefs? What if insulted her? Who would come to her aid?

Leah took a step back and felt the railing against her spine. *I don't require anyone to come to my aid.* Jutting her chin in a grandiloquent manner, she replied, "Yiddish, sir, is a language that Jewish people speak throughout Russia and Eastern Europe."

He scratched his square chin that she had, but a moment ago, found so arresting. "A Russian Jewess, you say?"

Without realizing the action, Leah stomped her foot and huffed. "Yes, that is correct. Your astonishment at my lineage is quite disquieting, sir. Allow me to suggest a visit to the ship's library. I am certain you will find a book or two which will enlighten you on the subject. And now, you will please excuse me. I am afraid I've been too long away."

The stranger studied her face once more, and then coming to his senses, began apologizing profusely. "You must forgive my ignorance, but you see I had no idea..."

"No idea of what?"

"Well, the *rusos*—the Jews on board—they are below deck. They travel in steerage, at least, that was what I believed," he said guiltily. "Your dress, your speech—your entire person, Miss Abramovitz, tells me you are a lady of quality."

"You, sir, are truly ignorant," Leah replied. "For as you see, I am Russian and I am Jewish *and* I am traveling in First Class—very likely in a far more luxurious cabin than you have claimed for yourself!"

Without so much as a by your leave, she turned to walk away, but he scandalously reached out, touched her elbow, and stayed her departure.

"I did not mean to offend you, *señorita*. I own that I am quite the imbecile. May I have an opportunity to prove my sincerity? Perhaps tonight, after dinner, we might take a stroll on deck," he suggested, smiling provocatively inducing his dimples to appear. "The stars are beautiful at night on open sea, although not as beautiful as your eyes…"

Leah, surprising herself and the Spaniard, started giggling. First he insulted her and then he wished to woo her under a moonlit starry night. Leah shook her head declining his offer.

"I think it best if I returned to my family, *señor*," she said, gratified that she hadn't fallen for his charms. "I believe we will have reason to celebrate this evening, and you know how we *rusos* become when celebrating. Quite bacchanalian, you know!"

She very nearly skipped away—pleased with herself and thrilled with the experience that Life had presented, even if the dashing stranger turned out to be an ignorant buffoon. What a sense of empowerment, she thought, to have given the Spaniard the cut direct without need of assistance or approval from parent or guardian. She felt as if she was not only sailing to a new home, but to a new era of liberation and independence. In Argentina, she would strive to shed the old stifling ways that contained her, that regulated every thought and movement. Naturally, she enjoyed the niceties of polite society, and even dreamed of being a fine renowned lady, but she would obtain these ideals on her *own* terms.

Recalling señor Maldonado del Castillo's disdain for the rusos below deck, Leah flinched at his disparaging words. Those *rusos* were blood of her blood—they were her people sailing towards a new life on the same vessel. She realized, of course, that in Odessa, their lives couldn't have been any more different. Argentina would be their equalizer. The status of being a green immigrant, fresh off the ship, would put them on a level playing field. She grimaced and thought, *well, not exactly*. Her brothers had purchased a palatial new home and had grand plans for their advancement. Her brethren traveling in steerage faced an altogether different scenario, but as mamá had always said, 'Man plans and God laughs.' Who truly knew what lay ahead, once they reached the shores of Buenos Aires?

In the meanwhile, Bluma had been hard at work using every ounce of courage and strength at her disposal. In the hours that had transpired, Malka and Gitel supported the laboring mother in the ways that were as old as time. A sisterhood had formed among the women, a kinship forged out of pain, trust, and the sense of wonderment in witnessing a new life being brought into the world. Bluma had been safely delivered of a son, small though he was. Malka believed him to be a tiny warrior—*this one will fight— he will survive*. And then, she quickly added, *may it be God's will.*

Gitel bathed and swaddled the child, while Malka prepared a tea for the new mother. This time it was to be Blackberry, as she knew it to be an astringent which would prevent hemorrhaging. Although it had been a premature birth and they were caught unprepared, things had gone smoothly. They had much to be thankful for: a new child for Bluma and Avram and a new life awaiting them in Argentina.

"Hashem has been good to us," Malka said aloud. "May we be blessed in our New Jerusalem."

Chapter Seven

April 1901 ~ Buenos Aires, Argentina

*J*ust when Leah was at the point of desperation—daydreaming of throwing her nephew overboard as he spewed forth another bit of trivia of the famed argent waters—crewmen and passengers heralded the sighting of *Puerto Madero*. Duvid added his voice to the jubilant calls of *land ho* as their friendly and always-eager-to-please steward came scurrying by. With great pride, the man informed his young friend that they were in for quite a treat. The new port, which had been completed only four short years ago, could finally accommodate the modern larger vessels, such as the Sofia Hohenberg. This interesting tidbit naturally caught Duvid's attention and the steward found a willing audience. Duvid would hear the whole of it, as Leah rolled her eyes in exasperation.

Prior to the construction, the man expounded, passengers had to disembark onto barges and ferries which were small enough to circumnavigate the shallow murky waters of La Boca. A costly project was undertaken by government decree to construct a new port which would receive Argentina's newest citizens in proper fashion.

"First Class passengers are given priority to disembark at their leisure and you will be able to proceed directly to the landing through a separate gate. When your family is ready, I would be honored to be your escort."

Leah, taking advantage of the break in conversation, grabbed Duvid by his arm, thanked the crewman, and took off in search of the family. At last, they were going to get off the ship! As soon as they were given permission to do so, the Abramovitz family guided by their steward, descended the wooden ramp and stepped foot upon the docks. With chaotic orchestration, the passengers were coaxed into forming lines as officials shouted out instructions in a variety of languages.

"Have your documents in hand!"

"Stay within your group."

"Customs to the right. Medical examinations to the left!"

Several hours later, their documents stamped and approved, the family waited for Moishe and Yosef to locate their Argentine contact. The children grew restless and the adults began to imagine all manner of misfortune when, at last, the brothers reappeared. With solemn faces, they approached the elders of the group.

"We were unable to locate our man," said a grim Moishe.

"But," Yosef added quickly, "do not despair. He must be here somewhere. Considering the multitude of people, the Tower of Babel would appear to be orderly and intelligible."

Leah spied a group of Russian Jews gathered around a gentleman, dressed in a most peculiar costume. The man wore a pair of voluminous dark pants and a coarse white shirt with a colorful handkerchief tied around his neck. Upon his head, he neither wore a panama hat, nor a straw boater nor a felt derby, but a red *beret*. Recognizing the outfit from Duvid's book, she knew that the men of the pampas dressed in this fashion. Leah thought he looked out of place here on the docks, surrounded by squawking seagulls and the smell of the sea.

The group had divided into groups. The women and children, with their bundles and belongings, traipsed off to one side while their men continued to listen intently to the man in the diaper-style pants. However unusual his outfit, her compatriots were clinging to, and apparently, understanding every word. Leah signaled to her brothers and suggested they speak to the man sporting the red hat. Her brothers approached the group, and indeed, the *gaucho* was speaking Yiddish. Avram posed his question when given an opportunity.

"*Dis vus yid?*" he asked.

"*Yo,*" the man replied with a smile. "I am a Jew."

Moishe let loose with a brief, but illustrative accounting of the family's situation, explaining that they had made arrangements to engage Alberto Zanetti here on the docks of Puerto Madero.

Furthermore, Moishe added bitterly, they were supposed to have been escorted to the acclaimed Hotel Phoenix on Avenida San Martin once they had finished their business with the immigration officials. Yosef, coming upon the men, heard his brother providing the rudimentary details to the stranger.

"We have a bill of sale for the purchase of *Villa Esperanza*, an estate about an hour away," Yosef added. "We were to lodge at the hotel until the final papers could be notarized and recorded."

"*Villa Esperanza*? You say it is a colonial...about an hour outside of the capital?"

"Yes!" the men answered in unison.

"But gentlemen, that *estancia* is not for sale! It belongs to a well-known family from Castile. The descendants of the original owners—now millionaires in their own right—have donated the property to the new historical society," the man informed. Adjusting his red *boina* and tossing his forgotten cigarette to the ground, he muttered, "They may as well have sold you the Eiffel Tower."

The brothers, pale and dumbstruck, were unable to vocalize any dissent at the stranger's declaration. They had fallen for a tried and true game of deception, so often played upon the desperate.

"Look here. I am taking these other families to a *conventillo* where they will lodge for a few days," the Argentine explained. "Arrangements have been made for our newest colonists to travel to Basavilbaso in the province of Entre Rios. Why don't you come with me? I will introduce you to the people in charge. Perhaps something can be done."

"What of the money that was paid out to Mr. Zhirinovsky?" Yosef demanded.

"I'm afraid it is lost," a desolate Aaron responded. "I don't know if it was Zhirinovsky or this Zanetti fellow, but our money is long gone." He turned to face the Argentine, wishing to get further information. "Sir..."

"Please—" He removed his head-covering and extending his hand. "My name is León, León Goldfarb, or as I was known in the old country, Leib."

"Which old country might that be?" asked Avram.

"I was born in England," León replied, "I speak English, Yiddish, German, *and* Spanish. Which language do you prefer?"

"Right at this moment, I am not all too pleased with Spanish speakers," Aaron grimaced. "What has me completely dumbfounded is this...*this fraud* which has been committed."

"The word you are looking for is e*stafa*."

"I beg your pardon?"

"*Estafa*—it is the Argentine word for swindle," León clarified. "Some wise-guy *porteño* thought he'd pull a fast one—a *piolada*. There are many such men with a deep hatred and fear of the *rusos*."

He explained to the newcomers that, unfortunately, there were many people who did not appreciate the continuing wave of Jewish immigration. They needed a scape goat for the nation's banking debacle and, as usual, the Jews fit the bill. Ships arrived continually to the Port of Buenos Aires. The Sofia Hohenberg had docked nineteen times—always chock full of greenhorns needing food, work, education, and shelter.

"So, why pick specifically on the Jews?"

"Why, indeed?" León shook his head. "The Pope and his Church are always stirring up trouble! Not to mention, we have our fair share of anarchists, socialists—communists. Ignorant fools! That is my only explanation for their revulsion towards our people, for we have immigrants arriving on these very docks from *every* corner of the world. We've received immigrants from the British Isles since the early 1800's. The Irish populated the outskirts of the province of Buenos Aires and the south of Santa Fe. The Basque followed soon after. The provinces of Santa Fe, Chaco, and Entre Rios began receiving immigrants from across Switzerland and France. Russians and Germans followed suit and the Spaniards and Italians, well—they came in massive waves!" he said throwing his arms open wide. "We have a saying here: Mexicans descended from Aztecs, Peruvians descended from Incas and Argentines descended from ships."

Avram began getting restless. After all, he had a new babe and a wife to attend. They couldn't stand on the docks all night discussing history and politics.

"Can you direct us to our lodgings, Leib?" he beseeched. "Our family needs to rest. We have had a great shock—you understand."

Aaron stayed that request. "I don't think we should spend our limited funds at the Hotel Phoenix. We have no idea of where we stand. We need to make inquiries. We *must* see to our finances and seek legal counsel."

Moishe and Yosef agreed. The new hotel was all the rage, but not necessarily what the family needed at the moment.

"I can't promise you anything like the Hotel Phoenix; nonetheless, my offer still stands. Come with me. I will arrange for temporary shelter, while you make your round of appointments. I am certain that the people at the J.C.A. will be able to assist you."

The men concurred and retreated to gather the family, while León arranged for transportation. Divulging only a few details, Aaron made quick work of informing the family of the calamitous error in judgment they had committed in trusting Mr. Zhirinovsky and Mr. Zanetti. Leah, who had been full of hope and expectation, nearly collapsed at the sight of her dear mamá. Disheartened and weakened, Malka looked on the verge of tears, but then she happened upon her daughter's face, and her entire person was transformed.

Never prouder, Leah observed her mother as she straightened to her full height, pulled back her shoulders, and exclaimed, "Lodging, food and sleep— that is what we require. Tomorrow is a new day, and *Baruch Hashem*, we are all together."

Silently, Leah added to her mother's dictum. *Papá, please watch over us. We are in quite a mess!*

León Goldfarb returned to find the Abramovitz family huddled together in prayer. In due time, he was introduced to the matriarch, who shocked her more pious children when she placed her hand on the stranger's forearm.

"My beloved Solomon has sent you to us, Mr. Goldfarb, in our hour of need," she said, with great reverence. "Lead on, if you please."

León had never before witnessed such poise and grace in the face of such misfortune. He stuttered as he begged the lady's pardon for escorting her family to rather unsuitable lodgings, but given that the new Immigrants' Hotel was in the process of construction, he had no other choice. The J.C.A. had leased several *conventillos* to house the onslaught of newcomers. To his dismay, León admitted these were located in a seedy quarter of town. Duvid had been listening intently; however, he was greatly confused by the gaucho's words. *Were they going to stay in a convent?*

The man shook his head in a fit of laughter. "No, no! Not a *convento*, boy, a *conventillo*. It is like a large home divided up into smaller, living quarters. The best part, my friend, is the courtyard in the center of the building where you can play and breathe fresh air."

León began escorting the family, along with his other travelers, off the crowded docks towards the hired wagons. Leah was reminded of the hay rides through open fields near their *dacha*, but there would be no singing among fields of wheat and sunflowers today. The weary group settled onto their humble conveyances, and as the cool night descended, they went deeper and further into the bowels of the city. When the caravan at last came to a stop, León Goldfarb turned to the fine lady and spoke in hushed tones.

"Señora Abramovitz, advise your youngsters to avert their eyes. Your new neighbors—they are not clean."

"*Kurveh!*" Sara screeched, as she shielded her face upon spying a brazen woman practically hanging out of a window.

Leah was shocked at her sister's outburst and confused by Mr. Goldfarb's insinuations. What did

Mr. Goldfarb mean—*they were not clean*? Sara began to explain, believing she understood the world better than her younger sister, but her mother interrupted with great disdain.

"Shame on you, Sara. Do you think they chose this path for themselves? They were most likely abandoned or tricked by some evil person."

"Then why don't they leave and make a decent living?"

"I fear you cannot comprehend their fall from grace," Leon interjected. "You see, many were kidnapped from the old country. They are here without proper documentation. They have no money of their own, no means to return home. There is little hope for escape." He was filled with shame for having brought *such* a family to *such a place*. Greater still, was the pity he had for the women trapped in their hellish existence.

Quickly, he escorted the assembly into the reception area of the lodging. Greeted by *señora* Moretti, León first discharged his J.C.A. colonists to her care and then set out to arrange rooms for the Abramovitz family. Although it was certainly not the Hotel Phoenix, they were essentially under one roof, separated only by the central courtyard Mr. Goldfarb had previously mentioned. Señora Moretti served her guests heaping platters of *fideos con tuco* and baskets full of crusty, thick bread. The meal made Leah homesick for Mrs. Kraskov's *lapsha* noodles, and she found that she was grateful for the simple fare. When at last they were all safely tucked away for the night, *Thank you, Papá,* was her last thought before falling fast asleep.

Chapter Eight

*T*he Argentine sun hadn't had a chance yet to smile down upon them, when León Goldfarb was at the door ready to be of service. At Aaron's request, their first stop would be the bank. He had been able to acquire a letter of credit from their institution in Odessa and was informed that *Banco Nación* would be equipped to work with international customers. Aaron prayed that the process would go smoothly as he and his brother accompanied señor Goldfarb on their way to *El Centro*, the financial hub of the city.

Immediately upon entering the establishment, León pinpointed a staff member and made discreet inquires on the brothers' behalf. They were informed that señor Eduardo H. Aguirre de la Casas would be happy to be of service. The elegant bank manager greeted the party with great fanfare and flourish as he led them to his office. It was evident that señor Aguirre de la Casas was accustomed to dealing with people of quality, and in particular, foreigners. He spoke several languages; nevertheless, the Abramovitz brothers insisted on speaking Spanish.

Impatient with the niceties that accompany forming a new acquaintance, Aaron took a seat and began explaining—in no uncertain terms—that they had been deceived. It was yet unclear if the culprit was their Russian contact or the Argentine fellow. Perhaps they had colluded together, he surmised, but the deed had been done and he wished them both to the devil! Aaron divulged the family's reasons for leaving Russia in a bitter and clipped voice; and without further ceremony, presented his letter of credit. It was imperative that Banco Nación understand their predicament and recognize their status.

"You can well imagine we are deeply concerned," Aaron stated. "It is my understanding that you are able to prepare the appropriate paperwork, in order to transfer our funds. We wish to establish an account with your bank."

"Yes, of course. We offer a full range of modern services for our international clientele, and I would be honored to see to the arrangements myself. If you would permit me," señor Aguirre de la Casas reached for the documentation, "I will initiate the process by contacting your financial institution."

The men were asked to wait in the manager's well-appointed office. An attractive young lady wheeled in a coffee set, accompanied by a silver platter filled with pastries and sweet cakes. Nerves had the brothers on edge—the refreshments went untouched. When at last the banker returned, he found the Abramovitz men overcome with exhaustion and dread.

"I'm afraid, gentlemen, that I must be the bearer of bad news. We have received a telegram from a Mr. Evgeny Petrovich Kobseva..."

"Evgeny Petrovich?" Aaron barked as he jumped to his feet.

"You know him?"

"We have been doing business with his bank for decades, as our father had done before us."

The banker pursed his lips before begging his anxious customer to take a seat once more.

"It seems that your funds have been frozen until further notice."

"What?" the brothers cried out in unison.

"Mr. Kobseva indicated that the Abramovitz accounts are being audited. It would appear our hands are tied for the moment. Gentlemen, I am sure you can appreciate that these things take time—even under the best of circumstances."

Moishe turned to face his brother. "You know as well as I do, Kobseva and his bank officials will not allow us one *kopeck*. How do we fight this? It is our money, after all."

"Perhaps," said señor Aguirre de la Casas, "you might be interested in a loan until such time as your funds are released?"

The brothers declined the offer, having had the foresight of bringing along a limited sum of European currency, coupled with coin and trinkets. Aaron hoped that these reserves would allay the family's trepidation while they waited for the officials to complete their so-called audit. Privately, however, he battled against his deepest fears. Corruption and thievery ran rampant amongst those in power, and there was every possibility that the family's treasury was lost to them forever.

Having completed their business with the banking institution, the men continued on to the Jewish Colonization Association headquarters. Shaken to the core, Aaron and Moishe were unable to take in the sights and sounds of their surroundings. Who in their right mind could have paid any attention to the tree-lined streets or the elegant buildings after receiving such devastating news? A rapid stream of movement passed before their glazed eyes. Pedestrians and conveyances became blurred images until the carriage stopped in front of a five-story brick building. The men alit, and took to the stairs reaching the top floor harried and out of breath. A man was just coming out the door as they arrived. It happened to be the person León Goldfarb had meant to see.

"Yankel! Where are you going?" León asked. "I have brought these fine gentlemen to speak with you."

León proceeded to make the introductions, but his friend knew that such things were not done standing in the door's threshold. "It is bad luck to stand in the doorway," he chuckled. "Come in, come in!"

Once the party had completely entered the office, he extended his hand in greeting. "I am Jacobo Shulman; but my friend here, he calls me *Yankel* like the old man he is!"

The men shook hands and shared a nervous laugh. Jacobo asked them to be seated, as he brought a worn leather chair from behind his desk. "What can I do for you, gentlemen?"

Aaron looked at Moishe and nodded, affirming he wished the elder brother to speak. Without further prompting, Moishe let loose.

"My family felt compelled to leave Russia. We paid for our passage and purchased a home in the outskirts of Buenos Aires—that is to say—we thought we purchased a home. We have been swindled, sir. The transaction was fraudulent. We had planned to open a factory, you see, but our funds have been confiscated by our government. We find ourselves in dire straits, sir."

"That is indeed a remarkable story, Mr. Abramovitz. I offer my condolences for the manner you were received here in Argentina," Jacobo murmured, shaking his head. "That being said, I believe we can be of service to your family; although, it will not be what you were expecting. You will be settled in the provinces, of course. It seems God has a different plan for your family. At the very least, let us call it a deviation," he chuckled and got up to place a kettle to boil. "The JCA has already established several colonies, and you might consider yourselves lucky—even under these circumstances. Your family is arriving at a time where things have smoothed out a bit."

The men breathed a bit easier knowing that they would not be turned away, but Aaron was interested in understanding Mr. Shulman's meaning. *Why should they consider themselves lucky?* When Jacobo asked if they were familiar with the pilgrims of North American history, Aaron's curiosity was piqued more than ever.

"In 1889," Jacobo began, "the first wave of immigrants left their homes in Ukraine and set out to sea on a *Mayflower*-like pilgrimage lasting thirty-five days. The first colonists faced famine, locusts, and disease. These days, although we no longer have our beloved Baron Hirsch to guide us, we are functioning like a well-oiled machine. You will find it much easier than those first wayfarers."

Moishe asked if he could tell them more about the first colonists. How would their experiences differ from the founders? Jacobo was a walking encyclopedia, and there was nothing he enjoyed more than sharing the history of Jewish immigration to Argentina.

"Ten groups of fifty families were chosen from Bessarabia. These families settled in the Clara colony, in the province of Entre Rios. At the same time, forty families from Grodno were selected. They settled in Santa Fe, in the colony known as Moises Ville. Prior to the J.C.A. becoming a formalized organization, it was quite common for immigrants to be cheated—you are in good company on that score!" he said with a bitter laugh. "A man by the name of Palacios tricked the first group out of their land. Without proper organization and management, they found themselves sleeping in freight cars and begging for sustenance. The railway workers distributed food among the hungry children; but due to numerous factors, a typhus epidemic spread and sixty-nine children perished. Even after the J.C.A. was established and Baron Hirsch provided people to administrate and maintain order, the early colonists were subjected to many trials, losing all their crops through heavy rains or drought, infestations and their own inexperience."

"It sounds a bit like the Israelites exodus out of Egypt—plagues and all," Moishe exclaimed.

"Truer words were never spoken, but they had their very own Moses—*the Moses of South America*—to help them get to the Promised Land."

"Well said! Leon cheered. "Now, tell them about the co-ops..."

"*Co-ops*? Do you mean cooperatives?" asked Aaron. "I am a bit leery of these types of organizations. Would you label them socialist in nature?"

Jacobo laughed. "At first glance, one might suppose the ideology is rather *Dumasian*—all for one and one for all! The First Israelite Agricultural Society was recently established in Lucienville to assist struggling individual farmers. Together, they were able to fund the purchase of seed and harvesting supplies, and because they were ordering larger quantities..."

"They were able to negotiate a better price." Aaron nodded in acknowledgement. "I understand the concept, of course—"

"People will have their individual political views, but I cannot fault a group of farmers coming together to promote the well-being of their community. Look, I'm not going to lie to you. This undertaking *will* be demanding. Many immigrants struggle to adapt, but they are becoming more and more like the gauchos, their adopted brethren of the plains."

"Tell us more about these people," Moishe asked. "Do we have anything to fear from these men?"

The whistling of the kettle caught Jacobo's attention. While he prepared a tray with four cups and saucers, he happily enlightened his guests.

"The men travel across the plains working for land owners—moving cattle or training horses. Now that the colonists are arriving to establish farms, life as they have known it has drastically changed. Nevertheless, it is remarkable to note that–*in most cases*–a certain kinship has developed between these two peoples."

León nodded in agreement. "The gauchos are acclimating themselves to the newcomers, but more than that, they have also become their friends and teachers. They have taken it upon themselves to teach Jewish shopkeepers and intellectuals how to handle cattle, how to break-in horses, and even how to deal with sick animals. We are witnessing a new era, I tell you—the gauchos are learning to speak Yiddish and the Jews are wearing traditional gaucho garb and drinking *yerba maté*—but that is another subject altogether!" he said with a great bellow.

The men continued to talk over small cups of intense, black coffee and sweet pastries, León called *facturas*. Jacobo talked romantically of thistles and thickets; of land so vast, one might compare it to the wide expanse of an unending ocean. By the time they left, the Abramovitz brothers were waxing poetic about starry nights on the pampas. They were eager to tell the family what they had learned, and more to the point, what they could expect from this new adventure. León offered to accompany the men, just in case there were more questions to be answered. Moishe knew that his family would be prepared with long lists of concerns. He appreciated the offer and was glad to have made such a fine friend.

Upon arriving at the *conventillo*, they found the adults gathered around a long table having tea and *facturas,* while the children were enjoying an afternoon nap. Far off in the distance, the sound of rumbling thunder added to thickness in the air. An autumn storm was upon them. Anxious and uncomfortable, Leah was ready to receive both the news her brothers were about to divulge, as well as, the downpour the heavy clouds promised.

"Where are we to go?" she cried. "What have you arranged for us?

"There has been some unforeseen trouble with the bank, I'm afraid." Shouldering all the guilt for the failures and setbacks they were experiencing, Aaron began a painful declamation explaining their current financial status. He outlined a plan where they could set aside a modest sum for the establishment of a future textile operation, but for the time being, they would have to retrench. "And we have met with a representative of the Jewish Colonization Association."

"It seems that Yosef's dream to work the land will come to fruition," Moishe added, grinning at his youngest brother.

"What does this mean for our family?" Naftali enquired.

"We will sign a contract and incur a debt with the J.C.A. In return, as Yosef detailed, we will receive a home, land, and the basic necessities to survive as farmers."

"*A debt?*"

"At five percent charge of interest," Aaron responded. "Which, if looked at coldly, is nothing compared to what the Association has put out since the inception of the organization."

"What do I care about the Association?" How does this benefit us?"

"Our funds are frozen, Brother, for an undetermined amount of time. If we stay in Buenos

Aires, we will quickly eat our way through our limited reserves. Moving to the province will, at the very least, provide us with some stability, and we will leave a small amount of savings untouched for when the time comes that we may reevaluate our situation."

"Can you be more specific?" Avram asked. "What do you know of this place? Is there a Jewish school?"

"Are there shops?"

"Are there medical facilities?"

Moishe answered with patience and empathy, for his siblings had put their future in his hands. And after all, he and Aaron had had a few hours to acclimate themselves to the situation.

"We will be going to Basavilbaso—a small, agricultural town about 160 miles north of Buenos Aires. Just as other families, already established in the area, we will receive the same allotment—a contract to lease a plot of land. The J.C.A. will supply us with *one* cow, *one* horse and some chickens," he said with some sarcasm thinking of his cherished Abastor and the other animals they left behind in Odessa. "Materials and implements to work the land will also be provided. Mr. Shulman indicated that as the population continues to grow, the need for other occupations increase. So to answer your question, Avram, I am certain that your skills as a teacher will be most welcome."

"We do have visiting physicians and a small clinic in town," León added, hoping to set the family at ease. "We have been blessed by several Russian Jewish doctors who distinguish themselves by their devotion to both colonists and locals. Dr. Noe Yarcho, who came to Entre Rios in '93, is greatly esteemed by all the settlers. I urge you to take heart! Many of the colonists were small merchants and shop-keepers in the old country—most never engaged in agricultural pursuits whatsoever, but they have shown zeal and great enthusiasm for the project. They have *recreated* themselves to be agriculturists in the end."

The family murmured their interest, as well as their angst. It was not what they had planned. They had expected a cosmopolitan life in Buenos Aires, but under the circumstances, it seemed apparent that they had little choice.

"What about accommodations?" Malka asked. "We are a large family and are accustomed to living under one roof."

"I dare say that will have to change, madam," León said, removing his hat and approaching the gracious lady. "You will most likely find a small cottage on the land, in addition to a barn or perhaps a granary. You will have to make do, but I suspect your family will begin spreading out and occupying homesteads of their own."

"I would prefer for us to stay together," Malka said softly. "It was my husband's dying wish, but if my sons are of another mind—well, we did come here to start anew. For now, we will make do, as you say."

"I will make all the arrangements and Jacobo Shulman will prepare the contract. It will not be easy, but sometimes, one must take a leap of faith and know that God is in command."

"Yes. I am of that belief, as well. Hashem can change everything in the blink of an eye. I have no doubt, Mr. Goldfarb, that no matter how bleak something may look, salvation could be just around the corner."

Chapter Nine

May 1901 ~ Basavilbaso, Entre Rios

With no time to spare, the family prepared to board yet another train together with the other families headed for the colony. Leah had hoped that her brothers would have allowed her to see the sights—heaven only knew when they would be in Buenos Aires again—but there had been no time allotted for frivolities. The men had barely enough time to submit a formal report to the authorities with regard to señor Zanetti. The police did not relay any sense of urgency or empathy, but Moishe felt somewhat placated. At the very least, an official complaint had been lodged. The telling of the misfortune which befell them would, *perhaps*, prevent another ill-advised family from suffering the same financial disaster.

At the last moment, prior to leaving the *conventillo*, Leah had decided to wear her paisley traveling ensemble. Unfortunately, it needed pressing. Señora Moretti had come to the rescue with hot coals for the iron and a board. When Malka commented on the impracticality of the gown, Leah conceded it was perhaps not the best choice, given the mode of transportation or their destination, but she *would* have her way.

The family made their way to the impressive Retiro train station, alongside the murky River Plate. They boarded and were comfortably situated, although the accommodations were far different from those to which they were accustomed. Leah sat by her nephew who, again, had his nose stuck in a book. Such was his idiosyncrasy, and she was very much aware of this practice. It would have been uncharacteristic for the young man to have traveled without a collection of reading material, and she expected the trip would be dreadfully tiresome. The only conversation to be had, it seemed, came from Mr. Goldfarb.

"The colony of Basavilbaso is considered to be at the heart of Entre Rios' railway system," said Mr. Goldfarb. "Just six or seven years ago, they laid out tracks that reached Paraná, the capital of the province, Concepción del Uruguay; Gualeguaychu *and* Villaguay. The colony's growth is such that the J.C.A. had to purchase additional land. Just look out the window! All you will see, for miles and miles, is land—beautiful, rich land."

Leah brushed aside the heavy drapery and stared across the grassy plains. Mr. Goldfarb was partially correct. All she saw was land *and* fat cows. She reserved the right to withhold any commentary on the beauty, or the richness, of the vast terrain until such time she felt her family's decision to *schlep* out to the middle of nowhere warranted such high praise. Leah's meandering thoughts were interrupted, for Mr. Goldfarb was not finished with his exuberant tribute of their new homeland.

"The fertile terrain is well suited for corn, wheat, and oats. Some of the finest linen comes from the flax grown right here, in Entre Rios. It is a painstaking process to manufacture, but the fiber is very absorbent, and garments made of linen are valued for their exceptional coolness and freshness in hot weather. This is very much appreciated, especially by the *porteños* who suffer the humid summers in Buenos Aires!"

At the mention of this interesting tidbit, Leah showed a modicum of curiosity. At the very least, the man had spoken words which bore some semblance of interesting conversation. Unfortunately, his next offering reverted back to the allotment of land parcels and some such. Speaking directly to Moishe and the elders, Leon expounded on the colony's genesis when the J.C.A. purchased land for a group of immigrants from Bessarabia. The colony was named after their ancestral village of Novy Buk.

"They are actually two settlements, but we simply call them Novy Buk One and Two." León laughed at this practical solution before continuing. "Both are situated adjacent to the railway station. After the establishment of the sister settlements, new immigrants arrived. They were dubbed the Aquerman Group. Land was purchased for them, as well, just north east of the city center."

"Where are *we* to live?" Leah ventured to ask.

"My friend wired the local agent to arrange for accommodations, miss. But just where your family will be placed, has yet to be decided."

"So, what happens next, León?" asked Moishe.

"The J.C.A. will send their representative to greet us, as well as several men to assist with your belongings," León replied. Although the family believed that they had packed sensibly and with restraint, he valiantly suppressed the urge to laugh at the impressive quantity of luggage. "You will find the *peones* to be very helpful—you need only ask and they will be at your service."

"*Peones?*" Duvid repeated, suddenly looking up from his tome.

"That's right—hired hands that do menial work, as opposed to the gauchos, who are skilled animal handlers. I dare say your Spanish skills will come in very handy with the locals, but...ah, it is obvious that you have been trained by the rules of the *Academia Real Española*," he said with a hearty chuckle. "You will have to learn the *lunfardo* of the city folk and the *gaucho's* colloquialisms, in order to fit in."

Disappointed that he wouldn't meet authentic gauchos as soon as they stepped foot on the landing, Duvid returned to his book where he continued to read about his new-found heroes.

Leah closed her eyes and tried to drown out the chatter with thoughts of Buenos Aires, and all the *soirees* she'd imagined they would attend. She fought against the resentment that seared her soul and prayed to Hashem that He would illuminate her path. *Whatever would she do here?* Whatever could she hope to accomplish, settled so far away from the heart of culture and society?

As the train approached its final destination, the travelers became agitated and impatient. Men began pushing and reaching for their coats and bags. Women shouted at their children to obey and be still. Yiddish cries and Russian curses could be heard as chaos unfolded. The tension in the air was hard to avoid. The Abramovitz family began feeling the impulse to act out as well, but one look from the matriarch had everyone seated, shoulders back, and heads held high.

Once the conductor announced, *"Basavilbaso"* the travelers rushed out, as if the land would disappear if they tarried a moment longer. It was only when Malka turned to Moishe and Aaron with a slight nod, did the Abramovitz family alight. Mr. Goldfarb asked that the women and children gather by a specific post—it had a blue and white sign with the number 5 artistically scrolled upon it. The men were to accompany him to retrieve their numerous trunks and belongings; after which, they would meet with Adolfo Lipinsky, the J.C.A. agent.

Leah stepped off the train, wiping the dirt from her paisley print silk and grumbling over the many wrinkles and creases. Her throat was dry and parched and her was head pounding. Simple, as it surely would be, Leah was eager to reach their new home and looked forward to having a good long soak. *Would the cottage have a soaker tub?* She wondered.

It was then that Leah noticed a group of men standing near the appointed Number Five post. Assuming that they had been sent by the J.C.A., she thought it prudent to begin the process of loading the wagons with their hand belongings and the small children. After all, she was now an adult. She was eager to show her mamá that she could be relied upon.

"You there," Leah said, pointing to a tall muscular fellow as she adjusted her kid gloves. "Come assist us with our luggage."

As soon as she had articulated the words, Leah recognized her discourteousness, and immediately felt ashamed. She was tired and overwrought—she didn't mean any harm, but the man was a servant—*surely*. What did they call them here? A *peon*? Mr. Goldfarb had said they need only ask.

The man threw his cigarette on the dirt and grinned at his companions leaning against the post. Removing his black felt hat, he placed it over his heart and bowed.

"Yes, of course, *princesa*," he said, gazing at the elegant young woman appreciatively—brazenly. "I am at your command."

He picked up her belongings and signaled for his companions to help the others. Mr. Goldfarb and the Abramovitz men arrived with the trunks trailing behind in large carts, and found that the women and children had all been assisted onto several conveyances. Yosef was then confused, when the J.C.A. man arrived, huffing and blue in the face and begging pardon for being late. He had several men trailing behind him.

Leah, perched high above on the wagon, asked the J.C.A. agent if the men standing by the post worked for the organization as well.

"Ah—no, *señorita*," he said. "They are from the *estancias*. These here are my men," he stepped aside and the peones began loading the heavy travel trunks onto empty wagons.

"But *they* came to my aid," Leah said weakly. "That man there—I insisted..."

"That tall fellow? He is no local peon. That is Joaquín Ibáñez, or, as he is known around here, *El Moro.*"

"I beg your pardon?"

"His father was a descendant of the Moors. El Moro works at one of the neighboring ranches. The others work with the cattle, but he is the lead *domador*—eh, how do you say it—a horse trainer."

The men made fast work of loading the various trunks and crates. Spreading out a map on a handy table, the agent signaled for the Abramovitz brothers to gather around, as well as the *doña,* referring to the matriarch of the family. He turned once again, and asked two couples, who had lingered behind, to now approach. The agent introduced *señor* and *señora* Lipovesky from Novy Buk One and *señor* and *señora* Rabinovich from Novy Buk Two.

Removing their *boinas* from their heads, the men bowed as their charming wives approached bearing gifts. The Lipoveskys presented the family with an assortment of fruits and vegetables, various selections of cheese and several bottles of wine. The Rabinovich couple generously offered large sacks of sugar, salt, flour, and coffee beans, along with loaves of freshly baked bread.

"We understand that an unexpected turn of events has caused you to join our colony. We hope you accept this small token of friendship and our best wishes," said *señor* Lipovesky. "May the good Lord see that you always have the necessities of life."

"Bread," interjected señora Lipovesky, "so that you shall never know hunger."

"Salt—so your life shall always be flavorful," added *señor* Rabinovich.

"And Sugar," said his wife, "so that your life should be sweet."

Leah watched, overcome with pride, as her mother accepted the colonists' hospitality and good wishes. With grace and humility, the Abramovitz matriarch acknowledged that the loaves of bread, fruits and cheese would make for a welcomed evening repast. She listened as her mother promised to store a piece of bread, salt, and sugar in the corner of a cupboard, in keeping with the ancient custom of inviting good fortune to reign in a new home.

"Lipovesky and Rabinovich are originally from Novy Buk," Lipinsky said. "Their families were some of the first settlers in this area. Although they are close to town, the lots are relatively small. Their homes are of simple design and function."

"Are there lots available in Novy Buk Two?" asked Moishe. "Is that where you mean to place us?"

"No, not quite. Thanks to the assistance of the agronomist, Eusebio Lapin, new settlements have been developed in the southernmost regions of the province, namely, Lucienville. The lots are larger—there is more room to spread out. I have a certain parcel of land in mind for your family. You will receive 150 hectares, instead of 75, and the land comes with a corral."

"*Lucienville?*" asked Avram. "I thought we were to settle in the main area."

"These new parcels are simply an extension of J.C.A. land. When Baron and Baroness Hirsch lost their only son, their response to the outpour of sympathy was only to further their aid to the Jewish people. The baron said, 'My son I have lost, but not my heir. Humanity is my heir.' I only tell you this so that you will understand. Lucienville was named with much respect to the Hirsch family. Indeed, the J.C.A. is under the guidance of philanthropic men. In fact, you will receive a credit of 3,000 *pesos* to get started, and you will receive a monthly stipend until you can get on your feet."

"What is this?" Avram demanded. "Are we now to be considered children, with our hands stretched out, begging for *gelt* and treats as if it were Chanukah?"

Lipinsky immediately regretted his words. It had not been his intention to patronize the newcomers. This family had arrived under far different circumstances than the vast majority of the other colonists; but he felt it his duty to explain what the Association was able to provide, and the role it played in their daily lives. He begged their pardon, but insisted on elaborating. In the earlier years, each adult colonist received eight pesos per month. and each child was entitled to four. The assistance was gratefully received, for the colonists' endured back-breaking work in extreme conditions.

"Are we to slave away for absent land barons, who throw some coins our way while our land is plagued by sick cattle and infestations?" Avram spewed. "Are we now indentured servants to the Association? Aaron, what have you gotten us into?"

"That is quite enough!" Malka exclaimed. "I am ashamed of these outbursts. Should we not have faith in the Administration? Perhaps they know best..."

"Forgive me, Mamá, but I hope that this monthly charity will not be necessary," Aaron interjected hurriedly. "If the time comes—*heaven forbid*—that we require further assistance, I assure you señor Lipinsky, I will come to you at once."

Leah observed her brothers' faces. Angry and frustrated, their patience had grown thin.

"Perhaps tomorrow, we can revisit the contract, and all of its ramifications," the agent said. "Your journey has been quite a strain. Let us escort you to your new home, and allow you a night's respite before further discussion.

Looking at their beleaguered clan, the brothers recognized their only recourse was to accept Lipinsky's offer. Once they had time to rest, the family would review that matter and make a final decision. Lucienville, after all, couldn't be as bad as a *shtetl* in the Pale.

Seeing that her brothers had come to a decision, Leah settled back in her seat as they prepared to leave the station. Fussing with her wrap, she turned, and noticed just then, that the men she had erroneously subjugated were *still* lingering about. The man they called, El Moro, removed his hat and bowed dramatically as the wagon caravan began to pull out. When he lifted his head, Joaquín Ibáñez found himself staring directly into Leah's eyes. He smirked. She gasped. Embarrassed, Leah quickly turned away, too flustered to return his gaze.

Chapter Ten

The procession made its way across the small town passing fields where cattle lazily grazed. Leah, convinced that it was her sisterly duty to do so, turned around only once to survey how the children were faring. She was mortified to see that El Moro and his men continued to follow the wagons, as if they were faithful musketeers escorting a royal convoy. Duvid and the other children waved to the men on horseback. Restless and eager, the youngsters stirred this way and that, not wanting to miss any points of interest in their new homeland. Leah, however, sat arrow straight and refused to show any outward curiosity towards the flora or fauna. Nor or towards the gaucho who was following her home.

What had he called her—*princesa?* An outrageously impudent manner of address for a simple hired hand. But, then again, he *was not* a simple hired hand, and she *did* order him in a rather imperial tone. Heavens!

It had been an honest mistake and, if she had the opportunity to do so, Leah decided, then and there, to apologize to the man. She would not, however, allow him to make her feel as if she were a misbehaved child. Having an assortment of siblings, who daily reminded her of her shortcomings and of what was considered proper conduct for a young lady, Leah refused to add an impudent horse trainer to her list of tormentors.

Having traveled several miles deep in her own thoughts, Leah suddenly realized that the chatter and excitement, stemming from both the children and the adults, had decreased significantly. Turning her head ever so slightly to the right and then to the left, Leah witnessed the cause for the abrupt change in her family's emotions. Lonely homesteads spotted the terrain. Farmland and open range was all one could see.

As if he could read their minds, Yosef called out from the head wagon. Cupping his hands around his lips, so that his voice would travel down the line he exclaimed, "Remember—we are free to come and go as we please. This is not the Pale of Settlement and there are no inspectors, revizors or *Okhrana!*"

At that precise moment, Leah found Yosef's astute observation very small comfort, indeed. Slow and steady, the oxen ambled on for what seemed an eternity before señor Lipinsky held up his hand, signaling the drivers to come to a stop. They had arrived.

The Abramovitz men jumped off the wagons and handed down the women and children. Dismayed, they stood solemnly in place and quietly took in their surroundings. A dilapidated wooden fence, in dire need of sanding and a new coat of paint, marked the property. As señor Lipinsky had promised, the lot and the dwelling appeared somewhat larger than those seen on the previous homesteads. León Goldfarb had mentioned that they would most likely have a cabin or a cottage, depending on their luck, along with a small barn and granary. His assumption had been correct.

"I cannot believe that we trekked across Mother Russia through Europe and across the Atlantic Ocean to end up here—to live like *krepostnyye!*" Naftali bellowed.

"We are not serfs, Brother. We will work the land for our own benefit—not for some nobleman," replied Yosef. "*And* we will live in peace."

"We might as well have gone to Siberia," was Yaacov's grim reply. "We are in the middle of nowhere."

"'If only we had died by the hand of the Lord in the land of Egypt, when we sat by pots of meat, when we ate bread to our fill!'" Ysroel recited. "'For you have brought us out into this desert, to starve this entire congregation to death'—does that sound familiar? We have not yet been here one full day!" exclaimed the pious brother. "Where is your faith?"

Malka nodded her agreement. "It is quite fitting that you quote Exodus, my son, for are we not the epitome of Israelites wandering in the desert? But the Lord will provide—of that I am sure!"

Señor Lipinsky cleared his throat and the men turned towards the agent. Aware that the Abramovitz family had begun their odyssey with a different plan in mind, he did not begrudge them their displeasure. He could only imagine the life they had led in Odessa in the upper stratums of Jewish society. It was quite a different scenario than the vast majority of colonists, but not completely unheard of. The agronomic engineer, Miguel Sajaroff and his brother-in-law, Doctor Noé Yarcho, were both learned men of means—certainly known and admired among the colonists. They, too, had come from rather illustrious origins.

Señor Lipinsky gently reminded the family that they were on the outskirts of town but, there *was indeed* a thriving town—a Jewish town. The children would be required to attend public school in the morning; but the town was proud to boast of their own *cheder,* where Yiddish and religious studies were taught in the afternoons. The community had shops, a synagogue, a cemetery and a social hall. They would soon meet their neighbors and establish friendships with the *criollos* and the *yiden* alike.

"We—the Argentines and the Jews—live together in peace," he said. "God has made it possible for us to make a good life here."

"Of course, señor Lipinsky and we will do the same—may it be Hashem's will," replied Malka, as she turned and took in the full view of their new land. "Are these fruit trees? The orchard seems to have been abandoned, but with some work, we will have a bountiful harvest next year. This reminds me of when I was a child. It will be good for the *kinder* to get their hands into the dirt."

"You most likely will find peach and plum trees. At home, we also have mango," the land agent boasted.

"What is a *mango*?" Duvid asked. "May I try one?"

Señor Lipinsky laughed. "Yes, of course *boychik*! When you taste it, you will think it is a slice of heaven. Sweet and tangy, it is like biting into a peach and an orange at the same time."

"Come now, children," Malka said, as she marched to the door. "Let us enter our new home with uplifted spirits and gratitude in our hearts."

With their mother and señor Lipinsky leading the way, the Abramovitz clan followed suit. Leah trailed behind. She willed herself not to turn around, but curiosity overruled. The gauchos were still there—*he was still there.*

From atop his steed, El Moro removed his hat once more, and placed it over his heart. Knowing she owed him apology, she sunk into a deep curtsey, as if he were the Tsar himself. He laughed, not in a disparaging fashion, but with full appreciation of her good sportsmanship. He let out a triumphant holler, as the men turned their horses and raced away. Feeling herself blush, Leah laughed as well and quickly caught up with the family now entering their new lodgings.

Her mother, having removed her hat and gloves, was inspecting the building, which could not be compared to anything but the gardener's cabin back home. Leah could see her mamá's mind at work. She could only imagine the list of duties that soon would be imparted to each and every one. When she heard her mother speaking of chemical compounds, Leah began to understand the true magnitude of the undertaking.

"I will need a fair amount of the product, if we are to paint these walls *and* the fruit trees," Malka informed the J.C.A. agent.

"Yes, of course," Lipinsky replied, agreeing with the fine lady's assessment. Many of the colonists applied whitewash to the trees in order to prevent sun scorching.

"My father was known to paint the entire tree trunk, not just the bottom portion, as he insisted that it kept the tree from blooming prematurely."

"We are going to *paint* the trees?" Duvid asked.

"Yes, as well as the house," said Malka. "If we can purchase a bit of blue dye—perhaps a local laundress might have a decent supply—we can color the calcimine and end up with a lovely shade of pale blue."

"Lovely. It will be our very own Winter Palace," added Leah in jest. Having only known the luxury of living on a grand estate, she hadn't a clue of the benefits of whitewashing; and although she had enjoyed her lessons with watercolors, the idea of washing the grimy stone walls sounded exhausting. Noting the sarcasm in her own voice, Leah winced and waited for the certain rebuke. When none came, she decided it was in her best interest to pay attention to her mamá.

"We will cover the walls with this compound several times a year, my dears, for the coating has hygienic properties. Once we have added successive applications, layers of scale will build up on the roughhewn walls, and the flakes will fall off. Then it is simply a matter of sweeping away any remaining debris," she said, running her finger along the wainscoting. You shall see...with fresh, clean paint, colorful curtains, and cheerful wildflowers on the table, we will feel quite at home."

"It will be like visiting the country house!" shouted Duvid with delight.

"It will be better than visiting our *dacha*—we will be home." replied Yosef.

Although the décor would certainly be addressed, the fact of the matter was with only four bedrooms, it would be impossible to house the entire family under one roof. Adolfo Lipinsky had informed them the lot and the dwelling were already larger than most. The previous family, who were Volga Germans, had seen to that. With increased prosperity, they added on to the original two-room cabin, and had the granary enlarged, as well. But as many of their compatriots had settled in Colonia General Alvear, they abandoned their homestead and chose to settle amongst their friends.

"Homesick, they were," said Lipinsky. "The Bornemanns were dedicated hard-working people. They arrived much like this young man here," he said pointed at Yosef, "full of heart and idealistic sentiments, but they lacked a key component. Making this *chacra* a success requires more than an understanding of farming or husbandry—for which they had none, by the way. It takes a desire to work as a team—to see the entire colony succeed and prosper. The Bornemanns kept to themselves. They made money, but did not make friends. They neither asked for help, nor did they give it. They only pined for their own kind, and so they left. The J.C.A. was more than happy to purchase the property, for it only could improve the overall prosperity of the colony."

Noting that his audience was overwhelmed and quite intimated by what they had undertaken, the kind man added words of encouragement.

"You might be inexperienced with this lifestyle but, know this: you are not alone! We have all come out of the mire of self-doubt and recrimination, uplifted by our fellow colonists. *Ask for help*. We will gladly provide it. Oh—yes, I was telling you about the previous owners. No love for the land in that lot, to be sure! They were experienced carpenters and woodworkers. You will notice some details in this pioneer home that your neighbors are lacking...the second floor, additional bedrooms, decorative wood carvings and some such. When you say your prayers tonight, you may thank the good Lord *and* the Bornemann family."

Leah followed her mother and sisters as they toured the rest of the home. Malka had released the breath she had unwittingly been holding. Grateful to note they did not have dirt floors, she said her first prayer of thanks. The walls were wainscoted—that was most definitely in thanks to the Bornemanns' artisanship. The upper portion of the walls revealed bare stone, hence the need for the whitewash compound. Off to the right, in what must have been the original main room, stood a large enveloping chimney. The layer of dust and cobwebs would be easily cleaned away, and the room would eventually make a warm and inviting parlor. A modest, but well-equipped kitchen adjoined the room and a large ranch table divided the space.

The women followed Malka as she opened a door to a bedroom. It was simply furnished with the bare necessities. The sturdy staircase led them to the other rooms. Although señor Lipinsky intimated that a second floor would be considered a luxury amongst their neighbors, the women, each alone in their own thoughts, couldn't help but remember the stately staircase that complimented the entry of their beloved family home.

The Bornemanns were evidently a large family, for the women note three additional rooms, each housing two sets of bunk beds, in addition to one double-sized bed. The rooms were utilitarian and unassuming. There was neither a need nor room for anything more.

"This will do very well."

"I don't see how, Mamá," replied Sara. "Where will we all sleep? Not to mention, there is no salon, no library, no dining room…"

"Sara, dear, there is a difference in between what is *desired* and what is *necessary* and; while beautiful things and pleasant accommodations are quite lovely indeed, there is something to be said for simplicity. The children can sleep in these two rooms—the baby will stay with Bluma, of course—and the women can sleep in the other two. The men will sleep in the granary…"

"What? Impossible!"

"Why ever not?" Malka replied with a smile. "I recall many a time where I stole an afternoon nap on mounds of fresh hay, while my father tended the barnyard animals. The men will manage very well in the granary. Perhaps sharing the close quarters will inspire a bit more camaraderie amongst my boys. They have allowed their differences of opinion to mar their fraternal relationships."

"I believe it will be quite beneficial to all," said Leah with a gleam in her eye.

"Yes?" questioned Rivka. "What possible benefit could there be?"

"I am supposing that the discomfort, *and* the fact that they will be sleeping away from their wives, will be excellent incentive."

"Leah! That is not an appropriate observation for a young lady," Sara exclaimed.

"But it is not far from the truth, is it? The faster they build onto this house, or even move on to their own lot of land, the happier we will all be!" Leah said with a burst of laughter.

"Well!"

"Bickering is of no use at a time such as this," Malka decreed. "It will be nightfall soon enough and, I for one, wish to have a comforting bowl of soup and a clean bed to lay my weary body upon. I suggest we roll up our sleeves and get to work."

Having come to an understanding, the women set out to do that which had been habitually done by a houseful of servants—dusting, sweeping, cleaning out the fireplace and changing bed linens. Other than having Gitel to assist them, they were on their own. Malka went straight away to the kitchen, and organized a staff made up of eager grandchildren outfitted with brooms and dustpans.

She realized immediately that maintaining a *kosher* kitchen would prove to be exceedingly difficult, given their current circumstance. How would she manage to transplant traditional Judaic dietary laws to the Argentine pampas? If there wasn't a *shochet* to slaughter the meat under the strict observance of their ritual guidelines, they would have to resort to purchasing meat from another town, and risk it spoiling before it was delivered.

Malka was grateful for the burlap sacks which had been presented them at the train station. They were chock full of onions and root vegetables, along with many other useful staples; but the kitchen was most certainly not kosher, and the process of making it ritually clean was almost beyond the realm of possibility.

Malka called for Duvid asking him to bring buckets of water from the well, and when Leah joined in, they made quick work of the kitchen detail. Gitel began unpacking various utensils, pots and pans. She enlisted the children to assist as they organized and divided the kitchen into two separate areas, one side for meat and the other for dairy. Surveying what had been accomplished, Malka allowed herself a sigh of absolution. It was not her kitchen in Odessa, but it would simply have to do.

"Gather around, *kinderlach*. We are going to make a hearty vegetable soup," she said to the children. "With the fresh bread and cheese our generous neighbors provided, it will be a meal fit for a king!"

As she began with the unfamiliar task of helping prepare their meal, Leah felt a sense of pride and wonderment. Of course, she had known of her mother's humble existence as a child, but the tales had seemed like ancient history—places and names and events that happened to other people so very long ago. And yet, Leah thought, here they were in very similar circumstances. She closed her eyes for a moment and thought back. How many times had her mother mentioned meager meals of borsht and herring? How many times had she retold the stories of eating potatoes three times a day yet, recalling those meals with nostalgia and longing? Leah tried to imagine being raised on boiled potatoes and a bit of fried onion. Her mother had survived it—Gitel too.

"What are thinking of, my dear?" Malka questioned, as she witnessed Leah standing with eyes closed and an unpeeled carrot in her hand.

"However will we manage, Mamá?"

"One must be prepared to face Life's challenges as they present themselves, my sweet one. Life has taught me many lessons, Baruch Hashem. I know how to economize and I know how to feed my family. We *will* manage."

Outside, the men surrounded Adolfo Lipinsky as he went down a detailed list. Each colonist in the territory received an assortment of fowl, a cow, two pair of ox, along with a sulky, a wagon and wooden plow. The J.C.A. agent was aware that these men were used to a different breed of horse, and needless to say, they had no skills whatsoever with the oxen used to do the heavy work on the land. He emphasized the importance of learning to deal with these *bueyes* and repeatedly instructed to use caution when working with the horses, some of which could still be considered rather wild and unaccustomed to the tasks required of them.

"Your neighbors, the *criollos,* will be glad to help."

"This word—*criollo*—I am not familiar with the term," Aaron stated.

"Some people equate the term *criollo* with a native, but that would be a mistake. An indigenous native is one thing. A criollo is native to Argentina, but he has European ancestry." Lipinsky paused and gave the newcomers a quick, once-over. "I will send some men over tomorrow morning. You'll want to take on help, as soon as possible. There is still some fall harvesting to be done, and with their help, you'll be able to start planting your winter small grains."

"Meaning *what* exactly?" Moishe asked.

"That would be your winter barley and cereal rye, but again, I urge to hire a few local fellows. It is surely an extra expense. In the end, however, they will be your salvation."

The men listened in a sort of mixed state of awe and fear, as Lipinsky spoke of completing the soybean harvest by June, followed by sowing corn and sunflower seeds by late September.

"Sunflower seeds?"

"Yes, we grow them here and in the northern part of Santa Fe. The first colonists pined for their flowering golden fields left behind in the old county— it seems they couldn't do without their favorite treat. A sort of craze caught on, and now, it is a sought after commodity."

"Well, Duvid will be happy, at any rate." Moishe grinned. "I've never seen anyone eat sunflower seeds with such enthusiasm as my son."

The men completed a quick tour of their parcel of land. It became quite evident that they would need to expand; neither the lot nor the house was meant to maintain a family of their size. Having put an ocean in between themselves and the Tsar, the necessities of sheltering themselves together under one roof began to diminish, and they began to consider other possibilities.

As they entered the barn, Duvid raced to his father's side, inadvertently flustering a flock of wandering hens. He couldn't contain his excitement and shouted out his grandmother's decree: the men would bed down among the fowl and livestock that night. Moishe, waving away a scattering of loose feathers, laughed at his son's impetuous entrance.

"Well, if Noah could share the ark with every manner of creature, the Abramovitz men should be able to manage quite well with this mangy crew."

Moishe let out a dramatic sneeze as a feather tickled and floated by, causing the ox to bellow low in reply.

"Papá, you have insulted our new friends," Duvid cried in jest.

"Quite the opposite, Duvid!" Moishe laughed. "The great beast is acknowledging the truth of my statement. G'nossem tsum emes! You know, if a sneeze follows any sort of declaration, it means the speaker has stated a truth."

Adolfo Lipinsky, gladdened to witness a bit of levity among his new neighbors, began shaking hands and bidding all a good night. Assuring the men of his return the following morning, Lipinsky left the men as they began cleaning out the stalls and laying fresh hay.

They'll be alright, he thought to himself. *A bit upper crust, but—God willing—they'll be alright!*

Chapter Eleven

*L*eah found herself with ample time to continue her studies of all things Argentine, while the elders attended meetings, purchased supplies, and attempted to bring order into the utter chaos that their lives had become. She understood that soon, she would be put to work, but at present, her only responsibility was to mind the children. Once she settled them down with lesson plans, she slipped a book from Duvid's collection for her own perusal and quickly became enamored with a chapter of the great ladies of Argentina's history.

One grand dame in particular caught Leah's attention, as she had been the leading *salonnière* in the early days of colonial Buenos Aires. Mariquita Sánchez de Thompson inspired Leah's imagination, much as Judith Montefiore had done, for the lady patriot had been quite well-known and admired by many.

With great attentiveness, she read that during one particular *tertúlia*, where only the most charming and most influential citizens were in attendance, the Argentine national anthem was sung for the very first time. Leah pictured herself in Mariquita's salon, draped in a Spanish lace *mantilla* and donning a *peinetone* a foot tall and wide. Standing at attention, they would have sung the inspiring words in unison, as true patriots. Swallowing a great lump in her throat, Leah quickly recognized the parallels in-between the *Shema*, the cornerstone of Jewish prayer, and her adopted country's anthem. One cried out: *Hear O Israel! The Lord is our God. The Lord is One!* The other beckoned: *Hearken mortals the sacred call! Liberty! Liberty! Liberty!*

In her day, señora Mariquita had answered a frenzied appeal. She stood bravely at the forefront and paved the way towards a new life. Leah wondered if she could match that sort of resolve. To hear the call and recognize the path that she was meant to take. And, to have the mettle to see it through.

Leah's next project was to tackle a snippet from José Hernandez's poem, *Martín Fierro*. The famous work provided all the romance, mystery, and heartbreak she desired, while creating a heroic figure of the Argentine gaucho. She read, with some astonishment, that the North American cowboy, known to many as Buffalo Bill, had long been an admirer of his South American counterpart. This delighted Leah to no end, for her dear papá had once returned from Europe with a story book of the Wild West and the renowned William Frederick Cody. She read the section with much enthusiasm thinking how pleased her father would be to see her share his interests.

Duvid's book coincided with her father's explanation of how Bill Cody rose to stardom due to his accomplishments as a cowboy, and his famed traveling circus. In one of those tours, Buffalo Bill recruited gauchos to perform alongside the American cowboys. Leah was enthralled to find, that while performing a show before none other than Queen Victoria herself, a wild horse escaped the corral and raced towards the vicinity of the royal box. Amidst the pandemonium, a gallant gaucho hurled his *boleadora* through the air, and stopped the rebellious horse before any injury could come to the Grandmother of Europe.

Leah prepared to set aside her reading material for the afternoon, but not before she came across a famous Argentine saying: *A gaucho and his horse are one; but a man on foot is only a half a gaucho.* The image of Joaquín Ibáñez, so handsome and proud, strutting down the streets of Lucienville as a mythological centaur caused her to laugh until her side ached. It took the better part of the day to get her mind back on task.

With Malka at the head, Moishe, Aaron, and Yosef had organized a cohesive and dedicated detail of men, women, and children. They had soldiered through the initial days, exhausted and overwhelmed. The Bornemanns had left behind a sturdy house; Malka was well pleased with the special detailing and the layout of the rooms. They could have been faced with much worse. Realizing she would need help in, and around the house, she hired Magdalena Fernandez, a woman recently relocated from Dominguez who was seeking room and board. Malka declared their agreement quite providential, and laughed when the woman confessed that she had not been worried about finding work.

"It is as we always say, *señora*: *Que sea lo que Dios quiera*. Why worry, when it is in the hands of the Lord."

Malka nodded and explained that she shared that philosophy. "My children are forever hearing me say the same exact thing: Be it Hashem's will—what will be, will be."

The men, acknowledging they were quite useless in the fields, had immediately hired several locals to teach them their new trade. Ignacio Cervantes and Faustino Padilla, or, as they were known by the friends and neighbors, *Nacho* and *Tino,* were a welcomed addition on the farm. Tino noted the family's cramped accommodations, and echoed the suggestion once offered by the J.C.A. agent. By purchasing a discarded wagon from a retired train, they could outfit the structure as sleeping quarters for the men. Tino wasn't sure if his new employers would be insulted by the suggestion, knowing that the townsfolk had nicknamed the family 'the aristocrats', but he stayed his ground, and reiterated that Basavilbaso's station was sure to have one or two wagons in storage.

The brothers thought it a sound idea. It would serve them well for the time being, and it was certainly better than sleeping alongside the animals. Moishe chuckled, as he shook hands with his hired help. The *aristocrats* would acclimate to their new surroundings and be grateful.

After the first several weeks of mayhem, Leah found herself being shuffled from one task to another. With a legion of adults, unskilled and amateurish, it had been decided to create a roster of duties. Everyone had to try their hand at any given task at least once. Leah's hands were soon rough and raw, and it seemed no amount of her mother's lavender and honey ointment could alleviate the redness or pain.

In the evenings, after completing her chores as scullery maid, Leah would help put the children to bed before stumbling, aching and sore, into her own awaited oblivion. Although her sisters were equally ill prepared for the various responsibilities suddenly thrust upon the family, it did not dispel their need to find fault with Leah's execution. When, one fine morning, she accidently burned Magdalena's breakfast pastries, she was booted out of the kitchen.

"What have you done?" Sara reprimanded. "You were supposed to keep your eye on the oven."

"I'm sorry. I thought they needed another minute and I became distracted…"

"You're just like a cat: always under foot and in the way. If you cannot be of use in the kitchen, why don't you find another way to be of assistance—preferably doing something where you won't burn down the house?"

Rivka tried to soften the blow, quietly whispering that Sara was just using her as a scapegoat. They were all struggling with their new responsibilities and the harsh conditions to which they were not accustomed.

"Besides," Rivka said with a grin, "you know that Sara has always been a bit jealous of Father's favorite."

"Do you mean me?"

"Of course, silly. Little Leah, with her dimpled chin and golden curls could do no wrong in Papá's eyes. Now that we find ourselves in the midst of this new adventure, as Mamá refers to it, Sara has found a way to outshine you. She is becoming quite the homemaker. Who knew she was such a *balabusta!*" Rivka laughed. "Go on. Grab your things and go for a walk. It will do you good."

Finding herself quite at liberty to explore the neighborhood, *sans* tormenting brothers or censuring sisters, Leah took advantage of the temporary reprieve and decided it was high time to venture out and explore her new community. Scurrying out of the kitchen before anyone could take notice and assign another menial task, Leah ran to the room she shared with her sisters, and quickly closed the door.

Washing with the now-tepid water left behind in the basin, she wiped her face clean and fixed her hair. She stepped out of the simple work dress, tossed it aside, and contemplated her wardrobe before finally deciding on a forest green walking skirt, a silk paisley cummerbund, and a crisp white cotton blouse with just a whisper of lace about the collar. Not wishing to appear condescending to her new neighbors, she hoped the simplicity of her attire would be acceptable. Gathering up a wicker basket and a wrap, Leah walked off the family property and turned down the dusty road.

With some curiosity, Leah spotted one or two sophisticated structures similar to what the

Bornemann family had created, but in keeping with the rural surroundings, the vast majority of the landscape was dotted with modest dwellings—simple, wooden shacks with patches of hay covering dull, tin roofs.

As her skirt rustled among the gold and crimson leaves, she was, again, bemused to note autumn was in full swing. Would she ever grow accustom to the seasonal cycles of the southern hemisphere? Back home, the month of May brought bright poppies, periwinkles, and blossoming chestnut trees. For a moment, Leah allowed the melancholy to hold sway as she recalled Odessa in the spring; but just as she brushed away a rogue tear, Leah heard a friendly *hola*! She turned to find neighbors waving a distant greeting from their fields. Although they had yet to be introduced, Leah found comfort in their salutations. At least she could look forward to meeting new people and hearing their tales. Where did they come from? Why did they leave their home?

She continually wrestled with her own family's decisions. She had felt impotent against their unwavering authority, but fighting against her natural instinct to rebel, Leah sought to find solace in her brothers' speaking points. They had provided good reasons to immigrate. She had nothing to refute their motives, other than emotional attachments and the heartache of seeing her own plans put to the wayside. Perhaps in this new country, with their seasons turned backwards and upside down, Leah thought, she would be able to make something of herself.

Coming upon the town, she noted the simple layout of the streets, and the surrounding homes and business. Leah was drawn to the few women she spied, and immediately felt out of place. The *criollas,* with their braided hair and colorful ribbons, wore full ruffled skirts and peasant blouses. Their shoes were the simplest moccasins made of cloth and jute. Serviceable yet appealing, Leah paid close attention to their utilitarian attire. It allowed the women freedom of movement, yet addressed the feminine need for charm. How different from her own distinctive form of dress.

Until recent events caused an upheaval of tradition and custom, she had been restricted and constrained with bustles and corsets. Unable to lift her arms in any sort of functional manner, and impeded by flowing skirts and trains, Leah realized that her garments imparted the illusion of a lady of leisure. Her look was meant to exude luxury and refinement— a lady of quality had servants to lift, bend, carry and toil. She laughed at the thought, for now, *she* was the one to carry and toil. And, she had the hands to prove it. But while Leah found humor in her silent revelry, a shot of electric energy raced through her veins, as images began formulating in her mind's eye. Could it be possible to incorporate fashion with function, and would anyone here—*in the middle of nowhere*—be interested?

She continued strolling about town, nodding a silent greeting to anyone who looked her way. She recognized the Jewish women who were busily scurrying about the streets, but, they too, were dressed simply with no lace or silk on their persons. A woman of the twentieth century could be—*should be*— a contributing member of society; and yet, she should be elegant and fashion forward. Leah made a mental note, tucking away these new concepts, along with her other aspirations for future implementation.

Wagons rolling down the lane created murky clouds of dust. Merchants busied themselves carting boxes in and out of their stores, and polishing windows that Leah assumed would never retain their sparkle. From a café she spotted on the street's corner, came the sounds of a guitar and an enthusiastic singer. She couldn't make out the words, but the melody was lively and the accompanying clapping indicated that the audience appreciated the tune. So entranced was she with the cacophony of sights and sounds, she didn't notice as a wagon approached from behind. Coming down the road at a high speed, the horses kicked up the muck from the street, and Leah found herself splattered with mud and grime.

It was impossible to believe that no one witnessed her humiliation. Already, Leah could hear children laughing, and someone shouted from a not-too-far-away window, "Welcome to Lucienville, *señorita*. You have been baptized *al estilo criollo!*"

Leah removed a crisp white handkerchief from her reticule. She patted her face, and then attempted to wipe the dirt from her skirt. It wasn't that bad, she thought. She held her head high, and smiled awkwardly at the onlookers. After all, she wasn't to blame. It could have happened to anyone. Not wanting to look like she was running away in humiliation, she attempted to moderate her speed and continued to stroll down the block until she found that the street suddenly came to an end. Leah looked about and attempted to get her bearings. She daren't get lost. She would never hear the end of it! Believing she was turning in the right direction, she began walking down a country lane, and hoped to return home before any further embarrassment came upon her.

She walked for what seemed an eternity, but before too long, Leah had to admit that she *was* lost. Each field seemed much like the other, and she realized then, she would have to deviate from the main road. Surely, she would soon cross paths with a colonist or farmer. With this new plan in mind, she followed a side pathway lined with tall chinaberry trees. Surprised not to find herself in the midst of wheat or corn fields, Leah appreciated the lush green pastures, and was delighted to spy a large barn looming in the not too distant horizon. A chestnut mare, with an ambling gait, crossed from under a copse of trees to greet Leah as she approached the wood posts, fencing in the periphery.

"I'm sorry, pet," Leah said, as she scratched the mare's nose. "I do not have any treats for you."

The horse followed her as Leah continued down the lane with the hopes of running into a helpful *campesino*, but upon witnessing a very odd and unexpected sight, Leah came to a sudden halt. A man was on the ground laying aside of a great beast of a stallion. She observed the gaucho's gentle movements, and attempted to close the distance which separated her from the pair. Too late, she realized that her efforts for discretion had failed. The man had heard her approach.

"Well, good afternoon," said Joaquín Ibáñez, nonplussed as his eyes met with the young lady.

No! Not El Moro!

"Good afternoon, *señor* Ibáñez," she replied, blushing furiously. Leah stood frozen, unable to think of a single clever thing to say.

"Princesa, what are you doing all the way out here?" He paused and looked her up and down. "And *what* has happened to you?"

She suddenly remembered that she had been showered with mud and muck. Having walked, for a mile or two, in the afternoon's sun had made matters worse. Her lovely green walking skirt was all but ruined. Mud had caked into the folds and along the delicate trim. Leah's golden curls, which had been properly pinned, were now spilling out from under her hat, caressing a dirty face smudged by her handkerchief.

"I was inducted into society—*criollo* style," Leah replied, and explained the turn of events that brought her to the pasture. Mortified that she was standing before Joaquín Ibáñez in such a disheveled state, she hoped that he would behave as the noble gaucho in her storybooks, and come to her aid.

Joaquín burst into laughter, inadvertently frightening his steed. He held fast to the reins and allowed the animal to bring them both up onto their feet. Leah tried not to notice his broad shoulders, or the muscles rippling underneath his work shirt. Untying a swath of red cloth wrapped around his neck, Joaquín wiped his face before coming to stand toe to toe with her—*much* to her chagrin.

"You are a mess!" he declared. "What has happened to the regal young lady of the train station? Have you come all this way to issue another command, princesa?"

"I have apologized for my rude behavior at the station, señor Ibáñez. It is ungentlemanly of you to reproach me on the matter yet again," she stated with as much dignity as she could muster.

"I do not recall an apology...Ah yes. I do seem to remember a smile and a condescending bow of your pretty little head, but that does not an apology make! You wish to instruct *me* on proper etiquette? Allow me to point out that *you* have interrupted my work. *You* have paid a call without an introduction, without an invitation, *and* without a chaperone."

"As I clearly stated, only moments ago, I was on an outing and lost my way. I had no intention of paying a call; therefore, I did not breach any manner of protocol."

"Your visit to the Vasquez *estancia* might have been unintentional—I will allow that—but your lording about orders at the train station was quite deliberate. I stand by my accusation that you, *not I*, require further lessons on decorum."

Ill prepared to answer such a claim, Leah fumbled to find a way to excuse herself.

"Please understand, señor Ibáñez, we had been traveling for so very long. I was overwrought. My siblings are forever complaining that I do not take on enough responsibility, so when an opportunity arose for me to do something useful, I acted upon it. I believed that you and your friends were laborers sent to assist us, and so, I asked for your help. I was only trying to be of service to my brothers who were occupied with other matters."

"You didn't ask. You *demanded*."

Leah nodded in agreement. "Yes. You are right, but I apologized once before, and I am apologizing yet again and—and now, I am exhausted from my walk and I am...muddy!"

"I am very sorry to see your fine apparel ruined on your first excursion into town, princesa."

"Why must you call me that? I am *not* a princess!" she said, stomping her foot. "I'm not a spoiled Romanov!"

"I do not mean to be impertinent, but a young lady, such as yourself—so elegant..."

Furious that he continued to tease, Leah interrupted with a question of her own.

"Never mind that. I saw you—you were whispering. *To your horse*! Whatever were you doing?"

"We are just getting to know each other better. It is a technique I have learned throughout the years when making new acquaintances. Shall I demonstrate?"

Leah could only stare at him. Was he speaking of the horse, or was he insinuating that he meant to whisper in *her* ear? Surprised at her reaction, Leah blushed wondering what it would feel like to have such a man leaning over her cheek...

"Every horse has his own temperament, just like human beings." Joaquín continued as if he hadn't noticed her agitation. "The key is to learn how to understand the animal—to understand his body language." He paused and allowed his eyes to gaze at the lovely young woman before him. Clearing his throat, he continued. "I have to establish a basis of trust and confidence, while letting him know who is the boss. Just like with people," he added with a grin.

Leah harrumphed in an unladylike fashion. "It seems most uncommon."

"The old ways of training simply do not work. Yelling at the animal or staring him down—even using spurs—all of these things only cause fear which leads to unacceptable behavior. Señor Vasquez, the owner of this ranch, has hired me to correct these problems. He recently acquired this fellow here," Joaquín said, pointing to his mount, "in addition to a few others. The horses had been mistreated, and so, they try to assert their dominance by bolting, kicking, and biting."

"And how do you correct that? Don't tell me by whispering sweet nothings into his ear."

"There are different ways to work with a horse," Joaquín chuckled, "but first, I try respecting the animal—something to which he is not accustomed."

"Respect, you say? You might want to try *that* with human beings, as well." Swiping yet again at her ruined skirt, she couldn't help but ask him to explain further.

"There isn't one specific thing," he replied, surprised by her interest. "Horses are curious and affectionate, but people really should learn to wait and judge the animal's disposition. Once he understands that I mean him no harm, I look at him, eye to eye. I speak softly, or offer him something to eat from my hand. Sometimes, it takes a gentle massage across an aching back or strained leg, but eventually, we can break a violent habit or a rebellious pattern."

"It all sounds a bit dangerous. What if he rejects you?" she asked, with growing admiration. "What if you try to mount him and you are thrown?"

"These things occur from time to time, but there is a give and take to this line of work. The horse and I...we come to understand each other. To tell the truth, my job is not only to train or dominate the horses. My job is to train *the people* who surround them."

Joaquín handed her a small apple, and nodded towards the horse that had followed Leah down the path. She accepted his offer, and turned to the chestnut who happily received the treat with gentle nibbles. Leah patted the mare's nose once more, and whispered gentle encouragements to her new friend while Joaquín looked on. As she turned, he held her gaze with such intensity that Leah found herself to be quite undone.

"I think it best that I take my leave now, señor Ibáñez. Would you be so kind as to help me find my way home?"

Removing his hat, El Moro bowed low.

"As you wish, princesa," he said softly. "I am at your command."

Chapter Twelve

Celebrating the Sabbath had become that much sweeter for the Abramovitz family. It hadn't taken long to note that, after enduring back-breaking toil throughout the week, *Shabbes* was not to be ignored. Ritual clothing might have been put aside, and dietary rules might have been adjusted, but Saturday indeed, remained a day of rest. The *Sabbath Queen* was welcomed, as the sun finally set upon the golden fields. Homes were aglow with the light of candles, as fathers blessed their children and husbands extoled the virtues of their wives. On Saturday afternoons, neighbors would pay social calls, and the *aristocrats* soon found themselves welcomed into the fold.

When the prayers of *Havdalah* were recited, the colonists marked the end of their sanctified rest with dancing and songs of old. No one was happier than Leah when the elders clapped along. Their approval resounded, as the folk songs were celebrated with joy and abandon. She was also pleased to see that the locals were welcomed at these gatherings; although she couldn't help but wonder, what did the criollos think of her people with their peculiar language and their melancholic music written in minor keys? Her answer came in a gestured fashion. Rather than being disconcerted by their differences, the criollos picked up the guitar and *bandoneón,* and joined in the merry-making.

Joaquín Ibáñez had long ago made it a habit to join in the Saturday evening celebrations, but now with the addition of the Abramovitz family, he suddenly felt the need to show some restraint. The *aristocrats'* adaptation to the land and its traditions was yet new and untried; and although he would rather not miss an opportunity to visit *la princesa*, he wished to respect their customs. But, a*hijuna*, the woman was dynamic and full of vigor!

He found Leah delightfully alluring and feminine, and was rather astonished when she began paying calls to the Vasquez ranch. He taunted her for her boldness. Leah would explain that she was just passing by and she was always properly accompanied, of course, by her companion, Gitel.

When he felt that sufficient time had lapsed, and his presence wouldn't call any due attention to the señorita, Joaquín allowed himself an evening to partake in the rusos' festivities. Leah sought him out from among the others and invited him to join her on an evening stroll. Languid from the meal, but refreshed by the soft breeze, Leah continued to petition the mysterious gaucho with her unending questions.

"How is it that I can understand your speech," she asked, "but I have such difficulty making out what the others say?"

"What *others*?" Joaquín probed, attempting to mask his jealousy. "With whom have you been speaking?"

"The locals—who else?"

Joaquín sighed with the understanding that no other man had tried to win *his* princesa. She was simply inquiring, trying to comprehend the culture... something the young lady did with great determination.

"You are picking up on a particular lilt to their speech," he explained. "They speak with a certain cadence, and frequently contract their words. For instance, someone might say *p' usted* instead of *para usted*. You'll get used to it, but I suggest you do not attempt to emulate them. Your mamá would not appreciate these new skills." He laughed, tossing his cigarette and grinding into the ground.

"But you do not speak as they do. In fact, your vocabulary and modulation are—*aristocratic*." Leah chose the adjective quite intentionally.

"My friends and neighbors speak a mixture of *Tehuelche*, Spanish, or Basque, along with other native languages. President Sarmiento, while an early proponent for education—even for women—was unfortunately misguided with regards to the...let us say, the rural population. He considered Argentina's indigenous people culturally backward. They were perceived to be uneducable, and were excluded from public schooling."

"How do you fit into this rather dreadful picture?"

"It is complicated, princesa." Seeing that she would not relent, he sighed before continuing. "My father's ancestors came to Argentina, long ago when they were expelled from Spain. The Moors were not considered Spaniards, or at least, they were looked upon as impure. My mother's people, on the other hand, were well-to-do Castilians and were not pleased when my grandparents immigrated to Argentina. When my mother informed her family that she had fallen in love with a descendant of the dreaded Moors, they all but disinherited her. They begged her to return to Castile, where presumably she could make an appropriate match, but she declined. I was not given a choice."

"How so?"

"Upon my twenty-first birthday, I was shipped off to Spain, having been informed that my great grandmother had set aside a sum of money for my education. I spent some time with my relatives, studying at university and traveling throughout the country. I was presented to nobles and offered money, titles, and even their daughters, if I would only remain. My heart was heavy, and I yearned for home. *La tierra*—the land called out to me, and so I returned to Argentina."

"I understand. You missed your family and friends...your horses too, no doubt."

"I missed my *freedom*."

She nodded an acknowledgment. "But when you returned, why did you not continue with your studies? With your background, there's no telling what you could achieve."

"I was not born to be enclosed within the walls of a library or schoolroom," Joaquín protested. "I need to be out in the open. Besides," he said with a chuckle, "I learn everything I need to know from my horses."

Leah laughed as well, but there was something about Joaquín's smile that didn't quite reach his eyes. He had meant to enliven the conversation and to bring humor into his speech; nevertheless, she perceived that the initial sorrow and passion he expressed was still very much present.

They returned to join the others, as the families began gathering their children and their belongings. The evening's pleasure had come to a close. The colonists had celebrated the peace and sanctity of the Sabbath and had acknowledged the separation of the holy from the mundane. Tomorrow, the week began again in full measure, and that meant rising before the crack of dawn.

Leah completed her morning chores with unusual alacrity. She had asked Aaron for a bit of spending money with the intention of purchasing supplies for her new project. The women had found it necessary to make some alterations to the lavish fashions they had in their possession. Even the simplest of skirts and blouses were vastly inappropriate for their daily work. The fine materials, along with the design and fabrication, hindered their movement and deterred any zealous plan of action. Leah was confident that here, at the very least, she could prove useful as she happily marched herself into town.

As she entered an unpretentious shop, Leah tried not to recall the fine establishments on the streets of Odessa. The very memory caused a knot to form in her chest, but she refused to give in to tears. With quiet determination, she approached the woman standing behind a glass-topped display case.

"Good day," Leah said with a smile she hoped the shopkeeper found amiable. "I am in need of fabric, patterns, and notions. I wish to dress more in keeping with the locals. I trust that I have come to right place."

The woman nodded briskly, and with a great smile of her own, welcomed the young lady. "Yes, of course—you most certainly have come to the right place! There is no finer establishment in any of the neighboring colonies. You have come to Basavilbaso under the auspices of the J.C.A.?"

Leah bowed her head in acknowledgement. "Yes, my family and I are living on the old Bornemann lot. We are new to the colony. and I readily admit, I am fascinated by the charm of the criollas."

The shopkeeper proceeded to lay out bolts of fabric, and as she opened drawers filled with colorful ribbons and embroidered trimmings, she spoke in a friendly, but pragmatic tone.

"Firstly, señorita, allow me to clarify your choice of words. We locals, charming as we may be, are as diverse as any other woman of the world and dress according to status, our daily rituals, *and* our whims, I dare say. The woman of Basavilbaso, as you will soon come to understand, cannot be categorized so easily. We carry fashion plates for the woman who works in the fields, as well as the woman who receives guests on her fine *estancia*."

"Yes, yes—of course. I have a tendency to be quick to judge. I do apologize," Leah said, having the decency to blush upon realizing her blunder. "I do feel quite the fish out of water. We are far from home and my wardrobe is filled with garments wholly unsuitable for our new way of life."

"Never fear, señorita. It will be my pleasure to help you acclimate to your new surroundings. I only wish I could provide you with a few ready-made samples. You see, up until recently, we had a talented seamstress on hand, but she married and moved to Concordia."

Leah set down the patterned chambray she had been rubbing in-between her fingers and gazed at the shopkeeper. Ambition sparkled in her eyes. "Are you thinking of replacing her?"

"As a matter of fact, I had high hopes that Esmeralda would return to make her home here. With the town growing so very quickly, I was planning on augmenting my inventory by offering a complete line of ready-wear, just as they do in the capital. We receive a few fashion plates, every now and then, when they deliver the publications from Buenos Aires. Sometimes we even get those fancy periodicals all the way from Paris! But, that is neither here or there. Why did you ask about Esmeralda's position? Do you know of someone looking for work?"

Leah smiled. "Yes. Yes, I do."

While she folded and unfolded a length of blue and white striped cotton lawn, Leah spoke hurriedly, as she explained her family's background. Her nerves got the better of her, and she began intermingling Russian with Spanish and Yiddish to boot.

The shopkeeper, raising a hand, laughed and begged her to stop. "I lost a word or two, here and there, but I believe I understand that you are a qualified seamstress *and* a fashion designer, and that you are being held against your will as some sort of indentured servant."

"I suppose something *did* get lost in the translation, but that is very close to my meaning!" Leah responded in a fit of giggles. "If you allow me the opportunity, I can prove that I am more than capable."

"I wouldn't be able to pay you much."

"Oh, I am certain that whatever amount you decide upon will be quite fair. This little excursion into town has proven to be a blessing in disguise, for if I truly can come to work in your shop, I can finally find a way to be of some use to my family. Nothing would give me greater pleasure."

The woman smiled and nodded. "What would you suggest for this new bolt of cream linen?"

Leah inspected the material and immediately thought of the peasant blouses the girls wore back home. She described her vision of light colored blouses with embroidered stitching about the décolletage. She would pair them with skirts of diverse fabrics and vivid colors all trimmed layers of ruffles.

"I think a capped, or even a loose-fitting sleeve that covers the forearm, would suit splendidly," She said. "Perhaps a touch of lace or embroidery would be appropriate for when the lady is at leisure or for a special event."

"We *do* enjoy dressing up for our local dances and assemblies. We are drawn to color, and tend to favor ruffles trimmed with gold or silver thread," the shopkeeper said as she held out a bolt of crepe de chine for Leah's inspection. "Many of the local women have roots in Spain or the Iberian Peninsula. We enjoy a certain flair for the dramatic, even in the most rudimentary garment."

Leah appreciated the lesson and nodded enthusiastically. "What of the length? It would be rather scandalous to show my ankles in Odessa."

"Ah—yes, but our skirts usually extend to just above the ankle, and they tend to be full capacious designs. It makes for a pretty presentation when dancing, and it is infinitely more practical when riding or working in the fields. And of course, our footwear is of a pragmatic nature, as well. For the most part, you will see the *alpargatas* made of cotton with soles typically made of jute or hemp. The cobbler can provide you with leather button-down boots, if you prefer, but the breathable material of the glove-like shoe is more practical—certainly in the case of house work," she concluded.

The two became fast friends, so much so that the owner insisted to be called by her first name. "You may call me Paulina—or better still, Poli. There's no need to stand on formality here, and if your family has no reservations about your accepting employment, I will expect you next week at this same time."

After sharing in a midmorning snack of *maté* and *bizcochitos*, Leah purchased two pair of the unusual shoes and enough cotton and chambray to make three sets of blouses and skirts, before returning home. Now that she would be earning wages, she hoped to gain some respect in her sisters' eyes and approval for the garments she would create. Certainly, their daily routines called for such a change. They were no longer the Abramovitz sisters, leisurely drinking tea in their Odessan parlor. Life was now centered on the fertile land, not decadent tea services or lavish dinner parties. As she made her way home, Leah prayed that she would be allowed to accept Paulina's offer and

found herself repeating Magdalena's favorite phrase—
que sea lo que Dios quiera.

Awash with anticipation, she could barely contain
the sense of pride and satisfaction. To think, she, the
youngest of the Abramovitz children—and a woman at
that—would be bringing home a few extra pesos to
help the family meet their needs. Sara had been right.
Everyone had to do their part, and with this new
opportunity which had seemingly come out of the
blue, Leah felt a sense of purpose that filled her soul
with satisfaction.

Leah awoke with a start. Dawn, it seemed, had
brought an ominous interruption to their daily
routine. The animals could be heard bellowing, but it
was her brothers' curses that caused her to awaken.
Still in her dressing gown and slippers, Leah ran
outdoors to find her brothers rushing about, as Nacho
and Tino shouted instructions. She looked out at the
horizon, and blinked several times trying to
comprehend what was before her disbelieving eyes.
The sky was blue and clear, but coming towards their
home was a singular black cloud. She cried out to no
one in particular. "What is it?"

It was Duvid who shouted to her, as he ran behind
the men, "Locusts!"

Driving in from the north, the cloud seemed large
enough to encompass the length of the horizon. The
air was crisp and the leaves were still. Leah noticed
the birds had stopped chirping and then she heard it—

a whirring, *rasping*, sound. Aaron called out for the women to close the windows and to secure the doors, as the men lit raging bonfires to abate the assault. Leah and her sisters threw quilts over the vegetable garden on Magdalena's instruction, while Duvid and Ysroel ran to cover the family's well. Their drinking water had to be protected from the onslaught, but their efforts were all in vain.

The chaos that unfolded for the next several hours hit the entire community. No one was spared, as the pestilence devoured the crops, the leaves on the trees, and every blade of grass. There was no manner of defense against this powerful force of nature.

In the weeks that followed the infestation, there had been little time for anything other than salvaging and rebuilding what was left of the farm. Money, which had been so carefully set aside for their future endeavors, was required to meet their immediate needs; and as each day passed, with the grace of God—coupled with the support and camaraderie of the entire community—the family pieced together their lives once more. What could not be so easily pieced together was their collective resolve.

The family, along with their friends and neighbors, began to question the feasibility of producing a profitable harvest under such dire conditions. They were in a constant state of flux, continually surveying the price of grain, watching for signs of plague or storm. In Odessa, the Abramovitz Manufacturing Company had to deal with the Tsar and his bureaucrats. They battled against unreasonable international trading policies, taxes, jealousies and prejudice but in Entre Rios, the brothers faced another sort of brutal adversary—an adversary as old as time, and that was Mother Nature.

From dawn to dusk, the Jewish farmers and the criollos worked the fields of wheat and corn which lined the plots of land from one colony to the next. Still, it seemed, it was not enough. The demand for product, and the flow of new immigrants descending into the province, necessitated the J.C.A.'s continual expansion. The farmers plowed and sowed until their own sweat and tears watered the ever-growing fields; but even with this great effort, they could not keep up with the goals set by the founding organization.

Joining with a committee of experienced and long-suffering colonists, Moishe and Aaron took their complaint to the J. C. A. They expounded on the need to adjust the organization's business plan. Argentina was considered the old-world's breadbasket, but the J.C.A. was not taking advantage of the opportunities. The colonists proposed adopting British acumen by diversifying into various business schemes, and exporting crops back to Europe. The local administration, including Adolfo Lipinsky, recognized that the colony would not reach their aspired goals at the rate they were going—a fact which would indubitably cast doubt on the entire philanthropic endeavor.

When next they met, the administrators informed the good people that a series of negotiations with the prominent British owned, River Plate Dairy Company had concluded efficaciously. With their help and the colonists' approval, Lucienville would soon be at the epicenter of creamery production. They would begin with the manufacturing of butter, but the long term goal was to establish a series of full-fledged dairy factories.

After a brief discussion, the men held a vote. With the knowledge that they would have the support of the

River Plate Dairy, along with Abramovitz brothers who were practiced businessmen, the colonists agreed to the scheme. The matter demanded full cooperation and dedication if they were to be profitable, warned Adolfo Lipinsky. He immediately called for a volunteer to oversee the local management. The men offered Moishe's name.

Looking to his side, Moishe glanced sheepishly at Aaron before standing up in front of his fellow *Entrerrianos.* "Gentlemen, I readily admit that I know nothing of the production of dairy products—I am just learning the difference between the front end and the back end of our cows."

The men roared with laughter at Moishe's self-deprecation, knowing his humor was a nod to the moniker they affably bestowed up the famous Odessan fabricants.

"I would be honored," Moishe continued, "to take part of a management team. But, I could not serve you well on my own and we *need* this to succeed for the good of all the community. Come now—who among you will join me as a team leader? How about you, Roitberg? I see you in the back, Kupersmit!"

Within minutes, the men had organized themselves. Roitberg did indeed accept to work with Moishe, and suggested that they write out a plan with equitable work schedules for each man. Kupersmit, not wanting to be outdone, advised that they would need to locate and purchase large amounts of milking cows.

"Make sure that they are not skinny, dried up beasts like the J.C.A. provides us!" shouted one of the men.

After some preliminary figures and logistics were discussed, the men set off to their respective homes, eager to share the news with their families. With much to do, and even more to learn, everyone would be expected to help, as their very lives depended on the success of the colony's newest enterprise. But the Abramovitz brothers had become decidedly divided and entrenched in their own visions for the future. Avram, Yaacov, and Naftali declared that they didn't care much for working the land, and with a new dairy production in the works, they felt it was time to act. The three men, scholarly in the secular world as well as the religious, were ready to set out on their own. They had written to varies colonies across the great expanse, each seeking to serve Hashem.

Avram had found work nearby in Pedernal. Surprisingly, Bluma and his son had acclimated well to their new lifestyle, and he didn't wish to move too far away from what had become a happy home. A short train ride would allow them to visit frequently, while affording him the opportunity of directing his own school.

Naftali had accepted a position in the province of La Pampa where he would live in the colony of Narcisse Leven. The director warned that the work of the gauchos, called out to the adolescents far more than the ancient scrolls and scholarly commentary. Naftali would have his work cut out for him, but he was eager to have a go at it. He would find a way to merge both cultures—there was time for everything under the heavens.

Yaacov would head northwest to the province of Salta where, surrounded by eighteenth century cathedrals and Inca ruins, he would teach *Torah* and *Tanakh* in the small Jewish community. The brothers were resolute in their decisions to leave home, and it seemed, to Malka at the very least, that their plans were indeed heaven sent.

Having settled the matter for the scholars in the family, Aaron, Ysroel, Efraim, Benjamin and even young Duvid, reaffirmed that they too had found their calling. Upon setting foot in Entre Rios, they had dedicated themselves body and soul to the land and its bounty—much like the original colonists. The brothers never tired of hearing tales from the old timers, many of whom had their own offspring abandon farm life and migrate to Buenos Aires in search of new challenges and opportunities.

"What else could they ask for?" cried a sage settler. "They had everything they needed right here. Perhaps this is not the Garden of Eden, but we have everything to sustain ourselves and be happy with our lot!"

The founding pioneers dubbed their antsy offspring *luft menshen* for, in their eyes, their children lived with their heads in the clouds. The four Abramovitz brothers, having had their fill of big cities and fast-paced lifestyles, couldn't have agreed more. They had planted their feet firmly in *Entrerriano* soil.

Chapter Thirteen

"*Esta noche hay peña!*" Someone shouted as he galloped down the lane, his broadcast filtering through the kitchen window. *Tonight there will be...* Leah, unable to translate the last word of the man's declaration, turned to Magdalena as she kneaded the dough for a batch of *empanadas*. The flakey pastry filled with meat had become a new favorite on the Abramovitz farm. In truth, it was easy enough to incorporate the Argentine staple, as it reminded the family of the *pirozhki* from home.

"A *peña* is a night of singing and dancing," explained Magdalena. "It is a night of *música folklórica*, where the guitar and *bombo* drum reach deep into our very souls, and the food and wine fill our bellies!"

"I wonder if Mamá will allow us to attend," Leah said, as she stirred the seasoned meat in the cast iron skillet. "Does the entire community participate? That is to say, is it only for the criollos?"

Magdalena shook her head and chuckled. "No, *señorita* Leah, everyone is welcome when there is a *peña*. As you have witnessed with your own eyes, there is very little that separates your people from the locals," she said, wiping the flour from her hands on her multicolored apron. "We have a saying here, '*El que nació pa' chicharra tiene que morir cantando.*' Do you understand its meaning? The *chicharra* is an insect that makes a sort of music by rubbing her hind legs together. She does this without thinking, it is a natural process. And so is it with us. We are simple people. We work hard, we love our families. We live together in this small community, sharing our joys and our sorrows with those who know us best. It is a natural thing, we do it without thinking."

Leah smiled, and gave the woman a quick hug transferring the flour from Magdalena's apron onto her own work clothes. They shared a laugh, as Leah went off in search of her mother. Surely her mamá would allow them to attend such a joyful community event. It would appear rather like a snub if they did not!

Walking towards the clothesline that had been strung across two cypress trees, Leah began formulating a case to convince her mamá. So focused on developing a strong argument, Leah did not notice that her brother, Yosef, was just leaving her mother's side. He waved to his preoccupied sister, as he walked away. Malka turned just then, smiling with a mouthful of clothespins. When she placed the final damp item on the line, Malka faced her daughter once more and raised her hand, in effect, stopping Leah before she began her diatribe.

"I know all about it, and, *yes* you may go," Malka said. "Yosef, Sofia and a few others will be attending the festivities, so mind, you will not be going off willy-nilly."

"Oh, thank you, Mamá!" Leah cried. "Magdalena gave me quite a speech and I was going to repeat it word for word, in hopes to sway your decision."

"What did Magdalena have to say?"

"Something about not going against the nature of things, and how we all live together and how it is right to share our sorrows and our joys. Thank you, Mamá!" And with that, Leah rushed back indoors and ran to her room. What to wear? *What to wear?*

As the sun began setting, the Abramovitz family heard the wagons rumbling down the dirt lane. Their neighbors and friends had already begun the short journey to the appointed open field. The ladies traveled seated on bales of hay, and the men followed alongside on horseback. Yosef, seeing it was time to head out, emulated his fellow colonists by arranging wagon and beasts.

With many hands assisting, they made quick work of the necessary preparations, and soon, with Malka waving them off, the Abramovitz contingency was on their way. Leah was anxious, and urged her brothers to hurry along. She so wanted to catch up with the others—she could hear them singing up the lane.

Yosef laughed at his sister, but urged her to sit still. Her fidgeting was causing him some difficulty controlling the team of sluggish oxen. Nonetheless, they managed to meet their neighbors as the caravan began to bottleneck at a particularly thin stretch of road. Leah stood to see how much further they might have yet to travel. The wagon, trudging down the uneven road, was already unstable, and when she shifted her weight unexpectedly, Leah lost her footing on the slippery hay.

"Sit down!" a man bellowed from behind.

Leah turned abruptly to see who was shouting and nearly fell off the wagon. In an instant, she felt a strong arm holding her upright. El Moro! Where had he come from? How did he know she would need his assistance? Heavens! How brave he was! How silly she felt.

"Are you alright?"

She nodded, feeling her face furiously burn in the evening's light.

"Perhaps I should ride alongside you. I see your brother struggles yet with the oxen. It wouldn't do to lose any precious cargo before arriving to the *peña*," he said with a devilish wink.

Yosef now managed to control his team, and turned to see the gaucho accompanying the wagon. If he had any reservations seeing El Moro with his sister, Yosef kept them to himself; however, he couldn't help but note his wife's stern expression. Sofia was none too pleased.

Finally arriving to the plot of land where the festivities would unfold and continue through the dawn, the family joined the others already arranging blankets and chairs around an improvised wooden planked stage. Men tending the *asado* were sectioned off to one side, while several women were seen laying out the accompaniments on multicolored table linens.

As Yosef situated his wife and family, Leah asked for permission to investigate the complex and strange proceedings. "Might I go, Yosef? I promise not to stray."

"Perhaps your brother will allow me to escort you, señorita Leah," Joaquín offered.

Yosef nodded his assent, and instantly let out a yelp when his wife nudged his ribs with her pointy elbow. Leah, already on El Moro's arm, failed to witness the display of marital castigation.

"I am thankful," Leah timidly began, "for your assistance earlier. Clearly, I wasn't thinking. I would have never done such a thing back home in the *troika*. Moishe would have had my hide."

"And I am thankful that I was there to prevent any injury. You must always be alert and aware of your surroundings, *princesa*. You might have been crushed had you fallen."

Leah nodded, but was so taken in by the delightful aromas, she nearly wandered off on her own.

"I see you are already in love with the *asado*."

"In love?" she giggled. "That is rather a strange comment to make about a slice of beef."

"No, not really. For us the *asado* is a matter of the heart. It is prepared with passion and tradition, and it is offered in this manner—with love."

Leah gasped as they turned and were awarded an unencumbered view of the gauchos preparing their meal. She had not been prepared to see dozens of carcasses held vertically over an open flame.

"This style of grilling is called *a la cruz,* for the obvious reason of the whole carcass being cooked upright on an iron cross," Joaquín explained. "The men tend the meat for hours. It will be quite tender and flavorful, although they only use salt and some herbs—nothing fancy—certainly nothing like French cuisine, or anything you were used to in Odessa."

They continued to walk along the roped area where a multitude of gridirons—*parrillas*—were filled with various cuts of meats. Leah, recognizing Adolfo Lipinsky among the other men, shouted out a greeting. He was more than happy to explain what he was doing in the midst of the experienced *campesinos*.

"*Ay caray!*" He said with a great belly laugh. "I took to the asado like a Russian takes to vodka. Now, look here," he said, removing his white scarf from around his neck and waving it down the line of *parrillas*. "You don't want to eat any of this, young lady. The *chorizos, morcilla, chinchulín*—these are not kosher meats."

"Do not worry yourself, señor. I will keep to the cuts Mamá has already approved," Leah said, thinking all the while of the many concessions the family already had made. The Argentines ate all sorts of meats, pork, goat, lamb, and of course beef—and nothing went to waste. This didn't necessarily fit the dietary laws of the *Ashkenazim*.

"You know, many of us *yiden* have stretched the rules a bit. Some of us struggle to keep kosher at home, others keep kosher for the holidays and some of us—well, some of us apparently are criollo at heart. The good Lord will know how to forgive us when we meet Him someday. Besides, if He didn't want us to eat this," he said, spreading his arm across the wide expanse of the grills, "He wouldn't have led us to the land of the gauchos!"

Leah laughed as she turned to look upon the sea of men dressed in their gaucho's *pilcha*, and laughed again realizing how the vernacular terms had become interwoven in her thoughts. Working for Poli had been a God-send, as it had pushed her out into the new environment. Small as the colony was, it still was a world onto itself and Leah had come to know the townspeople, as well as, those who lived far out in the country.

She learned to recognize the various styles of *ponchos* that the men wore to keep warm, and could even determine from which province they hailed by the color or cloth. She learned to sew the baggy pants, so popular with the working men; it was an easy enough task—quite similar to whipping up a batch of nappies for the babies! The *bombachas* were held up with a strip of woven wool. On special occasions, such as the peña this night, the gauchos would wear wide leather belts adorned with silver coins, to hold up their trousers. The men strutting around in their finery reminded Leah of the competition between the ladies of old, and their sky-high peinetones.

The sounds of music had begun to fill the night air, and Joaquín eagerly directed Leah towards the stage. Uncertain of the flow of events, or what would be expected of her, Leah suddenly became apprehensive. Unable to look directly into his eyes, she reminded Joaquín that her mamá had not given her permission to dance.

"Ah princesa, never fear. Tonight, you shall see for yourself that the *campesinos* respect modesty, as much as the rusos. Look now—the handkerchief dance has begun! Pay close attention to the pantomime they act out."

Leah was held spelled bound by the unfolding performance. She listened to Joaquín, as he described the meaning behind the choreography.

"The handkerchief represents the emotion shared between the dancers," he said, "and ultimately the man's desire to attain his lady's love."

"It's as if they are speaking to one another with their hands—as if the handkerchief is transmitting their feelings," Leah whispered.

She watched the lady's shy response, as her partner attempted to woo her. Delicately moving the handkerchief to cover her face, Leah sensed the lady's timidity. They couple performed intricate steps, but rather than being scandalous, the lady always maintained her modesty, and they never touched. The silky swatch of material, held by its tips, transformed into a triangle as they twisted one way or another.

Joaquín leaned in to whisper in Leah's ear. His soft breath on her skin caused her to quake. She had to force herself to concentrate on what he was relaying...something about how the twisting of the handkerchief was symbolic.

"There. You see? He twists the triangle inwards, and it is as if he has kissed his lady. And now, with the next few steps, she will turn in the opposite direction, and the triangle will twist outwardly signifying that she has returned the caress."

The chivalry and grace exhibited on the dance floor had taken Leah's breath away. She listened intently as Joaquín explained what was transpiring, and her heart raced in anticipation. The dance came to a close as the lady released the fabric. Leah watched as the gentleman dancer gently took hold of the four corners and placed it above the lady's head.

"A fitting conclusion, don't you agree?"

Leah waited for his clarification.

"The lady has bestowed her greatest gift—her love," Joaquín offered. "The caballero responds by crowning his *reina*—his queen. What did you think of our dance?"

Leah spoke without thinking. "I wish I had a handkerchief." She gasped at her own wickedness.

"Are you saying you wished to be kissed?"

She hadn't the courage to answer.

"As always, I am at your command," he murmured. Taking his wide felt hat from his head, Joaquín shielded their public display as he gently brushed across Leah's soft lips.

Leah scarcely had a moment to experience the pleasure which had stemmed from her shocking behavior, when they were startled by shouts and applause. To her relief, *they* had not been the cause for the uproar. The audience simply had begun greeting the next set of dancers approaching the stage.

"We best pay attention, Joaquín. Did you not reprimand me earlier for not being aware of my surroundings? I do not wish to be heralded as the next act," Leah said, feeling quite emboldened. "Perhaps now, we might find my family, and observe the performance with them."

"Whatever you say, princesa," he replied. "I am at your..."

"Yes. I know. *Don't say it!*"

Although they had searched among the crowd, they were unable to find Yosef. Leah decided it was quite appropriate to take a seat along the others. Surely her brother would not find anything improper i conduct, if she was surrounded by neighbo: friends. While her heart still raced, and he: ... tingled from Joaquín's gentle kiss, Leah desperately tried to portray herself as her mother would wish. She must be a lady with a modicum of decorum, no matter the location or the occasion. Joaquín interrupted her thoughts, once again, explaining the next dance with great enthusiasm.

"These dancers will perform *El Gato*. Although you see couples forming, they will dance without embracing." Joaquín motioned with his hands—his palms, at first, together and then held wide apart.

"Good," she giggled, "that way *you* will not get any ideas." She blushed at her brazen attitude; after all, it was *she* who had prompted him to behave with such impropriety.

The music began and Leah clapped along as the men pursued their ladies by performing impressive jumps and complex *zapateo*. She had never seen such dance steps.

"Why is it called *El Gato*?"

"Watch. He is as a cat, chasing after his prey. While he tries to entice her with his strength and personality, his *china* relies on her grace and modesty to keep the upper hand."

Realizing that although her vocabulary had proven to be exemplary, Leah hadn't understood his choice of words and Joaquín continued with his tutelage. "You see, a gaucho calls his woman *his china*. I know you are thinking of the oriental country, but I am not referring to China," he chuckled. "The word comes from the Quechua language. It simply means female."

"I suppose I still have quite a bit to learn."

"And I would be happy to teach you," he answered with a sheepish grin. "Speaking of which," he said, clearing his throat, "do you ride, Leah?"

Surprised at his use of her name, she smiled and nodded.

"What do you say to seeing a bit more of the country side? Do you think your mamá will allow it?"

"It seems that my family has forgotten I exist. Even Yosef apparently is not overly concerned with my presence this evening. With everything that has transpired since we arrived, no one has the time to worry about my comings and goings. As long as I complete my chores, I do believe—for the first time in my life—that my siblings and Mamá are quite content to give me free reign."

"Well then, I am at your disposal."

Just then, the *bombo* player began beating out a new rhythm, as the stage was taken over by a new set of performers. Leah fiddled with her skirt and brushed a few loose curls back into place as she sighed, settling against the sweet-smelling hay. Joaquín, accepting her silent invitation to make himself comfortable, reclined and stretched his long legs before him. Folding his arms behind his head, Joaquín conveyed his own unspoken message. Content to share the rest of the evening simply enjoying the music and the moonlight, Leah and the *domador* sat quietly each lost in their own thoughts.

It was much later after the asado had been enjoyed, and the performers had finally said their farewells, that Yosef, Sofia and the rest of the Abramovitz clan found Leah standing next to their wagon. Bidding everyone a good night, Joaquín swept his hat across his chest and bowed like a caballero of old. Leah felt her face flush, and quickly boarded the wagon with the others. While her family chattered away, she kept silent. Heavens! She would be up all night reliving the evening's events and planning for tomorrow's outing.

Leah knew at once she could not—she would not—wear one of her riding habits from home. It would be completely inappropriate! How would it look to be riding alongside a handsome gaucho dressed in a Parisian ensemble? She would look like a princess out riding with her stable groom. That would never do! By the time the rooster advised everyone it was time to arise, she had decided she would ride like every other woman on the pampas. She would ride like a *china*.

Leah and her sisters gathered in the kitchen, as they did each morning. They had developed such a routine, one would think that they had been born to the life. Fresh eggs had been scrambled, and Mrs. Kraskov's *maslenitsa* recipe was transformed to Argentine-style *panqueques* with the addition of the sweet dairy spread the locals called *dulce de leche*. Sweet buns, jam, and fresh milk were set out on the table as the men began wandering in. Magdalena brought the *maté* and kettle, as well, trying to get the rusos to develop a taste for the traditional herbal tea.

The men ate quickly, talking with their mouths full and gulping down cups of steaming hot coffee. There was much to do, and as they still relied on the help of Nacho and Tino, they were eager to return to work and do their share.

Leah waited for someone to ask her about the prior evening, but her sisters were occupied with refreshing the platters and admonishing their children. She expected her mamá to enquire of her plans for the day or, at the very least, to give her a list of duties, but even this was overlooked among the chaos.

"I'm going riding today," she said to no one in particular.

Moishe raised an eyebrow in her direction. She offered a brief response. "I've been invited to tour the countryside with El Moro...with señor Joaquín Ibáñez, that is."

Moishe nodded his sanction, and returned to arguing with Aaron about the necessity of purchasing sheep. When her morning chores had been completed, Leah washed and changed her dress. Finding she finally had the courage to wear the skirt and blouse she had concocted weeks prior, Leah was giddy with excitement. She braided her hair like the girls in town, and tied each section with a matching ribbon of sky blue. Her purchase of the alpargatas completed her ensemble. She looked like *a china!* Suddenly hesitant to make her debut dressed as a local, she hoped to sneak out of the house without discovery; however, when she entered the parlor, Leah found her mother waiting there. Malka set down her needle and thread to gaze at her daughter.

"My dear, you look quite charming," she said with genuine delight. "Is this the same girl who wore silk gowns and emerald pendants?"

"I thought it would be nice to try to fit in with our friends."

"Indeed. Will this be your new look, then?"

Leah giggled. "I don't think I can give up my fitted frocks and lovely fabrics entirely, but *as I am going riding* today, I thought it would be appropriate," she said, emphasizing her planned activity.

"Oh yes," Malka replied. "I heard you mention something about touring the countryside. Do be careful, and do not dally the day away. Your sisters will not think too kindly of it."

Kissing her mother's cheek and grabbing a shawl, Leah opened the front door and began the now-familiar trek to the Vasquez ranch. The road narrowed to a lane with a riot of flowers, growing alongside a creek. Leah looked up to the sun and felt the warmth on her face—it was a lovely day. Who would have thought that Leah Solomonovna Abramovitz would be walking leisurely by fields of grain and cattle dressed like a *krest'yanka*?

As she approached the Vasquez estancia, Leah hailed the gaucho with a shy wave of her hand. Joaquín, holding the reins of two horses, came up to greet her with a courtly bow.

"*Buenas días.* I have brought the horse you befriended on your first visit. See?" he chuckled, as the mare sought out Leah's hand for a treat. "She remembers you well."

As Leah nuzzled with her old friend, Joaquín took a moment to glance at her unexpected attire. He knew he wouldn't be able to hide his amusement *or* his appreciation.

"You look very pretty in your new outfit, princesa. I thought for certain you would be dressed head to toe in a proper riding habit, with a plume in your hair and a whip in your hand."

"I decided that if we are to live on the pampas, it wouldn't make sense to dress for the Avenue des Champs-Élysées."

He laughed, accustomed now to her witticisms, until something quite suddenly dawned on him. Leah's criolla skirt was not nearly long enough to cover her properly. At least, not in the manner that she most certainly was accustomed—not if she was going to straddle the horse.

"I don't know why I didn't think to ask before, but Leah, do you ride astride?"

"Heavens! No!"

Joaquín felt a complete fool. Thinking only of the pleasure of spending time with her, he had come ill-prepared. Perhaps he could yet save the day.

"If you are willing, I will teach you to ride like a true criolla, but let me warn you: you will be sore by the end of the day. Every muscle you have ever used and then some will cry out in protest, but it will be well worth it."

Leah agreed, bravely stating that she was not so easily intimidated. They walked to a nearby open meadow, and there began his patient instruction. It didn't take long for Leah to feel a bit more at ease in the strange position. With no one around to pass judgment, she felt at great liberty to do as she pleased. After all, she was old enough to make her own decisions and strong enough to face the consequences—good or bad. They continued to meander over an unending sea of green pasture until Leah turned to her instructor and shouted, "I'll race you!"

Off she went, flying across the plains, her curls loosening from their braided restraints. *What freedom!* Her skirts blew in the wind, and without a corset inhibiting her movement, Leah breathed freely and laughed shamelessly as Joaquín came galloping up from behind. When she tired—her muscles were already beginning to cramp—they dismounted, and began retracing their path back home.

"You lied to me," he said straight-faced. "You are no Russian princess—*you are Argentine* through and through!"

"Perhaps I can learn to be both." Leah laughed and bowed her head graciously. "In all seriousness, it is truly remarkable to see how the *yiden* have acclimated to their new environment, and how well they are accepted by the locals."

"It is to everyone's benefit. We all share the same concerns—food in the belly and shelter from the sun and the wind. Working together, the town prospers. The problem is that sometimes, we get along *too* well."

"What do you mean?"

"We men," he said with a grin, "we are only human. A pretty face, a charming accent—what can I say? More than one gaucho has fallen for a *sheine meidelach*."

Leah laughed at his use of the Yiddish words. "And who taught you to say that? How many *pretty girls* have succumbed to your charms?"

"Oh, we pick up a few words here and there. And you have to admit, it is a good idea to know how to flirt and say *piropos* in many languages."

"Does it happen very often—Jewish girls flirting with gauchos?" Leah asked, barely having the courage to lift her eyes.

"Not very often, as well as you can imagine, but there was that one love story. It happened years ago.

People still talk about it. *Caramba!* People still swear that they see..."

"See what?"

"It's not a happy story, princesa. This is the land of music and poetry, and we are a tragic people."

"I'll have you know I am an unabashed reader of Russian novels, and they are nothing, if not heart wrenching tragedies. Go on—*tell me!*"

He acquiesced with a shrug. "There was a young Russian girl—Tzipora was her name, but they called her Palomita, because she was a graceful, peaceful creature."

"Yes. Go on."

"Palomita was a beautiful girl, porcelain skin and fair hair—not quite as lovely as your golden locks. Your hair reminds me of wheat, waving in the breeze, glistening in the sun..."

"Joaquín! Please!"

"Ah, princesa, you must learn to enjoy the language of romance. It is a dance in and of itself."

"If you do not tell me the story, I will not walk another step."

And true to her word, Leah plopped down on the grass and refused to go any further. Joaquín laughed at this childish display but, after securing the horses, he too sat down alongside her.

"Where was I? Ah yes—Palomita was a lovely girl. The men couldn't help but notice her—couldn't help falling in love with her. Of course, Palomita's parents guarded her closely. They would not have approved of their daughter finding love in the arms of a gaucho."

Leah, identifying with the story herself, was more than curious. She prodded him to continue.

"*What happened*?"

"Nothing happened. That is to say, Palomita was a dutiful daughter. She knew that a romance with any of the local men would have been out of the question. But she was a sweet girl, and had many friends. Pepe and Cacho were two young men that counted themselves amongst her acquaintances. It was said about town that Palomita had eyes for Cacho. He was a tall, handsome young man. Although she never acted on her emotions, Cacho fell in love with her. *But, so did Pepe*. For months, they vied for her attentions. They showered her with gifts—flowers from the fields, silk ribbons for her hair. She would not accept them, of course. Palomita was an innocent; she was not aware of the repercussions."

"I should think not. A young lady of good family and reputation…"

"You forget yourself. We are not in a prim and proper parlor in Russia. We live without your aristocratic restrictions. The men acted out of passion, out of *macho* competitiveness, but more than that; they acted out of love."

Leah tried to imagine this girl, this Tzipora—caught in between two men—two *forbidden* men. How would she have acted if she had been in her place? Would she have turned her back on her family and traditions, or would she have turned away from love?

I don't have to imagine the scenario. I am heading down the same path, she thought to herself.

"One day, as Palomita crossed the field that bordered her home, she saw Pepe and Cacho. They were shouting, and when she heard her name, she knew that they were fighting over her hand. She quickened her pace to reach them—hoping to repair whatever damage had been done—but peaceful resolutions were too late. The men were past talking. Knives were shining in the bright sun when she finally reached them."

"Knives? What were they thinking?"

"They weren't *thinking*. Passion had taken over!" Joaquín exclaimed. "Palomita stood frozen as she watched the men play out their fatal dance."

"Why didn't she stop them?"

"Nothing could have stopped them. We do not wield a knife, unless we mean to use it—*unless we mean to kill*. In a split second, each man had pulled his *facón* from behind his back. Within an instant, the men ripped off their ponchos, and with a flick of the wrist, wrapped the material around their forearms— effectively shielding themselves from their opponent's blows.

The men circled each other—unaware that their little dove watched from afar. Pepe lunged first. Cacho whipped the fringed poncho off his arm and across his opponents face. Pepe lost his balance, and Cacho's knife left its first brutal mark. Pepe's shielded arm went to cover his face, but with a slight of hand, he unraveled his poncho. As Cacho lunged forward, he stepped onto the woolen cape. Pepe ruthlessly pulled back on the material, downing his rival in one fell swoop. With purposeful aim, Pepe thrust his *facón* towards Cacho's stomach knowing he wasn't strong enough to tear through the man's ribcage and reach his heart. A knife to the stomach was the surest way to end the battle. But just as Pepe's knife plunged through flesh, Cacho's own weapon found a final resting place."

Leah was sickened by the thought. "What sort of men fight like this?"

"What is the difference between a gaucho with his *facón* and a cavalier and his sabre?"

She could only shake her head in response.

"When Palomita saw both men fall to the ground, she let out an agonizing shriek—alerting family and neighbors from across the fields. They were not quick enough, however. Palomita ran to the men and embraced their stilled, bloodstained bodies. Coming upon the threesome, the *campesinos* heard her cry out, "It is because of me. They died because of me!""

"Poor, poor girl! How could she go on?"

"That is the real tragedy of the story. Blinded by shock and remorse, Palomita picked up Cacho's knife and plunged it deep into her own heart."

Speechless, Leah held her head in her hands and tried to hold back her tears.

"I have shocked you, Leah. I apologize but, the legend is very much alive among the *campesinos*."

Joaquín stood up and extended his hand. Leah reached up, and allowed him to help her to her feet.

"Come with me," Joaquín said. "I want to show you something."

Grabbing hold of the horses' reins, they walked a short distance until they reached a shaded pond just beyond a copse.

"Do you see that *ombú* tree over there, beyond the mossy rocks?"

Leah, with rogue tears glistening on her cheeks, silently nodded her head.

"Her parents buried her there. It was a favorite spot. Palomita loved to picnic under the ombú and gaze out across the pond. The people of the colony have seen her ghost here."

Leah's head snapped to attention. Her eyes wide open now, she glared at Joaquín. Was he teasing her? Had the entire story been in jest? "Her ghost? Come now, Joaquín, do you take me for a fool?"

"No, never that. They say her ghost comes to this place. She cries out to young lovers."

"Truly? What does she say?"

El Moro eyes grew dark and solemn. "I see that you do not believe me, but we are a passionate people. We cry irrationally, we hate vehemently—we love *ardently*. These are powerful emotions. Her cries are to warn others not to play with matters of the heart."

Uncertain if he meant to caution or mock her, Leah grew uncomfortable in the intimate surroundings. Perhaps she was not quite as grown up as she thought.

"I thank you for your story. It has been quite...*enlightening*," Leah allowed. "Perhaps we should return. I will be expected home soon."

He nodded and said quietly, "As you command, princesita."

Chapter Fourteen

April 1903 ~ Lucienville, Entre Rios

*I*n the past two years since they had been courting, for in her mind, that was exactly what they had been doing, Joaquín had yet to make a firm decisive resolution—at least, not where Leah was concerned. *It was for her own good.* His last words were still ringing in her ears, although they had walked in silence for quite some time—he, with his horse trailing behind and she, with her reed basket full of wild flowers. She should have known by now that Joaquín was nothing, if not accommodating. She should have thought ahead, and better prepared for his refusal to *injure her expectations.*

As it occurred, they had been strolling down a side path leading to the Abramovitz home, when Leah approached the delicate matter of their future together, and had been taken aback at his response.

With a small tentative voice, Leah now attempted to break the uneasy silence that hovered over the couple.

"I do not understand. I thought I meant something to you."

"You do! Of course, you do, but I am not the sort of man that marries and settles down—neither am I the kind of man that would ruin a girl."

"Therefore, one might presume, you *are* the kind of man that would purposefully entice a girl with no honorable intention."

"Leah," he sighed, "That is not altogether fair. I have enjoyed every moment in your company, but you must have noted that—that I have not..."

"Have not *what*, Joaquín? You have not defiled my person? Is that what you mean to say?"

"It was not for the lack of wanting, I assure you," he said sheepishly. "I simply couldn't allow for things to get out of hand."

"Out of hand? We have spent every free moment together..."

"Yes," he interrupted with some frustration, "but I would never have presumed to insinuate myself into your life."

"I think it is too late for that! Joaquín! I believed we had an understanding. I thought I was your...your *chinita*."

"No, Leah. Never that, *mi princesa*. After everything I have done to show my respect—my reverence—I could not allow it."

"But, I want to share my life with you."

"My life revolves around the horses, Leah, and the land. You know it well. But, what is it that speaks to your heart?"

Leah sighed and closed her eyes. Again, he sidestepped the issue which she most wanted to address. It was not unheard of these days. Mixed marriages between the Jews and the criollos were inevitable, living lives so intertwined. Leah, of course, was concerned how her family would react, but then again; no one had the time or the inclination to pay her much mind anymore. Her siblings had had an opinion on every detail of her life when they lived in Odessa, but now, what with running the farm, building onto the homestead, raising their own children without the help of servants and nannies, Leah found herself unimpeded by her family's overzealous guidance.

Now Joaquín's question had her disconcerted. He asked what spoke to her heart. She always assumed she would marry, but in her dreams—where no one could pass judgment—Leah also envisioned herself as a designer of fashion.

"I've been reading fascinating articles from Buenos Aires, London, and Paris," she began with some hesitancy. "Fashion today is beginning to reflect the practical needs of the twentieth century woman. I want to be a part of that world, but to do so would mean a move to the city."

"You see," he smiled, "that is exactly my point."

"I don't understand—*what* is your point? Our love is stronger than you will allow. We could combine our two worlds and be stronger for it. Have you not ever thought of owning a ranch of your own? That would mean a stable home for us both. Or would you consider moving to Buenos Aires? Perhaps there is a future for you with the British in their world of polo."

Joaquín gently took hold of her hands and shook his head in disapprobation. "I do not want an *estancia*, Leah. I am not ambitious in that way. I cannot, and would not, wish to live in the city—Buenos Aires or any other. My life is here."

She tried to interrupt, but he had captured her hands and held her gaze. "I am a gaucho, *querida*. I do not stay in one place too long. As it is, my time is almost up with Vasquez. I do love you, but you must understand, I am not willing to change my way of life. It is impossible. I do not ask this of you. Do not ask it of me."

Leah's tears flowed freely as she walked the final steps back to her home alone. They had parted with many things still left unsaid for, he had no desire to crush her heart, and she had no need to hear further denials of their love.

Not wanting to face her family, Leah avoided entering the house that would afford her so little privacy, and instead went off to have a good cry amongst the oxen in the barn. When she was finally spent, Leah nestled in a bed of fresh hay and resolved that nothing was more important to her than Joaquín. She would find a way to make him understand. She would find a way to make their lives fit—even if it meant compromising her own dreams. *There was still time*, Leah thought. Tomorrow, she would think of a brilliant plan, and he would come to see the right of it.

Shaking off the loose pieces of hay from her skirt, Leah attempted to pat her hair back into place in preparation for facing the family. Her eyes, red and swollen, would certainly give her away. But there was nothing for it. Leah was expected at home.

Holding her head high and suppressing a rogue hiccup, she opened the front door only to find her siblings huddled in the small parlor. Surprised to see so many family members together at once, she immediately noticed their own tell-tale eyes. With one look at her mother, Leah knew that they had received terrible news.

"What is it? Was has happened?"

"Yosef brought us the latest newspaper from Buenos Aires," her mamá replied. "It seems there has been another *pogrom*. This time it was in Kishinev."

Leah looked towards her brother. With his head bent and held in between his hands, Yosef filled her in with the details. "There have been expulsions, arrests, and beatings—not only of the poor, but even of the middle class and the Jewish intelligentsia. Hundreds were injured, even more were rendered homeless and destitute. The never ending tyranny of the Romanovs has left our community with one hundred and eighteen men, women, and children dead."

"Was there no one to come to their aid?" Leah asked, knowing full well the answer.

Yosef answered with disgust. "There were over twelve thousand soldiers in Kishinev, but they were ordered to stand down. They did nothing to stop the violence for two full days."

Leah observed her mother, weary with anguish and disbelief, as she stood and walked toward Yosef. How much tragedy had her mamá witnessed in her lifetime, she wondered. How much more would they have to bear?

"We could have been there—trapped and without aid *or* hope for the future, if we hadn't followed your lead, my son. I praise Hashem daily for giving you the wisdom to see our path to salvation." Malka kissed his head, still bowed in bereavement, and went off to seek the solace of her room where she could grieve in private.

Quietly, and without further outburst, the others began seeing their way to their own evening quarters. Although they still did not share a roof, they were together and that was all that mattered. The days and nights that followed were filled with the solemnity of the catastrophic event. Leah could not help but feel guilty, for her heart was also in anguish over the quarrel she had had with Joaquín.

Although she would not have believed it, her mother was not blind to these emotions. Malka had been aware of the growing attachment between her daughter and the handsome gaucho, but she had not wanted to interfere. What Hashem had planned for Leah was yet to be seen, and in the meantime, there was a joyous event to be celebrated within the community. In keeping with Jewish tradition, a wedding could not be postponed due to a death in the family, and while the community was in mourning for their brethren in Kishinev, the nuptials would be celebrated as planned. Leah had no desire to attend, but Malka insisted that the Abramovitz family participate in the *simcha* as a whole.

"This is life, my daughter. As it is written, 'Everything has an appointed season, and there is a time for every matter under heaven.' We must go on with the matter of living."

They dressed appropriately for the occasion. Not too fine as to outshine their neighbors, or the bride, but neither too shabbily as to not differentiate between their daily tasks and the happy event. In keeping with local tradition, the wedding would begin on Wednesday, allowing family and friends enough time to come from neighboring colonies, and giving them a day or so to return before the onset of *Shabbes* on Friday night. If a celebrant lost track of the day and time, he would have to find lodging until Saturday evening, when the appearance of three stars announced the end of festival. Not that it would be too troublesome—any colonist would make room for one more.

The Abramovitz family, children and all, walked down to the main road and joined the others, as they headed towards the town's center. The groom had been accompanied by family and friends to the appointed place, and all waited in anticipation for his intended to arrive. Leah noted that, although the *chuppah* was plain in comparison to the bridal canopies she had seen in Odessa, the love and pride of the community more than made up for the lack of elegance or finery.

Music could be heard now, coming from up the road. With lanterns held high illuminating her path, a regal entourage escorted the bride, as if she were a queen approaching her throne.

Gauchos on horseback lined the streets, as they observed the proceedings. Leah wondered what they thought as the rabbi chanted the blessings. There were so many customs that would appear odd. She watched as the bride circled her groom seven times, as dictated by tradition. Would they think her subservient? Leah recalled the explanation her mother had provided years ago and smiled—it was actually quite the opposite of what an outsider might think. Men were taught to create an impression of impenetrability, to never show any signs of weakness. They had to build a protective wall around their true self. But a wise woman, Malka had explained, could pierce this defensive wall. When the bride completed the seven circles, it was reminiscent of the walls of Jericho tumbling down. Her husband's heart would now be released, and more importantly, empowered by his bride's strength and love.

Leah watched as the groom lifted the bride's veil and brought a goblet of wine to her lips. He then lowered the veil and partook of the contents. The goblet was returned to the rabbi who carefully wrapped it in a handkerchief, and placed it under the groom's foot. The young man forcefully crushed the glass with one powerful stomp, as jubilant cries of *mazal tov* rang out from the congregation. It was then, amongst the cheers and applause, that Leah spotted Joaquín in the crowd.

He smiled from a distance and held her gaze. Leah blinked back her tears, hurt, and confused. *What did he think of all of this*? Leah did not return Joaquín's smile. She didn't understand the meaning of it—was he attempting to apologize or was he saying good-bye?

The sudden burst of sound stemming from a *klezmer's* clarinet announced that the evening's celebration had begun; but Leah, numb and resolute, watched as Joaquín rejoined his companions and disappeared down the dark road. The family did not stay overly long for the festivities would continue throughout the night. There was much work to be done before the final autumn harvest, and the men, still relatively newcomers to the entire scheme, needed to be rested and prepared.

They had heard the stories. The old-timers were quick to share their tales about the fires of '87, or the flood of '92; but the Abramovitz family could not allow themselves to become paralyzed with fear, each time the winds blew or menacing clouds formed over their fields. It wasn't until weeks had gone by, with little to no rain, that Aaron and his brothers began to allow their alarm to settle. And they weren't the only ones.

The local co-op called for a town meeting, where the practiced farmers and leaders of the community discussed the possibilities of a prolonged drought. Many had lived through the loss of crops in seasons past. They knew the tell-tale signs and forewarned the newcomers to prepare.

Leah and the family followed the lead of their friends and neighbors. They stockpiled supplies as best they could, ensuring they had feed and water for the animals. The men built ditches alongside the fields, in the hopes that they would be able to hold and contain any rainwater that would bless the land. The women, with the help of Magdalena, thought of ways to conserve water in the kitchen and throughout the home. When they learned that locusts tend to follow long dry periods, it was all they could do not to run away in a fit of hysterics! The family relied on prayer and their community to help see them through yet another natural calamity.

"We have done all we can. We've purchased supplies, and we will make do as required," Aaron said. "In short, we have prepared for the worst, but we should pray that it doesn't come to that."

"All the preparation does help relieve some of the anxiety," Duvid offered, "but it doesn't take away the frustration and the sense of failure."

"My dear boy, these are the moments in time when you have to admit that things are not in your control," Malka said gently. "We have done our best, and now, we must wait and see what we will have to deal with. That is the secret. We cannot control the wind or the rain, but we can control how we react to the circumstances. We must have faith that all will be for the best."

Each day that passed brought stronger winds and scorching heat. Many surrounding farms began sacrificing their livestock, selling them to ranch owners in neighboring provinces. Others were obliged to ship in grain and hay to feed their stock. The Abramovitz family watched in desperation as their own supplies lessened day by day. Leah observed her brothers, as they attempted to hide their worst fears from the women, but there was no hiding the cracked parched landscape that was their home. The children were beginning to show signs of dehydration, and it had been several weeks since they had been at school. *What was to become of her family*?

The locals assured the newcomers that the dry spell could not last much longer. But with no real manner of foretelling the future, their assurances soon became maddening, and Leah, at the end of her rope, found it difficult to hold her tongue.

Yet, even in this irritable and weakened state, she found that she could not put Joaquín out of her mind. *Where was he*? Why hadn't he come? She had been certain that they would be able to sort things out. If only it would rain, and they could get on with their lives. She prayed for it daily, and felt guilty in doing so. Rain! *Dear God, please send rain*! Then, she would see things right with Joaquín. Then everything would be as it should. And finally, at long last, her prayers were answered.

It started slowly at first, just a few sprinkles that hit the parched ground, and instantly created tear drops of dust. As the downpour began building in strength, the rhythm beating out on the granary's tin roof alerted the household of the gift from above. One by one, the family came from every corner of the homestead, laughing, crying, and cheering as they rejoiced in the storm. When at last, they were spent and covered with mud, Malka began ushering everyone to get cleaned up for dinner. They would splurge that evening, digging into supplies that had been carefully monitored for weeks.

When a rider and his horse were spotted trotting up the road, Moishe and Aaron went to the gate to investigate. They couldn't imagine anyone paying a social call, not under these circumstances. It was, indeed, not a social call, but Adolfo Lipinsky coming to check on the family he had taken under his wing. The men brought their friend indoors where he was offered a towel and a hot cup of coffee.

Standing by the entrance, not wanting to drip over Malka's rug, Adolfo began explaining his self-appointed task. "Thank God, the rains have come!" he cried.

"*Baruch Hashem*!" the family replied in unison.

"Now listen, my friends. This storm will provide some immediate relief, but it may take weeks, or even *months* before our lives return to normal. You must be vigilant. Any new vegetation can turn to dry tinder. A spark from someone's chimney, a discarded cigarette, or a bolt of lightning could swiftly ignite our fields into raging wildfires. We are all too familiar with this disaster here in the colonies."

Leah had heard enough. She simply wanted to change out of her wet things, and not worry about any further catastrophe. She left the men to discuss the particulars, and seeing her sisters in the kitchen with the meal well under way, Leah went to her room. Now that the worst of it was seemingly over, she could plan on her next course of action. She would give it a day or two, but then, Leah would pay a visit to her gaucho. She would make him understand. She was in love with Joaquín. Nothing was impossible.

The following days transpired with a whirl of activity. Everyone was needed to put things to right and Leah fell into desperation with each new assigned task. She couldn't complain, for even the children worked dutifully at their parents' side, but Leah counted the minutes to when she might have the freedom—and the strength—to walk to the Vasquez ranch. At last her brothers were satisfied and called for a much needed break.

The cessation of work saw her family collapse in exhaustion, but Leah took the opportunity to rush to her room and see to her attire. Quickly, she washed and began choosing something appropriate to wear—discarding one option after another until finally settling on a modest, pale green skirt and matching blouse. As she arranged her hair in a simple braid, Leah heard her mamá quietly enter the room.

Having noted her daughter's swift departure when the men had called for a period of rest, Malka followed Leah out of concern, and was now surprised to find her preparing for an outing. Retrieving a light shawl she found atop of the bed, Malka draped it over Leah's shoulders as she astutely chose her words.

"I haven't said much on the subject, but I do wish for you to know that I am very much aware of your relationship with señor Ibáñez."

Leah had the decency to blush. "It is true, Mamá, my friendship with Joaquín has blossomed into something quite dear—to me, at least."

"I see." Malka turned and began to straighten the discarded clothing her daughter had tossed aside in haste. "You have *always* had a mind of your own, my dear. It is also indisputable that your life's journey has been so very different than that of your sisters. You are faced with opportunities, and challenged with choices, that were unheard of in their youth."

"Please, do not trouble yourself—"

"I am not troubled. I would counsel you, my dear, but, there is something telling me to hold my tongue."

"I did not set out to go against your wishes, Mamá. Your blessing means more than I can say. It is just, I need more time to understand my own heart."

"Very well, my sweet one," Malka said, as she peered knowingly into her daughter's eyes. "May Hashem guard you and guide you as you make your decision."

Leah walked the familiar road passed the fields and surrounding homesteads wondering what she would say when she faced Joaquín. Living in polite silence had not solved anything, and she had always preferred speaking her mind and clearing the air. She didn't have much time to ponder her choice of words, as she easily found Joaquín putting a horse through his paces. Leah waved as he glanced up in her direction and came hesitantly to her side.

"Hello, princesa," he said with an awkward grin. "I have been concerned for you and your family. How have you fared?"

"Well enough, I suppose, under the circumstances. Our farm, like the others, was hit hard, but we will recover and survive. I—Joaquín—I have missed you."

"I have always been right here."

Leah did not reply to his comment, for if she did, they would end up arguing over semantics, instead of the real purpose of her visit. She began to speak, but he cut her short.

"It is good that you came to see me today." Joaquín loosened his hold on the reigns, and he continued, although the tenor of his voice was detached and straightforward. "I have been called away, and will be leaving for La Pampa."

Barely able to put two words together, Leah responded in breathless despair. "Leaving? But why?"

"I go where there is work."

"Would you have gone without telling me—without asking me to go with you?"

"Leah, I have behaved without honor. I was convinced that I could put a stop to this—this hopeless fantasy—before either one of us could be hurt." Joaquín clicked his tongue and beckoned the horse to his side. "I was wrong. And while I cannot undo the damage to your heart, *or mine,* I will not permit any further transgression. I will not allow you to ruin your life traipsing after me."

"How dare you?" Leah hissed. "How *dare* you decide for me? Have I no say in the matter? Even my brothers, who have tortured me with opinions and instruction, would have respected me enough to hear me out. But you—*noble gaucho that you are*—are honor bound to protect the innocent and long suffering maiden. Is that right?"

"Princesa, please..."

"Do not call me that infernal name! My name is Leah Solomonovna Abramovitz, and it seems, I have been played the fool once again!"

Silently picking up a brush, Joaquín began grooming the great beast that now stood between him and the fiery rusa. The symbolism of the animal's stance was not lost on either of the two, but Leah would not be put off.

"You attempt to use your caballero's integrity to push me away, but I reject your definition of honor, and instead, call you a coward!" Leah cried, accusing the man she had thought to love.

"Please *querida*. I can't bear to see you cry."

"Why not? *Argentines are a passionate people*. We cry irrationally, we hate vehemently—we love ardently. Isn't that what you told me? You should have heeded Palomita's warning not to play with matters of the heart."

Joaquín refused to answer; his silence only spurred her on. "You are right. *I have pursued you!* Never have you sought me—never have you approached without me first giving you leave to do so! And this foolish name—*princesa*," Leah said with disdain, "you are forever subjugating yourself to my command, as if I wished for you to be under my rule! I do not want a man servant, Joaquín, nor do I wish to be subservient to your desires. I want to be your equal."

"*Cariño,* can you not understand my position? If I didn't approach you until bidden, it was out of respect for you and your family. I, *of all people*, understand the differences in our lot."

"Differences?" She laughed bitterly. "After all this time, you still view me as an aristocrat?"

"Never forget who, and what, I am."

"What are you, exactly? Tell me, what is this great difference between our social spheres?" Leah moved around the great beast which had separated the two, forcing Joaquín to face her—daring him to say what she would not address.

"I am but a lowly crossbreed that follows roaming herds from one estancia to another. You are a rare exotic bird—I *will not* be the one to clip your wings before you even have a chance to take flight."

Leah wept unashamedly, not knowing if her tears were from anger or defeat. "Your staggering lack of faith in our future together is an affront to my heart. You could not have injured me more deeply had you not wholly dismissed the strength of my resolve. I am only sorry that your perception of me was so limited— so infinitely small."

Heartbroken, but determined to walk away with her dignity intact, Leah turned from El Moro for the last time, not wishing to witness his astonishment nor his despondency.

As she marched away, taking out her emotions on the soft yielding grassland, Leah poured out her heart to the open and welcoming pampas. Returning home, spent and undone, she hoped she would be able to scurry up to an empty bedroom; but upon opening the front door, Leah instead was welcomed by her mother's warm smile and the soothing aromas of chamomile tea and Mrs. Kraskov's *kamishbroit*.

"Have a cookie, my dear," bid Malka. "They are not as good as our beloved cook's, but I do believe I am getting closer to her level of perfection."

Mystified, and yet comforted that her mamá would know she'd need consoling upon her return, Leah decided that it was now, indeed, the appropriate time to confide all. While her mother stroked her hair, Leah explained the entire sordid mess, but as the concluding words were spoken and the final drops of revitalizing tea were sipped, she made one last fateful declaration.

"I will never marry, Mamá. My destiny is in my hands—my hands alone!"

Chapter Fifteen

January 1904 ~ Lucienville, Entre Rios

"*I*t is beyond time for me to do this," Yosef decreed. "We have struggled for years now, and if it weren't for the dairy and its production, we would have starved. We didn't leave Odessa to merely survive day to day. Don't you see? Working for Singer as a traveling salesman, I would be able to supplement our income. And who better to sell sewing machines than an Abramovitz?" he said with a sheepish grin.

"We still may hear from the bank. Our funds may soon be released," Benjamin said.

"Do not be foolish, Brother. That money is never leaving Russia. We can no longer believe that our fortune will be returned. I have no qualms of becoming a *cuentanik* for the time being. Who knows, I might be able to convert this job into something more substantial. Who is to say that the Abramovitz brothers might still have a place in the world of manufacturing?"

The discussion continued on with the family contributing their varied and heartfelt opinions, but Malka was not happy to see her youngest son leave home. As a cuentanik he would have to travel across the provinces, selling sewing machines from his catalog and collecting payments upon delivery. Of course, she knew he would be successful. Yosef always found a way. His background with fabrics and design would be more than enough to ensure his success, but would he be happy so often away from home? *Oh Solomon*, Malka thought, *what advice would you have given?*

In the end, Yosef packed his meager belongings and kissed his Sofia goodbye. Promising his absence would be short lived, Yosef joked that he'd be back before the lot of them even realized he had been gone. Leah knew his humor was meant to soften the somberness of his departure, but the reality was that Yosef would be sorely missed. They had walked him into town and waved goodbye as the train departed. Leah, not ready to return home, asked to stay behind. She was not eager to be among melancholy that was sure to descend their home.

Choosing a secluded bench situated on the side of the depot, she gazed out on the tracks and imagined the various little towns Yosef would visit and all the interesting people he would meet. Upon hearing someone chattering with a distinct British inflection, she turned and was pleasantly surprised to see her friend, Juan Carlos discharging his duties for the day.

Juan Carlos Bartholomew had made Leah's acquaintance one blistering afternoon when he stormed Paulina's shop, shouting at the top of his lungs. Paulina had unwittingly informed her new and eager seamstress that an important client, a British engineer, had placed an order for two waistcoats. Leah, eager to please her employer, imagined what a man of quality in Odessa would wear, and proceeded to create a fine vest in a rich brocade and another in a striped silk.

Señor Bartholomew was not pleased when the package had been delivered to his rooms, and when he burst into Paulina's shop, he showered the shopkeeper and her humble staff with a few choice words. Leah, dismayed at the customer's dissatisfaction, was momentarily rendered speechless. She was certain that any of her brothers would have been pleased. Certainly any educated, refined gentleman of Odessa would be proud to be seen in either offering.

"I asked for two waistcoats, Paulina—*for work!*" the man bellowed. "I can't be seen wearing these. The men will think me a popinjay!"

Leah couldn't bear for her kind employer to take the blame. Pushing herself away from her sewing machine, she glared at the man and—forgetting her embarrassment—poked him solidly in his shoulder.

"Stop harassing poor Polita! I am the one you wish to insult and berate, although I cannot understand why you would do so. These waistcoats are of the finest quality and style. Any man of means would be proud to wear my creations."

Juan Carlos Bartholomew stared at the young upstart, his curiosity piqued. "Did *Polita* tell you my line of work?"

"Yes, she did. She said you were an engineer. I was well acquainted with several gentlemen of that profession in Odessa. They went to university with my brothers and they were always dressed smartly."

"I am a railway engineer, *nenita*." He roared with laughter and slammed his hand down on Paulina's fragile countertop. "I don't design the trains, I drive them."

As comprehension and humor combined to diffuse the situation, Leah offered to create two new waistcoats—serviceable, yet fashionable—and to cover the cost with her own wages. The señor would have none of that.

"I will keep these fine samples of your work. If ever I pay a visit to my relatives in England, or my father deems it appropriate to visit his renegade son in the Argentine, I will have something appropriate to wear."

Seeing Leah's confused expression, he proceeded to explain that, although he had been born and raised in the country, he had broken with his family when they returned to England. His father, a British industrialist, and his colleagues had formed the Western Railway Company back in '55; and while he had expected to make his fortune in the South American territories, he never expected his son to stay behind. Juan Carlos stunned his father by choosing a simpler life driving trains up and down the Argentine countryside.

"Haven't seen or heard from him in years, but one can never lose faith. Who's to say he won't be on the next 5:15 from Buenos Aires? And won't dear old *pater* be impressed as I strut around, proud as a peacock, in one of your fine vests?"

The two immediately became fast friends. Leah enjoyed listening to his stories about life on the rails and about the many friends he had made along the way. Juan Carlos had met people from all over the world, for everyone was chasing the rainbow to find their pot of gold in Argentina.

Leah had often pondered this concept. In this new country, anyone could make something of themselves. It was just a matter of finding a niche in the multilayered fabric that made up the population. Somehow, she would *make* herself fit. She would find a way to meld her Russian heritage, her Jewish faith, *and* her new Argentine identity into one unique young woman.

Deciding that she had allowed enough time to pass, Leah said goodbye to her friend and started for home, but not before stopping at the kiosk for the evening paper. She knew Yosef would approve. Perusing the headlines, Leah gasped and quickened her step down the familiar road. By the time she reached home, Leah, breathless and with a stitch in her side, burst through the door shrieking, "Russia has gone to war with Japan!"

As Rivka fanned her with a dish towel and Sara brought a much appreciated glass of water, Aaron quickly read from the periodical. Of course, they had been aware of the pressure Russia had placed on China for dominance in Manchuria. Russia had sought to hold the sea port for numerous reasons, access for the Trans-Siberian Railroad being chief among them. By occupying the peninsula, Russia had forced Japan to relinquish their rights over the land.

Aaron read aloud, with much repulsion, but little surprise. Russia reneged on her agreement to withdraw its troops from the area, while Japan had been steadily expanding its army. Now with the upper hand, Japan made her move.

"Once again, allow me to say it, *even* if Yosef is not here to take credit," Aaron declared. "I thank the good Lord that we are out of that quagmire—no matter if we lost our fortune, no matter if we have to face locusts every year."

Leah agreed with her brother's passionate speech, but even so, she said a prayer for her friends in the old country. So many young people...would their lives be spared? As the days marched on, the family continued on with a blanket of solemnity hovering over their daily chores. With so much work to be done, it was easy to forget oneself with the task at hand; however, in the evenings, there was some respite when they gathered together for their meal. Someone would inevitably attempt to enliven the conversation with an amusing anecdote or by sharing a good piece of news.

It was at such a time, when Gitel, who had been quietly eating her dinner in the corner of the room, suddenly announced she wished to speak privately with the *barynya* and Leah—now her dearest friend. The women sequestered themselves in the main floor bedroom, and after being seated, waited for Gitel's explanation.

"I am to be married."

When neither of the women responded, Gitel repeated her comment. "Rafael Vasquez has asked for my hand in marriage, madam, and I wish for your blessing."

Astonished, Leah shook her head in disbelief. *Rafael Vásquez?* But, that was Joaquín's employer! Gitel blushed, as she looked at her dear friend, and explained that she had inadvertently met the owner of the impressive ranch on one of their impromptu visits to El Moro. That first meeting led to other assignations, of course, Gitel added quickly, they were always in public view and quite proper.

"I would not wish to bring any dishonor to your family, madam, but you see, he loves me and accepts me as I am."

"What do you mean, he *accepts* you?" Leah demanded.

"I only mean that I am a poor orphan—housekeeping and manual labor are my only skills. But on the other hand, he is a man without family or faith. Señor Vásquez, I mean, Rafael, has promised that I may keep my kitchen per our traditions, *Barynya* Abramovitz, and if we are blessed with children—be it God's will—he agrees to raise them as Jews."

"Of course I only wish you happy," Malka declared. "If he is a good man, as you say, and you have thought through all the repercussions of marrying outside of your faith, I will not withhold my blessing."

"He *is* a very kind man and, although he is wealthy and powerful, he is sorrowfully lonely. He doesn't wish me to work—can you imagine it? I am to be *la señora de la estancia*! It is rather laughable really..."

"What will you do with so much time on your hands, Gitel, my dear?"

"I have had an idea for quite a while, and now, thanks to the generosity of my husband-to-be, I will put it into action."

"Yes?" Leah asked enthusiastically. "Do tell!"

"Those poor women in Buenos Aires—do you recall? You had said, mistress, that they were trapped, without documents, without skills. Tragedy and disgrace had befallen them through no fault of their own. I remember thinking at the time; I could have followed down such a path…"

"Surely not!" Leah cried.

"It is true—had I not come into service, who knows what kind of life I would have led. I had no other home, no one to care for me. I was completely lost and without guidance. As it happens, God had a plan for me all along," Gitel said, looking very pleased indeed. "My good fortune will be put to good use, for I plan to free as many women as possible from their evil masters and bring them here to Entre Rios. Rafael's generosity knows no bounds. He has offered to build a home for my refugees on a lovely parcel of land."

"This is a splendid idea!" Malka exclaimed.

"The women will have time to heal their bodies and their souls. Rafael and I will share our various talents and skills so that, in time, they may find good honest work. My future husband knows someone in Buenos Aires that will help with their legal documents, and those wicked men who tricked them into a life of degradation and slavery will see their evil work undone. And I, my dear *barynya*, will finally feel that I have repaid your kindness."

Malka wiped a fallen tear as she looked pointedly at her daughter.

"You see, Hashem always had a plan. We may not be able to discern it, but in the end, things have a way of working out."

"Divine Providence *again*, Mamá?"

"Yes, Daughter," Malka smiled and kissed Gitel soundly on both cheeks. "Hashem might have a thing or two to say about your destiny, as well. We shall leave it in His good hands. Now, I too have some news to share. We've had word from Yosef. He arrives on the afternoon train tomorrow and will have just enough time to stop in for dinner before continuing his journey."

Leah had missed her brother—taunts and all—and was happy to know he'd soon be home to share a meal with his wife and family. They would enjoy a quiet repast and share what little time they had together before Yosef headed north.

The image Leah had painted in her mind's eye did not quite develop as she had planned. Rather than a pleasant evening spent enjoying each other's company, they participated in a classic family deliberation, for Moishe and Yosef brought up the beleaguered subject of their imminent relocation.

"Papá's wish was for us to be successful and thrive. We can't do that here in the colony—at least *I* can't. The purpose of starting over in this country was to reestablish the family name in our field of expertise. I cannot see a way clear to that goal as a lowly cuentanik. In my travels, I have discovered an entire district of jewelers, manufacturers, wholesalers, and retail establishments in the center of Buenos Aires. That is where Moishe and I need to be."

"The family has already seen three sons go off on their own," said Sara. "Our numbers are dwindling. Soon, this little house will be empty!"

"I am staying put," Duvid boldly interjected. At seventeen, he was practically running the family dairy on his own. Besides, he had recently met a charming, blue-eyed brunette from Bessarabia. Needless to say,

Duvid had high hopes of becoming better acquainted. "I can think of nowhere else I'd rather be."

"Then, it is settled. Moishe and I will venture to Buenos Aires and...

"And I will come along," Leah interrupted. "As everyone is chiming in with their plans, I don't see why I should be excluded. Moishe knows I am more than capable, even if you don't have any faith in me Yosef."

"I never have discounted your work. Moishe may have allowed you to create your first fashion plates, but I have always applauded your determination. That being said, I do still have significant reservations."

Leah sighed. "Go on—what are they?"

"Our funds are limited," Yosef explained, "I can't vouch for the sort of accommodations we might have to let. I don't know what sort of work we will have to accept, or how often we will eat, for that matter! To that end, Devora and Sofia will have to remain here and wait for us to call for them. As will you, I am afraid."

"But, I could help you! I have given the matter considerable consideration and believe I have useful, *profitable* ideas." Leah stressed. "Of course, because I am a woman, you do not wish to hear them."

"That is simply not true. We are perfectly willing to listen."

"I want to open my very own Russian Tea Room. I envision ladies engaging in conversation and refreshment, while I entertain them with a strolling fashion show—just like the House of Worth in Paris. This would be an extraordinary vehicle to promote my designs *and* your fabrics."

Moishe beamed with pride. "It is an excellent proposition, but the pesky little matter of finances still looms over us."

Malka, understanding the difficulties that lay ahead, both financial and emotional, intervened.

"Please take your brothers' words into consideration, Leah dearest. You would not wish to be a burden to them, and your continued presence here would be of great use to me."

"Why must I always put my plans on hold?"

"I realize you are eager to find your purpose in life," Malka stressed, "but we must remain faithful and know that everything is as it should be. I know that Buenos Aires is calling out for you. When Hashem dictates it is your time to leave, there will be nothing to hold you back."

Chapter Sixteen

January 1908 ~ Buenos Aires

*I*t had taken four years for Leah to return to country's capital—four long years on the farm, where she had been housekeeper, cook, nursemaid, and even dairymaid, but the time had finally come. Leah was determined to see her dreams to fruition.

As the conductor announced their imminent arrival, her fellow passengers began gathering their belongings and preparing to disembark. With all the commotion unfolding on the platform, Leah was hard pressed to recall when she had ever seen such a chaotic orchestration of people coming and going.

Having had the pleasure of experiencing museums, theater, and ballet in Odessa, Leah looked forward to the cultural events that Buenos Aires was sure to provide. She hoped to visit the Museum of Fine Arts, as well as *Cabildo* and the presidential center of government, *la Casa Rosada*. But mostly, after finding a tourist pamphlet on the train and reading it from cover to cover, Leah was eager to visit *Teatro Colón*.

The cornerstone for the theater had been laid nearly eighteen years ago on the anniversary of the Argentine revolution. Given that it was named in honor of Cristobal Colón, the architects had had every intention of inaugurating the building by October 12th 1892, which would have coincided with the 400th anniversary of the discovery of America. But, as Leah had read with increasing curiosity, the construction had been delayed. Time and time again, the work was put off by disagreements on locations and plan designs; by an unending stream of financial difficulties; and most shockingly, by *mysterious deaths*! With this information tucked away, Leah was that much more resolved to visit the famous, or rather *infamous* venue.

She stashed away the pamphlet, with the periodical that had kept her company on the long trip, and settled onto a bench in the passengers' vestibule. Wondering whatever could have detained her family from meeting her upon the train's arrival, Leah fought to keep her emotions at bay. The fretfulness of leaving her mamá and siblings behind in a far-away province, the excitement of her new surroundings, and the apprehension of finally putting her plans into action, had taken their toll. When at last she was in her brothers' warm embrace, and the initial excitement of being reunited had subsided, Leah finally released the breath she had clenched deep down in her core.

With the men dashing away to retrieve her trunks, Leah linked arms with Devora and Sofia as they led her towards the hired carriage.

"I find my brothers quite transformed," Leah stated. "They are no longer prim Russian industrialists, nor are they homesteaders from the pampas."

"Truly?" Sofia asked. "How so?"

"There is a certain air about them," Leah admitted. "They look like true *porteños*. I doubt if the family would recognize them if the crossed each other in the street.

"Do you mean their mode of dress?"

"Yes, but—there is something more. I can't quite put my finger on it."

"Moishe had several—let us say—*disagreeable* encounters when they first arrived in town," Devora offered. "They were seen as foreign interlopers and were given the cold shoulder by some of the local manufacturers."

"Naturally," Sofia laughed, "that only served to accelerate their assimilation to city life. Yosef believed that if they were to be accepted as businessmen—not only businessmen for the *rusos*—they would have to adapt their fashion and mannerisms."

"They are still our Yosef and Moishe, dearest. They have not changed their hearts," Devora said gently. "Your brothers will always have a *yiddishe neshama*.

"Indeed! Yosef has become more and more involved with various Jewish societies. In truth, many *kehillot* have come into existence to address the needs of our community."

Devora nodded in agreement. "The government, which is fairly run by the Catholic Church, is certainly not willing to assist."

"You probably were not aware that Yosef was working with the *Chevra Kadisha*?" Sofia said.

Stunned at this piece of news, Leah simply shook her head.

"Upon arriving to Buenos Aires, our men were bombarded with invitations to join various organizations, some political in nature, others religious. Yosef can't seem to help it—he *must* involve himself, in particular when he sees an injustice being committed."

"But the *burial society*? I can't imagine why..."

"It is simple, really. Jews are not allowed to be buried within the city limits. There is but one, far-away cemetery and officials have allocated an area there for *dissidents*. Can you imagine? Yosef is working with the *Chevra Kadisha* to purchase land in a place call Liniers. Soon, our community will have a consecrated final resting place."

"So you see, Leah, while they look the part of a dandified porteño, their Jewish souls remain intact. Their commitment to our community has never been stronger."

Leah nodded her approval as her brothers returned to their side. The happy assembly headed for home chattering away—hungry for news of family and friends. Yosef, eager to show off to his sister, breathlessly extolled the virtues of their new neighborhood.

"We've chosen, with great purpose, a particular street in the eleventh district to house our manufacturing works," he explained. "While most of the owners live above or behind their businesses, we decided to utilize the entire lot to produce, showcase, and sell our fabrics—"

"Yes, and in doing so, we staked an important claim amongst the mélange of industrious immigrants of the city," Moishe added.

"If we do not reside on the property, where *do* we live?"

"We were lucky. We found accommodations in an unpretentious, yet suitable building several blocks away on Avenida Corrientes and Pueyrredón."

"And Leah, there is ample room for you to work in the attic," Yosef said with a grin. "Not to mention, we've cleared a small corner of the storefront for your use. I'm sure you will make it your own and be quite comfortable."

With tears glistening in her eyes, Leah simply kissed her brothers with humble gratitude. It seemed, for once in her life, she found herself at a complete loss for words. Devora and Sofia quickly filled in the void with chatter and interesting tidbits, while Leah composed herself.

Looking at the carriage window, as she was prone to do, she tried to focus on the many sites; but everything was so grand and imposing, she soon became overwhelmed *Where to look first*? As the vehicle came to a final stop, she did have the presence of mind to notice the plaza directly in front of their building. It was a charming park with lovely trees and pathways, but Leah was most surprised to see a group of gypsies lunching by a great fountain. She was not a little ashamed when Sofia noticed her reaction and laughed.

"There is every sort of person here in this city. Even the Roma gypsies have found their way to the Argentine!"

Leah's thoughts of gypsies, and her beloved Molly, were quickly interrupted when Moishe jumped down from the carriage and raised his hands out to her.

"You've come to the city just at the right time. Today's headline in *La Nación* announced that the International Exposition, scheduled in honor of the Centennial, will be held in two years. The article says preparations for the celebration are to begin immediately. Imagine that! If they need two years to prepare, that means *we* will have two years of good, solid work!"

Yosef, carrying packages and cartons, came around and placed a kiss on his sister's cheek. "Don't worry, dear. We are not all work and no play! We have made many friends here, business associates as well. As soon as you have settled in, we will begin introducing you around."

"And speaking of introductions," said Sofia with a giggle, "we—Devora and I—think it's high time you married."

"What?" Although she had years to heal after Joaquin's departure, Leah's heart was not ready to contemplate marriage. "Do you think we are in the old country? I've come to the city to work—not for you and Devora to play matchmaker. The last thing I need is a *shidach!*"

"It's not *so* terrible—being married that is," Yosef grinned.

"That is easy for you to say. You are a man, so *you* can work and be married at the same time! A woman is not afforded that luxury. I want to focus on my plans—"

"But there are so many eligible bachelors in Buenos Aires. Perhaps you could…"

"I don't need to be a fine, married lady of the haute society. I'd rather be a famed designer such as Worth, Doucet or Poiret. To aspire to be as good as any one of these designers, one needs time and seclusion to concentrate, to work, *to create*."

Yosef leaned in and now placed a noisy kiss on his wife's cheek. "Leave her be, Sofia. When the love bug bites, she will sing a different tune. Since you require *seclusion*, Sister, I do believe our attic will indeed suit your needs. Would you like to tour the new Abramovitz factory now, or shall we wait a day or two until you have had time to rest?"

Hoping to curtail the subject of her proposed nuptials, Leah eagerly accepted Yosef's offer. To further illustrate her sincerity and determination, Leah made much work of opening a rather large, heavily-bound package.

"I have brought tools of the trade, along with a few knick knacks and souvenirs. They were Mamá's. You could well imagine, I couldn't bear to part with them," Leah said holding up a vintage treasure. "Just look at this charming, silver parasol, Sofia. It's quite delicate, but when you release the mechanism," she said showing her delighted audience, "it opens and reveals a case full of needles. And of course, Mamá's rosewood thimble—you remember her collection of thimbles? Papá would bring one from each European city he visited. I also have a set of millinery needles for basting and pleating, colored pencils, tablets of sketching paper, and who knows what else!"

"I'm sure it all will prove to be useful, but, I sincerely hope you do not hide yourself away in that attic," Sofia pouted. "There is more to life than work."

"Yes that may be true for you, but I am completely focused on making a name for myself. And as this decade is coming to a close, there are many, exciting changes in fashion. Just look at this new corset," Leah said, holding up the fashion magazine she acquired at the train station. "It shows off a woman's tiny waist, or *produces* one if she has indulged in too many sweets!"

"I *do* prefer the softer fabrics and pastel colors they are promoting this season," Devora allowed.

"We'll have to ask Moishe to create a variety of delicate shades. Now look at this periodical," Leah added quickly, before either of her sisters could interrupt. "Paul Poiret is all the rage this season. I must incorporate some of his design. See this narrow silhouette? So simple, and yet, complex...he must use a different form of corset—oh dear! It appears that this design calls for a natural waist—so liberating—but it is cut shockingly low on the bust..."

"Do take a breath Leah. My head is spinning!" Devora exclaimed. "Besides, can you not think of anything else besides fashion? Are you not in the least bit interested in seeing the sights?"

"Yes, of course! I most certainly wish to be shown about and become acclimated to my new home. There are so many fascinating places I wish to visit. What was that impressive structure we passed on the way home from the station? Could it be the theater I've read about?"

"I believe you are referring to *Teatro Colón*—the new jewel of the city," Devora replied. "Opening night is to be on the 25th of May, in honor of the Revolution."

"I do so wish we could attend."

"You will have to do more than wish. Tickets will be quite dear, I'm afraid."

Sofia laughed as a thought came to mind. "Why don't you ask the gypsies in the plaza for a tarot reading? They can tell your fortune, don't you know? Perhaps they can see if you are meant to attend the opening!"

Leah turned away, pretending to be engrossed in the fashion journal she desperately clutched. Tarot cards? Gypsies? Once again, Molly was at the forefront of her mind. Perhaps a meeting with the gypsies was meant to be. Perhaps they could be of use to her, as she made her way into the business world. But, Leah had been warned not to delve into that mystical world. Mamá had proclaimed that Molly's dalliances with such inexplicable manifestations had been meant for her alone. Tossing aside the magazine, Leah picked up another box ready for the unpacking, and focused on the task at hand.

I am not Molly, she said to herself, as she fought with an impossible knot of twine. Molly, with all her education and unprecedented freedoms, had been shackled by her insecurities and fear of failure. *I have faith in my abilities. I will succeed!* With renewed determination, Leah disavowed the need for esoteric experiences to illuminate her path. She would rely on her own strengths.

Chapter Seventeen

May 1908 ~ Buenos Aires

"*B*y what miracle did you come by these tickets?" Yosef laughed, as he looked up his brother's sleeves and under his hat. "What magic is this? They are astronomically pricey and nearly impossible to obtain!"

Moishe chuckled at his brother's antics. "*Gelt gait tzu gelt*—money goes to money. All of Buenos Aires will be at Teatro Colón..."

"So?"

"*So*—I thought it was a good idea to be seen among high society. We need to set ourselves apart from the cuentaniks and other low-end fabricants. It's time we dress up and play the part. Besides, the girls have earned a special night out..."

"Oh yes!" Leah interjected. "For one night, let's pretend we are back in Odessa. Let's recreate something of what was left behind."

"No more pretending, little sister. We *are* the Abramovitz Manufacturing Company of Buenos Aires, and unlike that Grimm's fairy tale you used to love as a child, you will not have to return the glass slipper at midnight." Turning to his beaming wife, Moishe asked, "So, my love, what say you? What will you wear?"

Leah practically squealed with delight. At twenty-five years of age, she knew her youthful exuberance would be considered gauche in polite society, but considering they were nestled together in a most familial manner; Leah grabbed her sister-in-law's hands and together, they twirled about as children.

"Never you mind," Leah said with much glee. "I have the perfect dress for you, Devora. It is the loveliest shade of plum, which will be ever so charming with your eyes! I used a luxurious velvet for the body of the gown, but it has a delicate lace bodice and tulle edging on the sleeves. I am certain you will be pleased! And for Sofia—oh, let's leave the men! We have ever so much planning to do."

The women disappeared into Leah's workshop; their gaiety and delight brought smiles to the men's faces. For the next two weeks, Leah was kept hard at work, completing Sofia's silk charmeuse in pearlescent rose, and applying the finishing touches on a gown of her own. Thankfully, the pieces had already been designed and their construction initiated, while she was still at work in Paulina's shop. Leah had hoped to schedule a fashion show to debut her designs, but what better opportunity to display her work than at the grand opening of Teatro Colón!

The highly anticipated evening finally arrived and found Moishe and Yosef, elegant in their eveningwear, waiting patiently for their wives and sister to appear in their small parlor. Sofia and Devora opened the bedroom door, at last, and paraded about for their appreciative husbands. Leah graciously waited to hear their oohs and aahs come to an end, before coming forth herself. Not having a husband to wax poetic over her own beauty was a fact to which she had grown accustomed. Besides, Leah thought, she had two dashing brothers who would bestow their praises upon her. And praise they did!

In her satin gown of aquamarine, Leah appeared to be a sea goddess. She had painstakingly beaded the net insert at the bodice and hand stitched the gold lamé waistband. The flowing trained skirt, decorated with a metallic gold cord, provided the final regal touch. With compliments to the designer and her models, the men gathered their beauties and escorted the party to the conveyance waiting below.

They traveled through the crowded streets, leaving behind the hustle and bustle of Avenida Corrientes, and turned onto the famously wide boulevard with its elegant architecture and majestic trees. Peering through her window, Leah observed with marked curiosity as the line of carriages came to a standstill. One by one, they made their way through a narrow lane, which led the elegant passengers directly to the theatre's main entrance.

It had been made known to the driver that the side streets of Toscanini and Cerrito were to be avoided. The entrances there were for artists and labourers, and of course, the doorway on Calle Tucuman was meant for those ticketholders that would stand in the upper levels already nicknamed *Paraíso,* in reference to that section's great, *almost heavenly,* height.

The Abramovitz family entered through the main doors, along with the rest of Buenos Aires' high society. With necks craning to see every corner and heads turning to note each detail, Leah suppressed an urge to giggle at the shocking lack of decorum displayed by the city's elite. Her brothers continued to escort their party through the main hall, which had been created in a horse-shoe fashion enabling the spectators to stroll easily in either direction.

Leah noted the classic Italian and French influences with great appreciation, recalling many happy hours with her father in his library, listening intently as he explained the various European styles. Approaching the grand staircase, they ascended three flights, until finally, their party reached their reserved seats.

Leah's eagle eye took great pride in noting that more than one, or two, fashionable ladies had looked their way. Their appreciation of quality and style was clearly observed. Such was her excitement, Leah failed to see that her family had already situated themselves within the box—leaving her on the edge of their row.

Sneering at her brothers for not allowing her to sit alongside the women, Leah gracefully took her seat hoping not to crush the satin gown, while offering up a prayer that the last empty seat to her left would remain unoccupied. Alas, her prayers were left unanswered. An elegant gentleman soon approached.

"Pardon me, madam," the gentleman said, "Are you expecting another to join your party? I do believe this is my seat..."

Moishe, Leah noticed with some disconcertion, didn't bother to stand, but merely craned his neck to observe the unexpected activity at his sister's side. "By all means, sir," Moishe said, as he gestured amiably towards the vacancy.

How ghastly! Could her brother not see that she was most discomfited by the awkward situation? Moishe should have, at the very least, changed places with her! Handsome as he may be, the gentleman was a complete stranger. Leah had hoped that the intimate accommodations of the theater's box would allow for a pleasurable evening *alone* with her family. She flashed a scowl at her brother, but Moishe's eyes were already distracted. His eyes had locked with the interloper.

"Ernesto?" Moishe exclaimed. "You sly dog! Whatever are you doing here?"

To Leah's dismay, the stranger returned her brother's enthusiastic greeting with one of his own.

"Moishe? And Yosef too? This is a grand surprise!"

The men stood, shook hands, and pounded each other on the back, as men often do. Yosef nearly stepped on Leah's delicate shoes in his eagerness to greet his friend. Leah looked to her sisters and returned their questioning gaze with a most unladylike shrug. Neither Moishe, nor Yosef, noticed anything awry until Devora cleared her throat and smiled at her husband.

With a boyish grin, Moishe begged to be excused for his atrocious lack of manners and made the presentations to the party at once. A gentleman of their acquaintance since the Abramovitz brothers arrived to Buenos Aires, Moishe now introduced their friend, *Ernesto Blumental*—otherwise known as Ernst

Bloomenthal of that famous haberdashery, Bloomenthal's of London.

"The *porteños* have a devilish time pronouncing the man's name, so he has adopted an Argentine moniker," Moishe explained in between chuckles.

Leah remained uncharacteristically quiet throughout introductions and the overly zealous reactions of her brothers. Sofia and Devora, usually lively and amiable themselves, were surprisingly restrained. Something was not quite right, Leah thought. In truth, it seemed her brothers were playing a part. The question was *for whose benefit?*

She retraced the last few moments in her mind and came to the conclusion that her brothers purposefully had maneuvered the seating arrangements. They had wanted her to sit next to the vacant seat because...*they knew* it wouldn't remain vacant for long. Heavens! Her brothers knew that Mr. Blumental would be attending, or worse still, they had invited him to attend in order to meet their spinster sister!

Leah cringed at the thought of her brothers scheming behind her back, but stopped short at believing her sisters had been included in the imbroglio. They seemed quite surprised—*even* taken in by the handsome gentleman. There was one component Leah could not quite explain. Mr. Blumental, point in fact, was completely ignoring her. If, indeed, her brothers had planned the assignation, would the gentleman not be more *attentive* to the lady in question? While he did briefly acknowledge her presence with a patrician salutation, he quickly turned and spoke directly to her brothers extolling his good fortune.

"How providential to meet you, tonight of all nights!" he declared. "I have been remiss—it has been far too long. My trip to London was quite productive, however, and I know you both will be interested in hearing my news."

"You must come by and visit us soon. The shop is more conducive to business," Moishe said gesturing with his hand across the theater's expanse. "I'm sure the ladies do not wish to hear our discourse this evening."

"Certainly," Mr. Blumental agreed. "I would, by no means, wish to suspend their pleasure."

Her brothers resumed their seats, but not before Leah witnessed a silent exchange between Yosef and the gentleman. She was certain they had communicated a message to one another—*fete accompli*, perhaps? Leah glanced up through her long lashes to spy on the player Moishe and Yosef contracted.

Ernesto Blumental stood taller than her brothers, and *they* were at least a head taller than Leah. His formal wear was well tailored, and she couldn't help but notice how nicely his broad shoulders appeared under the fine cloth. With the glow of candlelight, it was difficult to discern his coloring; but there was no doubt, the man cut an imposing figure. That fact alone did not impede Leah's mortification at having been foisted off on a stranger!

After the disgrace of believing herself to be in love with Lieutenant Yegorov, and her heartbreak with Joaquín, had she not suffered enough at the hands of handsome men? Leah gasped when, at once, the gentleman's eyes came upon her. She had been caught staring. She would add that to her list of humiliations for the evening.

"Are you quite well, Miss Abramovitz?" he asked.

She nodded.

He continued to gaze at her, as if noticing her for the first time. Leah shifted uncomfortably in her seat.

"Sir, the stage is directly in front of you."

"Oh—yes. I do apologize."

Unable to put two words together, Leah nodded—*again*.

"This is quite pleasant, isn't it?" he continued. "I hadn't planned on attending this evening, having just returned from London, but at the last moment, I thought it would be good for business to be out and about. And here I am now—amongst friends."

Leah finally found her voice. He needn't make up stories to make her feel more at ease. "Come now, Mr. Blumental, there is no need to feign innocence."

"I beg your pardon?"

"I can only assume my brothers have acted with the best intentions; nevertheless I do not require their assistance, nor do I seek to enter into an *understanding* with any gentleman at this point in time."

"Miss Abramovitz, I haven't the slightest inkling of your meaning."

"Oh, but I believe you do, sir. Furthermore," Leah hissed, "I believe you have been sworn to secrecy by my meddling brothers."

"Are you implying that I was asked to join your party, only to feign surprise upon meeting you here?" he whispered in return.

"Yes, that is precisely what I am implying. And there is no need to deny it, Mr. Blumental. It is shocking behavior—I do not know when I have ever been so affronted."

"Let me assure you, Miss Abramovitz," he said matching the young woman's volume, "I am not in the habit of incommoding young ladies in order to make their acquaintance."

He looked down upon her and was about to offer another denial, but he stopped short when he noticed her pretty dimpled chin held high, almost daring him to rejoin. Her fiery eyes were aglow with indignation and, if he was not mistaken, *anguish*. He would have abandoned his place in the box and made his excuses to his friends, had Yosef not stayed his intended action.

"Are you two becoming better acquainted? You know, Blumental, my sister has just recently arrived from Lucienville. This is her first real night out on the town."

Speechless at her brother's declaration, Leah could only glare at Yosef and hoped he understood that there would be retribution. *How could he*? He made her sound so very provincial—a county rustic playing dress up in the big city. Indeed!

"Is that so? And how are you enjoying Buenos Aires?" Ernesto stated, raising his voice so that the others might perceive the topic of conversation. "How do you entertain yourself while your brothers are at work? Are you musical? Do you read?"

"Yes. I read, Mr. Blumental," Leah muttered. "I find I am quite capable of filling the hours in the day." She certainly was not going to enumerate her accomplishments—her brothers probably already had done so!

"My sister is an unabashed novel reader," Yosef offered, impervious to Leah's animosity.

"Do you have a preference for a particular genre, Miss Abramovitz?"

"My sister has read everything tragic," Yosef again interjected, speaking over his wife's head.

"And yet," Leah said, shooting daggers at her brother with an uncompromising gaze, "Given my druthers, I now prefer to read about a *new* sort woman. I'm tired of the tragic heroine."

"To which heroine do you refer?" Mr. Blumental asked innocently enough. "Juliette, perhaps?"

Leah groaned. *Naturally, he would think of Shakespeare.*

"In fact, I was thinking of Tatyana Larina. You are familiar, of course, with Onegin's work. Oh—perhaps not. I dare say you have read *Anna Karenina*? Are you familiar with Nastasya Filipovna of *The Idiot*?"

"That sounds rather a brutal title," opined the gentleman.

"Ah, but that *is* Russian literature in a nutshell. You see, the heroine, Nastasya Filipovna, is a quintessential study of Dostoyevskian complexity," Yosef offered. "She is an exploited woman and a victim of her own beauty. It's horrid stuff, really— orphaned as a child, she is raised by an older man who later keeps her as his mistress. She attempts to break free from this wretched life, but in typical Russian form; she finds herself powerless to determine her own path. Eventually, Nastasya succumbs to her miserable destiny and her inescapable tragic end."

Leah grimaced at Yosef's vivid explanation. "As I just expressed, Brother, I no longer care for these women who simply give up and refuse to take hold of the reins!"

Thankful that the musicians began tuning their instruments, Leah begged the gentlemen to draw their attention to center stage. After all, they had come to witness the opening of this grand theater, and needless to say, *Aida* had more than enough tragedy to satisfy even the most ardent admirers of Russian literature.

Taking advantage of the present breach in small talk, Leah planned on how she would address the issue of Mr. Blumental with her brothers—once they were secluded in the privacy of their own home. How they believed she would succumb to their trickery, was beyond her comprehension. The other question that loomed heavily upon her was *why* they thought it necessary to trick her in the first place! Leah attempted to focus on the evening's entertainment. Her brothers might have set out to find her a match, but she wasn't obligated to comply. By the time the final note was sung and the last *encore* was uttered, Leah's ire had significantly subsided and the evening continued without further vexation.

In truth, Leah had reason to be overjoyed in the success of the family outing, for as they committed themselves to the throng of people attempting to make their way to the grand lobby, a matronly lady wrapped in a black lace mantilla approached the party, begging for a moment of the señorita's time.

"Please forgive my intrusion," said the woman. "As *duenna* to señorita Alfonsina Pereyra, I have come to make your acquaintance on my mistress' behalf."

Leah, intrigued beyond measure, simply smiled and bowed her head in acknowledgement. Her party— brothers and sisters, and even Mr. Blumental—stood by Leah's side with genuine curiosity.

"It is not the custom of the Pereyra family to approach strangers, you understand, but the señorita has only recently arrived in Buenos Aires to announce her engagement and—" the woman paused and lowered her voice to whisper so that only Leah could discern her words. "You see, her clothes were ruined in the crossing. We had a most disagreeable voyage."

Leah, showing the appropriate signs of concern and empathy, interrupted the woman who was quickly becoming distraught. "How can I be of service, señora?" she asked.

"My mistress begs me to inquire—if you would be so kind as to share a confidence—who is your *modista*?"

With all the decorousness she could summon, Leah reached into her reticule and produced a card.

"Please tell señorita Pereyra that I would be honored to share my secret. I designed my gown, you see, and those of my sisters," she said gesticulating towards Sofia and Devora.

The woman accepted the card and performed a deep curtsey in her billowing antiquated skirts. Flittering off quickly to her charge's side, the abigail left the Abramovitz party in quite good spirits as they continued to make their way through the multitude.

"*Mazal tov*, Leah!" Devora said with tremendous admiration. "Mark my words, that young señorita will be the first of many customers."

"Yes, well done!" said Mr. Blumental. "I had no idea—"

"That is correct, sir. You had no idea," Leah scoffed with a tart reply. "You assumed that I sat at the piano for hours on end, or worked on my needlepoint while my brothers toiled away in the factory, but as you see, I have my own vocation to occupy my time. No doubt, you do not approve."

Yosef cleared his throat, and in an attempt to change the topic of conversation, again insisted that Ernesto visit the Abramovitz factory at his earliest convenience. The gentleman graciously accepted the offer, and with a final bow to the ladies, bade the party a good evening as he returned a nod to an acquaintance—who quite advantageously—appeared to be waving at him from across the salon.

"For heaven's sake," Yosef reproached as they continued on to their way through the throng. "Did you have to be so brutal with the man?"

"My goodness! *I* should be reprimanding the lot of *you*! How could you do this to me? Am I such a burden that you felt it necessary to match me up with the first gentleman of your acquaintance?"

Moishe frowned in utter confusion. "Explain yourself Leah, with the minimum of circumlocution, if you please."

"With pleasure! But, I would have you recall my first day in town. I had barely the opportunity to set down my belongings, when the four of you set out to marry me off to the first eligible bachelor!"

"Nonsense!" Moishe summarily dismissed her account.

"Do not attempt to refute my interpretation of the events. Do you recall what happened next?" Leah asked. "Quite propitiously, you appeared with tickets for the grand opening of Teatro Colón! And we were not situated in the so-called *Paraíso* section with the multitudes of tradesmen and lower classes, were we? No! We had the luxury of a private box, however, it was not *quite* so private. I had my first suspicion that something was awry when you allowed me to sit next to a vacant seat. You would never had done so in Odessa."

Flabbergasted, Moishe was only able to look at his wife for assistance, but Devora was rendered speechless as well.

"The dissimulation of your actions was clear," Leah continued, "when I witnessed *the look* Yosef shared with Mr. Blumental..."

"Now, see here!" Yosef interjected. "What look?"

"The two of you exchanged a *knowing look*. I don't know how to explain it exactly, but I certainly can put two and two together!"

"Leah, you have obviously been too long from society! Moishe exclaimed.

"Or she has imbibed rather too much champagne," Yosef suggested.

Sofia attempted to calm the party, as they had begun attracting attention, and it was not the sort of publicity they had intended. "Leah dearest, I can see how you have come to these erroneous conclusions; but in truth, Mr. Blumental's arrival was a complete surprise to us all. Why would we participate in such egregious behavior?"

"Because you wish to see me married!" Leah cried.

"Well— yes, of course. But not in this manner. For heaven's sake! Mr. Blumental is a businessman and a good friend of your brothers. I have long admired your brilliant capacity to comprehend the nature *and* humor of society. You possess a great deal of spirit and sagacity, dearest. It would behoove you to implement these characteristics to resolve this evening's misunderstandings."

Leah was left mute at Sofia's soliloquy. She bowed her head in deference to her sister-in-law, but silently continued to ruminate upon the events of the evening. Yosef and Moishe, hooking their arms on either side of their sister, wished to have the last word on the subject.

"Come now, Leah! Be reasonable. I wager that this contretemps will be forgotten in a day or two. Thanks to señorita Alfonsina Pereyra, word will spread like wildfire. Miss Leah Abramovitz will be the talk of the town!" Yosef avowed.

"And you will be too busy to give Mr. Blumental, *or* your purported meddlesome brothers, a second thought," Moishe added.

Befuddled, Leah stood altogether humbled before her family. "From your lips, to God's ears."

Chapter Eighteen

Leah had not been the only one to benefit from their outing to the opera for, not three days had transpired, when a gentleman of the highest ilk came to call on her brothers. Explaining that he overheard a conversation in the theater's foyer, señor Alberti admitted he had made certain enquires. He had been informed that the fashionable party, addressed by a member of Pereyra's staff, were the rusos known as The Abramovitz Brothers of El Once.

"You will forgive my colloquial terminology—I have no time or interest to debate the usage of derogatory remarks towards your people," señor Alberti stated in a matter of fact tone. "I am a business man and I do not care one iota if you are Russian, Polish, or German. You rusos know business and you Abramovitz, in particular, *know fabric*. I am here to make you a proposition, and if you truly are such good businessmen, you will accept!"

Moishe and Yosef listened intently to the man's diatribe without putting forth two words together. Their business had indeed expanded with the passing of time, and quite naturally, their name had been promoted within the community. But to have a man such as señor Antonio Alberti address them in their own establishment and to propose a partnership, was quite extraordinary. *Casa Alberti* was known to every gentleman of means throughout the province. The establishment's tailoring had long been revered for its cut and quality. Its work was comparable only to that found in London's Savile Row.

Señor Alberti found himself in dire straits. He was in need of fabric—in large quantities—ever since Argentina begun bucking the trend of importing textiles from England.

"This country is growing, but the industry is not keeping up with demand," Alberti said as he puffed on a pungent cigar. "If the government would get out of our way, we could make millions, but instead I have to battle against import restrictions that impede my production. You fellows here," he said with another puff of smoke climbing up to Leah's workstation, "you have the right of it. With only five or six textile manufacturers in all of Argentina, you will rise to the top in no time. You have stiff competition in Brazil, you know, but if I can't get fabrics from England, I'm certainly not going to do business with Brazil. I'll buy it from you and in copious amounts!"

Leah, having overheard the entire exchange from the staircase, was clapping her hands and sending up a prayer of gratitude for her brothers' good fortune. When the front door opened and closed, she assumed that the gentleman had departed and proceeded to sprint down the stairs to congratulate Yosef and

Moishe. Leaping off a step and skipping the final treads, she landed quite soundly and found herself in the arms of *Mr. Blumental.*

"Miss Abramovitz! Are you quite alright?"

Adjusting her skirt and patting back a few loose curls, Leah desperately attempted to regain her composure. She could hear her Mamá's chastising censure, "A modicum of restraint, my dear."

With a quick look over her shoulder, Leah spied into Moishe's office. The door was ajar, which explained how she could eavesdrop. The men appeared to be completely engrossed in their conversation, and Leah realized that she would have to face *him* on her own. Heavens! After her outrageous behavior the other evening, Leah was at a loss on how to proceed, but she had to say *something*.

"How clumsy of me, Mr. Blumental," she murmured. "I do apologize. I—ah...what brings you to our shop?"

Ernesto had followed her gaze, and noted her brothers were ensconced with a renowned business magnate, infamous for his indecorous behavior, as well as his industry acumen. Sensing Leah's unease, he was hesitant to proceed with his social call, but that censure had come too late.

"Good afternoon, Miss Abramovitz," he stated in an awkward attempt to start afresh. "I had an appointment on this very street, and if you recall, your brothers had invited me to pay a visit."

There was no need to remind her of the events at the theater. Leah remembered the evening with great clarity.

"Yes, of course, but my brothers are occupied at present. Perhaps you would care to return on another occasion?" She almost held her breath waiting for his concurrence.

"Certainly, if you think it best." He began advancing towards the door, but stayed his retreat. Turning about, rather abruptly, he handed Leah a package carefully wrapped in brown paper. "Miss Abramovitz, I hope you do not think it too presumptuous..."

"What's this? I cannot accept a gift."

"Please—it is a simple token. I remembered your comment regarding Russian tragedies and such. I thought you might enjoy this British authoress. My sister finds Miss Austen's heroines to be quite daring and highly intelligent."

Humbled by his thoughtfulness, Leah carefully opened the package and found an aged book entitled, *Sense and Sensibility*.

"It is not exactly about today's new woman, as you had mentioned," he acknowledged. "I believe it was published nearly a hundred years ago, but the author's popularity is growing exponentially—at least, according to my sister, who knows of these things."

Leah found herself hard-pressed to turn the visitor away. She had already humiliated herself the other night at the theater. She daren't bring any further shame upon the family by being rude to their friend once again.

"Thank you, Mr. Blumental. Although it was completely unnecessary, I appreciate the thought," she said with a gracious smile. "I haven't a clue how long my brothers will remain closeted with their client, but if you would care to join me for tea, perhaps you still might have an opportunity to meet with Moishe and Yosef this afternoon."

Leah gestured to the courtyard where a small table and two chairs had been positioned. "Please be seated, Mr. Blumental. I will only be but a moment." As she turned towards the kitchen in the backroom, Leah suddenly remembered that one of the chairs had a faulty leg.

"I beg your pardon," she called out, "but would you mind assisting me? There is an extra chair over by the staircase. Would you bring it out, while I attend to the tray?"

Ernesto followed her instruction and located the aforementioned chair with ease. He noted the fine construction and design, and wondered why it hadn't placed in the front room. Upon returning with a tray laden with a porcelain service, Leah offered a brief explanation without having been pressed.

"Yosef was supposed to have fixed this old pine chair last week, but they have been terribly busy of late. We have this spare—it's actually the last one of a set of four. It has some sentimental value, you see, I can't bear to forsake it."

Ernesto lifted a brow and watched as Leah carefully served the tea. He made no further comment as she seemed reluctant to discuss the furnishings, and decided to return to the subject of Yosef.

"I am happy to hear that your brothers have been occupied. Business is booming, then?"

Leah nodded slightly and smiled. "Things are progressing, to be sure, but there is still much to be done before obtaining the level of success we enjoyed in Odessa."

Thinking to set her at ease, he asked Leah to tell him more about their business in the old country. Although he had heard most of the tale from Moishe and Yosef, it seemed a subject that the Abramovitz family enjoyed recounting.

Leah explained the history of the works and extoled upon the virtuous manner in which her brothers conducted business. They ran the factory with only the most honorable of intentions; their father's memory was at stake, so they placed integrity and commitment to the customer, as well as to the employee as their top priority.

"When my father was alive, and the government allowed it, he traveled extensively across Europe learning the tools of the trade and how others made their fortunes. Moishe and my other siblings were not able to indulge in traveling as much as they would have liked, but they learned much through reading and from their colleagues living abroad. They heard of these so-called sweatshops in London and New York," she said with disgust, "and knew them to be dangerous outfits—especially for women and children. Their employees were poorly paid and mistreated. We paid a decent wage. Our employees didn't live in squalor, and because they were well fed and well looked after, they produced a better product for our customers."

"Your brothers employed women and children?"

"The children had to be at least 16 years of age— Moishe was adamant about that point. As far as employing women, you must know that there are limited options available for the working class.

Needlework is one of the few occupations considered acceptable, and so, our family took the matter one step further by training the women to work on the looms."

"Ah—yes. My sister mentioned this point when reading Austen," he acknowledged. "Something about the need for women to find suitable work—other than being a governess or..."

"Yes. Precisely so, Mr. Blumental," she replied quickly, sparing either of them the need to speak of other unseemly occupations. "Some of our workers were highly skilled and had experience with the intricacies of lace and bead work. Whenever possible, Moishe would help secure positions for them in a reputable house of couture. A seamstress of this caliber is infinitely more respectable than a worker at a loom—of course, society has always held *tailors* in higher esteem," Leah said with some disdain. "This is how it's always been. I find it rather appalling to note how little has changed since Miss Austen's time."

"I am familiar with this tendency. In London, the dandy trend has quite stimulated the profession. Savile Row has never been quite as busy."

Leah was not pleased to hear Mr. Blumental's concurrence with her remarks, for that only punctuated her displeasure at the disparity of the matter. "Be it a seamstress, or a tailor, both deserve their proper accolades. In any event, I have my own thoughts regarding the woman of today."

"Are you a Suffragette, then?"

Leah shrugged her shoulders. "Are you familiar with the term *Gibson Girl*? Charles Gibson's concept is extraordinary. This new woman doesn't see herself as *only* someone's wife, nor does she want to be a servant, or a factory employee...or something worse," Leah said, feeling herself blush. "I, for one, am excited to see how far she can go."

"I am intrigued, Miss Abramovitz. You certainly have put some thought into this. What do your brothers think of your ideas?"

"Naturally, they think me naive and somewhat audacious. But I will not allow their opinions be an impediment! My vision has more to do with empowerment. Of course, I mean the empowerment of women, in general, not just for myself. The idea of being self-reliant—of knowing that, at the end of the day, one can be satisfied with what one has accomplished. I wouldn't wish to waste away the hours that God has allotted me on my life's journey. I wasn't meant to sit idly by. I have plans, Mr. Blumental, and I mean to put them into action!"

Ernesto sat back with his cup and saucer and listened as the lovely young lady chatted on. Her cheeks had turned a delightful shade of pink and her emerald eyes glowed with fervor. It appeared she had forgotten that he was even there, so lost was she in her enthusiasm. He nodded attentively as she explained that the future of fashion lay in a versatile suit.

"...and the summer months in Buenos Aires are unbearably humid! We cannot wear the same heavy material, the same brocades, and heavy velvets of seasons past. I envision gauzy white fabrics for summer blouses and dresses. I would have them embroidered with white silk thread and lace—and even have the lace cut away to reveal a little bit of the neck and the arm. I know it is quite provocative, but for heaven's sake, how is a woman to work if her clothes are weighing her down?"

"And have you thought of the cost, Miss Abramovitz?" Ernesto asked, his own enthusiasm increasing as he listened to her speak.

"Well, yes—of course," she replied, his interruption causing her to moderate her tone. "Couture items, such as these, would be extremely expensive, but they could be bought ready-made quite reasonably. I would change out the fabric to cotton and linen. The garments would be both affordable and practical for a working woman."

Leah picked up her tepid tea, and returned to a seated position more in keeping with her mother's instruction. Her back rod straight, shoulders back, and chin slightly inclined, Leah now attempted to hold her tongue. To be sure, she had been far too outspoken. The poor man was probably shocked!

"I have known your brothers to be most helpful," Ernesto admitted, "but our conversation this afternoon has been positively illuminating. I realize now that I still have much to learn."

With the tea consumed, and the sweets left untouched, it became quite clear that the conversation had come to a close. Moishe and Yosef had yet to conclude their meeting, and Leah feared that they would continue on well into the evening. Feeling quite self-conscious, she lightly dabbed the corner of her lips with a delicate linen napkin, unknowingly drawing Ernesto's attention to that certain attractive spot.

He sputtered and set down his own napkin alongside the cup and saucer. The *tête-à-tête* suddenly seemed inappropriate and had gone on for far too long. Ernesto had learned his lesson well on the first night of their acquaintance, and he was not inclined to experience her derision again.

"Thank you for tea, Miss Abramovitz," he said, surprisingly himself, as well as his hostess, with his curt announcement. "Please convey my regards to your family."

Bowing elegantly, he took his leave without another word. Leah remained seated and watched his hasty escape. Repeating the conversation in her mind, she was mortified in the manner of her conduct. She behaved abominably on their first meeting, and then so soon after making his acquaintance, she relentlessly plied the man with her thoughts and schemes. He barely managed to get in a word edgewise! Obviously, Mr. Blumental couldn't wait to make his escape.

Chapter Nineteen

May 1909 ~ Buenos Aires

While the vast majority of the city was enmeshed with preparations for the awaited Centennial celebrations still a year away, there were many others who only busied themselves with matters of politics and upheaval. With immigration numbers continuing to rise, the clash of cultures and philosophies made a volatile mix. The Abramovitz family, either in Buenos Aires or in the surrounding provinces, stayed out of the fray, for their immigrant experience was not on par with the less fortunate.

The climate among the poor and uneducated masses was ripe with belligerence, and the city watched in shock as anarchists waged campaigns against their employers and anti-labor legislation. The situation had come to a fevered pitch as the brutality of the militants was matched equally by the authorities. Each group incited the other to greater atrocities, until they clashed on one fateful day in May.

El Once was awash with the news being heralded across the city. There had been a demonstration starting in Plaza Lorea, and it was said that the rabble-rousers were not the sort of society usually found in that part of town. Frightened residents whispered among themselves as protesters dressed in berets, neckerchiefs, and patched trousers paraded across the affluent park chanting, "Death to the bourgeois!"

Reports were being passed around that a recent immigrant of the Ukraine, nineteen year-old Simón Radowitzky led the demonstration, organizing the militants to stock pile weaponry, to destroy private property and to harm innocents going about their daily lives. The Chief of Police, Ramon Falcon, had heard of their plan to bomb the tramways, but he brought their terrorist acts to a standstill. His might was felt when the police finally suppressed the rioters, leaving Buenos Aires to face eight lamentable souls dead and forty more wounded.

The Abramovitz family had remained secluded in the shop for the better part of the day, although, Moishe had decided against bringing down the metal roller blinds to secure their livelihood. It seemed pointless. The streets of El Once appeared rather ghostly, with only the occasional neighbor popping in to share another piece of news. Yosef kept busy supervising the flow of work in the back rooms. Their dedicated employees remained at their stations—the machinery provided a continual humming sound that calmed the family's nerves.

Attempting to portray a composed demeanor, Moishe remained at his desk, but was unable to concentrate on the outstanding invoices or neglected purchase contracts. He was startled out of his stupor when the front door suddenly flew ajar. Thinking he would have to protect his family and property, it was with much relief that Moishe let out a shout upon recognizing the intruder.

"Blumental! What on earth are you doing here?"

With a fierce slam of the door, Ernesto strode to his friend's side and deposited the afternoon's paper upon the desk with a great whack. "Why haven't you locked down the shop?" he demanded. "Where is everyone?"

"Calm yourself, my friend. Yosef is in the back room and the women are upstairs," replied Moishe. "What are you doing out and about? We heard horrific news of riots and demonstrations."

"Yes, yes—that's why I had to stop by. I was in the neighborhood and I was concerned. I...ah, I also have another book for Miss Abramovitz' collection."

"*You were in the neighborhood?* And you were concerned—for us? But *you* are the one running up and down the streets. We are safe and sound, as you see. What's this about a book for Leah?"

Ernesto grimaced. "You make it sound foolish, but I had an appointment, and was not aware of the mayhem until I completed my meeting. Once I was mindful of the situation, I felt it only proper to ascertain the wellbeing of my friends, and since I had the book already on my possession—"

"You scared me near to death when you came barreling through the door," Moishe laughed. "I suppose you are right. I should have closed down the shop and escorted the women to our flat; but once we arrived and got to work, it seemed unnecessary. With nothing to do but wait for more news, we would have been at each other's throats at home."

"What is all the commotion down there?" Leah called out.

Moishe summoned the family, as he meandered to the kitchen to set the kettle on and find the plate of potato *knishes* Devora had made the night before.

"Well, well. Who do we have here?" Yosef said, smacking his friend soundly on his back. "What brings you to our shop today?"

Moishe hollered over his shoulder, "He wanted to check on us and he has a gift for Leah."

Coming down the stairs in her usual spirited manner, Leah heard her name mentioned just as her eyes met with Mr. Blumental. Sofia and Devora followed behind in a more demure fashion, but were, indeed, as eager as Leah to have a pleasant interruption to the tense afternoon.

"Good afternoon, ladies." Standing at attention, as if a military man, Ernesto held his arms behind his back and bowed.

"He's brought you something, Leah," Moishe announced with a grin.

"I brought *you* the afternoon paper, as well," Ernesto said, glaring at his friend. "No need to make such a commotion."

"Don't mind him, Mr. Blumental," Leah responded with a mischievous gleam in her eye. "We are all a bit jumpy today."

Realizing he still held his bowler hat in his hand, Ernesto set it down, along with an unnecessary umbrella. Free of the extraneous accouterments, he presented Leah with a brown paper package tied up with a thin string.

"This one is called *Pride and Prejudice*, he related, slightly discomfited as the family watched on. "My sister and I find that the characters, and storyline, are very well executed. She assures me that you will enjoy Miss Austen's work. I certainly hope so."

Leah accepted the gift with sincere gratitude. She had yet to understand the workings of the man. One moment he was everything amiable, and the next, he was the most infuriating man of her acquaintance.

As several seconds passed in uncomfortable silence, Ernesto blurted out the first thought that came to mind. "I was reading an article in *La Nación* today. It's most scintillating, really. Why don't you read it aloud, Moishe, and entertain us all."

Thinking it would occupy their harried minds with something light and engaging, Moishe gladly acquiesced. Clearing his throat and stretching out the paper so that it was *just so*, he began:

From: The Argentine Minister

To: The Acting Secretary of State

Sir: A law of the Argentine Congress has ordained that, through the medium of the executive department, the Governments of America and Europe, which have representatives accredited to the Republic, be invited to participate in the celebration in 1910 of the first centennial of its national independence. In accordance with said ordinance, I have been charged with the exalted and pleasant duty of inviting the United States Government to take part in said commemorations, trusting that the nation which, ahead of every other nation, hastened to recognize Argentine sovereignty, will honor, by its representation, an event so intimately connected with its own history. In the hope that I shall have the good fortune to transmit to my Government acceptance by the United States Government of the invitation, I have the honor of tendering to your Excellency the compliance with the instruction referred to. I avail etc., Epifanio Portela

"Why, it is most exciting!" exclaimed Devora amidst a round of applause.

"Wait," exclaimed Moishe, "the newspaper has printed an acceptance from the Americans!"

From: The Acting Secretary of State

To: The Argentine Minister

Sir: I have the honor to acknowledge the receipt of your note of the 15th in which, by direction of your Government and in pursuance of the provisions of a law of the Argentine Congress, you extend to the United States an invitation to take part in the celebration of the first centennial of the independence of the Argentine Republic. In reply, it affords me pleasure to say that the Government of the United States, which was the first to recognize the Argentine Republic as a sovereign State, and which has observed with particular satisfaction the steady growth of its power and prosperity, is glad to accept this courteously extended invitation. Alvey A Adee

"Now read the response from the president himself," Ernesto pressed on.

Moishe nodded, and with great theatrics, cleared his throat before continuing.

From: The White House—Washington, D.C.

To: The President of the Argentine Republic

In the name of the Government and people of the United States, and in my own, I send cordial felicitations on this centennial anniversary of the birth of your great nation. The United States of America has observed with sympathetic interest the marvelous development of the Argentine Republic, not only in material things, but in the highest aims of nations, and it is our hearty wish that this sister Republic of the south may ever flourish and prosper. I also offer to Your Excellency personally the assurance of my own high regard and good wishes.

WM. H Taft

"No doubt, this will be the event of the year!" said Leah.

"It will be the event of the decade," replied Yosef, in his usual informative manner. "The world-wide exhibition will host pavilions from Paraguay and the European nations of Spain, Italy, Germany, England, Switzerland, and the Austro-Hungarian Empire."

"American and British ships will be invited to participate in the festivities and will be docked in the neighboring city of Bahia Blanca," Ernesto added. "It fills one with pride—quite exhilarating, that."

"This is all very interesting, Ernesto, but have you forgotten *your mission*?" Moishe implored, while setting down the periodical and snacking on a savory knish.

"My mission?"

"The purpose of your residency in Argentina—what news of *your business*, man? Have you found a property? Have you even been looking?"

"Yes, yes. Of course! I visited the neighborhood of Retiro with my agent recently, but I became side tracked by the construction of the railway stations. Did you know the building is the design genius of several British architects? They imported the steel structure directly from Liverpool—I tell you, this will be considered the finest example of structural engineering in all of South America! I will go even further; architecturally, it will be one of the finest buildings in the world."

"My friend, you must concentrate on the business at hand. What will you tell your father when he writes and asks for an update?"

"You are quite the task master, Moishe, but of course, you are right. I did have the opportunity to familiarize myself with the *barrio*. As far as fashionable districts go, Retiro would do quite nicely— probably bested only by neighboring Recoleta. Of course, *Gath y Chaves* is situated most propitiously in the downtown area. I will have to keep any eye on that company in particular. Next to Harrods, they will prove to be my strongest competitors."

"Have you considered any other locations?" asked Leah, as the women brought out a tea tray. "El Once, perhaps?"

"No, forgive me, Miss Abramovitz, but I do not believe this locality would suit—"

Leah harrumphed and did not allow the man to continue. "Far be from me to presume to understand..."

"Leah, dear—" Devora interposed, as she handed her sister-in-law a cup of tea.

The gentleman left further discussions of business ventures to the wayside, as the party continued on with delicate topics of the weather and the upcoming winter holidays. Devora mentioned *Shavuot* would be late this year, and of course, before they knew it, it would *Rosh Hashanah*. The women shared a laugh acknowledging that once they had commemorated the receiving of the Ten Commandments at Mount Sinai, the High Holy Days would indeed be upon them in short order.

In truth, Leah had noted, that with all their activity, keeping track of holy calendar events was becoming more and more challenging. Their lives had become complex, and their integration into Argentine society had modified their religious observation. Happily, this year's celebration of *Rosh Hashanah* would bring a long-awaited visitor, for along with Duvid's weekly update, Leah had received word from her mother. If everything worked out as planned, her dearest mamá would be traveling to Buenos Aires by mid-August, with plenty of time to bake the *challah*, *lekach*, and all matter of sweet treats to welcome in the Jewish new year.

And indeed, Devora had been correct. The crisp, autumn air quickly blended into the cool, gloom of winter—the season made brighter only by her mamá's anticipated arrival. Their days were joyfully full of activities then. The women went from baking and preparing holiday treats to visiting the city's many theaters and museums. They toured the famed shops of Calle Florida, cafés, and even the green-domed Palacio del Congreso—the mammoth structure which housed Argentina's national Congress.

On one unusually clear and sunny afternoon, the women strolled through the famed rose gardens of Palermo, and after tea, were joined by the men for an exhilarating adventure at the *hipódromo*. While the men focused on their favorite horses, Leah peeked through a pair of silver plated binoculars and indulged in her own spectator sport. Attending the races was to hobnob with sport heroes and society's elite. The women in the crowd were dressed to the nines for the evening's high profile event. As she scanned the crowd with a trained eye, Leah gasped as her gaze settled upon *Ernesto Blumental*.

Seated with a group of elegantly dressed men, Leah observed his actions from a safe and comfortable distance. He was certainly quite animated and enjoying his conversation. She wondered what he found so amusing—he was usually so very serious whenever she was about. As she had remained nearly frozen in her current state of astonishment, Leah had awoken her mother's curiosity.

"What has caught your attention, my dear?"

Leah muttered an oath and allowed the field glasses to drop to her side. Unable to make out her sister-in-law's mumblings, and inquisitive to the core, Sofia begged the binoculars for herself. Scanning the area which had been so mesmerizing, it only took a moment before Sofia let out a most unladylike snort.

"Why, it's Mr. Blumental!"

"The name sounds vaguely familiar." Malka smiled and looked upon her children with interest. "Might this be the gentleman you mentioned, Yosef? The one who came to your aid?"

"You must mean the gentleman that *Yosef and Moishe* have aided, Mamá. Ernesto Blumental is forever coming to the shop and continually interrupting our work with his questions and plans."

"Leah—*really*!"

"I don't seem to understand," said Malka, turning to her son. "Isn't he the gentleman who introduced you to señor Alberti?"

Leah snorted in response.

Yosef laughed at the women. "You two are sounding more and more like street urchins with all that screeching and grunting."

"What is this about Mr. Blumental and the Alberti account?" Leah demanded.

"I don't know what has gotten into you lately, but, to answer your question, Blumental *was* the reason we secured the contract—and a very lucrative one it is. He wanted the matter to be kept under wraps, but if you must know, Ernesto spoke to Alberti that night at Teatro Colon. I'm sure you recall the grand opening."

"Yes, of course I recall the event, but I don't understand the connection. Why would he have spoken to señor Alberti on our behalf?"

"Why wouldn't he? Ernesto knew that our business desperately needed some sort of catalyst to make our name known among the *bon ton*. Having had just returned from a visit home, Ernesto learned of the strained dealings Alberti was having with his English exporters, and he decided to put our two parties together."

"There was no need to involve himself in our affairs."

"No—you are right Leah. There was *no need*, and yet, his intervention proved to be a God-send."

Malka peered at her daughter's face, taking notice of her flushed appearance, and glistening eyes. "It is rather providential that we were able to find Mr. Blumental among this throng of people. Is it not? I would like to meet the gentleman and personally thank him for assisting my family."

"Mamá, he appears to be otherwise occupied," Leah said hurriedly. "Perhaps another time..."

The horses, and their zealous riders, deemed it necessary to interrupt the family's discussion as they completed the last lap of the race with great fanfare. With the ensuing excitement overshadowing their present conversation, Leah was glad to escape the necessity of introductions and the social niceties that were sure to follow. It gave her the opportunity to revisit Yosef's assertion—they were *beholden* to Ernesto's intervention. She would need time to contemplate the man's actions *and* his stipulation that the matter be kept confidential. But Leah would find that her days were filled with activities and preparations for the holidays. There would be little time for pondering the attributes of a certain English gentleman.

On *erev Rosh Hashanah*, they made their way, along with hundreds of other Jewish families to Lavalle Square where the great Templo Libertad was situated. Leah and her siblings were shocked when their mamá requested to have the carriage brought about—instead of attempting to walk to services, as tradition dictated. In practical terms, the distance *was*

rather daunting, and the family reluctantly admitted that their level of observance had taken quite a turn. Not unlike other Jewish immigrants, as their assimilation into Argentine society deepened, their traditions and rituals began evolving into a more accommodating practice. And while residents of the city had been attending the grand Israelite Congregation of Buenos Aires for over a decade, Leah was further stunned when her mother revealed that she much preferred the *heymish*, unpretentious style of the Novy Buk synagogue in Basavilbaso. It was quite an unusual start to the new year's commemoration.

When services concluded, the Abramovitz women made their way down the crowded staircase. This led them from the segregated women's section to the men's sanctuary on the main floor. Devora and Sofia, hoping to find their husbands in short order, walked on ahead. When two exuberant young girls raced away from their mother's grasp, their mischievous behavior nearly caused Malka to lose her footing. Leah, reaching out to stay her mother's fall, missed the final step herself and tumbled onto the marbled floor. In an instant, she felt a hand at her elbow and an arm about her waist. Turning to thank her rescuer, and to reassure her mamá that she was unharmed, Leah came face to face with *Ernesto Blumental*.

"Where did you come from?"

"Are you quite alright?"

They questioned in unison.

"From the sanctuary."

"Yes, I'm fine."

Again, they spoke as one.

Malka hid a smile behind a gloved hand. "Leah, my dear, if you are quite sure you are not injured, might you introduce me to the gentleman?"

"Yes, of course." Mortified, and attempting not to grind her teeth in pain, Leah turned to face *him*. "Mr. Ernesto Blumental, may I present Malka Abramovitz, my mother."

Pleasantries were exchanged very prettily, while Leah managed to shift her weight to her other foot. Stubbornly, she refused to admit that her ankle was throbbing, but as they began moving away from the stairwell, Leah nearly fell once more.

"Miss Abramovitz! You *are* hurt."

"I assure you, it is nothing."

"Nonsense. Take my arm and allow me to escort you to your carriage."

Seeing her mother's countenance fraught with concern, Leah had no other recourse but to accept. Leaning on his arm, she limped towards the main lobby that led outdoors, noting how the more pious women looked on in astonishment. An unmarried, lady holding onto an unattached gentleman's arm, *without benefit of an understanding*, was unheard of—unless, of course, the lady was an elderly spinster or infirmed. Grimacing at the notion of being perceived in such a manner by Ernesto Blumental, Leah was even further perplexed by her own thoughts. When did she begin worrying about *his* good opinion?

"I will find your brothers and inform them of the mishap," he said, executing a quick bow before darting away.

"He seems quite a nice, young man."

"Oh Mamá! Please don't start..."

"I am not starting anything of the sort. After all, it was not *I* that put these events into motion..."

The men came bursting into the carriage, followed quickly by their wives. Their attention turned to Leah's discoloring, and increasingly inflamed, ankle; but not before Sofia further embarrassed the patient with a small package—courtesy of a concerned gentleman.

"He sends the book with his sister's compliments and his best wishes for a complete *refuah shleima.*" Giggling, Sofia unwrapped the book while her husband inspected Leah's ankle. "This one is entitled, *Persuasion.*"

"I wonder if you might be *persuaded* to stop that chortling, Sofia, and climb aboard. I wish to go home." Leah reclined against the plush cushioned seat, while covertly eyeing the latest addition to her Austen collection. *What could he mean by these gifts?*

With not another comment regarding Mr. Blumental's timely appearance *or* his offering, Malka settled back and happily observed her children attend their youngest sibling. *All would be well*, she thought, and let out a weary sigh. Indeed, it seemed that the hustle and bustle of the city had taken its toll on Malka, and she was ready to return home.

The grand dame of Odessa had become blissfully provincial; but then again, she had come from humble beginnings and her life, it appeared, had come full circle. She was pleased with her children's progress in Buenos Aires, and was certain that things were well in hand. Encouraged by such *naches*, in just over ten days' time, it was a relieved Malka who boarded the northbound train on a cold and wintery afternoon.

Chapter Twenty

October 1909 ~ Buenos Aires

*E*ven with the advent of her mother's capricious holiday, Leah had found time to complete Miss Austen's book, and wondered if Mr. Blumental would bring around another to discuss. Not that they truly *discussed* the books, for he always seemed too eager to capitulate, and she, too eager to dispute. There was something about the man that set her teeth on edge; nonetheless, Leah had determined to put aside her woolgathering. With so much work to do establishing a good name about town, she could not spare more time contemplating Mr. Blumental *or* Miss Austen's fine work.

The city was in constant motion now. Just last month, the British residents of Buenos Aires offered a gift to commemorate the upcoming Centennial and held a grand reception to honor Sir Ambrose Macdonald Poynter of the Royal Institute of British Architects. Naturally, the announcement had been well received in the Abramovitz household for, as Leah had hoped, each mew event necessitated a new ensemble for the ladies of high society. Ernesto Blumental reacted to the announcement with great enthusiasm, as well, but for entirely dissimilar reasons.

With each visit paid to the Abramovitz shop, Ernesto extoled the vision of Sir Poynter, the architectural design of his fellow countrymen Hopkins and Gardom, and even the fact that his compatriots were importing the raw materials from England. When Leah took exception to this unnecessary extravagance, he proudly refuted her opinion. The stone from Dorset was incomparable for its color and texture, he declared, and the bricks—made from the red clay of Gloucestershire—were exceptional.

"These authentic materials are necessary, Ernesto said pointedly, "to recreate the thistle of Scotland, the English rose, the Welsh dragon and the Irish shamrock."

Moishe glanced at his sister as she silently mimicked his friend's pedantic monologue. He knew Leah would not be able to hold her tongue much longer. "Enough!" Moishe laughed, slapping his friend soundly on the back. "There's work to be done! Go home, Englishman."

"Work to be done, indeed!" Leah huffed as they witnessed the man's flustered departure.

In truth, there was no time for such nonsense, for Yosef and Moishe would not be at peace until they regained a status comparable to what their father had created so long ago. Together with Leah, they kept their shoulders to the grind stone and their eyes on the goal. Unfortunately, the outside world was spinning out of control and each day brought diverse and disturbing news.

"Another *guerrilla* attack!" Yosef said, tossing the periodical into the trash bin. "This time, they bombed the Spanish consulate in Rosario."

Sofia gasped. "Do the officials know who is to blame?"

"Not yet, but it's the work of an anarchist, to be sure."

"Why do they attack public places, where innocent people conduct business and simply are going about their lives?"

"These radicals are being manipulated by powerful organizations," Yosef answered bitterly. "This so-called, patriotic student's group, for example, cries about injustice and inequality, but the Church feeds the fire with anti-Semitic rhetoric and malicious gestures against capitalists."

"Do you think there will be trouble at the Tradesman Ball?" Leah interjected. "We've so been looking forward to attending the opening of the Majestic Hotel this summer."

"Who's to say? That is the whole point behind these cowardly attacks. They want to terrorize the public and shut down the country. I, for one, refuse to live my life in fear. We will attend the ball as planned, and I'm sure that the Abramovitz women will outshine the haute society of Buenos Aires."

Leah laughed, encouraged by her brother's brave stance. "We don't wish to outshine the ladies of the *ton,* Brother dear—we wish to inspire them and entice their patronage!"

When in November, another terrifying act occurred in the city, the family was caught again ill-prepared. The May demonstrations had not been forgotten by the belligerent sects of the population. To exact revenge for the brutal way in which the chief of police had suppressed the rioters, Simón Radowitzky hurled a bomb into a carriage bearing Falcón and his personal secretary. Both men were killed and Buenos Aires was again thrown in an uproar of chaos and mayhem.

Unaware of the situation unfolding, Leah had decided to take her tea and settle down by the window for a bit of a respite, when the front door of the shop flew open.

"Is everyone alright?" Ernesto called out.

"Mr. Blumental!" she exclaimed, spilling the hot liquid upon the latest fashion magazine. "Whatever is the matter? We are all well. Thank you for your kind concern."

"Do not mention it, Miss Abramovitz. I was in the neighborhood, paying a call to Tito Kaplan, when I was advised that the police were out in full force."

Leah shook her head and groaned. "Not again?"

"Unfortunately, yes, there has been trouble. Where are you brothers? I understood they were headed downtown," he said, scanning the shop and noting calm activity.

"What is it, Leah?" Yosef called, as he darted from the back of the warehouse. "Blumental! What brings you around?"

With her brother's convenient entrance, Leah attempted to make her excuses and quit the room; however, she was detained by the gentleman holding a brown paper package.

"Do stay a moment, won't you, Miss Abramovitz?"

Yosef cackled. "Don't tell me you have brought her another book, old man?"

"With my sister's compliments, however, be warned. She writes that *Emma* was her least favorite."

"I will be sure to enjoy the novel, and will write her at once to offer my thanks. Heaven knows, I will be grateful for the distraction. What with such unsettling news, I find Jane Austen's wit and philosophy to be a breath of fresh air."

"I am certain my sister shall be pleased, indeed."

Moishe, entering from the back room, looked upon the party and was reassured that all was well. "I thought I heard shouting."

"My apologies. I entered in haste, but was quickly assured that everyone was present and accounted for." Ernesto said sheepishly. "Were you able to make your delivery? Did you speak with manager at Gath y Chaves? He seemed quite interested—"

Moishe waggled his eyebrows and nodded with satisfaction. "Yes. It was a productive outing."

"Why don't we sit down to tea?" Yosef suggested. "I'm famished already."

Leah agreed and offered to prepare a light repast. They kept the small kitchen stocked with tea and maté. The corner *panadería* provided them with freshly baked breads, cakes, and pastries. When, a few minutes later, they were situated comfortably around the table, Leah thought to offer an easy subject of conversation, hoping to keep Yosef from the tedious topic of politics and the events of the day.

"I find Elizabeth Bennet's qualities to be quite delightful. How does *Emma* fare in comparison, Mr. Blumental?"

"I would not wish to give away all of the author's secrets and delights, Miss Abramovitz. You may wish to discover all of these things on your own, when you have had the opportunity to read the novel."

Leah would not be put off by this circumvention and attempted another course of questioning. "And what did you think of *Persuasion*?"

He smiled at this. "In truth, we found it quite moving."

"Don't tell me *you* are familiar with Miss Austen's literary canon?" Yosef teased.

"My brother is of the mind that gentlemen have more refined interests, such as the classics and political philosophies, and cannot be bothered to read anything as low as a novel."

"Then he will be surprised to note that, in fact, I have read all of Miss Austen's work." Ernesto grinned as he stirred his tea. "I enjoy any opportunity to engage in easy banter with my sister."

"Do you realize that you never speak of her except when you bring about these books? Is she something of a bluestocking?" Yosef asked, continuing to torment his friend.

Ernesto set down his cup and saucer. His hesitation struck an uncomfortable pause. "Judy is almost a full decade my junior. Unfortunately, she has been assigned to a wheelchair these past five years."

"I do apologize, old man—"

"No, don't…it is my fault. I should have explained about Judith long ago. It is a difficult subject to broach, as you can imagine. It is difficult *for me* at any rate. She is rather remarkable."

"What happened, Mr. Blumental, if you don't mind me asking?" Leah whispered.

"It was a riding accident. Judy was quite a horsewoman. She lived for all manner of outdoor activity, much to Mama's displeasure. For her seventeenth birthday, Judy rejected a grand party, or any sort of celebration for that matter. She simply requested a new saddle and a full day of riding."

Dragging a trembling hand through his hair, Ernesto released a heavy sigh before continuing. "It was that *damned* saddle! She was used to riding aside, of course, but those infernal objects are not designed for a woman's safety. Heaven forbid her modesty come into question!" he said with bitter sarcasm.

"You don't have to say anymore, my friend. We should never have asked."

"No, it is quite alright. I probably should speak of her more often, rather than hide the story away—as if Judy had done something shameful. The long and the short of it is that Judith was—*is*—a headstrong girl. She sped off before anyone of us had a chance to mount, and well, she had ample time to race ahead. We, my brother and I, were still at quite a distance when we saw that she meant to take a risky jump. Ah—but I presume too much. You *are* acquainted with equestrianism?"

Leah allowed her brother to reply in the affirmative. They, of course, had kept a small stable on the estate; but it wasn't until they lived in Entre Rios, that Leah did take to riding. Those memories were wrought with emotions, and she preferred not to recall them at this time—certainly not in the middle of Mr. Blumental's own declamation.

"Yes. Well, you are aware then, that a man's saddle is designed to throw the rider free from his mount in case of a fall. A blasted side saddle, however, does not follow suit," Ernesto spewed. "Judy hadn't sufficient flexibility or control; so when her mount failed to complete the jump, she was not able to manoeuvre the horse. She was trapped underneath the beast!" Ernesto, sinking into a chair, brought his head into his hands. "My sister broke her back in the fall. She will be an invalid for the rest of her life."

Distraught by his unexpected display of emotion, Leah contemplated the man she had judged so harshly. Anxious to ease the lingering discomfort, she sought to lead their conversation towards a lighter subject, but found that it was not quite so simple. How does one delicately back away from a topic so full of anguish?

"You mentioned that Miss Blumental shows an eagerness to succeed. You must be very proud of her vivacity and cheerful disposition."

"Yes indeed. She is quite an example to us all. She finds many ways to occupy her time. She volunteers to help the young children of the village with their schooling; she loves to follow Cook around in the kitchen and enthusiastically writes down all of the family's favorite recipes; and *she loves to read*. Jane Austen happens to be her latest favorite. As Judy is quite enthralled by these books, I make it a point to read the material and understand it well enough to carry on a transcontinental conversation."

"How delightful," Leah exclaimed—happy that he seemed to be at ease once more. "I would be very pleased to meet your sister one day, Mr. Blumental. She is a young woman that speaks to my own heart."

"I know that she would be delighted to make your acquaintance."

"I must admit that I find myself relating to Elizabeth Bennet far more than another other of Miss Austen's characters. You seem to be an expert on the subject," Leah teased amiably, attempting to continue with the calming subject. "Tell me, Mr. Blumental, why is *Persuasion* your sister's favorite?"

Ernesto hesitated a moment wishing to formulate an intelligent response. "Miss Anne Elliot possesses a certain indelible strength—quite possibly, it is the main reason she resonates with my dear sister. She manages to remain true to her values, despite everything that goes on about her. I quite agree with Judy on this point; the heroine portrayed in *Persuasion* seems to be a forerunner to today's modern woman."

"A *modern-day* woman you say? In a Regency novel?" Leah challenged. "I hardly think so. Perhaps, you would care to elaborate...?"

"I believe you have misunderstood my meaning, Miss Abramovitz. I meant no disrespect to any of the beloved, but fictitious ladies."

Leah shrugged. "Fictitious or not, it is of little matter to me. I believe Miss Austen's style could be compared, in some small way, to that of the *Peredvizhniki*, for these artists strive to mirror true and natural life in their work. Surely, you can see the similarities in your compatriot's creations. Miss Austen fills her novels with ordinary people and then exposes their flaws to make fun of—*or criticize*—society."

"But that is precisely my point. In discussing the Austen novels, my sister and I have noticed that her heroines all find their salvation, if you will, by marrying well-born gentlemen. They marry someone of means—a man with property or a long history of family wealth. Furthermore, the gentleman is usually several years the senior of the lady."

"What are you saying, Mr. Blumental?"

"Miss Elliot made an emotional commitment, and remained constant, to a self-made, younger man. My sister insists that this distinguishes Anne from all other of Austen's heroines."

With a raised brow, Leah begged to differ. "I dare say that each of Miss Austen's ladies had their particular reason for choosing such high-born men. I wouldn't assume that they *deliberately* set out in some sort of mercenary fashion..."

"Nothing as avaricious as that, to be sure. But Anne Elliott had formed an attachment with Wentworth *before* he came into his own. Even Elizabeth Bennet had a moment of regret when she first toured Pemberley, if I recall correctly. It was something about how she could of been mistress of 'all this.'"

Leah's astonishment was beyond expression. Sighing, she placed her napkin upon the table and clasped her hands together as if in prayer. "Mr. Blumental, I struggle with the notion of Anne Elliot being a modern woman. She was little more than a servant in her own home—always at the beck and call of one sister or another. She played nursemaid and housekeeper and was constantly belittled by her dote of a father! These are not aspiring qualities...*and what of Lady Russell*? What good opinion would you have for a woman who allowed herself to be intimidated in such a manner?"

"You make a valid point, however, my first impression of poor Anne improved upon completing the novel—"

"Ah—you had a change of heart. Wasn't Darcy accused of forming implacable first impressions? Are you saying you are to be admired for that quality which escaped Miss Austen's beloved protagonist?"

"Miss Abramovitz, you have a way of misinterpreting my words."

Leah laughed. "Not at all, sir. I am simply trying to understand how you imagine Anne Elliot in the role of a modern Gibson Girl."

"My sister helped me to see that it was *not* a flaw on Anne's part to be persuaded by Lady Russell. It was *her choice*. Anne weighed the information available to her at the time and made an educated decision. I leave it to you to agree or disagree."

"You are not addressing the fact that her own family treated Anne with disdain."

"And you are choosing to ignore the character's intelligence and quick thinking. Recall that it was Anne *and* Lady Russell who figured out a new plan for the family to retrench. Anne showed independence, courage, and good judgment throughout the book. We witnessed her growth as she became a self-reliant determined woman who knew her own mind."

"As charming as I found the novel, I cannot agree on your hypothesis. Anne was manipulated and deprived years of happiness—her own dreams were pushed aside to accommodate the needs and desires of her family."

Yosef stared at his sister in disbelief. "Leah! You're reading too much into the storyline or—*is it possible*—you see your own life mirrored in the pages of that book?"

Ernesto, suddenly ill at ease, rose to his feet. Unsure how the conversation took such a turn, he felt a swift departure was necessary in order to avoid any further unpleasantness.

"I do not wish to argue with you, Miss Abramovitz—certainly not about this. Clearly, I do not understand the intricate workings of a young lady's mind, and as you are an ardent advocate for designing one's own destiny, I will refrain from further incommoding such educated company with my humble opinions."

Finding his hat, Ernesto bowed to Leah and her brothers. "Please, do excuse me. I am unpardonably late for a meeting." And with that, Ernesto removed himself from the Abramovitz shop.

"Oh *that man*! I thought we were having an intelligent dialogue. That *is* what one does in a conversation—there is a give and take of ideas. This is so typical of his nature. He believes he knows *everything*!"

"Do be fair," Moishe replied. "You asked for his opinion. You practically dared him not to share his thoughts and then, you *ridiculed* his commentary."

"Yes—well, I might have taunted him a bit, but only because I didn't agree with his observation. He needn't be so...infuriating!"

The long awaited Tradesmen Ball was to be a gala affair and Leah had prepared her gown with extreme care. Personal opportunities for mingling with the city's newest industrialists, and modeling her designs for their wives, were few and far between. She had chosen an emerald green silk satin for this creation. The gown had been designed with the new fashioned bodice draped over a boned understructure. Complementing the neckline and the short, net sleeves dripped silver and black beading. The simple train, shortened to a functional length, was covered in matching black net, sequins, and bugle beads in a stylized floral pattern. *It was stunning.* Leah wouldn't have considered attending such an affair with anything less grandiose.

The gala had been scheduled for December to commemorate the beginning of the summer season. That was deemed quite apropos since the investors had requested that their institution's logo—a dazzling sun—be displayed throughout the building, and in particular, on the towering cupola. In honor of the various unions and tradesman, who had dedicated four long years to the Majestic's construction, the grateful hoteliers were hosting the grand ball. It was most certainly the talk of El Once.

While Yosef and Moishe had provided raw materials for draperies, linens, and the like, they had not seen the completed project. As the Abramovitz family entered the structure, they, along with the other attendees, were quite duly impressed. The regal design of the building was befitting the hotel's designation. Imposing bronze statues received the visitors in the foyer as they ascended the Majestic's grand staircase, and as Leah raised her eyes to the first landing, she was awarded a most exceptional prospect of the imported stained glass.

Every detail was completed with the utmost attention to design and quality. Leah appreciated the fine marble floors, as well as, the exquisite French chandeliers and sconces; nevertheless, her greatest pleasure was in spying the luxurious draperies and wall hangings. Her brothers' fine work would be on exhibition for years to come.

Reading from the souvenir program, Leah noted the guestrooms—all 150—were unique unto themselves, and had been purposefully fashioned with the upcoming Centennial celebration in mind. An entire wing had already been reserved for important dignitaries who were expected to attend the festivities. It was said that the Infanta Isabel de Borbón of Spain would be honoring the hotel with her presence. *Heavens! We are coming up in the world.* Leah allowed a giggle to escape her lips, envisioning the robust Spanish princess sleeping upon a bed of Abramovitz linens. *The Princess and the Pea*, she laughed aloud, before being startled by an impetuous shout.

"Yosef! Moishe!" The party turned as one to greet Ernesto Blumental, looking quite dapper in his white tie and tails.

"Well met, old man," Yosef exclaimed. "I say Ernesto, do you have another book for my sister?"

Leah began to protest, but her clever sister-in-law interjected before either sibling could create further chaos. "How delightful to meet you here, Mr. Blumental," said Sofia. "Have you come prepared for an evening of fine dining and dancing?"

"Indubitably madam," he replied gazing at Leah with controlled anticipation.

The party, now six in total, continued to walk towards the grand salon. The lavishness of the foyer was, of course, continued throughout the ballroom. With intimate table accommodations, flowers and candlelight, the stage was set for an evening of pleasure and romance. Finding a table comfortably situated by a wall of French doors, the gentlemen assisted the ladies as they took their seats. Leah attempted to hide her apprehension at Mr. Blumental's presence but being neither, a good liar nor a fine actress, the situation was quite provoking.

How will he behave, she thought? And how would she react? Would she spend the evening with a petulant and dour 'Mr. Darcy,' or would the perfectly amiable gentleman make an appearance this night?

The orchestra invitingly played the first few notes of a waltz, calling eager participants to the floor. Ernesto stood and gallantly petitioned Leah for the honor. Grateful that her family had long ago accepted the concept of mixed dancing, she accepted graciously, if not with some trepidation. Ernesto guided her to the center of the dance floor where, surrounded by dozens of other couples, he focused only on Leah's demeanor as he gently took her hand in his. With her eyes cast downward and her body strained, Ernesto was dismayed realizing she was uncomfortable in his arms.

"Miss Abramovitz, have I offended you in some manner?"

"Not at all," she said with a tilt of her head. The candlelight, catching her movement, shimmered over the jet beads woven throughout her golden curls. "Whatever makes you believe I am offended?"

"It seems that my company puts you ill at ease. Dare I ask? Do you have an aversion to my presence in particular? Would you welcome another suitor's entreat?"

Leah sighed, and the action caused her to relax in his arms. Whether it was an act of capitulation, or in preparation for further confrontation, was yet to be seen. "I'm well over the age of being in the market for a husband, Mr. Blumental, and more to the point, I am persuaded that my happiness lies with my work. My brothers wouldn't allow their wives a career. Why should you be any different?"

"Do you not wish to form an attachment at some point in your life?"

"You do not seem to understand what I am saying. To speak plainly, I will not be deterred by impractical notions or romantic gestures."

With slight pressure on her lower back, Ernesto whirled her about, circling the other dancers until finding an isolated corner of the ballroom. "Ah, but you err in your estimation of my character, Miss Abramovitz. And—if I may be so bold—you have a marked misconception of my desires. I am not at all like your brothers."

Leah looked up upon hearing his specific choice of words. His eyes held hers for a moment as she contemplated the significance of his *desires*. The moment quickly passed, however, and she focused, once again, on elaborating her beleaguered point. "I have never had much power over my life—save what was permitted me. That must come to an end. I will not allow anyone to dictate my life, especially now—

now with the *beau monde* focusing on a monumental international event. You see, I used to be a part of that world. In Odessa, I would have been a star in my own right, but Providence has provided me another venue to shine. If I am no longer to be part of that sphere, I would have my presence known through my work. I mean no disrespect to you, sir, but I do not believe that we would suit."

"I respectfully disagree with you on that point, Miss Abramovitz. I believe we have never been able to overcome our initial encounter. For my part, I admit to being overly restrained and unapproachable throughout the course of our acquaintance. If you could only understand my history—my upbringing— you might forgive me my ineptitude. Your innocent misunderstanding of how we came to be seated together that night in the theater, and your subsequent attempts to overcome your discomposure, only raised my esteem for your courage and vivacity. I wish you to know how deeply I feel..."

"Please," she whispered, "do not continue in this manner."

"You would reject my offer before hearing me out?"

"I am not so heartless as to allow you to believe we could have a future together. I am not prepared to accept the honor of your attentions, Mr. Blumental. My mind is focused elsewhere."

The waltz had concluded, and with the finality of her words, Ernesto had no other choice but to release Leah from his arms and escort her back to her family. The promise of the evening had come to a brutal end.

Chapter Twenty-One

January 1910 ~ Buenos Aires

The *Exposition Universelle,* celebrated ten years prior, showcased the achievements of the new century to nearly fifty million people who visited the Parisian fair. *Art Nouveau* had been unveiled to the masses. Foreign exhibits, as well as national displays, presented new-fangled machinery and inventions to a captivated population. A fledging nation, in the new world, could do no less. The call for expert craftsman, artisans and engineers was heard across Argentina and no one answered as eagerly as the Abramovitz brothers.

Moishe and Yosef had reached some acclaim. Their textiles were in hot demand as the city began its preparations in earnest for the Centennial, now only five months away. The fact that they had achieved this coveted success, without their funds still held in limbo, only added to their satisfaction. If the Russian banks refused to release their hard earned treasury, so be it! The brothers understood that they had been penalized for daring to break free of a system that no longer worked or could provide for its citizens. They had been penalized for daring to be Jewish and having the audacity of surviving the venomous vitriol thrown their way. Their adversaries had not judged wisely; they hadn't taken into account that the Abramovitz brothers were made of stronger stuff—as was their little sister.

Leah's keen eye kept tabs on all the advertised festivities, and in this manner, she stayed one step ahead of demanding customers who required fashionable ensembles to debut at the *haute société* events. Too late, however, Leah failed to realize her tea salon and fashion shows would not fare well in her brothers' shop. That it took her so very long to come to terms with the fact, had her quite alarmed. It was a lesson in humility to own it.

Seeking inspiration, Leah proclaimed that a day of site-seeing was in order. There were several illustrious *confiterías* in Buenos Aires, but there were two establishments she determined would be most suited to her needs. Both Café Tortoni and Confitería Las Violetas were purported to be quite charming— sufficiently posh, and yet, warm and convivial. She was bound to be motivated by their famed beauty and ambiance.

Although walking from El Once to Almagro was an option, Leah elected to travel on an electric tram. At the furious speed of thirty kilometers per hour, the ride would make short work of the distance separating the two neighborhoods. She enjoyed traveling through the city and relished the vibrant mood of her fellow passengers. The diversity of the people crowding the thoroughfares was intriguing, and Leah couldn't help but be proud of how her own community was represented among the citizenry.

Recently, while attending a Shabbes service, she had overheard the name Alberto Gerchunoff repeated among the congregants. A woman explained, with great pride, that the author had written a novel about *gauchos judíos*. His work showcased how these immigrants solidified their place within the national fabric in less than one generation. Leah made a mental note to look up the title with her next visit to the book store; but while she was bumped and tossed about as the trolley made its way down the street, she had an epiphany. While it was true that the fledgling society was growing at an accelerated speed, it lacked a cohesive national identity. Paris and Rome had a style of their own—Buenos Aires deserved no less. And she was the woman who would blaze the trail!

Just then, as if the outside world could read her thoughts, Leah looked out the tram's window and saw a series of placards plastered on the scaffolding of a rising structure. The advertisements promoted tango singer, Carlos Gardel and his upcoming performance. Leah had heard about the man in muted conversations around the neighborhood. Tango had been born in seedy pubs deep in the immigrant suburbs, but according to the gossips, Gardel was single-handedly bringing the music and life style to the posh salons of the upper class. By taking the European style and integrating the criollo influence, Gardel was creating a unique Argentine sound. What with this music craze and a decidedly *porteño* fashion statement, Leah was motivated beyond measure as she disembarked the tram at the corner of Rivadavia and Medrano.

Viewing her surroundings with more than a little self-serving eye, Leah took into consideration the pristine sidewalk, the cast-iron bistro tables and chairs, the cheerful potted plants, as well as the enticing aroma that beckoned one to enter the curved glass doors of Las Violetas. It was all quite welcoming. A waiter in formal livery greeted her at the entrance, and immediately escorted her to a table happily situated by the illustrious, stained-glass windows. The ornate woodwork and gilded details reminded Leah of home, and the waiters crossing to and fro with heavy trays of pastries and cakes made her mouth water.

Refined literary and well-known political figures had made the café a popular meeting place, and with its marble columns and magnificent light fixtures, Leah could well appreciate that the room was more than apt to receive such notables. Knowing that Café Tortoni was comparable, both in design and social standing, left her pondering the inevitable question— how on earth would her little tea room compete with such extravagance?

Returning her focus to the comings and goings in the café, Leah observed customers lingering over their sumptuous plates of crème filled pastries and *dulce de leche* cakes. She noted the ladies wearing day dresses and walking suits of the highest quality, if not the most modern design. The gentlemen were suitably attired; some were taking tea with business associates while others, it appeared, were accompanying their wives for the afternoon.

Making a mental note of the space in between each marbled table, along with the foyer and walkways, Leah imagined a scene were elegantly dressed models glided passed customers, as she announced each *ensemble*, describing the rich fabrics and expounding on its style and versatility. It was a lovely dream, but the vision disappeared as Leah heard her mother's familiar admonition: 'Trust in Hashem and His plans. He is sure to send a sign.'

I only hope I can recognize it when it comes. She laughed at her own musings, but the smile immediately transformed to the shape of an *O*, when Ernesto Blumental sauntered into the refined establishment. British elitist! Naturally, he would come to Las Violetas for his afternoon tea, she thought. She was instantly ashamed of herself, but it seemed she was never in control of her baser emotions when that man was in her midst. She was still uneasy around him—ever since their very first meeting, when she had behaved so abominably.

Fussing with adjusting her napkin *just so* upon her lap and averting her eyes, she hoped against hope that Ernesto would not look her way. When she thought enough time had elapsed—*surely, he has been seated by now*—Leah resumed a natural pose, only to find herself looking straight into the man's azure eyes.

"Good afternoon, Miss Abramovitz," he said, bowing slightly and immediately returning both hands behind his back.

Stunned to see Leah sitting so prettily by the famed windows, Ernesto blinked several times to ensure he hadn't imagined her there. He had hesitated a moment before approaching her—he was still uneasy around the young woman—she had such a fiery, outspoken way about her. He wasn't quite sure how to speak intelligently when he was in her midst, and after being dismally rejected the other night at the ball, Ernesto almost turned around and walked away. Almost—but not quite.

"Good afternoon," she mumbled, as she pushed the cup and saucer to the center of the table. "What are you doing here?"

"I live here. That is to say, I live across the street. And you?"

"Taking tea, of course."

"Unaccompanied?" he blurted and immediately regretted.

"I am of age, Mr. Blumental, and I am quite safe in these surroundings," Leah pronounced, her eyes daring him to offer a dispute. "I—I assumed you lived in El Once. You always seem to be about."

Ignoring her obvious rebuke, he surprised himself, as well as the lady, by asking if might join her. Leah simply nodded, attempting to curtail any further biting remarks. "It is true—although I live here in Almagro—I frequently find myself in your neighborhood. I value your brothers' expert opinions, you see; and as I believe I have finally found a suitable location to build my family's business, I need their help more than ever," he admitted. "What brings you here to Las Violetas, if I may ask?"

Leah pondered how to respond. Dare she confide in him? Cautiously, she began explaining what she had envisioned: an elegant tea salon to display her designs. In paying a visit to Las Violetas, she had hoped to contrive a new plan, for she had now come to realize the impracticalities of sharing her brothers' space. Ernesto, thanking the heavens above for the providential opportunity he had been afforded, decided to speak his mind. She had not given him leave to address the matter fully the night of the ball. Perhaps now Leah might listen, and see the possibilities he had envisioned for their mutual benefit.

"You honor me, Miss Abramovitz, in sharing your thoughts. I do believe I might be able to help."

"How so?" she asked with a sinking feeling in the pit of her stomach.

"As I mentioned, I believe I have found a suitable resolution for my father's plans, and as you have just revealed that your brothers' location is wholly inappropriate for your tea shop scheme..."

"Does your plan involve repeating that which we have already stated, Mr. Blumental?"

"On the contrary, Miss Abramovitz, if you would only spare me a moment of your time."

"By all means."

"Inaugurate your salon in my department store."

"I beg your pardon?"

"Your customers will think they have been transported to the finest establishment in Odessa. And as I plan to dedicate an entire floor to ladies wear, I would be proud to showcase your line." He would have continued, but noticing the abrupt change in Leah's complexion, Ernesto allowed his offer to stand without further elucidation.

"Are you attempting to *bribe* me, Mr. Blumental?"

"I am merely suggesting you have no real interest in running a tea salon—"

"And you have no interest in running a grand department store."

"You are truly the most exasperating woman I have ever met."

"That is a rather curious declaration, especially since you recently asked for my hand in marriage and have, just now, proposed a business partnership."

"The sentiment does not preclude the offer—*either* offer."

"I don't believe that I can accept..."

"Why not? It is a perfect solution. You can design and showcase your collection, and I will honor my father's request by building a store to give Harrods a run for their money. We could make a success of it, I have no doubt, and I would be honored to assist you."

"That's just it. I don't want your assistance. I don't want *anyone's* interference. I don't need a knight in shining armor to come to my rescue."

"Why reject the help when it is offered with nothing but the most honorable of intentions?"

Leah sighed at this. Would she forever have to explain herself? "As you well know, I was raised in a large, tight-knit family. I have been cherished and protected to the point that I fear I may not be able to function independently..."

"I don't see—"

"Allow me to finish!" she insisted, and then, softened her tone. "You asked me, the night of the ball, if I was put off by your intentions or by all gentlemen callers. Do you recall the moment? I admit that I can still feel the tightening of my heart upon hearing those words, for you see, I *have* loved. I have loved foolishly. I cannot—*I will not*—give in to that emotion. To be smothered in such a fashion that I lose myself, that I give up on my dreams again. I *must* see if I have it in me to succeed on my own."

Ernesto sat quietly for a moment, allowing her words to settle within his very bones. Leah's heartfelt speech only inspired a deeper level of respect, a yearning to share his life with such a woman. Could he find the right words to make her understand? Would she listen?

"You have been fortunate to be blessed with such a family—my own differs in too many ways to enumerate," he said fiddling anxiously with the silverware. "Nonetheless, my sister and I share a unique relationship. I have grown accustomed to being her protector, as well as her confidant, and she has taught me the true meaning of strength and the importance of having faith. It is because of this relationship, I can see what a loving family is meant to be. It is because of my acquaintance with you, and your brothers, I can envision my own happy home."

As Leah attempted to interject an objection, he raised his hand to stay her comment. "I do not wish to be your knight. I've not come to save you. I wish for a wife. I want to fashion a life *together*—with laughter and love, and yes, even with passionate disagreements because; at least, one knows that there is fire in the blood and a thirst to succeed! My offer for your hand still stands, Miss Abramovitz. Say yes and make me the happiest of men."

In spite of the turmoil she was experiencing, Leah could not deny that the gentleman had done her a great honor. In opening his heart, he was at his most vulnerable, and she truly had no desire to injure him further. She simply could not allow herself to accept. To do so would feel as if the last ten years of her life had been pointless.

"I thank you for the compliment you have paid me, but I cannot accept."

"It seems that my offers, either matrimonial in nature or in business, cannot find favor in your eyes," Ernesto softly replied, grimacing at the sound of resignation in his own voice. Adjusting his suddenly-too-tight necktie, he composed himself. "If you are quite done with your tea, perhaps you would allow me to escort you home?"

"There is no need, I assure you..."

"It would be my pleasure," he stood and stoically held out his arm.

Seeing no other recourse but to accept, Leah allowed herself to be escorted by the now silent and ever-so-proper gentleman.

The air was thick. They made their way back to El Once under threatening clouds and the rumble of thunder. When at last they reached her doorstep, Leah found herself in the awkward position of having to invite him into the family's home. What would her brothers say? Sofia and Devora would most likely jump to conclusions and find it necessary to notify the rabbi at once. Leah was spared the unnecessary upheaval, as the man tipped his hat, and begged she convey his regards to her family.

"I have a business meeting to attend, Miss Abramovitz. Please tell your brothers I will be paying a call in the next few days."

"Of course."

Lowering her gaze, Leah fidgeted with the silk tassels of her reticule. "Good afternoon," she whispered as she stepped passed the threshold into the foyer—just as the heavens opened and released their heavy bounty.

Chapter Twenty—Two

May 14, 1910

The inhabitants of the port city found themselves in the clutches of an autumnal downpour. That, alone, brought on a deep sense of melancholy as Leah recalled the many stormy afternoons spent in the library accompanied by her dearest papá. Solomon Abramovitz would welcome his young daughter at the edge of his great leather chair, as he shuffled and rearranged drawings into a cohesive catalogue for his customers. On occasion, he would pull out a sketch for her inspection—encouraging her to choose a certain shade or particular fabric to match the design. Now, closeted behind a slip of crushed velvet, Leah listened as her brothers' voices coincided with each clap of thunder. Their forceful rumblings, matching the violent storm, chased away her bittersweet memories and kept her from concentrating on her proposed task.

Even as a young girl in Odessa, Leah had been certain it was her destiny to join ranks with the exclusive set of renowned designers, but it seemed her dream was not meant to be, at least, not yet. And with the numerous distractions she had been facing this day, not the least being the inclement weather and the ruckus her brothers were *again* creating in the main salon, Leah was having a most difficult time scrutinizing the Society pages.

Much to Yosef's delight and Moishe's annoyance, the men were heatedly discussing a particularly sensational topic. To say that her siblings were riled over last year's murder of the Chief of Police, would be belittling the tempest brewing in their midst. Had it been it an act of anarchy, or was it a desperate deed instigated by a misguided eighteen-year-old boy? Although Leah had a passing interest in politics and current events, she had not planned on spending her afternoon listening to their raging debate.

"Simón Radowitzky assassinated Ramon Falcón," insisted Moishe. "That is a fact!"

"I am not contesting the fact that Falcón is dead," Yosef rebutted, "I am merely pointing out that the *impetus* for Radowitzky's actions merit further examination!"

"The country, much like a fledgling toddler, is yet in leading strings," interjected another, yet more restrained, speaker. "There is a battle of philosophy raging through Argentina's populace, and with the hodgepodge of classes that make up the citizenry, it is no wonder. Labor unions are hard pressed to pick between the socialists, who are clamoring to gain control, and the outright communists. All the while, the government is struggling to maintain the vision of the Founders. A nation *cannot* function in this manner. The rule of law must be respected."

With only a thin curtain acting as a barrier between her pine desk and her brothers' workshop, Leah was perturbed by the boisterous dialogue. It was not her intention to eavesdrop, but as she did not wish to abandon her office—and she refused to call it anything else *but* her office—she had no other recourse.

Moishe and Yosef were certainly capable of engaging in such a passionate discourse. Their guest, however, was not known to display such fervency. Ernesto Blumental, as was his custom, quietly refuted each point, or rationally played the devil's advocate by presenting an alternative perspective.

"I don't take issue with these fellows bringing their cause to light," he said in a measured and precise tone, "but I feel the officials are well within their right to curtail radicals and their violent schemes."

Hearing this last utterance, Leah could not contain herself and popped her head out from behind the burgundy divide. "But surely, if the workers have legitimate complaints..."

"Miss Abramovitz." Mr. Blumental immediately came to his feet and executed a perfunctory bow. "That's the rub. Their legitimacy is negated; at least in my eyes, when they become criminal, when they become *murderers* and cry for Jewish blood—ah, do forgive my strong language. This certainly is not a topic for mixed company."

She opened her lips to respond, when Mr. Blumental abruptly suspended the conversation.

"What's this?" he asked, peering over her shoulder. "Are you expecting visitors?"

Mr. Blumental was the first to notice a coach and four coming to a standstill at the shop's door. Leah, now catching a glimpse of the imposing vehicle, gasped her astonishment.

"That is no plain coach!" she exclaimed. "That is a *barouche* and I know that lady. I read about her in today's periodical. To be sure! That is *señora* Aragón-Peña!"

In her haste, Leah made a mad dash to the front entrance, inadvertently bumping into bolts of fabric as she collided into Moishe's arms. Putting a hand to her hair, she tucked an errant curl back into place and straightened the ribbon at her collar, just as Mr. Blumental came to her side.

"Might I suggest, Miss Abramovitz," he quietly pronounced, "that you moderate your enthusiasm?"

"Thank you, Mr. Blumental," Leah quipped, "but I do believe I know how to behave in front of polite society."

Without another word, Ernesto Blumental walked to his friends' backroom and returned with a mahogany high-back chair. "Put this alongside your desk and remove the pine one. The woodwork is exquisite and the embroidery on the cushion is tastefully done. A lady of her distinction will appreciate the craftsmanship."

"Really Mr. Blumental..."

"And offer her a coffee," he continued, "or better yet, tea. I know that you keep a fine Russian set of porcelain. Do you, per chance, have *masas finas*?"

Insufferable man! Did he think her so provincial? How dare he insinuate that she would offer her guest anything less than her best? Of course, the Londoner would look down his nose at her, but she was no county bumpkin. She was Leah Solomonovna Abramovitz, daughter of an Honorary Citizen and member of the First Merchant's Guild. Unable to hold her tongue, Leah found some release in her flippant rejoinder.

"I thought we would sit around a campfire like real gauchos—sipping *yerba maté* and munching on *bizcochitos.*"

"Leah, as usual, you are overdramatizing the situation," Moishe reproached. "I'm sure Ernesto is only trying to ensure your success."

She glanced out the window, and then, whipped back around to face her nemeses. With seconds to spare, she halfheartedly apologized to the man and quickly reversed course as the grand lady's dove grey skirt swooshed through the door.

"Madam," Leah purred, bowing her head slightly, "it is an honor to receive you in our humble establishment."

With not too little satisfaction, Leah noticed the look on the men's faces as she escorted the lady to her private retreat. Once her customer had been accommodated, she graciously offered tea, accompanied, of course, by petits fours and other dainty, confectionary treats. The Rubenesque customer did not decline. Not only did she accept the refreshment, but much to Leah's perturbation, the señora did indeed remark on the fine workmanship of the grand chair. In point of fact, the woman was quite entirely taken by the rusa's charm and manners. She had not been prepared to be received by such a genteel young lady and was not ashamed to admit it.

"I am very pleased to say that you quite exceed my expectations, señorita. You speak with a slight accent, of course, but I appreciate your well-mannered tone and excellent vocabulary. I was not at all certain what sort of creature to expect! You see, I have little experience with people of your...heritage."

"You honor me, *madame.*" Leah, curtailing her habitual acerbity, bit her tongue as the woman commented on her accent. It was a point of contention, to be sure, but now was not the time to pursue the issue. "I am exceedingly grateful for my tutelage in all the arts. French, as you may know, is practically the national tongue among Russians of a certain class; and although I am working on perfecting my enunciation, Spanish has come quite naturally to me."

The grand lady situated herself comfortably in the well-appointed chair, and accepting another cup of tea, began explaining how she came to visit the Abramovitz shop on such a cold and miserable day. Leah was certainly aware, the señora said, that festivities were fast approaching for the centennial celebration. The fact of the matter was that she, Leticia Maldonado Alvarez Aragón-Peña, could not be outdone by her friends.

"Great Britain withdrew their delegation from participating, of course. The sudden death of King Edward VII threw the empire into mourning, don't you know. Nevertheless, other foreign dignitaries will most certainly be commemorating the anniversary of our nation's revolution."

"Yes," Leah said, attempting to get in a word edgewise, "I understand that Isabel de Borbón—"

"Precisely so! *La infanta*, the Princess of Asturias and *the* most popular member of the Spanish Royal family will be in attendance. So, you see, I cannot be seen in just any haute couture when presented to such society. I require something new and fresh—*inspired*."

Leah's guest went on to divulge that a close friend had discreetly mentioned how a 'young rusa' had created a ball gown for Alfonsina Pereyra's engagement party and another for Borghetti's daughter's debut. The bead work, the quality of the lace, and the modern design had been the talk about town.

"I *must* have my very own gown created by the, so-called, 'up and coming Jewess'—*even* if it entailed visiting you on this dreary day in this bastion of haggling and trade. But, on second thought," she paused to take a much needed breath, "perhaps the change in the weather has been providential. None of my friends will be out in this storm, so I do not run the risk of being seen. I do not suppose you are acquainted with...?"

From under her long full lashes, Leah observed her celebrated, yet *gauche* customer. While the woman chattered on about international dignitaries and her husband's important contacts, Leah's heart pounded wildly and feared that Mr. Blumental had indeed been correct. She had to restrain her enthusiasm, otherwise even the lacings of her modern corset would surely burst. But heavens—she *was* bursting with joy!

The wife of an industrial magnate had condescended to visit their establishment on the *Avenida Azcuénaga*. That was quite something!

Already, from the corner of her eye, Leah could see busybody neighbors, merchants, and shoppers alike gawking at the elegant barouche stationed at the Abramovitz door. No doubt, the entire block would be speaking of the affair for days to come, for although the neighborhood bustled with activity, it most certainly was *not* for posh clientele.

On any given day, harried passengers traveled on jam-packed trolley cars, while push carts weaved in between horse-drawn conveyances and cuentaniks lugged their suitcases filled with merchandise across the cobblestone streets. Noises and aromas filled the air as newspaper boys cried out the headlines and waiters stood by the doors of their corner cafes, enticing pedestrians as they passed by. That a lady, of such high standing as señora Aragón-Peña, would consider visiting a shop *not* located on the tree-lined streets of Recoleta or Palermo was a testament to Leah's talent—and she was going to take full advantage of the opportunity!

Realizing that the lady had finished her monologue, and that she herself had been woolgathering rather than attentively listening, Leah decided it was high time to get to work. Setting down the teacup and pushing aside the plate of cookies, she stated, "Now then, señora, would you care for me to sketch a few designs?" And with that, sounds of oohs and aahs emanated from the private alcove for the better part of an hour. Leah came out from behind her wine-colored screen only once to collect a variety of fabric samples. At the end of the appointment, the grand lady was enchanted and assured *la rusita* that she would return for more.

By then, Ernesto Blumental had concluded his business and requested that Yosef extend his best compliments to his sister. Leah, relieved to hear of the man's departure, rolled her eyes as she put back the fabric samples and stored her colored pencils.

"I don't understand why you should dislike him so," questioned Yosef.

"Who? Oh, you mean *Mr. Know-It-All*? I find him irksome, to say the least," Leah said purposefully picking at nonexistent threads on her shirt sleeve. "And that accent! His *Castellano* is perfect, but there is no hiding his British urbanity."

"Leah, you have always admired all things British," Moishe said. "What has gotten into you?"

"He is not called *ruso*, is he? Oh no! That charming designation is just for us *Eastern* European Jews."

"You are being childish and it is not becoming of a woman your age."

"A woman of my age?" she snickered. "That is quite fitting, isn't it?" She wouldn't admit that being considered on the shelf at twenty-seven years of age was hurtful, but as she had pledged not to marry after suffering through one too many painful experiences, the epithet was aptly applied. Realizing that to continue to fret over the matter might lead her to divulge her recent dealings with the man, Leah reverted to her tried and true grievance. "Why is he *always* here? Exactly how much business can he possibly need to discuss?"

"And all this time, I thought you found him— debonair," Yosef teased.

Leah grabbed a roll of ribbon and threw it at her tormentor. "Whatever gave you the idea I thought him handsome?"

"Aha!" Laughing, Yosef rushed to the other side of the room. "I didn't say handsome. I said *debonair*— not quite the same thing. That being said, I'm not quite sure what he makes of you."

"His good opinion is not of the slightest concern."

"My dear girl, what good opinion may he have when your tongue drips with sarcasm and your eyes, *brilliant emeralds that they may be*, cast daggers whenever poor Ernesto speaks?"

Moishe interrupted their childish shenanigans, his voice calm and steady. "You know very well that his family wish him to establish a business in Buenos Aires. Ernesto has long confided that his skills—his interests—lie elsewhere. He seeks us out, because he values our experience. Furthermore, all that business about changing out the furniture and suggesting you serve refreshments, was only meant to help you succeed with the señora. He has been groomed to work with this class of society."

"And I have not?" she seethed.

"No, Miss Leah Solomonovna Abramovitz, you have been groomed to be *in* society."

That was a lifetime ago, she thought, *before you tore me away from my home.*

Persisting, Moishe waved a thick index finger in his sister's face. "They have ears, but do not hear."

"What do you mean by that?"

"You are ignoring the obvious, sister dear."

"Putting all that aside," Yosef interjected, "Ernesto has always been nothing but thoughtful and well-mannered. In short, he is an exemplary example of a true caballero."

Leah willed herself from countering her brother's flowery commentary. It was that word—*caballero* which brought forth painful reminders of youthful escapades. How foolish she had been. A soldier in the Russian army, Lieutenant Dmitry Yegorov was not the gallant knight she supposed him to be. Her heart had been broken, and what's more, her pride had been hurt. Years later, she had met a gaucho with more chivalry and integrity than those high born. She had misjudged this caballero as well, for in the end, his honor meant more to him than their shared affection. No—she had had enough gallantry to last a lifetime, and thought it best to allow the conversation to come to an end without further derision from her sharp tongue.

There would be no more talk of Mr. Blumental that evening. Moishe intimated that the hour was late and returned to the back room to shut down the machinery. Yosef bellowed a reminder across the patio, "I have a meeting. Tell Sofia. I will be home late!"

As her brothers prepared to take their leave, Leah collected her sketches. She walked through the courtyard, which separated the storefront from the factory, and climbed the spiral staircase, jutting up from the center of the space. The room wasn't much— certainly nothing as charming or welcoming as the attic of their home in Odessa—but it was hers. When she first had arrived to Buenos Aires, Leah had appropriated a large oak table to set out her fashion plates and fabrics, as well as a midsized cabinet to house several keepsakes she inherited from her mamá. Some tools were from the ancient days of tailoring, and Leah kept them on display for inspiration and ambiance. Others were handy items that she put to good use whenever she needed to be designer, seamstress, and tailor all at once.

Setting down her sketches, Leah organized the tools of the trade about her. She desperately wanted to concentrate on the señora's ensemble, but her mind wandered back to *that man*. She couldn't quite determine what it was about him that set her on edge, but Leah never felt at ease in his presence. He was forever standing at attention whenever she entered the room, one arm clasped behind his back so as not to appear too forward—too intimidating in front of the *delicate* and *innocent* young lady. *Miss Abramovitz this*, *Miss Abramovitz that*...they lived in a modern 20th century nation, but Ernesto Blumental preferred a bygone era. He favored an antiquated mentality which Leah discarded long ago with other mannerisms of Imperial Russia.

Leah shook off any further thoughts of Ernesto Blumental, and instead, focused on her drawings, knowing she would have to work swiftly if she expected to complete the gown in time for the opening gala event.

She was pleased with her vision for the gown. With black netting and velvet trim, the cream embroidery she planned would provide a delicate relief. An aqua silk would be just the right amount of color—not too bold or brash. Laying out the various fabrics, and completely engrossed with the task at hand, Leah was unaware of her employee's approach. With a box of steel pins balancing in the palm of her hand, she sat back on her heels as she considered the proper placement of the silk on the model's form. Magdalena's sudden entrance into the room startled Leah, and her brusque movement upset the precariously held mother-of-pearl pin box. Its lethal instruments scattered across the mosaic floor.

"*Caramba!*" Leah cursed. She had pricked her finger trying to save the box, and quickly lapped up the drop of blood before it stained the precious silk.

"*Ay Dios mío!* I am terribly sorry, señorita! I did not realize you were still here," Magdalena cried. "I thought you had forgotten to turn off the light. Has señora Malka's box been damaged?"

"No, no, I didn't drop it—just its blasted contents! If I had ruined Mamá's gift, you would have had to truly cover your ears!" Leah giggled as she scooped up the pins.

Magdalena crossed her arms, scowling at her employer. "You should be ashamed of yourself—cursing like a man."

Leah laughed at the accusation. "It was not as bad as all that! My brothers say much worse *and* in many different languages!"

"Not señor Avram," stated the woman, "Nor señor Yaacov or Naftali for that matter. I do not know where you learn such language!"

"It was a harmless curse. Anyhow, if I hadn't pricked my finger, I might now have asked you to pinch me. I still can't believe it—my gowns are being sought after by the crème de la crème! Soon, all the ladies of Argentina's high society will be waltzing about in my designs."

"That is all well and good, but do you have any idea what time it is? I am only here because Nacho is finishing up an order before *Shabbos* tomorrow."

Leah smiled at that. Ignacio Cervantes was a good worker. Just as Magdalena, he had followed the family from his provincial hometown of Dominguez in Entre Rios. Nacho, as he was known, had been of great help on the farm in the early days; and although he was the grandson of Spaniards and a good Catholic, he had become acquainted with Jewish rituals and respected the traditions. Although no longer strictly observant, the Abramovitz family still kept the Sabbath, as did many of their customers and competitors in El Once. If the work was not complete before Friday afternoon, the delivery would be delayed until Sunday, and the customer would be inconvenienced. Leah recognized how blessed they were to have such dedicated and loyal employees. In fact, they had become more than employees; they were friends. And as her friend, Magdalena continued her barrage of criticism.

"Nacho is walking me home, yet you—you think it is acceptable to walk the streets alone. Have you not heard the news?"

"My goodness Magdalena, I don't need someone else lecturing me. As you can see, I've been busy with this new project. Once I cut the pattern, you—as the head seamstress—will complete the work and señora Aragón-Peña will have her gown in time for the renowned Jockey Club's ball. Things are finally going my way. I can't be bothered by hovering siblings or fretful friends..." *or meddlesome—distracting—men.*

"But señorita..."

"In any case, I am done for the evening. You may stop attempting to be my nursemaid."

Grabbing her hat, Leah embraced the distressed woman as she walked towards the full length mahogany-encased mirror she had lugged upstairs herself. With a mass of golden curls teased and piled high in the contemporary pompadour, she expertly secured her hat while recalling Yosef's taunts. *"You might as well place a latke on top of your head. Your hair looks like a squashed potato pancake,"* he had said. With a wry grin, Leah adjusted the hat pin and thought, what do men know anyway?

She sighed noticing the woman still hovering over her shoulder. "Very well. Tell me your news, although I can't imagine what it could be. I haven't heard anything out of the ordinary today."

"That doesn't surprise me. How could you hear anything at all when you are slaving away, up here, like a servant girl? The whole world could be coming to an end..."

"Halley's Comet is supposed to crash into the earth—now *that* would mean the world was coming to an end. Do stop exaggerating and tell me what this is all about."

"Jacobo came back early from El Centro where he had been delivering an order to that nice new store, you know the one—on Avenida 9 de Julio?"

Leah nodded and moved her hand as if she was rolling up a bolt of cloth. "And?"

"There are men rioting in the streets and the police have warned that the violence might spread across the city. It is dangerous for a young lady to be outside," Magdalena said on her last breath. "I am surprised that a curfew has not yet been imposed."

"What nonsense! It isn't the first time that the miscreants have raised a ruckus and we are miles away from downtown. Besides, I am not an innocent girl terrified of walking home alone in my own neighborhood. Listen to me—we are preparing for a national celebration in just a few days' time.

Dignitaries and royalty will be descending upon the *Paris of South America*, for heaven's sake. We are not in Russia where we need to quiver and quake every time the peasants have a bit much to drink!"

Taking a quick look again in the mirror, Leah adjusted the bowtie on her smart damask blouse and buttoned up the coat of her cranberry wool suit. Satisfied with the sophisticated presentation, she turned and gave Magdalena a quick peck on the cheek. "You're right, of course. Go tell Nacho to close up—it's late and you both should be home." Heading down the stairs, Leah waved an absent-minded goodbye.

"Very well, but please, do not tarry."

Raising her hand to cup her mouth, Magdalena yodeled out to her companion, "Roll down the blinds, Nachito! Let's go home before the police close down the streets."

Chapter Twenty-Three

Leah's heels tapped out a staccato beat punctuating the eerie stillness of the neighborhood. Clouds, now silent and spent, hovered high in the night's sky, shielding the moon with their silvery haze. She thought, surely upon reaching the main thoroughfare with its modern electric street lights, the usual hustle and bustle of El Once would resume. As it was now, Leah passed store after store shut down tight for the night; their proprietors all at home safe and cozy.

Pulling on the collar of her coat, she inhaled deeply attempting to regulate her flustered breath with fresh crisp air but instead, Leah began coughing as smoke tickled her throat. *Fire?* A blaze of any sort could quickly turn into a monumental disaster in the district.

Instinctively she sought out the flames, though from where she stood, Leah couldn't determine the source. Her anguish grew as she heard the clamor of raised voices shouting out in the night. It differed from the usual, boisterous neighborhood commotion. There was something about the tone....they were chanting.

Footsteps clapped on the wet pavement as ominous figures came running from behind. Caught off guard, she had no time to seek shelter as two men, blinded by their own urgency, brutally pushed her out of their path. Leah cursed at them, fiercely and without shame, as they sped away. The street, unnaturally illuminated by the glow of weak electricity, was empty again except for the shadows that danced across the brick walls.

Looking over her shoulder, Leah realized she had come too far to return to the shop. Clearly, it was imperative to cover the remaining blocks to her home as quickly as possible. She picked up her pace, nearly stumbling onto the street, when she heard the distinct sound of glass breaking. Men were hollering in victory; she could hear them from around the corner.

"Death to the rusos!"

"Out with the foreigners!"

Leah feared for friends and their livelihoods. Whose store was being vandalized? Down the block a dog was barking—probably giving chase to a lowly criminal. She pressed herself against the side of the building, holding her breath as a man raced by. Telltale sounds of crashing glass were quickly followed by earsplitting reverberations. Gunshots? Dear God, she thought, could it be a *pogrom?*

Bereft of any remaining bravado, Leah attempted to run, but her long slim skirt barred the necessary movement. Realizing that she would have to pull the material up to her knees, Leah bent to grasp the hem when she witnessed a mob running towards her. Terrified, she froze as they approached her position hurling objects at yet another storefront's window display. Leah ducked her chin and swerved hoping to avoid being hit; but when she felt the blunt force of a projectile weapon graze her brow, she cried out and collapsed.

En masse, the men rushed wildly by—running towards some unknown destination. Leah gingerly brought a gloved hand up to the injured site. Her fingers came away stained with blood. With a trembling hand, she attempted to retrieve a handkerchief from her handbag; when suddenly, she felt someone grab her arm and lift her up. Leah screamed as the man pulled her towards him.

"Let me go!" she desperately wrestled against the stranger with failing strength.

"Come away! Quickly!"

Struggling, she pushed to no avail.

"It is I, Miss Abramovitz. Calm yourself!"

Lost in a moment of panic, Leah continued to fight. Pounding on the man's chest, she attempted to break free until remembering to use her legs. Long ago, just prior to boarding the ship in Trieste, Yosef had warned her to be wary of sailors and unaccompanied male passengers. He taught her how a precise kick could bring a man down. Leah attempted the action, but again, her modern skirt prevented the movement and she was only able to manage a swift kick to his shin. The man roared like an injured animal, but refused to unhand her. With a firm grip, he maneuvered an about face and Leah found herself running alongside the stranger.

"Where are you taking me?" she cried out. Her hat had long fallen away in the mêlée. Pins had given way and her hair spilled over her shoulders and onto her face. Weak with fear and exhaustion, unable to see through her curls, she railed against him with her last ounce of courage. "Let me go!"

"Leah! *Stop fighting me*. We must get off the streets."

Suddenly recognizing the familiar accent, she realized the man had used her name. Leah snapped out of the hysteria and looked upon the familiar face of Ernesto Blumental.

She allowed him to guide her through an alley, as he unlocked the back door of unknown location. Ernesto slammed the door shut with such force, several items shattered as they fell off of a nearby shelf. With the entrance locked and secured, he permitted himself to feel the intense emotion he suppressed during the confrontation. *She could have been killed!* Still gripping her arm, Ernesto crossed over the debris he created, found a worn wicker chair, and proceeded to unceremoniously deposit the obstinate, *careless* woman there. His alarm had left him quite speechless. Never had he experienced such terror. Ernesto hovered by the doorway, scowling for several minutes, until finally, he found his voice.

"Forgive me, madam, for being so blunt but what in God's name are you about?"

Avoiding the intensity of his glare, Leah attempted to adjust her skirt which was now in a complete state of disarray. Rather than succumb to sheer helplessness, she allowed the emotion to transform into something more familiar. How often had she allowed her frustration and vulnerability be replaced by rage and indignation? As he glowered at her, Leah was able to catch her breath until finally finding she had just enough strength to bellow a reply.

"Do forgive me Mr. Blumental, but I was simply conducting myself as any independent young woman would by walking home after a long day at work," she said, pulling herself up to her full height. "I had no idea that Buenos Aires had suddenly become a *shtetl* in Ukraine."

Ernesto could only glare at her in response. How dare she respond to his enquiry with her customary sarcasm? *Was the woman daft?* Attempting to regulate his breath and control his tongue, Ernesto tried to reconcile what he had witnessed moments ago with what the woman was blathering about. He had seen her—*had tried to call out to her*—but with all the commotion, she had not heard his warning.

Moments after leaving his appointment just up the block from the Abramovitz establishment, Ernesto had sensed that the streets were not safe. Rather than seeking a hackney cab, he choose to run back to see if Miss Abramovitz was still in the company of her brothers. In the two years he had been acquainted with the enterprising woman, he had come to know that she seldom left her workshop at a reasonable hour.

Ernesto convinced himself that he simply wanted to confirm she had been properly escorted home. When he saw that the blinds had been secured, and the shop had been suitably padlocked for the night, he decided it best to seek shelter for himself. He sprinted to Tito Kaplan's warehouse and *that's* when he spotted Miss Abramovitz—alone and facing an angry, advancing mob.

His heart had yet to return to its natural rhythm, even now as the headstrong—*infuriatingly beautiful*—woman stood before him, her head bent as she ridiculously fiddled with her torn skirt. Deciding that they both needed another moment to collect themselves, Ernesto turned to investigate their surroundings, and upon finding some lighting, he busied himself with that task.

"Do they not have electricity in this place?" asked Leah, disturbed to hear the shrill demand in her voice.

The dark room was damp and clammy. She recognized the telltale smell of fabrics that had retained too much moisture. Her brothers knew how to deal with this problem—evidently, the owner of this shop did not. The musty odor and the lack of proper lighting were clear indicators to the woman experienced in the world of textile manufacturing. They were not in a competitor's establishment, of that she was certain. "Where, may I ask, did you shelter us? The proprietor should not be so careless with his product."

"Careless? How so?" Ernesto relaxed a bit. If she was able to blurt out questions in that challenging tone, she would be alright.

"Mold, Mr. Blumental. Mold survives on organic materials. Can you not smell it? The textiles are particularly susceptible in these damp conditions and the proprietor risks damaging his merchandise. That musty odor is a sure giveaway. I am certain if you were to look closely—that is to say—if there was *sufficient light* in this workspace, you would be able to ascertain a veritable rainbow of stains on the fabric."

Ernesto grinned, as he lit a wick and replaced the glass globe of an oil lamp before replying. "Set your mind at ease, Miss Abramovitz. We are in Tito Kaplan's warehouse, or rather, *my* new property. It is rather fortunate, is it not, that I happened to sign the final paperwork this day and was presented with a set of keys. The old chap decided to try his luck elsewhere. I dare say fungal growth was the last thing on his mind before he took off to the Patagonia. Apparently, the tittle-tattle Kaplan picked up around the neighborhood was more than just idle gossip. He feared there would be trouble, and tonight's rabble-rousers proved he was rightly concerned."

Cupping the side of her face, Leah leaned against the door and willed herself to regain a modicum of control. She refused to give in to raging emotions which threatened to overpower her weakened state. Instead, Leah thought it best to continue conversing as if nothing out of the ordinary had taken place.

"Did I hear you correctly? You *purchased* Tito Kaplan's property?"

"Yes, precisely so."

"But why?" Leah turned to observe his expression, for she had never known Mr. Blumental to be insincere, but the sudden movement caused her to sway with an attack of vertigo. She stood deathly still, hoping the episode would pass before she caused herself further embarrassment.

Occupied with rearranging the sparse furnishings, Ernesto was ignorant of her malady and continued moving two chairs together while booting a small round table to the center of the room. Setting the lamp down, he gestured for her to come closer. When

Leah refused to move, he came to her side and gently placed a hand on her elbow.

"Come Miss Abramovitz, do take a seat and rest a bit. This chair appears considerably more comfortable. It seems I have a developed a penchant for moving furniture about," he said, trying to bring some levity into their dialogue.

He waited for her stinging reply, knowing how he had vexed her earlier in the day, but she merely stared at him. Her befuddled expression tore at his heart, but when her golden tresses shifted and exposed her face, Ernesto felt the air leave his lungs.

With the room properly illuminated, her injuries were now plain to see. A nasty gash above her eye needed tending. She might even require a stich or two, he thought to himself. Puzzled that she had not complained of pain, Ernesto took the handkerchief from his breast pocket and began gently dabbing the wound. Much to his surprise, Leah offered no resistance—no claims of being a strong, modern woman without need of his manhandling. Instead, she gazed about the room with a glazed look in her eye, until finally settling once again upon his countenance.

"What has happened? Has the world gone mad?"

"I am not altogether certain, Miss Abramovitz. You do recall that your brothers and I were speaking of union workers. I would not be too surprised if that new group, the *Juventud Autonomista*, wasn't behind this mayhem," he said, as he created a bandage for her wound out of a length of clean linen. "The imbeciles! It is the Church that feeds into their prejudices, while the Government incites their fears. What's worse is that they believe all Jews are Russian and all anarchists are Jews! After the murder of the Chief of

Police, you will recall that several nationalist groups attacked *La Protesta* and *La Vanguardia*, not to mention the Biblioteca Rusa," he continued. "They shut down the production of those two newspapers, as they destroyed the treasured books of the library in the Plaza Congreso."

Running a hand through his hair, Ernesto shook his head in disbelief. "I am not saying that I approved of those newspapers, but I do not support the burning of books or the impediment of new ideas. If we are not free to debate opposing views, *what is the point*?"

"Why can they not leave us in peace?" she cried. "Have we not proven ourselves? We have worked hard for everything that we have achieved in this *goldene medina*. To be labeled Bolsheviks and cast as trouble-makers...it is simply unacceptable!"

"I am in agreement with your keen observations, Miss Abramovitz. Those characterizations are indeed degrading. We, of the *colectividad*, deserve to be respected, not objectified."

Leah, yet in shock from the fright that had befallen her, was stunned to hear Ernesto Blumental speaking of matters he rarely broached with such fervor. As an Englishman, he would never have been denigrated as a lowly *ruso*, and yet, he had just self-identified with her community—with the *colectividad*.

Coming to his senses, Ernesto realized that this was not the moment to discuss politics; after all, the woman was shaken and injured. "I do apologize, Miss Abramovitz. The events of this evening have caused me to act in an unchivalrous manner. We should attempt to make ourselves comfortable. I believe we will have to barricade ourselves here for the night."

"All night? But my family will be worried. Yosef and Moishe—"

"We cannot risk going outside, not while those drunk, brainwashed hooligans are still out in full force. They were driven to this violence by men in great power. They will not be stopped quite so easily."

Overwrought with concern for her brothers, Leah began to pace. "I—I cannot stay here. I must go home. This *is* a pogrom! We left Russia for this very reason. We risked everything to escape this sort of obscene behavior, and yet, here we are again embroiled in a nightmare. Papá!" she gasped unexpectedly. "Papá had *warned* us all to remain together. I must go!"

She managed to open the door only to hear once again: "Death to the rusos!"

Chapter Twenty-Four

Ernesto was behind her instantly, firmly shutting the door—gently guiding her back to the center of the room. "Come away, Miss Abramovitz. Please, remain seated. To be sure, your brothers would want you to seek shelter at a time such as this. Your safety would be their main concern, and therefore, it is mine as well."

Leah nodded her head, grimacing at the pain she had inadvertently caused and allowed a nervous giggle to escape her dry lips. She realized he was right. Wandering out of doors in an attempt to reach home would be counterproductive, to say the least. She also realized that he was doing his utmost to be pleasant...*charming,* really.

He was actually conversing with her, a welcomed change from his customary assumptions and curt commands; and with his hair disheveled and his suit in disarray, Ernesto Blumental didn't appear so high and mighty after all. Somehow, she found his altered appearance and new demeanor rather comforting and felt her level of apprehension subside. She paused, suddenly stricken by an epiphany. *If he can pretend everything is well, so can I.*

"I agree with your assessment of the situation," she said, cautiously patting her bandaged wound, "but, would you mind terribly if we dispense with the formality? If we are to be quarantined for the night, you must promise to call me by my given name. Tell me, *Ernesto*, do you think Tito kept a kettle in this place?"

"You have the right of it, Miss Abra...*Miss Leah*," he compromised, turning to search the warehouse for supplies. "I'm certain the chap kept a stock of tea and biscuits, at the very least." Scrounging around, he found various tools, bolts of fabric, and machine parts—probably replacement bits for the new-fangled sewing machine, Ernesto speculated—until finally coming across a cupboard with pantry items.

"Look here." Ernesto beckoned her to the table where he had laid out a plate of shortbread cookies, a jar of preserves and a maté service. "I have found a few treats for a proper *merienda*."

"You know very well it's too late for tea," she teased. "But, as I am hungry, I will ignore the antiquated protocols and accept your invitation. Do you know how to serve maté, or shall I take the lead?"

He took a moment to look at the woman, awkwardly attempting to put up a brave front for his benefit. Of course he knew how to *cebar maté*, but he wouldn't dream of taking the honor away from Leah. There was a decided pageantry in serving the beverage and Ernesto hoped that the familiarity of the routine would have a calming effect—on *both* of them. "By all means, please proceed," he said with an innocuous smile.

Leah prepared the bitter brew, and then, sneaking a peek at the man from under her long eyelashes, suspected that he knew more about the process than he let on. Attempting to keep the gravity of the situation at bay, she determined to taunt her host and reached for the sugar bowl. He quickly tried to stay her hand, but not before she sprinkled a healthy teaspoon of the sweetener.

"No sugar please," Ernesto blurted. "It alters the taste, don't you know."

"Oh dear, I'm terribly sorry." Leah continued by placing the silver-plated straw carefully in the center and began pouring the hot water into the gourd. "Here, let me stir it up a bit. The water's so very hot."

"No! Don't do that!" he said, surprised at Leah's lack of expertise. "You do not move the *bombilla* once it has been placed. The crushed leaves will be stuck in the filter. And—"

Leah was laughing now, holding the maté in one hand and her bandaged head in the other. "The water can never be *too* hot, isn't that right, Mr. *Ernst Bloomenthal*?" She asked in her best British accent, exaggerating the 'th' sound—nonexistent in Spanish. Leah finally passed the tea to the perplexed gentleman. "How do *you* know so much about maté?"

"It is the national drink, is it not?"

He took a few sips of the steaming hot liquid before returning the gourd to her—but he did not say 'thank you'. She would take the acknowledgement as an indication that he was satisfied and did not require another serving. Ernesto, most definitely, wanted to continue; however, he was becoming increasingly anxious at the thought of not having enough conversation to fill the hours that loomed ahead.

"I probably should beg your pardon now, Miss Leah. I fear you will find me dull. I'm not very good company..."

"'My idea of good company is the company of clever, well-informed people who have a great deal of conversation.'"

"Ah—you read *Persuasion*, after all."

"Yes, of course. Why wouldn't I? Did you think because the books were written by Miss Jane Austen, an English authoress, I would not be interested?"

He grimaced at her accusation. "Our acquaintance has had a somewhat precarious commencement, would you not agree? We have been plagued with one misunderstanding after another. Surely you could comprehend my hesitation in believing you enjoyed the gifts so humbly offered? Especially after our recent conversation—"

Leah lowered her gaze as she accepted the gourd in return. She was not pleased. Her attempt at levity had failed to keep the subject matter far and away from the conversation to which he so solemnly alluded. Not wishing to continue in that same vein, Leah struggled to turn the topic.

"Forgive my mischievous inclination, but *Dios mío!* I can't seem to help myself! You looked so serious just then—you always look serious. You are the consummate gentleman, so very formal and reserved. I suppose that's why I tease you, for I *am not!*"

"Yes well, that much I know. To your assertion of my being a *consummate gentleman*, one does aspire to be courteous and honorable, to be sure. As to my being *so very formal*, perhaps you will allow me to expound on that subject—seeing as we know so very little of each other. I was raised in a fairly strict household," he said uneasily. "Public signs of affection, or any sort of tomfoolery were frowned upon, you understand. Poor Mother and Father—they did *try* to do their best with us. When I first met your brothers, I was quite jealous, enchanted really. Coming from such a staid background, your family was a breath of fresh air. I am certain that your life has been far more fascinating than mine."

"I don't think I have ever thought of my family as enchanting. We are quite a rambunctious lot, even the serious ones whom you haven't met...Naftali or Avram come to mind." Leah grinned.

"Precisely! So large a family—twelve siblings in total, am I correct? I am fascinated by the endless variations of personalities in one household."

"Yes, well...I can attest to the fact that we do have *endless variations of personalities*. Mamá had hoped that we would all stay together—living out our lives in Entre Rios—but we, each of us, had our own hopes and plans to pursue. I understand that you set aside your own dreams in favor of your father's aspirations."

"That is not entirely accurate," Ernesto replied. "We have spoken of it, but perhaps you have forgotten."

Leah felt the heat come to her face. Once again, she had allowed the conversation to return to that uncomfortable tête-à—tête.

"It is not a matter of my father's plans not being to my liking," Ernesto admitted, "but, to be frank, my heart is not in it."

"Then, why do it?"

"It is a matter of honor. My parents expect this of me, and I am nothing, if not dutiful. In fact, I take pride in that attribute. A sense of duty to one's family—it imparts a feeling of purpose. My family expect me to establish a department store to rival Harrods of London. Our businesses have had similar beginnings and have been great competitors from the start."

"How so?"

"When Charles Harrod founded his wholesale grocery in East London in 1834, my grandfather opened a similar store on the opposite side of town. When my grandfather decided to move closer to Hyde Park in 1849, Harrods mimicked the move."

"My family and I are familiar with Harrods," she said, "although I had no idea that Bloomenthal's had experienced a similar genesis."

"Indeed, they have much in common. Both businesses benefited immensely by escaping the vice of the inner city. By the time the Great Exhibition was in full swing, both companies were showing a great deal of promise."

"I had asked Mamá—most fervently—to allow us a tour of London, prior to leaving the continent. My parents had visited the city during the Great Exhibition, you see, and it had been a dream of mine to follow in their footsteps. Mamá didn't think it prudent, and needless to say, I was outvoted by my brothers, as well." Embarrassed for having interrupted the man—he was usually so terse and to the point—she begged him to continue.

"Harrod's son took over the business soon after the Exposition, and my grandfather followed in his competitor's footsteps by bringing in his own son—my father. Both companies fought to outdo the other, but in December of '83—during the worst possible of times—Harrods suffered a great loss when a fire ripped through their buildings. I don't know if you're familiar with Dickens, Miss Leah, but after his novel, *A Christmas Carol,* was published, meeting the holiday rush was of the utmost importance. Harrods was able to fulfill all their holiday commitments, although, it was never quite clear *how* that came to pass. If my grandfather came to Harrods' aid— fulfilling a *mitzvah,* as it were—it has remained a secret among the two impresarios. I suppose, we will never know."

"To show such charity, such compassion towards one's rival—that *is* extraordinary!"

"To be sure, but soon after rebuilding, Harrods began exceeding everyone's expectations— Blumenthal's began falling short, and my father's concern became all encompassing. A little over ten years ago, Harrods inaugurated England's first moving staircase. Father and his team of managers were invited to observe the mechanism. I was a young man, just in my first year at university, but Father insisted I join the excursion."

"It must have been thrilling for you. What an honor to have been asked to join the party."

"Yes, well...the science behind the apparatus was extraordinary. The device was a woven leather conveyor belt-like unit—an impressive bit of machinery. I remember the balustrade was quite remarkable, made of rich mahogany and covered in a silver-plated glass material. It was a sight to see, Miss Leah; and I must admit, I could not hide my trepidation when I first stepped onboard. In truth, we were offered a brandy to help *revive* us after the experience! It was quite a success for Harrods, and we at Blumenthal's, felt it exceedingly.

All of which leads me to the reason the family feel we must outdo our competition with something quite unique. I was sent to school with this goal in mind. All these years, Father has been waiting for an opportunity, and well, opening a store in Argentina—a country that has burst onto *le beau monde* with wealth, style, and sophistication—would be quite the feather in his cap. As for the rest, you already know what I had hoped for. Perhaps it's best if we do not revisit the topic."

Ashamed for not being able to stop the conversation from leading—again—to such a delicate subject matter, Leah silently acknowledged that the man before her was a completely different specimen from that man of her acquaintance. With the exception of certain circumstances that seemed to providentially occur, her encounters with Ernesto Blumental were usually quite brief and to the point. And yet, here they were—in a most provocative situation, closeted together under dire conditions.

"What, exactly, do you wish to do?" Leah found that she could not help, but ask. "I mean to say, since your heart is not involved in running the business?"

"I had envisioned building something from the ground up, but my father advocated purchasing a ready-made outfit. As of late, it appears we have come to an understanding, which is how I came about purchasing this building. Now begins the real work. I will raze the entire thing and build it up from scratch."

"I must admit that I am stunned, and I do not believe it has anything to do with the bump on my head. Were you not against inaugurating Blumental's of Buenos Aires in this part of town?"

Ernesto shrugged, and without addressing her curiosity, continued outlining his plan. "I thought to import materials from England and possibly a stone mason or two. Of course," he teased, "I will be sure to eradicate the mold."

"Yes, but..."

"It will be quite an undertaking, but I welcome the construction and design aspect of it."

"Mr. Blumental," she insisted, "I distinctly recall your dismissal of El Once as a possible locality. What has happened to change your mind?"

"Nothing so earthshattering to recommend we continue speaking of me and mine. We've had enough of my story," he stated with some embarrassment and became grave once more. "I believe it is your turn. Tell me, if you would, how you came to live in this community. We do have plenty of time to while away—"

"You don't seriously want to hear my tale of woe," she mocked, but with such close proximity to one another, Leah couldn't help but notice the solemnity in his eyes. "Do you really think we will have to stay here all night?"

"I think it would be the safest choice, do you not agree?"

"Safety is relative, sir. Do not forget you will have to face my brothers in the morning," she said lightly.

Surprising them both, Ernesto allowed an errant chuckle to escape. "That, Miss Abramovitz, will be the charming price I have to pay for hearing your story. Now, please," he said with an unexpected twinkle in his eye, "be mindful of your responsibilities. I believe it is my turn—pass the maté and begin your *tale of woe.*"

Chapter Twenty-Five

May 15, 1910 ~ Buenos Aires

*T*he throbbing at her temple was a cruel reminder of the previous night's occurrences and an even crueler manner with which to be awakened. She cautiously opened one eye, and then the other, only to find Ernesto Blumental sleeping in the corner of the room. His large frame was awkwardly draped over a chair. *How could he sleep in such discomfort?*

Black unruly hair dipped over Ernesto's eyes while a soft snore escaped his lips. Leah tried to recall when they had finally fallen asleep. They had talked all through the night—*funny that.* She would never have dreamt that they would have found so much to talk about. What was it she had said—something about Anne Elliot and her idea of good conversation?

Leah had admitted to enjoying Austen's final novel. She most appreciated the fact that the heroine, *at last*, had found the strength to follow her own heart and map out her own destiny. Judith Blumental's opinion—and by default, her brother's as well—had been spot on. Anne's greatest reward was finding a true and constant life partner in Captain Wentworth.

Watching Ernesto now, as he stirred and stretched, was as if she was noticing him for the first time. *He is quite dashing, isn't he? Rather like a hero in a novel.* Could she have been so blind as to not notice his other heroic qualities? Ernesto's constancy had been legendary; his unselfish acts and noble character had been beyond reproach, but her vanity—her need to be right, to be in control—hadn't allowed her to see the value of the man who professed his admiration. All the declarations against love and marriage had distracted Leah from the truth of her *own* emotions. How could she have committed this error in judgment?

With full acknowledgment, Leah owned that as a girl of seventeen, she had disgraced herself chasing after Lieutenant Yegorov who neither respected her, nor cared for her. She recognized that she had been blinded by the romantic figure of the lone gaucho. She had wasted her time, not fully understanding that Joaquín would have never give up his solitary way of life. Then, as Fate would have it, *Ernst Bloomenthal* was placed in her path. Foolishly, she very nearly walked away from what could only be *beshert*—it was meant to be. What had her mother said long ago? When Hashem throws you a lifeline, you have a choice to grab hold, or not. *But was it too late?*

"Good morning," Leah whispered as she saw him awaken.

"Good morning," he croaked in reply. Stretching his sore muscles and rubbing a stiff neck, it took a moment for Ernesto to remember where he was and what had transpired the night before. Now wide-eyed, he gazed at Leah with concern. "How are you? Your injury—are you in pain?"

"I would kill for a hot bath and clean clothes," she replied, "but other than a pernicious headache, I am well. I—I would like to thank you for your kindness last night. I don't know what would have become of me had you not arrived. Were it not for your presence of mind to secure our safety—and to keep me preoccupied with conversation—I think I might have gone just a bit mad," Leah admitted ruefully. "I've been thinking of our conversation. I find that I am curious about one small detail. May I ask a question?"

Suddenly still, he responded with some hesitation. "By all means."

"Would you tell me now, once and for all, why *did* you buy this parcel of land—here in El Once?"

Laughing at his own trepidation, Ernesto found he could reply with great honesty. "If you must know, I owe this purchase all to you. Your tenacity has taught me a great lesson and I decided that, perhaps, it was time to reject the old ways of conducting business. I was convinced my father would not have approved my choice—that an address in El Once would not be able to compete with one in Palermo. It was witnessing your vision, *and your determination*, that convinced me. I could no longer allow my pride to stand in the way."

Leah was overcome with timidity at his gallant confession. Would her words fail her now—now, when she needed to reciprocate in kind? "I'm not certain how to respond to that declaration."

"There is no need to say anything." He smiled. "If you are ready, perhaps we should see about getting you home."

"Do you think it is safe to venture outside?"

Ernesto cautiously came to his feet, testing his long legs, rigid and unsteady. "I am quite certain that the residents of the neighborhood are preparing for a new day—as should we."

"I am a little hesitant to go outside after spending the night in here...*with you*." Leah's emerald eyes twinkled with amusement. "Whatever will my neighbors think? What will my brothers say?"

Ernesto paused, as he straightened his tie and focused on the woman before him. Did he dare match her frivolity with a rejoinder of his own? With a rakish grin, he continued to adjust his coat before uttering a sardonic reply. "My dear Miss Abramovitz, please do not distress over the matter. I simply will have to speak to your brothers. I am certain we can come to an agreement."

"An agreement?"

"As an Englishman," he stated portentously, "I do believe I know what is correct and proper."

"Mr. Blumental, how very droll," she teased. "*As an Englishman*, indeed! If not for this nasty cut on my forehead, I could be persuaded to believe that you designed this entire scheme." Leah paused and reflected. Perhaps now was not the time to continue taunting the man. She owed him an apology. *She owed him much more than that.* "They have ears, but do not hear," she said, quoting her brother's favorite psalm and suddenly finding the words she wished to speak.

"I beg your pardon?"

"I have been a fool, Ernesto. I had hardened my heart. I had made *my plans*, you see, and God laughed."

"What are you saying?"

"My insolence and lack of discernment nearly proved to be my downfall, but you—you vexatious Englishman—*you* have been everything that is good and honest. You have been attentive enough to make any girl swoon and patient enough to allow a girl to reconsider. And I have done just that. I believed that we would not suit, but I was wrong, and can now readily admit it. What do you say to that?"

"There comes to mind a certain quote some other *vexatious* English fellow once said: 'It is not in the stars to hold our destiny, but in ourselves.'"

"So typical," she teased, placing her hand in his. "*Must* you quote Shakespeare to make your case?"

"Madam, I will quote whomever you wish, as long as it—*and I—* fit into your designed destiny."

October 1910 ~ Derbyshire, England

*L*eah would have planned the entire event herself—*everyone knew she was more than capable*—however, upon returning home that fateful day in May, Devora and Sofia commenced the wedding arrangements before Leah could put two words together! Devora suggested a traditional affair held at Templo Libertad. Sofia preferred reserving the grand ballroom at the Plaza Hotel, or even possibly, the Savoy.

"But I—" Leah began.

"They have an embroidered silk *chuppah* at the Savoy that is simply exquisite!" exclaimed Devora.

"The imported one?" asked Sofia. "It makes quite a statement. We should invite all our neighbors and business associates—"

"I don't—"

Ernesto had plans of his own. He was of a mind to whisk his intended away to England, but there, Leah had put her foot down. She wished to be married in Basavilbaso where, surrounded by family and friends, she and Ernesto would stand under a traditional bridal canopy and chant the ancient vows. The family, now spread out across the country, would never have been able to travel to Europe, and Leah had always dreamt of her siblings accompanying her on her wedding day. Finding it easy enough to give in to her whims, Ernesto agreed to a ceremony in the colony. Nonetheless, he attempted to entice her once more— this time, with a wedding trip to Derbyshire.

"We will stop in London, where I will introduce you to my family. Judy will plan a wedding breakfast," he grinned. "It will be quite an Austen affair. Afterwards, we could tour the Peaks District. What do you say?"

Although tempted, Leah wished to remain on task. There was yet much to be done. "Would you mind terribly if we postponed the trip until after..."

"The Centennial?" they sang out in unison before joining in a tender kiss.

It wasn't long after, Blumental's of Buenos Aires had had its grand opening. The début of the tea salon had been received with rave reviews, and when Leah disclosed her new line of fashion, she became the toast of Buenos Aires. All of society was abuzz with her première. She had yet another, more intimate revelation to make; however, Leah was not quite prepared to share her news—at least, not just yet.

When, at last, the couple arrived in Derbyshire, Ernesto hired a horse and carriage and asked the driver to take them on a long quiet tour. Leah was charmed by the quaint village and dramatic landscape; but still, she was all aflutter. The time had come to share her secret.

Playing travel guide, Ernesto pointed towards the rocky outcrops on the horizon and the hills and lakes which painted a pleasing picture across the valley. The driver made a wide turn, passing through a gated entrance and continued for a half mile or so, until coming to a standstill. There, upon a hill, stood a handsome building surrounded by trees and all manner of natural beauty. Ernesto turned to face Leah—ready to test her knowledge of the grand estate prettily situated beyond a tranquil pond—but instead, was astounded to find his wife in tears.

"Are you not happy, my love?"

"The word does not do justice to my emotions! Who would have thought my life's journey would have led me to this contentment?"

"Your happiness makes my own complete," he said, taking her hand and gently placing a kiss there. "We are truly blessed. And to think, our journey has only just begun."

Laying her head on his shoulder, she softly whispered, "Dearest, you will need to make room for one more blessing."

Ernesto bowed his head in anticipation.

"I'd like to name our daughter Chanit, in honor of my grandmother," she said softly. "In Argentina, they will call her Juanita, but we shall call her Jane."

Acknowledgements

It is a truth universally acknowledged that I am an avid family historian and an amateurish genealogist. My books have benefited greatly by the memorabilia and anecdotes I have loving collected from family and friends. I gratefully acknowledge my husband and children for championing my writing endeavors and extend a heartfelt thanks to my great circle of family, friends, beta-readers, including Debbie Brown, Shanah Khubiar, Brooks Kohler and social media companions for their continued support and enthusiasm in my "scribbling."

Throughout this process, I have been overwhelmed by the magnitude of what my ancestors achieved. Had they remained in Russia, they would have, of course, suffered through the Revolution and the tumultuous period thereafter. If they survived Lenin and the Bolsheviks, they would have faced the Nazis. The truth of the matter is that while there was a small, but extremely successful Jewish aristocracy, the vast majority of the Jewish population in Odessa did not live like my fabled Abramovitz family. The fate of the Jewish community in Ukraine is widely known or easily researched. It is a horror story of monumental proportions. The fact that my ancestors left Imperial Russia and began new lives in Entre Rios and La Pampa, *and made a success of it*, leaves me in utter awe. Although anti-Semitism played a significant role in the life of Argentine Jews, they didn't allow this to deter their progress or their need to create a better life for their children.

I wish to pay homage to those who came before me and would have them know that I respect and honor their memory, their accomplishments—their lives.

In addition, please note the following credits in no particular order of importance:

The YIVO Encyclopedia of Jews in Eastern Europe
Online Edition

Immigrants of a Different Religion: Jewish Argentines and the Boundaries of *Argentinidad*, 1919—2009—A Dissertation submitted to Rutgers University John Dizgun

University of Wisconsin—Madison Libraries
Foreign Relations of the United States (FRUS)
Historical records declassified and edited for publication

The Jewish Manual; Practical Information in Jewish and Modern Cookery with a Collection of Valuable Recipes and Hints Relating to the Toilette
Lady Judith Cohen Montefiore

collections.ushmm.org/oh_findingaids/RG—50.590.0003_trs_es.pdf

coloniasjudiasarg.amia.org.ar/listing/lucienville/

kehilalinks.jewishgen.org/basavilbaso/

Sr. Adolfo Gorskin y el Museo Judio de Entre Rios

Miss Jane Austen

Thank you for your interest and support of this work. If you are so inclined, please leave a rating and/or a review on Amazon and Goodreads. As an "indie" author, I rely on word of mouth and visibility on these websites and social media outlets. Your feedback is of tremendous help.

Although I hope you will consider this a stand-alone novel, it is truly a sequel. You can read all about Molly Abramovitz (aka Marina Davidovich) and her trip to Odessa in *Becoming Malka*.

For more information, pictures and genealogical or historical resources, please visit me at:

http://www.facebook.com/mirtainestrupp

Or contact me at indieauthor4life@gmail.com